WHEN A SOUL STOPS RUNNING

The Autobiography of Brian M. Dixon

from

10-30-15

Brian M. Dixon
216-902-1725
440-317-0258

PAGE PUBLISHING, INC.
New York, NY

First originally published by Page Publishing, Inc. 2015

ISBN 978-1-68213-372-9 (pbk)
ISBN 978-1-68213-373-6 (digital)

Printed in the United States of America

Whenever compel into a corner allow fear
to become your most truest ally
-Brian M. Dixon

For Mr. N. Woods Rest in peace my friend, without you, where would my daughter be. I would never forget you Sir.

ACKNOWLEDGMENTS

There is just too many of you to list, but as you read this life story of mine, only you would know what part you played in my life to push me forward. My heart goes out to each and every one of you. Thank you.

Be blessed everyone and thumbs up to your hearts!

Special acknowledgments to the following:

The judges and federal judges of Ohio, thank you for giving me a second chance at life.

To all of the officers of the Cleveland Cuyahoga County Jail System, during my three-year stay with you guys, I know I was a handful, but not one time did you guys every do me wrong when you should have. Thank you.

To the Federal Air Marshals of The United States of America, we've had a lot of air travel time together, and there were times when I deserved to see what other uses those paratrooper boots could be used for, but you guys showed me nothing but respect. But! I must let you guys know that that black box around my wrist really made it hard to unwrap them peanut butter cheese crackers! :)

To all the beauty salons and barbershops of Cleveland Ohio that opened up their doors to me. Thank you.

Special thank yous to the following: To the Bedford Heights Police Department, to the Kent Police Department, to Portage

County Sheriff's Office, to the Family and Community Services of Portage County. I thank you guys for reviewing all the evidence first and not pointing a finger and convicting me of something I didn't do just because of my past record.

My heart goes out to Foster Parent Patty. When my daughter was placed in foster care, I prayed to God to keep my daughter safe, and now, you and I are friends. My heart goes out to two special officers of the Bedford Heights Police Department—Patrolman C. and Patrolman V. Gentlemen, that day over in Building C, I was lost. You guys were the first ones who guided me to my visitation rights.

To Sergeant H. of the Bedford Heights Police Department, sir, you have a place in my heart that can never be removed. You are my Detective Chestnut. You gave me a mission. You told me, "I've called Portage County and told them after a thorough investigation, we are not charging you with that crime and that you're on your way out there. Now you go and fight for your daughter, and when you get her, you be the best father you can be." Sergeant, five years later, I haven't skipped a beat.

To the Bedford Heights Community Prayer Group and to the individuals of Bedford Heights that prayed for and with me. You guys showed me the way to leave my worries in God's hands and continue living without stress.

Celebrity words of encouragement. To Queen Latifah. In 1998, while at the broad walk at University Studios, you tried to sneak past the crowd of people with your ball cap pulled down to hide your face making your way into the movie theater, but I spotted you and screamed your name, and you stop in your tracks. I didn't even pay for my tickets. I dipped under the ropes and ran straight to you with a white girl by my side. And how I cried at the Mann's Chinese Theater after the ending results of your character in the movie *Set It Off*. It was more than a beautiful sight seeing you in the flesh right before my eyes. Your last words to me were, "You can make things happen if you go for it." You gave me a hug, and I told you, "I'm Brian Dixon from Cleveland Ohio, and you will be hearing from me again." Well, it's 2015, and I just wanted to say hi and "Yes, I'm going for it! And something is going to happen" :)

To Marlon Wayans. When I met you at the Millennium Hair Salon in North Hollywood 1998, you were just as cool as they come. To Henry Winkler, when I met you at the gas station while you were filling your Classic Mercedes Benz, you shook my hands, and I was only thinking, "Wow! The Fonz from *Happy Days*!" As we started to depart, I told you that I want to be like you. You told me I can get it. I told you that you will hear from me again. Hello, Mr. Winkler. It's 2015, and I'm reaching to get it.

To Spice 1 and Vinny of Naughty by Nature and Mac, one night in Hollywood, you guys was posted up with a young guy from Cleveland Ohio in 1996. As the Ganja was being passed around, Spice 1, you were explaining to me that it's not hard to get. I just have to want it. Mac, you gave me a number to call, but I was running from the law. I just told you guys you would hear from me again. It's 2015, so what's it do Spice 1?

To Kevin Costner, there's no way I can explain to you in detail how much I loved your character in *Waterworld*, and your character in the movie *Bodyguard* began a newfound respect. But when I was working as an extra on the movie *Draft Day*, never in my wildest dreams would I have thought that I would be speaking to you and shaking your hand! I was one of the coaches inside of the war room. After rehearsing your part a couple of times, for no reason at all, you walked straight over to me and introduced yourself. I had the same feeling that I had when I met Queen Latifah. I couldn't believe that I was actually talking to one of my favorite stars. Later that day, under the tent where we had lunch, I saw you going to retrieve a plate. I couldn't help myself, and I was not about to miss the rare opportunity, so I got out of my chair and followed right behind you.

As I placed my left hand on your shoulder and shook your left hand with my right hand, I explained to you that I really appreciated and respected what you said about Whitney Houston. I told you my name was Brian Dixon and you'll hear from me again. It's 2015. Hello, Mr. Costner. :)

To you, the reader. One thing I'm pretty sure that we both can agree on, with life comes consequences. We all try to do what is right, but sometimes, we follow the path that makes life a lot easier for us. With doing so, we sometimes place ourselves in situations in which we are compelled to do things that we wish we didn't have to subject ourselves to. As we gain beautiful things in life, there comes a time when we lose them. That's when a soul stops running. (Cinnamon)

PART I

CHAPTER 1

IT'S A BOY

February 28, 1973. This was just one of the days that seemed just a little too odd to Linda from the last couple of days and the last previous hours. *As my mother sat up inside of the Metro hospital, located on the west side end of Cleveland in Ohio*, both parties were holding up their end of the argument, with neither side showing any signs of bending.

Once again, Linda was telling the doctor, "No! No, you are not putting them things around my son's head!" My mom was referring to the forceps that they wanted to exercise on me. She had already seen enough children's *deformities* from the use of that wicked device. And just my luck, *technology was not at its best back then. Forceps is an instrument used by doctors with long thin metal parts for picking up things*, but the aftermath that was left behind from the devastation for using such an apparatus on a brand-new baby, sometimes resorted into a child being left with a very odd shaped long head. And the appearance of your head would really be in trouble if your mom didn't know how to mold your cranium properly! That's why some children are nicknamed Egghead! *Thanks to my lucky stars that my beautiful mom loved me. It was too early in life for her to consider me just a thing*, and she's very serious about protecting a new born.

"No, no, no!" Linda shouted *as her strongest deer stare was coming into full focus!* The doctor and my mother have been going back and forth at each other about me coming into the world since January 29! And here we were on this day of February 28! Finally, Linda was getting tired of the shenanigans to which she was not accustomed to nor was she going to back down so easily. So with the exhaustion making itself present and known within my mother's body *she* used the last of her energy to deepen her voice like a man before she was totally drained!

"For the last time," she said in a quiet yet serious tone while being accommodated with a wide eyeballing stare that would stop a deer in his tracks. "He will come out when he is ready and no sooner." The doctors were trying to decipher this new desperate and spooky technique that Linda was using which was preventing them from doing their job, so they decided to leave her alone for a couple more days and went back to the drawing board to conjure up a technique of their own to win my mother over.

Finally on March 3, 1973, a day that should've occurred thirty-four days ago, I made my overdue tribute to the world. Holding me in her arms, Linda spoke very softly to her newborn son. "I told them over and over that you will come out when you were ready." Then, she softly kissed my forehead, then went to work and started molding my cranium. My mom said that I wasn't even wrinkled when I entered the world. And due to me being so late, *my mom said my hair was super fly long, and my fingernails was pimp pointing length. The doctors were even surprised by this lighter-skinned baby that came from such a browner-tone woman.* Because *I came out the same complexion as them* (and years later, I found out why).

At this particular hospital, I was an instant hit with the doctors and the head nurses as well. They even had a nickname for me, and thanks to the *forceps* not being used, it wasn't Egghead. Instead, they labeled me the "pretty baby." Now that I was finally part of this world, it was time for this little body to begin its first feeding into the growing process of life. But unfortunately that simple task that most newborns tackle on their first try turned into an obstacle, due to the fact that I was born *lactose* intolerant. So breast-feeding was a definite no-no for me, so I never received nutrition from my natural life source. I do believe that receiving nutrition from your birth mother does have some type of impact on a relationship between the child and the mother as time progresses forward. The nurses tried to give me Similac milk, but that was a no go as well. *The only milk my body would process* actually came from a goat (*I guess that explained a lot about my appetite*), but being *lactose intolerant* was only the tip of the iceberg. Because *I was also born with clubbed feet!* So *with my personal born into conditions*, I went from being called the pretty baby to being viewed as *the hospital pretty mascot*. (Real nice, hospital people.) >:(

But even with my newfound birth defects, Linda was very surprised and pushed off guard that a few people wanted to adopt me right then and there fresh from the womb, because they figured they could offer me a better life, than what my mom may be able to provide. *From my mother's understanding, everyone wanted me. First, there was the doctor. The doctor approached my mom very bluntly, and stated—not asked, but stated—"You should let me adopt this child."* But my mother politely refused his proposal.

There was another new mother that shared the same delivery room with my mom. My mother said that even as the other woman had just given birth, she could not help herself from staring in my direction as if she had forgot something on that side of the room. The new mother was trying to figure out why her baby wasn't receiving the same attention from the staff. *With all the commotion about me,* the curiosity of the cat was wide-awake, so *she got out of her bed* and readied herself to make it over to Linda, eliminating the feeling of soreness from her own birthing, *and asked my mom* in an artificial tone that made a wooden nickel seem very genuine, *"Can I take a peek at him?"*

Even as her warning signals was starting to fire up, Linda responded, *"Of course you can."* *As the curious mother approached the crib I was borrowing until my short stay was over, my mom began to sense a strange feeling over coming her. So before the new mother even got a slight glance at me,* my mother went into action. *"Do me a favor,"* *my mom said in a medium but commanding tone. "Push his crib closer to the head of my bed." And the woman didn't hesitate; she just responded without question.* Sore and all, she went straight to work. Now that her quick moving job was over, she was now *participating in her granted glance* at me, but suddenly, my mother noticed that *her glance transformed into a stare.* My mother was watching the different muscle spasms on this woman's face as *she looked across the room at her baby, then locked focus back on me. Then she slowly looked back over at her own baby* with an unhidden puzzling expression.

That's when my mom was like, "Okay, let's let these two guys get some rest. They've had a rough first day." Linda studied the woman as she was walking back toward her side of the room, and she noticed that the woman had her lips twisted to the left and biting on her bottom lip. *Once the new mother was settled back on her side of the delivery room, she asked my mom with a smirk mixed with a conniving grin,* as she was studying her own child's features, *"You want to trade babies?" My mom didn't* answer or show any acknowledgment of this silly young mother's pointless question. Instead, my mom recognized that her red flags wasn't just a test run. My mother found it to be pretty peculiar that this stranger was acting as if they had a *"new-found birth reason" to be best buddies. My mom just turned her inner body's security system on and just stared at the stranger for the rest of the night, without a sound* or taking a wink of sleep.

When the morning sun finally showed its face, my mother was expecting breakfast before anything else, but to her surprise, the bacon and eggs was not the first thing to come through the door. *There were two different sets of visitors in the room,* and she recognized the four of them with very questionable thoughts. *My mom's aunt (who was her mother's sister)* and *her husband.* Also *my father's dad and his wife* were in attendance. But my father was absent, and *my dad never showed up. It will be over thirty years* and some change *before I ever lay eyes on him. As my grandfather and grandmother were taking turns looking at me, my grandfather went over to my mother's left side* of the *bed,* so he could talk directly to her without anyone hearing his conversation. Then he *politely extended his arms and grabbed her hand,* just as gently and carefully as if he was holding a long-stemmed rose, with razor-sharp *thorns protruding from its greenery.* He started his attempt. "Will you let us adopt him?" he said.

Now my mother understood why the both of them displayed such nervous body energy as they were sitting inside of her *delivery room* playing super savior. *My grandfather was well-off financially in the game of life. Back in the day, he had two things going for himself. One, he* was of the visible mix nation due to his Chinese and white counterparts, *so that gave him a whiter skin tone,* which in them days gave you a visible *advantage.* So of course, he used that as a stepping-stone whenever opportunity presented itself. *He was also fortunate enough to own his own store* as well. And from what my mom told me, his store was actually *doing more than fairly well.* So now was this test to see if his stepping-stones could create a bridge with my mother. *My mom was young and already had a four-year-old son. So the fear of asking a black woman to give up her newborn baby was of no pressure at all to this guy.* For *all* that he was thinking, he would be doing this young black woman some good. Without showing any signs of anger, *my mom just told* him, "No, thank you." After hearing my mother's serious tone of an answer, they just gave me another smile, and that was the last time he ever laid eyes on me.

My mom's aunt, Mrs. Ann Faye, was a supposedly "good woman" (*church and all*). *She and her husband was well-off in life as well.* Even more well-off than my grandfather. They were pretty smart with life and were sure to play by the rules, only manipulating life structure when an extreme judgment call was totally necessary. *At the time of my birth, they owned a couple of stores and an apartment buildings* in various parts of the city. *They* also had sense enough to dwell within their own properties. *So they knew* the laws of making *and saving money.* Their philosophy was always "getting two birds with one stone."

Now Ann Faye did not like my father at all. From what my uncles told me later on in life, *my dad was a pure street guy!* He was *one* of the tough guys in the neighborhood. As far as their story goes, he really earned his street respects. My two uncles *were telling me how they watched him pistol-whip a fellow and smack the poor gun-eating guy's woman* for offering her poor man a helping hand. So I understood *why Ann Faye didn't like my father.* She believed in *her* heart that she was about to help my mother out and give her a lifeline in life, or *was it really the fact that she and her husband didn't have any children of their own and were at the age where they wouldn't have none naturally?*

So once again, since my mother was young and already had a four-year-old, did they honestly look at this as a self-interest opportunity of chance? So Ann Faye took her shot at shooting in the dark but wasn't really sure if she was going to *hit something. Faye grabbed my mom's hand* (just as smoothly as my grandfather had done previously and with a half-shyly but determined expression written all over her face). She finally said, *"You should let me and Buddy adopt him, Linda. You know he will be taken care of."*

My mom didn't want to offend them or get them angry, so she just said, "No thank you." *So Ann Faye tried to use a different approach, mixed with a conniving caliber of conversation.* (As if my mother wasn't who she was. *In a sense, she really tried to* downgrade *her as if she was weak* when it came to making choices in life since Linda already had two children with no fathers.) *Faye said "Look, let me adopt him, and you start staying away from his father, and we will give you whatever you want."*

Whatever Ann Faye was aiming for, it did not get a hit nor a graze of something. She was literally just shooting in the dark that didn't hold any type of target. I guess my aunt couldn't tell if *she* flicked my mom's security system on or not. *My mom just said no, while adding a little spice to her speech! And she did love her aunt, so my mom gave me a nickname after Faye's favorite cowboy.*

CHAPTER 2

LET THE GAMES BEGIN

My memory begins at the young age of three. That's also the time when I started truly noticing my father. He used to tell me stories later on in my teenage years how when I was three months old, he used to take wired coat hangers and bend them into a shape of a capital *U*, so he could slide them down into my left and right leg cast. He said that out of all the other remedies he tried, this was the only thing that he could do to stop me from crying so hard from all of the pain and very annoying irritation that was going on inside of my cast that was prohibiting me from being a happy child. And due to me being associated with clubbed feet, my mother was told that I would not be walking anytime soon. The doctors told Linda that I will never be able to run and skip like normal active children. (*Boy were they wrong.*)

My father said he was so crazy about me that he would take me everywhere with him even at the very young age of three months. He said that we would be gone all day. Just me and him! He had even given me a cool little name that only he would call me. It was Juice Mouth. My dad explained to me that I used to have so much saliva pouring out of my mouth that I used to leave him and his best T-shirts soaking wet. But he didn't mind at all. Besides, I was his little Juice Mouth. That's all that mattered to him. Even as he told me these little heartfelt (father-and-son) stories, there was still something that was not being said by this guy. Because his actions were not the same as the words he spoke, *and as I got a little older, I could sense the energy in my bones* that something was truly being hidden and untold. But just like most stories that's undercover, it will see the day of light.

My mom and my dad were great providers, even though we were proud to be of the food stamps and government cheese nation. (It's still very vivid in my mind till this day watching my mom and her closest sister standing in that food line, waiting to receive some of them powder eggs, with powder milk, and a big long block of cheese, sitting safely in a cardboard box, and let's not forget about the block of butter wrapped safely in the wax paper with the blue words typed on it.) But they knew how to make those elements work for the family. During Christmas season, we had everything a below-poverty child could ask for. We even lucked up on gifts that we didn't ask for, and for one reason or another, when we awoke the next day, just about all of our toys and the darn Christmas tree would be all over the place. Some toys would even be broken, but we still made it work. We were somewhat happy while living in a run-down apartment building.

My immediate family consisted of my dad, my mother, my oldest brother Earl, myself (Brian), and my little brother Slim. Earl was always the fighter/momma's boy, but this was okay because he holds the title of being the firstborn. Slim was the escape artist. My mom kept him in this baby crib that looked like it could accommodate a grown man, but my brother always found a way out of it every other night. And me, I was always just too curious! So I was always getting in trouble for just about everything.

At the age of five, I was very nosey, too hardheaded, very experimental, and wasn't too much afraid of anything. I traded my fears of life for figuring out my curiosities. Sometimes, I gained knowledge, and sometimes, I gained a right hand with a belt connected to it. For one reason or another (maybe it have something to do with me being a zodiac of the Pisces), my wonderful curious mind and I were always willing to test the hot-temper waters of my mom's patience. For example, Linda loved her Dentyne Classic chewing gum. She chewed that delicious sugary gum so often that she couldn't help but to develop a special talent for chewing. My mom would pop that gum so loud and fast, that it could be measured to the equivalency of a small-caliber machine gun.

One nice summer day, my mom decided that I would be the chosen child for the "mom and me" grocery store field trip. I was totally surprised! This would be my first time going. Earl was the one who usually rode shotgun. I guess she figured there was no need for all of us to partake in this great adventure. After we had finished shopping and me enjoying the views of the grocery store from my push-along captain's chair, we were falling in line with everyone else at the cashier checkout station. That's when I saw more candies than I can ever dream of! And that wonderful gum that she continued to split in half and share with me (But! that's only if I caught her at the right moment) was sitting there right in front of my face on the left hand side behind the cash register. It was like a super high calorie family reunion, because also located next to my mom's favorite gum was an assortment of other gums and candy bars to which I had no knowledge of. There was so many different colors of candies that I believe I was experiencing my first hypnotism. But this wasn't one of those times that I was going to let my curiosity kill the cat, oh no no no! Not this freaking time! So I went for what I thought was a very great and wonderful idea. *I grabbed it.* At the age of five, I had just committed my first theft. I knew what I was doing was wrong, but I just had to have it. For such a young a child, that gum was like a heroin addiction. I needed it bad! As we were leaving, I continued to display a polite, well-mannered child attitude as I waved good-bye to the grocery cashiers and took my place safely in the backseat of my mom's Pontiac Grand Prix.

We were living on E. Ninety-Third and Kinsman, and this part of the city already had its negative reputation. The building we lived in was not that great. It surely wasn't the worst concrete threshold in the neighborhood, but at the same time, it would never be anything to "write home to mom about." We lived in the bottom of the building, or to be more precise, our apartment location was considered "the dungeon" by the other children of the building. As a child, this is what I knew as home, so I was satisfied with the dungeon. As we were pulling up to the building, I was preparing myself for whatever my mom was about to do to me for my little "five finger" personal discount that within the next few seconds must be owned up to.

I watched as she hung her head out of the driver side of the car window, steadily searching for the oncoming traffic to make sure the car door (or herself for that matter) would not be knocked off and carried down the street. Just before she prepared to dart out, she gave me a quick glance and said (in her I'll-beat-your-butt voice), "Brian, don't you move!" Quickly, she safely navigated herself around the car. As my mom was making her way over towards my door, supersize goose bumps decided to appear up and down my little arms as if they were telling me. *It's getting ready to go down* was my train of thought as Linda's approaching was getting closer to discovering what was going on in the backseat of the Pontiac, I just watched as she was peering in through the window at me and shaking her head with a smiling frown and saying my name. The entire time, I was only thinking, *Now the party is about to begin* as I watched the car door being pulled open.

With a soft but stern demeanor, my mom initiated her interrogation on me. "Brian, who told you to go into my pocketbook and eat all my gum?" My mom was never one of those individuals that you would like to play stupid with, and trying to pull one over on her was out of the question and nowhere in the ballpark. She went straight to her purse to retrieve whatever I might have left behind of her own gum. And that's when I braced myself! Because I had "Illegal Stolen Gum Wrappers" spread around, all over the freaking backseat of her precious Pontiac! And Linda was about to find out that not one of those wrappers came from her purse. I had so much of that delicious pink gum in my little mouth that my eyes were watery, my mouth was hot, and my breathing was rapid. I was not ready for that much cinnamon flavor going down my young throat!

I nervously looked on with big teary eyeballs as she pulled her gum out of the pocketbook. In an instant, when she saw that her gum had not been touched, she grabbed my hand with the speed of lightning (I still don't know till this day where in the hell she got that big ass Afro comb from so freaking fast) and commenced to teach me and my hand a very valuable lesson in "Don't retrieve that to which don't belong to you!" Now even as a well-deserved learning lesson was given, but at that time it certainly wasn't totally learned. I just figured that the punishment was well worth its weight in gold. And I wouldn't hesitate to do another dance with that freaking Afro comb for that mouthwatering cinnamon flavored gum!

Within the next couple of days, my curiosities were back to their old tricks and were keeping me in even more undesirable hot water. My curiosity truly had a mind of its own! I mean it really went to work as if it really had a job and doing double overtime on the job came very naturally to my curiosity because it always worked for steam ahead with no lunch breaks. Now I was a pretty bright child for the most part, and that was honestly my problem. I knew darn well the biblical order of right from wrong, but I just couldn't follow suit when it came to doing the right part of the order. I can still remember my first untruthful statement to Linda that qualified me for a second date with the Afro comb. It was around the time when the all new Polaroid instant cameras were invented. This was the new thing of the century. A camera that develops photos for you. All you have to do is press a little red button. And—*poof!*—magic.

My mom loved her new camera, and we were not allowed to touch this camera for no reason at all. If it was on fire, let it burn. Her precious toy was totally off-limits to everyone that lived in that apartment. But like most children my age, or any age for that matter, we didn't listen too well or pay attention to any type of orders or demands when it came to something new that truly sparked our interest and eliminated the self-reasoning factor. After just getting into trouble for becoming a gum junkie (even though my mom was the one that introduced me to the sugary shit) I was finally allowed to get off of my bed from serving my punishment time. When I came out of my bedroom on that early morning, there was my mom's precious camera sitting on top of the dining room table. Now I knew it was wrong, like I knew a lot of things were wrong and I still chose to participate, but that bright red button was just staring me in my face. Then it began to call my name, and before I knew it, my little finger was up there pressing the red button as if I was trying to tell it to shut up! Because in my mind, I was trying to prevent it from calling me. Just as fast as I pushed in the little red button to make it stop talking, there was a bright white and blue flash to my face. Now after being attacked with very blurry vision, all I could do was to hightail it straight back into my bedroom in hopes that my mother would not find out. But how often does a criminal really get to escape and bury his crime (especially after I had just taken my first selfie)? :)

My mother, the self-proclaimed detective, was dead bang on it! She didn't skip, not one beat! As I was running to my room, Linda was coming out of her room going straight to where she heard the noise. As we passed by one another, I caught a glimpse of her eyeball staring at me. She was in the dining room for about a hot two seconds. Then, she was on her way back into her bedroom, passing by my room, not saying anything to me. She went back to whatever she was doing. Later that day, the evening hour was moving into its job position. The family had just finished eating dinner, and now it was time for dessert, but my mom didn't ask me what flavor of ice cream I wanted like my father and my two giggly brothers was asked. Instead, it was time for my interrogation.

"Brian, come here," she said. As I walked toward her, I knew she could see it all over my face. We both knew it was about to go down.

While sitting in the kitchen chair, she had me stand in front of her and lined me up face-to-face as if preparing me for a firing squad. "Didn't I tell you earlier not to touch my camera?"

I prepared myself to put forth a fictitious answer, and I knew there was going to be consequences. "No." I spoke in a deer-stuck-in-the-headlights voice.

"I'm going to ask you one more time. Brian, did you touch my camera?"

I looked away from her and was glancing at the floor. "No" was my weak spoken reply.

"What is this?" she asked me.

This was the first time that I actually saw what a Polaroid instant camera produces. She was holding a square-shaped piece of paper with a black plastic back, which was turned my way. She waited about five seconds, then turned it around. Now the back was facing her, and I was facing myself in that photo.

In the end, I got what I bargained for, and Linda got her work-out on. (And I'm not referring to a membership fitness center.) But little did she know I had more workouts in store as our lives would go on. I was fortunate enough to learn at an early age that there are bigger things in life, that's much worse than little old me. And my mom was going to make sure that I was held accountable for all my mischievous deeds.

CHAPTER 3

BYE-BYE NERVES OF STEEL

The first time that my mother decided I was older and bad enough to go to the yearly Carnival, she grabbed me and my oldest brother and we were on our way. It turned out to be a time that I will never forget. It was located up the street, very close to our apartment building, and sat across from the Fourth District Police Station on Ninety-Third Street and Kinsman. I was still waiting to turn six years old at this time, but I guess my mother figured that my "ego of badness" was much older than my age so she had no second thoughts about our little "scare the hell out of him" trip. And since my curiosity continued to keep my mother very busy with creating punishments and correcting me, and not offering her any apologies, I guess it was now time for Linda to truly get some get back that didn't involve a belt. My first trip to the Carnival really had me wondering what was really going on. Because my mother's vibes just seemed so totally strange and out of the ordinary from a regular day. The whole time we were walking over there, my brother kept telling me that we weren't going to a carnival. Instead, Mom was taking me to a "haunted house" because I was always getting into trouble.

As we were walking up the driveway into the carnival, we passed the "shoot the ball through the hoop" game and its cousin "toss the ring around the bottle neck and win you and extra-large stuffed animal that don't even fit in your car" game. But we traveled on past them two money gobblers without stopping to see if anyone would actually win. Linda was really on a mission because she walked straight past her favorite cotton candy and hot dog stand without even taking a glance. My mother made a beeline straight past all the cool stuff. Linda was walking as if she'd been here before because she was moving as if she knew exactly where we were going. The three of us rapidly moved forward while pushing through the crowds of people with me being dragged most of the way. That's when I noticed we were getting away from the brighter-lighted area of the carnival and venturing off into the dimly lit darkness.

We were making our way toward some type of a carnival ride called The Hammer Head. Now as a child, this was a very scary-looking ride. The two capsules of the ride actually looked like two hammerheads that will raise you in the air and spin you around very fast, and at my age and height, that will be considered nosebleed combined with a slight heart attack. And that ridiculous noise that the contraption of a motor made on this toolshed of a ride was truly terrifying to me as well. As soon as we passed The Hammer Head, we started walking up a makeshift wooden ramp that was constructed like something a pirate will make you walk off of and plunge into the deep sea. As we got to the top, we were met with a person standing inside of a box collecting money. My mom reached into her purse, handed them a couple of dollars, and we started walking toward the doorway of this makeshift building. As we entered, my brother said in his I'm-telling-on-you voice, "You are about to get it now, for always being bad."

Now let me explain to you guys what's really going on. By my brother being my mom's first child, he's automatically the baby for life, and boy oh boy did he played his role to the tee. So by lucking up and being the eldest of the children, he was fortunate enough to understand things better than me; so by him being around our mom more, he could actually comprehend some of her conversations while she was on the phone talking with her friends. Earlier that day, he overheard our mom discussing "yet another" one of my curious adventures. That always lands me in trouble. So now it was time to "pay the piper." Since I won't do right and she didn't want to kill me, she had decided on taking me over to Frankenstein's House so this legendary monster could teach me a lesson. And my brother continued to wear his serious face while he was telling me this spooky nonsense. As soon as we walked through the doorway, we were met by a stumbling bumbling raggedy rag dust encrusted walking mummy. I tried to run in the direction we just came from, but my mother was holding my wrists. I was trying to pull away from Linda, but she was much stronger than I was. I was tugging my hardest trying to break free of my mother's Kung Fu grip. So she decided to turn her gears up a notch and started the old dragging-a-child routine. My brother just laughed at me.

At that very moment, I was trying my best to promise my mother the entire world because she had definitely proven her point to me this time "loud and clear". Mom, mother, hey you! The person who provides me gum and teaches me right from wrong; I am now ready to sign my name on the dotted line Linda! Now I'm in cahoots with ya mother, that you were right every single time, because now I know it's definitely in my best interest to stop being so curious and be more into applying myself in a agreeing with you mom, and your wise "Mama bear to bear cub atmosphere". So for now on beautiful mother, the curiosity comes to an abrupt end right now! "I'm sorry Linda! I'll never do whatever I've previously done again!" But that wooden nickel of a promise went directly into one ear and did a Superman straight out of the other. She honestly didn't pay me any attention at all nor did she intend to! Because that broken record I was singing was getting no air play on her radio station! And boy oh boy was she prepared for my BS! Here it is in the middle of summer and she's the only one wearing boots. >:(But I continued to scream as loud as my vocal cords and lungs would allow me too; over and over I shouted in hopes of penetrating the deaf ears that my words were falling on, but her force field was strong as she continued dragging me with her Kung Fu grip being tighter then it has ever been before. Now we were actually inside the haunted house, which was deemed Frankenstein's House. As we turned our first right, a Wolfman ran straight toward us and stopped about five feet in front of us. He threw his left paw, turned, and disappeared while I started crying! Now we were making a left, and I could see the exit door. At this time, it will be a very good hypothesis to say, "I was scared shitless!" Trust me, if I was still in Pampers, they would've been put to the test at this very moment! Three feet away from the escape door, Frankenstein blocked our exit! But he didn't chase, and he didn't reach out to grab us. He just stood there staring at us!

I learned a great lesson from that experience. No matter how big and scary a person may be, unless they are making a move with the intent to harm, do not harm them. When our field trip of a "lesson learned" finally came to an ending, it would be a while before I asked my curiosity to come outside and play.

CHAPTER 4

BLOODY MARY

I believe for the young age I was, I had a considerable knowledge of where we lived. And this building was sort of a special, meaningful building for the family tree. The reason I said the building was of special meaning is due to the fact that most of my mom's brothers and sisters stayed there in the building as well. We had our very own beehive because everyone stayed busy in one way or another! Rather, you walked on the right side of life or decided to do wrong. This building catered to all different sorts of personalities that was blood connected.

My uncles and aunts had children as well. This meant for more than a few cousins running around creating chaos amongst ourselves and the non-Bloods. We called my mom's closest sister Aunt Ev. She was a second mom to us and had three girls—Sweet Pea, Tempo, and Nina. They were more like sisters to me and my brothers than actually being first cousins. My mom's eldest sister was there as well with her three children. My favorite uncle, we called him Sly, he lived in the meaningful building too with his wife and two children. As well as my uncle Red with his wife and three children. And I may be forgetting a few more members, but we were all there stuck in the sandbox together.

My uncle Sly was the first one fortunate enough to move his family away from the building, and we didn't notice until we didn't see them at church any longer. One thing I can say about all of our parents: they were very serious when it came to going to church. (They pretty much didn't have a choice due to their father's belief.) Sundays, you had no options but to put on your Sunday's best clothing because my grandfather was one of the head deacons. Which in turn aided us to be a close family at that time. We were so close that it was never a surprise to see one of us getting our backside introduced to the belt right before walking through the threshold of the church for being a "Noddy Soul, and right after the boring, "Child Get The Belt Show" to which we've seen far too often, we would be laughing about it in the pews as the pastor was speaking.

On the Sundays when we couldn't make it to my grandfather's church on time, we were fortunate enough that there was a store in front of church located right next door to our apartment building. I used to love going there. Just us children would attend the storefront ceremonies (this may have been a secret babysitting setup), and the only reason we did participate was due to the fact that the supposed to be pastor always gave us snacks before we left. He was never at a loss of Dan-Dee potato chips and Corn Twisties with peanuts and Kool-Aid. Sometimes, we'd get a surprise, and he'd have cake.

Yes, we were a spiritual family. Thank God, my mom even had us baptized. No one in the family had the big corporate jobs at this time, but the families were well-off. We all had something to smile about, even through the self-created gray cloudy days would always breeze through from time to time. My mom was a cheerful person for the most part. She was always singing and dancing around the apartment. I still can reminisce on one of her favorite songs that went something like this: "You don't have to be a star, baby, to be in my show." I used to love hearing my mom singing that song because if she was singing, that meant she was happy. (How I wish the singing had never stopped.) :(

But eventually, Linda's beautiful voice became a thing of the past. I never understood why some mornings when I awoke, our apartment always had things thrown around, and my mother and father always seemed to be covering up angered attitudes while dodging one other in such a small living quarters. Now, me and my mom share birthdays that are very close within the same month. And for some reason or another, she decided to have our birthday parties combined. At the time, I thought that was the coolest thing in the world. When the day of our party soundly arrived, all the family who lived in the building was there. The place will be packed like a bar mitzvah. My favorite uncle Sly, who was truly a street person, gave me a Spiderman gun for my birthday. This gun did not shoot darts. It did not pop caps, and it didn't shoot the little yellow BBs that we were accustomed to. This particular Spiderman gun was only a flashlight, but just like weed is a gateway to more harmful drugs, that flashlight gun that my uncle gave me was the beginning of my doorway to more harmful guns. And practice makes for perfect.

Growing up on Ninety-Third had its share of ups and downs. And in order for us to escape from the building, my little brother and I, and of course my younger cousins were allowed to be outside, as long as one of the bigger siblings was out there with us. There was some good and not so good that came along with that. For instance, my cousin Sweet Pea was a few years older than me. She was supposed to be one of the trusted protectors chosen by the parents to stand guard! But she kept us on silly little missions just for her enjoyment. I can still remember the one summer day she had all of us very sick to our stomachs. "Let me explain," in the backyard of our meaningful building, there was a fence that separated our building from the other houses on the next street over. This fence had some of the most gorgeous weeds that pretended to be flowers growing on it! And such awesome colorful flowers didn't exists in a neighborhood such as ours. That's when we learned that weeds don't just grow on the ground. They can also make the side of a building or house its home as well. But these weeds was living on this rusty steel fence! And they were so very beautiful! Most of the weeds looked like sexy little flowers that should be playing tagalong on a Hawaii belly dancer outfit, and with us children doing a little bit of detective work of our own, our investigation lead us to believe just how such weeds came into existence in such a terrible area. We discovered that it may have been due to the fact that the neighborhood drunks used that fence as a personal restroom. Not only was the fence assaulted by the neighborhood alcoholics, it had its everyday fights with the neighborhood dogs, cats, birds, and people who tossed whatever dirty water out of their homes on it as well, etc. So with all that foul play going on, when the terrible liquids were mixed together, it made the weeds have a pleasurable, intoxicating, and disturbing environment to grow in. The soil was so confused that it actually tricked the weeds into growing like they're meant to be something exotic.

Only Sweet Pea's mischievous self could make all of us think that those darn weeds was something delicious to eat. She called a few of us to the back of the building and told us that the flowers had honey in them. She ripped one of the weeds off the fence and started pulling a piece of the plant out of the middle, and to all of our surprise, she was holding the little stem with her pointing finger and her thumb, and at the end of the stem, there was one drop of some kind of yellow liquid, and we ate it. We cleared most of that fence in a matter of minutes. We ate so many of those perpetrating exotic flowers that we could clearly see over to the next street. We were all sick for that whole day with our naive, just-follow-the-white-rabbit selves.

Sweet Pea shenanigans always topped mines! I would never forget when she had all of us in the bathroom, chanting as she stared in the mirror, saying over and over, "Bloody Mary. Bloody Mary." When we entered into the third chant, she started screaming, and it was so dark that we couldn't see her scratching her own face. When the light was turned on, she had our dumb little butts believing that the woman came through the mirror and did a number on her, which, in turn, left us younger children in a traumatized state of mind for the next couple of months.

Since the parents put them in charge, they claimed to be the all mighty sibling protectors crusaders club (give me a break!). Now Earl was cool—I mean, real cool. You would really would have to be on your job to make him get angry. In order to get some type of negative reaction out of this dude, you would have to be good because he stayed on his square. But with all his coolness guiding his vessel, whenever the opportunity presented itself, the boy wouldn't hesitate to fight if all of the moral justifications was in the right place. I remember one sunny summer afternoon, all the children went into the building to have a quick lunch, and my brother left his one-of-a-kind Evil Knievel bike outside. This bike was awesomely handsome, I must say so myself. It was all chrome with all the Evil Knievel plastic on it to make it look like a real-life motorcycle. When we were done eating and went back out to play, it was gone. *Poof,* in the mist of the air, just like Houdini! Instantly, this young man's anger started building blocks within himself, but no emotions was there. You could just see it in his eyes.

Earl just so happened to be one of those people that you just don't want to see or make mad because that's when his animal instincts take over. It's like his brain just goes blank, and then, it goes into this silent loss of oxygen to the brain mode (or the Incredible Hulk syndrome, if you will), and you cannot explain anything to him. All avenues of reasoning is out the door! Asking him to be civilized is all the way off the menu because this crazy little bastard will turn on you as well, just as if he was your once loving, loyal pit bull terrier. So all of us children knew whenever my big brother hits his don't-say-shit-to-me zone, and we better not say anything to him!

He was so mad about that bike that he forgot that he was supposed to be watching us and darted around the corner. We didn't have the slightest idea what my brother was getting himself into on that other street behind our building where the older children lived. The rest of us were just standing there looking into the direction he ran, finally he was on his way back walking towards us. We notice that he was no longer upset. But one thing we did notice, was that he was wearing a very un-deniable wicked smile across his lips. When he finally made his way over to us so we can began asking him questions, he didn't give us the time to ask him anything. He just stopped in mid step and turned around then started focusing on the direction to which he had just came from. One of the bigger kids from around the corner came running up on Earl at full speed with an "I'm going to beat you down" expression written all over his face and speaking it with his body language. And you can tell that this child had a year or two and a couple of inches on Earl, which automatically gave this guy a true advantage. But when Earl turned and saw this guy running up on him, he didn't look afraid, he didn't look nervous, and he surely didn't look surprised. My big brother didn't look concerned at all. His face was as blank as a turned off computer monitor. He just silently stood there staring at this other guy from around the corner, just waiting to see what actions this bigger kid was going to bring forth.

When this guy finally came within inches of my brother he squinted his eyes hard enough to make his eyebrows formed into a unibrow, and with both of them within striking distance, this kid directed his statement directly at Earl's face! "That's my bike now and if you ever bring your little but around that corner again asking about anything, I'm going to punch you in your nose and ride circles around you on your own bike." Earl didn't say anything back to this bigger threat pushing guy. He just watched as this guy who came from around the corner turned on his heels and started heading back in the direction to which he came from and as soon as the kid bent the corner, Earl didn't even bother to look at us to see what we were thinking. He just ran into the meaningful apartment building and came back out with his favorite Bruce Lee fighting T-shirt on and his buddy tennis shoes laced so tight that his feet looked like a hand that was showing the symbol for the peace sign. I guess this was his display of what your feet should look like when transformed into ninja mode.

He looked at us while trying to control his nerves because his wicked smile was growling at us as if we had done something wrong, but to our surprise he spoke to us in a reasonable cool voice. He smiled and said, "All of you guys stay right here. I'll be right back."

Till this day, we truly do not know what happened around that corner, but as sure as we thought there would never be a black president in our lifetime, my brother came back from around that corner smiling and walking with his evil Knievel ride! His face wasn't touched but his knuckles were red and his Bruce Lee t-shirt seemed as if it had been in a fighting match with a blender. He parked his bike exactly in the spot where Houdini had done a number on him, and went back into the building to change his clothes.

CHAPTER 5

SCHOOL DAYS

My sometimes acceptable, but very confusing younger years was when I was truly introduced to the beginning of the negative side of life. Because the new children that I was starting to meet were little people who were growing up on a totally different steppingstones than the ones I was used to. Because they were saying things and doing things that I was too young to be doing or hearing. And this brings me to my first day of school. Well, to be more precise, let's make that my very unforgettable introduction to school! Now I was already accustomed to being around children, but that didn't count because they were all my relatives. Here I was, at my first day of school, and my mom didn't have the time or the pleasure of taking me to my very big first day. From the stories I was told in my later years, my mom has always been a hard worker. While holding down two jobs, she still had the energy to get off work and come home and multitask for her children. But with her home and job time zones not working together, she decided to ask her favorite sister to take me to school since she was like a second mother to all of her boys. My very first school, which is closed down in this present year, sat right across the Street from the fourth district police station. It was called Boulevard Elementary. I was so excited the night before, but when

I found out my mom was not going to take me, my excitement was minimized and transformed into a certain degree of fear. But due to the fact that my favorite aunt was taking me, I was still ready to go; but at the same time, I couldn't relinquish the feeling that I was really about to experiment with walking on the edge because I was going to this new place with new people without my precious Linda.

My aunt and I ascended up the stairs into this massive building. The scary side of me started to reveal its nervous face that early first day of a school morning, and without hesitation, my scary side prove that it was not shy about doing so no matter who I was in front of. Before my aunt and I could continue to the designated room we had to stop by the principal's office to make sure that all the paperwork was together. They gave my aunt the directions to the classroom, and we were on our way. Finally, we were at the classroom door. As we entered, I saw boys and girls playing and running around, but this did not encourage me in no type of manner to do the same as the other children were doing nor did it influence me to even like this place for that matter. One out of two kindergarten teachers came over to us. She politely introduced herself and walked us over to the coatroom area, which was not a room at all, just long pieces of wood with nails hanging out of them. After taking off my coat and hat, the teacher grabbed my hand and was talking kindly and softly to me, but of course, I took this lovely gesture from this stranger as a con game.

She said, "Let's go and introduce ourselves to our playmates." She ordered everyone to the middle of the classroom and stated, "Everyone, this is Brian, and he is going to be your classmate. Let's form a circle and take turns saying our names." I was super duper nervous now because being around children that I wasn't related to was a totally different part of the ballgame.

There was one main thing that caught my eye that I found to be very strange. It was two girls standing in front of me that looked exactly alike. I never knew anything about twins or heard anything about twins until this day. After all the children introduced themselves to me, I felt very comfortable and was now eager to stay... until my aunt told me that it was time for her to leave! That's when my comfort zone flew straight out of the window, and I suffered my first physical and very mental nervous breakdown. I grabbed my aunt's leg and once again started apologizing for everything that I had ever done in a mischievous manner. It all started with a "No! Please don't leave me. I will never do it again!" Did I know what I was apologizing for? No! Did I care what I was apologizing for? No! I was attempting to do anything within my power to make my aunt understand that it was a must that I leave with her. She was going for it for a second but only in front of the teacher. Just as we were getting closer to the door, it didn't dawn on me that we didn't stop at the coat rack; and just as I was starting to breathe in the fresh air of freedom, my aunt gave me a stern look and put me in place. And that's when both of our acting careers were over with! So I was given no choice but to stay with my new teachers and get to know my new playmates.

As I begun the process of learning new things in this very different environment, I didn't even notice the days and weeks or months for that matter that was passing by because the time was riding by so smoothly. I have really became fond of this school gig stuff! My mom was loving it. I was always getting stars or hundred percent for being on tasks and perfect attendance. Linda always made sure I was always on time, so I wouldn't miss the school breakfast. I fell in love with the peanut butter and jelly gram crackers with the small carton of milk. When it was doughnut day for that morning, I couldn't wait to get my hands around one of those glazed doughnuts wrapped in all that plastic that sucked the sugary coating from off the pastry. So once I finished the doughnut, I would lick that plastic until there was no sugar visible on it. By us not having too much money, I was able to receive my meals free. So if you were fortunate enough to get a green token that means you eat for free because that green token was your money baby. And from the looks of it just about every child had one, whose parents knew how to play the government game, which was pretty cool because it made just about all of us seem equal.

My classmates, each one with their very different personalities for one reason or another was all in love with me. But I did have a knack for making people smile even at a young age. And due to my own comical and sometimes overwhelming personality, going to school for me was like the beginning credits of the TV show called *Cheers* because everyone knew my name. I was always friendly and kind to everyone, even to the little boys who was mad at me from getting so much attention from the girls. I loved to make others smile or laugh, and acting out different characters came to me naturally. And learning and discovering new things became a breeze. But this wasn't in the textbook type of sense, no no no! Because I was a different type of child, every time I was introduced to something new, I would put it inside my first "mental box," which in turn dissected it, then transfer it to a my "own understanding box," then it's moved right along to another box that's outside of that box, which determine which box would take control of the situation at hand. So I was definitely lacking my full potential in school work because of the dreaming Pisces in me, but my common sense was developing into something magnificent.

In kindergarten, As, Bs, and Cs was not available on report cards. Instead, we received Es for Excellent and Ss for Satisfactory. Even though I wasn't focused on full potential, my report card never saw a satisfactory mark. My momma was so proud of me! With the way things were going at this new school, it really allow me to adapt and understand that this is a very important part of my life. As the time was nearing to move forward, I just knew that I will be skipping through first grade with ease, "mentally that is" and going forward to the second grade was pretty much a natural feeling as well. But I knew Mount Pleasant Elementary was going to be a different level of experience for me because the grade level started at grade 1 through grade 6, so now I was going to be around bigger and meaner children, and by me only coming in on a second grade level that meant that there's going to surely be some new challenges added to my already "jigsaw puzzle" of a young youth life. But all in all I was pretty much carrying everything that I learned from my previous school over with me, so maybe my smartness would win me over with some of the bigger kids? Not! :(, Fortunate enough my grades played copycat and being a good classmate was just in my genetic makeup. This was during the time when my grandfather and I started establishing a closer grandson-and-grandfather relationship. All the grandchildren adored grandfather. He had a gift for giving all the grandchildren a special name for themselves. We don't know if he did this because he could not remember all of our real names? Or it was because the memory bank he'd carry for so many years was running out of cash? But due to the love that I cherish for this beautiful man, I'm just going to say that there was a lot of us and our age range was not far from one another, but I honestly believed it was due to his age so it was probably a little confusing for him to remember so many freaking names. So I guess he created whatever fits the bill in his world. But come to find out, he really did have his own system when it came to identifying whichever grandchild he was talking to. Your name given by him would consist of whatever you had going on personally. For instance, he called me Foots due to the fact that I was born with clubbed feet.

Finally summer vacation was over and I was now entering into my new school, and due to all the hours my mother was working, my granddad was left with the awesome job of picking up most of the grandchildren once the last bell rang. And my grandfather did not mind this little job detail at all, which was fairly easy for him because most of the grandchildren attended the same school and my grandparents lived right around the corner. I can still remember the first day he was waiting to escort us back home. This also was the day when I found out what a middle finger meant. It's true that I've seen this gesture many times, but I never understood the meaning of it, and my cousin who was a little older than me who utilized this secret hand movement more often than any other child I saw with their middle finger raised high in the air, and he would not reveal its secrets to me. He will always tell me, "Brian you too young to do this, shoot, Linda would kill you and me." When Tempo, Nina, and I were exiting the school and walking towards our grandfather, we noticed two boys who seem to be in a heated conversation were in a dispute over a "priceless lunch token" and this was happening right in front of the path that we had to cross. As we were getting closer to the small crowd that had gathered together, we started wondering why the closer we got to the small mob that the crowd started split- ting straight down the middle like it was the Red Sea? But we quickly found out the reason behind the disbursement, it was because of that one stern look that my granddad gave to all of them. So I guess everyone's common sense kicked in and they realized that if it was going to go down he would definitely be the "HNIC" to intervene. One of the opponents, started shouting, and he stuck his middle fin- ger in the air and yelled the very unforbidden capital *F*-bomb word. And this guy couldn't have been no more than nine years of age. My grandfather looked at us, and without a word spoken, his facial expression said what his mouth was meant to say: "Ya'll will see the end of my belt if I ever see ya'll carrying on in that type of manner."

Due to our preexisting living conditions, it always allowed all the grandchildren to become a little closer. So we continue to play the role of brothers and sisters, and we protected one another. After a few weeks of attending Mount Pleasant Elementary, once again, the other boys in my class started picking with me because the girls were giving me more attention than them. The darker boys used to call me banana due to my skin color. But name-calling never bothered me at all because I got plenty of that at home. So I just continued to be a banana because whenever I looked at them, they continued to be jackasses. So fair exchange was never a robbery. Despite the obstacles at home, I was always a happy child, and I didn't like fighting. As they picked on me, each one with their signature taunting, I would never respond because they would have to aim really high in order to outdo my mother and father "Loveless words" that I've experienced more than once when they decided to show their "angered affection" towards one another. So as this specific school day was starting off with some real live "Jive Turkey" BS, my very first boxing match was wiggling its way into my young life. One of the boys got mad at me because of my "unresponsive actions" to his rude remarks, so with the girls now laughing at him instead of me didn't help me out much either. So he decided to follow me out of the building to teach me a lesson that didn't involve schoolwork, with a few of his flunkies in tow carrying the pom-poms. I guess he thought he was going to use their energy to cheer him on as he beat up and squash the banana boy.

One thing he did not know was that my grandfather did not always pick us up. It was a fifty-fifty chance that was split up into three ways between my granddad, my mom, and my mom's sister being the designated babysitter. On the days of their escort services, Linda and her sister would park on the side street located next to the school, and all of us siblings would meet them there. As I was walking toward my mom's car, because I was the first one out, the boy ran up and pushed me before I could reach the door handle. As soon as my mother saw it, she jumped straight out of the car, and my aunt moved just as fast as she did. She didn't say anything threatening to the little boy. She didn't even look upset. She didn't even ask him why he pushed me. She didn't even look in the direction where the other children's cheers were fueling him on. All she said was, "Brian, put your book bag in the car and get over there in that grass." Finally she turned her attention towards my future boxing opponent and spoke to the boy, "Since you pushed him, gone ahead and get over there in the grass with him and finish what you started."

The little boy did not look scared or afraid of my mom, instead I watched as his smirk transformed into an evil grin when he started taking his strides towards the grass. That's when quotes from Bugs Bunny started entering into my mind and his evil smirk was telling me, "I'm about to make mincemeat out of you!" After he climbed over the little steel fence, the imaginary boxing ring was created for everyone's enjoyment but mine. And I did not want this to go down in front of all of these little school people, because I already felt it in my bones that I had already lost this fight before it even got started! And I am more than positive that everyone could already see the yellow streak going down my back without me having to prove the coloring. And fortunate enough for this crowd, this little boxing match didn't require a ticket; they just needed to attend the same school. Now I was by no means a fighter at all, but this boy was, and he was very willing to demonstrate it. Without hesitation, he walked straight over to deliver me my first fight and punched me dead bang right in the middle of my nose. Instantly, my eyes began to water. Then, he tackled me down as if he was trying out for a football team. I twisted and turned and kicked a leg or two and somehow turned the table. Now I was on top of him feeling like a winner, but with my newfound accomplishment I really didn't know what I should do next. Shoot, I was still dazed from this little guy's punch, and just as fast as I was on top of him, he flipped the table and was right back on top of me, and he knew exactly what to do, and he wasn't playing.

Common sense told me to quickly cover my face! He started his assault of rapid punches on my forearms that was protecting me. I can still hear my mother's and aunt's voices in the background screaming, "Brian, you better kick his butt." I guess they didn't understand this was my first fight. This boy that was winning never met my cousin Sweet Pea, and he did not know she went to the same school as well, and she was one year behind in grade due to a bus strike. So there was no way he knew that she liked to fight, and her specialty was fighting boys. As I laid there being turned into a human punching bag, somehow, he flew straight off of me as if he had wings. As I lifted up and regained visibility, Sweet Pea was dragging him in the grass by the collar of his shirt as if he was a bag of dirty laundry. Once she had him far enough away from me, she pulled upward on his collar until he was standing on his own 2 feet, then pointing a finger at his nose and started talking to him so softly that only the two of them understood the conversation.

That guy never teased me again or any of his cheerleaders for that matter. Everything was going smoothly at school until the day I failed to be a protector (and my cousin still reminds me till this day of the incident). It was our grandfather's day to pick us up from school. Sweet Pea and the older siblings did not have to be escorted by my granddad. But Tempo, Nina, and I were not allowed to walk to my grandparent's house alone. Tempo and I exited the school together. We did not see Nina anywhere, nor did we see our granddad. The both of us waited on the corner of 116th and Union for only a couple of seconds. Tempo and I were trying to decide if we should take the chance and walk to my grandparents' house, which was only two blocks away. Reluctantly, I looked at Tempo and said, "Let's walk." So we started on our way.

The more we traveled into our journey, Tempo and I had no idea that this particular day will remain with us for the rest of our lives. Nina was still inside the school building, and by peering out of the window, she could see us as we were leaving. She started down the stairs going as fast as her little legs would allow her. She flew out of the building as fast as she could, working hard to play catchup! Without being escorted by a school traffic guard and not looking both ways, she ran straight out into traffic. :(Tempo and I made it to my grandparents' house safe enough, but for one reason or another, I started to get nervous when I began to knock at my grandad's door.

My uncle's wife answered and let us in. She was smiling, but her facial expression quickly turned into a look of concern. "Where is Nina?" was spoken with demand in it! We responded with a shrug and a dumbfounded "I don't know." She did not let us come all the way into the house. She left us standing in the foyer and hurried to call Tempo's mom. My aunt was at home from work as she listened to her sister-in-law explain that we walked to the house by ourselves and Nina was not with us. My aunt lived only five to ten minutes away, so she was there in the instant. And when my mother's sister came through my grandparents' door, she let it be known that right then and there I was not her nephew anymore! Mentally she had transformed me into her son as if we had shared a birthing together, and dealing with her was just like dealing with my real birth mother. So all I could do was prepare myself because what I was about to receive from her will be delivered to me as if I pressed the little red button on all the cameras in the world and stole a pack of gum from every neighborhood supermarket that carried that addictive cinnamon flavor BS. Like a strike of lightning with no questions asked, she begun taking her leather belt to me and her daughter backsides simultaneously, and she was doing a very good job at killing two birds with one stone! And there was no sugar coating added to this butt kicking the two of us were receiving. This woman wanted to know where her youngest daughter was at, so the beat down didn't last as long as I was anticipating.

As we were receiving our life lesson for being hardheaded, our rear ends and wherever else the leathery lighting struck, was rescued by a phone call. My uncle's wife announced that it was the school principal. I started to think, *Thank God. Anything to get this mad woman off of us.*

I just knew the principal was calling to notify her that Nina was left behind and sitting in her office. But that wishful thought would not become reality in this situation. This little walk from school had snowballed into something more severe than any thought pattern I was calculating.

As Nina darted into the traffic, trying to catch up with her older siblings, she was struck by a car and was helpless underneath until the vehicle completed its course over her entire body.

I wished I was more responsible at that time. Maybe I could have prevented this tragedy.

As the ambulance hastily made its way toward the hospital, my cousin slipped into a coma. With the grace of God, she survived that terrible ordeal.

As I'm sitting here reminiscing, I can still see her walking around my grandparents' house with all her bandages around her head and ice packs sitting on the tables. The driver of the vehicle was a family friend who accidentally ran her over. We gave praise to God that she was so small because while she was lying under that hot motor, the clearance of the vehicle in proportion to the ground protected her from being smashed.

CHAPTER 6

MOVING ON UP

After recovering from my cousin's ordeal, the last few incoming school days was running pretty smoothly than the previous ones and I was very thankful for that. But as the months passed, we entered the path of higher learning. And sometimes, that consists of a new school. My cousins and I were totally separated. Everyone was sent to a different school. I was transferred over to Woodland Hill Elementary, and my cousins were bussed and transferred to Rener Rainy Harper Elementary, and my other cousins was bussed to somewhere totally off the neighborhood map. I was now entering third grade. I do believe that transferring was the main contributing factor to why I never started smoking cigarettes. We lived too close for me to be bussed, so my mom was always dropping me off at school.

My mom used to load me into the car with all the windows raised up tightly. And as if she was doing her daily good deed, Linda would crack her window maybe five centimeters and fire up a Virginia Slim menthol light. The smell of smoke was so strong to my young nose, it always reminded me of the terrible scent from the older kids back at Mount Pleasant Elementary. The older boys at the school would go inside the bathroom and pee on the hot radiator just so they could hear their piss sizzle and watch it turn into a white pissy smoky mist. The smell was horrific, and they didn't give a damn who was breathing it in. Most of the bigger children didn't have a father at home, so that was always their reason for being dramatically over-the-top. I'm sure Guantánamo Special Forces could use that smell to get some type of answers from the captives. Now every time I see a lit cigarette, that smell will just enter into my conscience.

Woodland Elementary was located on Ninety-Third and Union, which was a straight shot from our apartment building, give or take a couple of traffic lights. Even though this school was very close to where we lived and I should've been feeling the presence of home, it turned out to be the total opposite. As I was surveying my new classroom, none of the children were noticeable from my neck of the woods. I did not know one soul in my class, which was perfect for me because this entitled me to a beautiful, new, fresh start, and with me being a natural, I started doing my thing. I became one of the teacher's favorites, and I didn't hesitate to jump on the honor roll bandwagon. So far, life as a kid at school was looking good.

Third grade was when I began noticing girls or a girl for that matter. I wasn't given the opportunity to remember her name, but for some reason or another, I always found myself staring at her during the school luncheon hours. When the weather was permitting, we were allowed outside to the school's playground for our lunch breaks. She was always smiling and laughing, and it kept my attention because I knew she was happy, so I figured she wasn't a victim to the same type of situation that I had going on at home, and I admire it. It had gotten to the point that the teacher would sometimes have to double call my name when she came to the playground in order to retrieve all of her class. As the rest of my classmates lined up to reenter back into the school, I would be holding up at the end of the line, looking at her, goo-goo eyes and all. If the butterfly kisses that was flickering from my eyelids were just a little bit stronger, I probably could've flown around in the air like "Dumbo", trying to get her to notice me. My teacher would just smile at me and say, "Come on, young man." Since we didn't share the same classroom, I didn't know if she was in a grade higher or not because she was a little bigger than me. But I did know that something inside me was telling me that I liked this girl! And this was a very weird feeling that was coming over me. My body knew what was going on, but my mind wasn't doing such a good job, and any reasoning of comprehension was at a total loss when trying to figure out these new feelings. I couldn't even describe nor understand what these new feelings meant because I've never honestly experienced it before and my comprehension of not understanding was at all the time high. But I was liking this very confused and unbalanced feeling! :)

At the time I was soaking it all in and trying to understand what I was experiencing, my teacher came to the rescue and explained to me that I had a crush on my lunch break buddy who doesn't have the slightest idea that I even exist. Now as the days were slowly going by, my mom and dad never did notified the children that they were working on a plan to move our part of the family away from the meaningful building and in doing so, the factor of that reality was also breaking our branch from the rest of family tree. The reason being that prompt this escape from our little dungeon was due to the fact that my dad had just landed a brand-new gig with an up and coming mega million working plantation called PPG. Now with Linda who always maintain more than one job at a time and with my father's new found fortune, the two of them together had made it to the point where they could actually do the George Jefferson shuffle! Because we were truly moving on up. They were singing the song and had us parading too even though we didn't know what the song meant. And when I found out, I was not ready to be a participant in this great adventure. I was not at all in cahoots with the lyrics to that song either, because as I listened closer to the words that was being spoken, moving on up also meant moving away from my cousin's and worst of all it also meant moving away from my grandparents. And now that the hamster was running around on the turning wheel in my mind at full speed I started to focus more. Oh my God! This moving venture would also mean being taken away (or kidnapped if you will) from my new crush that didn't know who I was! Which in turn is a double middle finger that was pointed directly at me! At that very moment I didn't know what to do about this newfound information. So I just tilted my face to the sky and ask one very serious question, "Why am I being hit with such a devastating blow at such a young age? Why! Why! Why!" But little did I know that that was just a very small preparation for the future to come.

My parents were only visualizing one view, (us children views didn't have a snowball in hell of a chance no matter how hard we wish to remain residing in the dungeon) and that's the "thank God Almighty we can afford a new house" view. Which actually was okay, because at the time they were figuring this would be beneficial for all of us. And one day, that very house, came into focus very unexpectedly for my taste. The daily hour was morning and I was getting into my usual routine readying myself for school, when my intuition told me to check my little jar to see how much change I had saved up. I believe to have had over two whole dollars. Now back in those days for a child of my age, two dollars was like having twenty dollars when it came to buying "delicious & juicy" penny candy. That two dollars would definitely guarantee me over 100 pieces of candy, so that would easily put me at first place when it came to being the man in third grade! And I had my eyes on only one very special prize to offer all my delicious sugary treasures too.

As the imaginary rooster made his debut in my mind for this day, I didn't have the slightest idea that I will be placing myself in such a foolish position! Because this was the day that I have decided to make my perfectly planned out "ingenious lovebird" move! I truly did my homework on masterminding my first big gig at initiating the Casanova that I thought was dwelling inside of me. It was nowhere near Valentine's Day, but I had orchestrated such a play within my thinking that I was going to treat my new crush as if it was that magical holiday for lovers. Now at the time my positive and outgoing personality had moved me into the role model student slot, I still had my ways, and hardheadedness came first place when I'm trying to complete a goal. Me being from off Ninety-Third, doing the wrong thing came very easily with very little conscience involved. As the bell rang, we were all sitting in the lunchroom enjoying our slimy fish sticks and refrigerator cold French fries, but mine was left untouched because I was more focused on my "super superior" Casanova mission that was now in the process of revving its engines and just waiting for the bell to sound off, so I can put my 007 into action. My whole train of thought was turned toward my master plan that this secret mission is a must! And it will be executed by all means necessary. The anticipation that has now made a home in the system of my nerves was so overwhelming that my whole body had pricked up into a shaken but not stirred drink with plenty of goose bumps masquerading as ice cubes. My little metal lunch seat was burning, and I couldn't wait to remove my rump off of it! My master plan had me dealing with much unforeseen anticipation on how this was really going to play out? But accommodate with full motivation as I waited very impatiently for that darn school bell to do its freaking job! Because as soon as I hear the fat lady sing that meant playtime for the other children, but it meant evasive action for me!

As the bell rang for the children to go outside into the school's playground to stretch their legs and burn off some of that energy so the classroom won't be overrun with little sugary filled bellies that's a little hard to manage for any teacher, I had already moved like Flash Gordon off of my hot seat and slid in line with another class that was first to go outside. As soon as we hit the playground, I walked all the way over to the end of the gate, and I was making sure to time my movements according to my blueprint. I hastily waited for the second wave of kids to come through the doors as the lunch maids were watching them exit. I separated myself from the group and hopped over the steel rails that separated the school from the public sidewalk and made my way over to the corner store, which sat across the street from a busy avenue. Before I darted across, I had thoughts of what happened to my cousin when she was laying up underneath that car. So I started initiating the imitation maneuver of Linda! When she hung her head out of her car window to make sure she was safe just before she beat me down with that Afro pick for taking that pack of gum.

I looked both ways as if I knew exactly what I was doing, saw it was clear, and started running for my life across the street. I did not stop until I entered the store. This was the very first very time that I was entering a store on my own, and without an adult guiding me as usual and telling me "No!" to every single snack that would lay its eyes upon me. But I was most definitely free now to taste whatever cupcakes and chips I pleased, and to my surprise now that I had the time to focus on the store's available tasty arsenal, I realized that there was so many different kinds of penny candies that I never knew existed! It was so many flavors before my face, I could feel the tears of joy welling up inside of my mouth. But within a split second all of that greedy nonsense was instantly pushed to the side because the little man inside of me just remind me of the mission that I was on, so I started pointing and giving off numbers. "Let me get ten Jolly Joes, three Bazooka gums… Oh yeah, give me twenty of those soft round Cherry Chewies. I need two boxes of Mike and Ikes and some Now-n-Later's [I was going to work with the little time that I had. It was destined for me to show this girl—whose name I didn't even know—that I was the candy man and I wanted her to be my candy girl.] Oh yeah, give me twenty Monster Chews and a box of Boston baked beans."

Now to top it all and finalize the deal, I ended my customize order with a few Reese's peanut butter cups.

Now it was time to seal the deal, so I ended my customize order with a few miniature Chico sticks, and with a wave of my right hand that struck like lightning, I snatched the brown paper bag from the cashier and quickly exited the store. I checked to make sure the coast was clear and quickly jumped back over the fence then slid right back in line with the other children that were running around. I was really fast for the clubfoot mascot that the doctor said wouldn't be able to run and jump like the other children. As the bell rang, I walked straight over to my no-name crush with my head halfway down because the shy guy in me didn't have the proper kahunas to even look her straight in the eyes, but that wasn't enough to prevent me from continuing on with my task. I handed over the brown paper bag full of all those delicious candies that I bought with my two dollars that probably took me almost two months of some serious saving up.

Then, in my coolest Casanova voice, I said, "Here, this is for you." After I made sure that she really had control of the bag, I ran my scared self straight over to the designated lunch line and started walking into the building with the rest of the children. As I completed my mission, I smiled to myself because no one was too wise of my actions. Except for my little candy girl, of course! While waiting for the clock to end the school day, I was wondering, *How will she be acting tomorrow at lunch? Will my hard work really pay off for what I was aiming for? Will I finally get to know her name?* So many thoughts of possibilities were floating around in my head that I really couldn't focus on anything else that was important. But we all know in reality, that only time holds the answers to most of all life questions.

Later that day, Linda picked me up from school with one of the biggest smiles tattooed on her face. Linda did not make the usual left to go down Ninety-Third so we can start making our way home.

She just kept straight up Union. So I was thinking we were going to my grandparents' house. But that was not the case. As we passed my grandparents' street, I didn't ask my mom any questions about where we were going because she always had us on a mission or two at any given time, so I was used to this, and more than likely, her answer would've been, "Stay in a child's place, little boy."

As we were making our way farther from home, little did I know that I would never see my candy girl or Woodland Hills School again. As we proceeded forward, I started seeing building structures that I had never laid eyes on before; and as our ride continued, the buildings disappeared and beautiful homes came into focus as we pulled up inside of a driveway.

Before I could even get a word out of my mouth, Mom said, "Brian, this is our new home." I would've passed out if I knew how to, so I went with the next best thing. I just stared at Linda with my mouth open. "Well, say something!" she said to me. "Why I be damn!" Is what I was thinking, but I wouldn't dare get smacked in the mouth at this time of the day, because I still needed my teeth in order to chew up my dinner. So I bypassed getting in trouble and answered with a very simple question.

"So you're telling me we're moving from the dingy apartment building into a new house?" was all that I could muster up because this was definitely bigger than Casanova!

Now it was time for one of my mother's "Mama bear to little cub" serious conversations before we exited the car. "Brian, you don't seem too happy?" I gave no response because I was still in shock. So Linda attempted to nudge me a little more forward with a puzzling smile. I was just sitting in the backseat of the car with no gum, staring at this woman as her lips began to move. "This is our new home, and guess what? You have your own bedroom now! We also have a basement my little bear." I managed to crack a small smile, since my mom was winning me over with her magic wand by calling me one of her pet names. She was really working hard to play the part of the good witch, as we both sat there knowing it was some BS somewhere within this mixing pot she was starring. I learn at a very young age about the, "unspoken truth" "Come here my little bear", Linda was whispering to me as she gave a helping hand and pulled my body over the headrests so I could sit in the shotgun seat where my father usually sits. "Now look directly in front of you little man, do you see the size of that garage?" I just nodded up and down yes. "We we'll be parking two cars in there with ease baby. And guess what Brian? We also have three bathrooms, no more being scared about wetting your pants baby, so come on now. Show your mama a bigger happy face!"

Everything sounded beautiful to me, but I was still a child, so those words of enhancements of having a new house didn't hold any merit with me other than "Woopy Doo for us." The only thing that was truly on my mind was the girl that I handed the big brown bag of candy too! Blah! :(

Since birth, I spent the majority of my time with my grandmother and my grandfather, due to the fact that my mom and dad were working on becoming stronger providers for their household. Only God Himself could've prevented them from taking care of their family, and I honestly believed that they would've given "The Almighty" a run for His money if it were such an option. So with that going on, I never followed the regular steps nor even used the words "mommy and daddy" when it came to referring to my parents. My grandmother became mom, and my grandfather became dad. And after hearing my grandparents calling Linda and my dad by their first name so often, my brothers and I really didn't have a choice but to follow suit. Till this day, we still call her by her first name, Linda! So there I was still sitting in the front seat waiting to be pulled out of the car by the good witch, with nothing but the thoughts of never seeing my first true love again (and remember this nonexistent relationship that I had with my candy girl is coming from a third-grader's perspective so no point in bringing this issue to my mom's attention), but I finally started realizing where we were sitting and what she was explaining to me. Did this lady just say that this is our new house? Like, this is where I'm going to be living forever and ever? Did this woman just say I got my own bedroom? Within three blinks of an eye, my whole theme of my candy girl was being diminished because of the sights of this beautiful home that I was finally breathing in.

I couldn't believe the results of that "unknowing where we're going" ride that we just took to get here! And now, I see that the experience was really worth it! Linda was just looking at me, displaying all of her "happy teeth" while smiling. She pointed and said, "Go in the backyard and check it out." As I walked toward the backyard, I noticed that the house had an aluminum coating, which made me think the house was made out of metal because I had never seen this type of material before. Every house that I've been to was made out of wood or bricks. The thick glass block windows that was installed for the basement was truly appealing. Them windows had me thinking, *Those are to keep the drunks out!* But by the looks of this neighborhood, there didn't seem to be any drunks around. Everything looked so neat and clean. (But that would surely change as the years go by!)

Before I could enter the backyard, I had to lift the latch off our pretty little green fence. This house actually came with a fence, and it wasn't covered with pissy, confused exotic weeds! As I'm walking into the backyard, it was such a sight from what I was normally used to. I saw trees that I'd never seen before. These trees grew straight up into the sky, and we had three of them. I ran over to my mom because now I needed answers. "Linda, what kind of trees are those?"

She looked me in my face, smiled, and said, "Those are pine trees. And that's where I'm going to put the garden."

I just continued smiling and took off running towards all three pine trees. As I peered towards the tippy top of their branches, I could actually see cones hanging off them! But to my surprise, the excitement was slid down a notch because the more I squinted my eyes to gain more focus I was thinking to myself, "Wow! Our pine trees must not be feeling too well, because they're producing the smallest pineapples I've ever seen." But I was still very satisfied and at the same time I was in need of some serious answers about the fruit I wanted to eat. So I ran just as fast back to my informational mother bear. "Linda! Something is very very wrong with our pineapple trees! Come look come look!" Now I was doing this not truly knowing if I was really concerned about the trees, or because I was hungry?

Playfully smiling, she said, "No, it's not, silly goose."

"Yes, it is," I responded with the seriousness written all over my face. "They're not fat and round like they should be, instead they're all like brown pears."

She just burst out laughing without giving any explanation whatsoever, so I just took off running again, and continued my exploring of this huge backyard. The next two trees that I encountered had berries growing on them, so I yelled in my "mama bear" direction in hopes of receiving some information this time around, "Linda look, exactly what kind of tree is this one?" Rubbing the old genie lamp seemed to have prevailed this time around and I couldn't believe that we actually owned two real live raspberry and blueberry trees! This was all so beautiful! And the anticipation of putting some in my watering mouth was killing me, because I knew this area was safe and nothing like what "Sweet Pea" had us eating! >:(And lucky enough I was given a second opinion that everything was safe (well at least that's what I thought) because I saw the bluest of the Blue Jays and the brightest cherries of the bright Cardinals landing on everything and taking a bite. I couldn't believe we had such beautiful birds flying around in our backyard! The birds were so colorful that they reminded me of enchanted soaring Disney. The longer I stood there taking everything in the feeling of being home was fading away, and was being replaced with the feeling of being the lucky chocolate bar winner to visit the totally awesome "Fruit Factory of Willy Wonka". Finally, I made my way to the end of the backyard and started making my journey through the scissor grass that was just as tall as me. And that's when I noticed with every step I was taking, the bottom of my tennis shoe soles was landing on top of fallen apples. Excitedly I screamed to myself, "Wow, I can't believe it! Our new house comes with a freaking fruit market!" As I quickly moved towards my mother with lightning speed, I could hardly catch my breath from running so darn fast and when I finally did catch it, I yelled as loudly as I could, "Linda, we have an apple tree!"

She looked at me with that stern "Afro Pick" glare (you know, the one that stops the deer in its tracks) and said, "No, we don't. That apple tree is our neighbor's who lives over the fence, and don't you go jumping over the fence touching her apples."

I said okay and started heading toward the garage because I knew I was going to get some of those apples, one of these days, as soon as the coast was clear. >:)

So far, we were doing great with this new house that came with eatable trees and a two-car door garage. When I finally entered into the garage, you could have never told me that garages come with lights and electrical sockets inside them. This garage was laid out to the fullest. It even had counters built on the inside so that whenever my dad got some tools, he would have somewhere to place them, and the garage was insulated with the Pink Panther puffy cotton ball stripy stuff. So much was going on in that backyard it had my head continuously flowing from left to right. As I prepared to walk out of the house for my mom and dad cars, that was when I finally noticed the back of our house. I was so super shocked by the natural environment that this place had going on that I didn't even pay attention to the back of this freaking house when I first entered through the fence. I was now just standing in front of the garage stuck in my darn tracks. "Good Goobly Zoo Zooland" my eyeballs were screaming!

I couldn't believe that this marvelous site I was gawking at belong to us. This house had an upper and lower deck connected to it and I mean they were large! I even noticed that the house had electrical sockets connected to it, for whatever reason I did not know but I was digging it! As my eyes followed the black beams that was protruding upwards from the lower deck and connecting themselves into the ceiling, I was only wondering if I could play "fire engine man" and slide right back down them. As the little mouse in my brain finally caught up to the wheel it was turning, I realized just how huge the upper deck was and was pretty sure (or positive if you will) that me and my brothers were going to turn that into our playroom in the sky. Quickly I spun around on my heels and completed a 360 maneuver as if I was the greatest "Cape Crusader" and thought to myself, "Well I be damn! We're moving into a freaking castle!" (Anyone would've had this feeling after leaving such a dingy dungeon behind, no matter what age you are).

My mom called me. It was time to go into the beautiful castle. When we walked through the door, my mom didn't even get a chance to direct me if she wanted to. I allowed myself to run free and explore this new strange place on my own, and Linda was truly okay with that. The first thing that came to light was the stairwell that led to the basement, and I ran for the gold. When I got to the bottom of the stairs, I had two options. Option one, open the door that was to my right and see what was in there, or option two, go through the little gate. So I followed option two.

First thing that came to sight was that this basement had a full bar that was at least eighteen feet long. It was made out of all leather with a wood grain top. In the back, it was all mirrors and mirrored shelves. After I finally made it to the top of one of the bar stools, I could see the reflection of the mirrors, and I was looking at the back of the bar, so I went behind there. There was a little refrigerator and a sink to accommodate it. When I exited from behind the bar, there was a little storage room right beside it. As I walked past that, I came to two doors. I opened the door to my right. It was a bathroom with a toilet, a sink, and a shower. I couldn't believe it. We had a basement with an actual shower and toilet! Wow! I couldn't wait to open up next door, but it turned out just to be another storage shed that lead under the stair casing. Now it was time for me to see the rest of the basement. There were speakers made into the walls and air vents everywhere. I continued further into the mist of this basement where I came upon three more doors. I opened door number 1! It was a room the size of a small bedroom. I made my way to door number 2! There were bookshelves built into the walls and as I slid the door open, that's where the gas meter and water meters were located. Now it was time for door number 3. When I opened door number 3, I stepped into yet another fairly large room, which was housing a washer and a dryer that sat on a concrete platform with a utility sink right next to them! Wow! Right next to the utility sink was a long wooden platform to fold all the laundry, but before I could step toward any of that, there was a door on my left! As I opened that door, which we will call door number 4, it was another fairly sized room for storage. I walked past the washer and made my way toward what we will call door number 5. That path brought me back around to the little gate that was on my right at the bottom of the stairs. I really enjoyed my "self-given tour" of the basement, but what really had my face smiling and singing a happy tune, was because we had so many places to hide when me and my cousins get together to play hide-and-seek!

Now it was time for me to make my way upstairs and continued this terrific journey. When I got to the top, I was in a hallway. I had two doors to choose from or go up a flight of stairs that led to another flight of stairs. So I chose door number 1. This turned out to be my mom and dad's bedroom. All I could think was wow! My mom and dad had a very big bedroom! It was bigger than our living room inside the dingy dungeon! And was my young eyes deceiving me? Linda and Ike had a full functional bathroom inside of their bedroom. Wow! I stood inside their beautiful bathroom soaking it all in. It was truly amazing. Everything was black marble with gray and gold sparkles! And mirrors from wall to wall! There was no way in the world you were going to be walking out of this bathroom with toilet paper hanging out of your pants! I walked out of their bedroom and entered into the living room, which was connected to the dining room, which was connected to the kitchen. This was really a big place to me.

Finally, I decided it was time for me to make my way up the two flights of stairs. First to my left, there was another bathroom. As I passed, I came to yet another room, which would later turn out to be my sister's bedroom when she's created. There was a very large den upstairs and two more bedrooms. I could not believe that we moved from such a dingy place to such a beautiful Palace. Finally the moon was showing its face in the darkened skies. As we all started winding down for the night and having our first dinner, my mother kept it simple with a fresh pot of spaghetti that she prepared in her new kitchen and Linda was smart because she made a very large pot of it. So we all knew with so much unpacking to be done, Linda will not have time to be cooking, so we were all prepared to be eating spaghetti for the rest of the week.

Life is good, I thought until my mom opened up her mouth and notified me and my brothers that we all would be attending a new school in the morning and that she now have a baby on board, which was an indication that there will be more snacks around for us to eat, Yay! (And sure enough a few months later, we had a little sister occupying that room upstairs.) Finally Linda said, "Time for you guys to go to bed. You young men have school in the morning."

CHAPTER 7

IT'S A NEW DAY

The saying "Out with the old and in with the new" introduced itself to me when I was on my way to Charles Dickens Elementary School which was located on E. 131st Street in Cleveland, Ohio. This was exactly where my life started its left turn towards the worse: I was entering into the third grade at Charles Dickens which shouldn't have been too much different from my previous school because I was in the third grade there, but this was a different type of third grade! Living on 131st is what we consider the "Up The Way" part of town, and these up the way children were really off the freaking chain. Shoot, they were already professionals at such a young age when it came to using cuss words and boy oh boy they really did curse a lot! I was hearing brand-new words that even my mother and father hadn't used yet! But the one word that really stuck in my head was combined with a capital *Mother* and ended with a capital *F*! Now, I've heard the four letter "F" word before, but I still didn't understand the exact meaning of this very interesting four-syllable word. And now that capital "F" was being combined with the word "Mother"? It just seemed to be a perfect "jumble word infusion" to me. But in my heart I knew that this sounded very wrong, but also it sounded so very powerful! And I couldn't wait to use it on my brothers and my cousins!

My first day at Charles Dickens was no ordinary day for your average third-grader that was coming from a less-advanced school because these little evil bastards were on a higher level of thinking. Nervously, I entered the classroom, following behind a smiley-faced secretary from the main office, and I knew right off hand before I could even sit down at a desk that these children were way out of my league. As I stood there watching the secretary who was so kind to me walk out the classroom door, I slowly turned to the right so I could try to get an understanding of where I was at and to what I was about to be dealing with. "In life, fair exchange is no robbery" because the whole classroom was returning the favor by staring at me! There was some snickering associated with some laughing, and of course, I knew this was going to be some type of ordeal for the days to come when I saw two little girls pointing a finger at me. Due to my past experience, I learned the powers of foretelling the future to myself (or at least that what I was thinking at the time)! First comes the girls pointing and smiling at me. After school comes the boys' frowns and trying to beat me up! Life really has its jokes at any age, I tell ya! >:(

As I stood there monitoring and supervising my own surveillance of these "little bad bastards", this one young guy stood out from the rest which raise my suspicion for some reason or another. His name was DeMarco. And he turned out to be a really cool cat. We befriended one another and became good buddies, and for a bonus he just so happen to have a little brother that was around my brother Slim's age. So whenever Ike and Linda started doing their dance number, my little brother and I would escape to DeMarco's house, and the four of us would always play with GI Joe's for hours. I don't know if it was fate or a hint of a learning experience for the future that's going to come, but I always ended up with the Cobra

Commander action figure. Even though DeMarco and I lived in the same neighborhood, his house was located far from mine, so we eventually lost connection. It was over fifteen years when I saw him again. Not only was it discovered that we both were of the same zodiac and had some ways alike, when we saw each other again, we started dressing like twins every single day, and it wasn't due to the fact that we were still so super cool. It was more of the reality that we had no choice but to wear the same outfit as soon as the correction officer shouted for us to come out of the prison cells for chow. :(.

My new teacher's name was Ms. Wheeler. She was an older woman who was probably working on a retirement at the end of the year. Not much of a prize for anyone, I guess that's why the title read Ms., instead of Mrs., and even at my age, I could tell she had a nervous condition due to old age. Sometimes, we all have our personal issues that give someone else the opportunity to laugh, and hers used to have me just about going into hysteria! She had very large jaws like the bulldog from off the cartoon *Tom and Jerry*. I think his name was Spike. And whenever the classroom set her pot to boil, she would shake her head so hard that her jaws would flap as if they were wings! With me standing on the side of her desk, Ms. Wheeler asked the children to quiet down and alerted them that I would be their new classmate. As she pointed in the direction of the empty desk, I started my walk through the rows of children with their brand-new gawking faces and for some reason, I didn't even find it surprising that I wasn't afraid of them. I actually marched to my desk while displaying a sprinkle of attitude on my "trying to be tough" face. As I continue surveying my surroundings, my first thought was "This is cool," so I started feeling right at home. A lot of this came about because I realized most of the boys in the class was no bigger than I was.

There were three things I learned on my first day of school at Charles Dickens. Number 1, Ms. Wheeler and I were not going to get along because she was too jumpy, and I already had bad nerves from Ike and Linda. Number 2, I'm going to fit in with these sneaky little children because every last one of them seemed just as curious as me. Number 3, I am not going to pass third grade with this group of animals because we all were too much alike!

Finally the last bell of the day was doing its job as it sounded off for everyone to start making their way to the start of "evening time life". Before I exited the classroom I thought to myself "this day went fairly well". :) As the second day was "snail sliding" to a poor start, my morning was already going sideways after inhaling all the secondhand smoke from my mother's love of the "good old nicotine". Yes there it was in my stomach and making its way throughout the rest of my body. You know what I'm talking about, because we all get it at one time or another, that uneasy feeling had made its way into my bones and I just knew this day was going to be tough on a kid. :(Let me explain the reason why! Coming from Woodland Hills third grade, we hadn't started on multiplication just yet. These kids cursed a lot true enough, but they were definitely smarter. And with so much negativity going on in my home with my mom and dad's cat and dog fights, I couldn't focus in school! I had no one to really take the time to show me proper arithmetic. I know all families have agreements and disagreements, but my mom and dad's agreements and disagreements were to an extreme! It was truly an everyday occurrence in one fashion or another! I hate that I had to endure this as a child! >:(

On this same second day of school, my dad decided we should all jump into the car and take a ride over to his cousin's house. And once again, it was about to go down! Linda and Ike were at it again with no holds barred in front of everyone. I do not know what initiated this argument because we were always told to stay out of grown people's business, and this argument was so overheated that my dad's people asked him to step out of the house and finish it outside. We all know that adding way too much alcohol into anyone's bloodstream can create a very negative, but memorable, event. My mom, just a little too harshly, grabbed my hand and started walking toward the door! I guess she figured Ike would look at me like some type of shield or security element for herself since I was his son, and just maybe, Ike's argument would settle down a little bit. Plus, we were outside in broad daylight. But that was not the case. The beautiful sun was shining its warm rays down on earth, which only heated up the situation more, and we all know that alcohol and heat do not mix! My mom continued pulling me along, walking toward her car. My dad followed close behind, talking real crazy and grinding his teeth. He always grind his teeth when he was trying to instill fear in someone, and it really worked on us because we didn't know no better.

My mom opened up the driver side of the car and quickly snatched me by my arm and pushed me into the backseat. She had to do this fast while trying to keep an eye on Ike. She was not trying to hurt me, but she had to hurry up and turn around and raise her hands in the air over her face because my dad was right behind her, grinding his teeth with his fists balled up. My mom screamed at my father, and you could tell she was sparing no vocal cords. It was released at the top of her lungs. "Just get into the car. Don't hit me! Just get into the car, please. Do not hit me, Ike!"

For some reason, my dad backed off but only for a split second. Ike was going to finish what he was starting on the passenger side of the vehicle. Little did he know that this will be the one rodeo that he would never forget about from riding shotgun next to Linda. Because my mother was going to let it be known, that sometimes "Fair exchange is a robbery".

As soon as he was in the car, he went straight to work grinding his teeth and staring at my mom like it was time to kill and eat something. My mother didn't look back. She just remained calm and cool as usual. That is, until he started making that noise that sounded like he was accumulating spit in his mouth. When my mother heard that sound, she looked him dead in his eyes, and with a venomous whisper, she softly said, "You better not spit on me, Ike."

My dad really had some very serious issues, and spitting on my mom was one of them. When Linda completed her whisper, she placed her hand inside her purse. She was now staring at him, with the venom transferred into her eyes, and with a glare that spoke what her mouth didn't say: "Today I'm tired of your shit!" My dad knew this look and backed down, but the liquor in his system was not having it. It told him to proceed forward, to which he foolishly continued to do. All I heard was the gargle of saliva, followed by a strong inhale, and a strong release that was pushed with a hard thrust of wind! In slow motion, I could actually see the spit flying through the air. His mouth was like a gun using his saliva as a very "disrespectful bullet" traveling in full force for the bull's-eye, and my mother was the target. And unfortunately enough; that foul play from Ike's mouth hit its mark. >:(

Before I could even comprehend what had just happened, the car was full of white smoke, and my nose was starting to burn from the stinging air that I had no choice but to inhale! As the tears began to fall from my eyes and the watery mucus that had built its self up inside of my nostrils drizzle into my open mouth with vengeance, I started choking from the chemically sharp smell of that fiery blast that had filled the entire car as if we were barbecuing inside of this Pontiac. I watched in total shock as this fast-paced episode had managed to slow my thinking down for a moment! But I knew exactly what was going on this time! Because my comprehension started moving at full speed from recapping on the Bonanza cowboy TV shows, that I used to sometimes watch with my dad. So everything became very vivid and totally understood instantaneously, and that's when I actually realized "that my mom had just shot my dad right in front of my eyes", and neither one of them was Cowboys or Cowgirls, but they was definitely playing the part of the shooter and the victim!

As the smoke started to retreat and my visual was gaining more site, the visual view I was viewing was starting to pull my tears up into a halting stance! And without hesitation a smile started struggling to break free from the crying and frowning that my face had accumulated within the seconds of this sad but purposely driven real life action movie! I watched as blood splattered inside of the Pontiac! I quickly turned my head towards "Mr. Pistol Mouth" just as his body was slamming into the passenger car door while he hastily grabbed and squeezed the upper part of his torso! And this time while he was gritting his teeth, he realize the pain he "evilly beg" for was afflicted upon himself only because of his mistreatment of a loving woman. And I was very proud of my mom for taking such a powerful stand against her husband! >:)

Till this day, I can still remember watching my mother's lips moving through the thin white smoke that was produced from her angered .38 snubnosed that was screaming to see fresh blood! My mom spoke to her freshly hit bull's-eye as the tears continue to run down her face with total control within her vocal cords, "I politely asked you not to spit on me, you dirty motherfucker! Now look at you, laying over there shot". I just sat there in the backseat watching this "Violent Circus" play itself out! I was definitely feeling numb but I was also slightly smiling because I actually learned something throughout this terrible ordeal.

Now I knew, that being called a "DMF" was way more sinister than being called an ordinary "MF".

CHAPTER 8

THE CANDY MAN

With all of my family physical and mental dysfunctions floating around and sometimes just hovering in the air waiting for an opportunity to make life more miserable, I was always embarrassed about how my school grades had tipped over off of the mountain top and was now just snowballing down the hill with no regrets. You could tell that math was one of the favorite subjects discussed in my new class, but I really had nowhere or anyone to turn to when it came to asking someone who was honestly willing to aid in teaching me arithmetic, so naturally, I started falling behind in school. To keep my mind at ease and not show signs of what was going on at home, I became the class clown and the class candy man. I was making all the kids laugh and had a desk full of candy that I would sell to the children who couldn't get to the store. Yes, third grade, this is where my life started going downhill and growing stronger on the negative side of life.

I can still remember one of Ms. Wheeler's nicknames that she honored me with. She call me a nincompoop. Once, she even told me that I was going to wind up in jail! The next day must have been when she had a heart to heart with herself, so she decided to call my mom to try to prevent my early imprisonment. I was sitting at my desk, being the joker that I usually was in class, with my back turned to the teacher. She pleaded with me to turn around, but as usual, her request fell on deaf ears. I had the crowd going; the back of the class was laughing so hard. Then all of a sudden, there was complete silence. I watched as everyone's eyes grew very big, and they all were looking in one direction, and that was the classroom doorway. The first thought that came to my head was that the principal had just stepped in to pay us a little visit and I was finally caught in the act with my buffoonery. But I truly could care less of any of the teacher or principal disciplinary actions because I wasn't getting parenting time at home like regular children. So if they decided to place a phone call to my "chaotic dwelling spot" and in hopes of retribution? They were really barking up the wrong tree. All I could do was wish them a very "good luck with that maneuver" trying to get some attention from Ike or Linda. Besides, with all the negative energy that they wasted on one another, they just might forget about that phone call before the receiver is even hung back up on its perching stand. But the more that I look at these "now quite" children with their eyeballs locked in on the classroom doorway, my common sense told me that whoever just entered through that threshold had to be the "perfect stranger"? Someone that they had "never seen before"!

As I slowly turned around to face the fears of my classmates, and wearing the expression on my face of knowing I was definitely caught in the act, I looked past the teacher straight to the doorway. I wish it was the principal or even Frankenstein, for that matter, but it was much worse. It was Linda! My freakin' mom. This is the same mom who shot my father in front of me! As our eyes met, I noticed that she had her stop-a-deer-in-its-tracks glance at half power. Thank God it wasn't at full power. One thing, even to this day, that I will always respect about my mom is that she does not hesitate to give an answer to an equation. The only thing that was running around in my head was, "MF! I'm in trouble now! Because she is about to put some parenting down on me! And right here-right now! In front of all of these little giggly fucks! MF!"

Immediately, she spoke to me in her your-little-butt-is-mine-mister voice, "Come here, Brian." As I slowly exited my desk and made my way to her, I was trying to brace myself for what was coming next because I truly didn't have the slightest idea what was about to occur while dealing with this woman. And a smack to the face wouldn't have been unexpected or a surprise to me for that matter, maybe to everyone else but not me. As I was making my way over closer to her, I had the feeling of walking the Green Mile and a pirate had his sword in my back as I was tiptoeing on his plank, whispering to me, "The water's all yours, *smart guy*, and you're not going to like it." Finally, I completed my imaginary journey, and now I was standing right in front of a serious-looking Linda. My whole thought was, "Wait for it, wait for it," but to my surprise, she just asked me to go stand over by the blackboard. She then turned her attention to my classmates while looking inside my desk, and I wondered what was going through her mind when she saw all that candy and all of that loose change that I'd accumulated. She lightly lowered my desktop without showing any emotion about what was going on inside of it. Then she spoke to my classmates softly but very sternly. "This is what's going to happen to you when you act like my son does in class."

While all this was going on, not one time did my mother introduce herself to my teacher. When she finally did, the conversation went like this:

"Hello, I'm Brian's mother. Do you have a yard stick?"

"Yes, I do."

"May I use it please?"

"Yes, be my guest," Ms. Creator of the Nincompoop said, with a smiling smirk mixed with vengeance and laughter written all over her, no-prize-of-a-face self. She was enjoying the fact that she was about to witness all of her revengeful-filled thoughts of me being played out right in front of her sad face. I'm pretty sure she was thinking, "There is a God."

I watched in semi-fear as my mom's eyeballs slid themselves back into the corner of her face while she was steadily making her way closer into my vicinity. She spoke to me a little rough and very commanding, "Turn around, young man, and place your hands on the chalkboard." I guess we can all say that this was my first "police search" stance, which would be followed by plenty more as my future went on. But I did as Linda asked. I followed her orders and spread-eagled on the chalkboard. I could hear her putting her purse down and taking her coat off. My mind was running at one hundred miles per hour. She was standing behind me with the yardstick. Peering out the corner of my eyes, I could see her hand raise the yardstick high in midair; and at that very moment, my mind that was running at one hundred miles per hour connected its thoughts to my legs, and I burned rubber!

Run, little nigga, run!

There was no way in hell I was going to let my mother connect that stick to my butt. (Shoot! Just the other day, one of my old third-grade schoolmates brought up the incident on Facebook! That was third grade, and I'm forty now!) That was the first time *when a soul started running*. I flew out of that classroom, then soared through the air down two flights of stairs, and ran straight out of the school building.

CHAPTER 9

ALLEY RED

Someone must've been praying for me to carry on into the fourth grade because I was actually leaving third grade behind with some of the poorest report card grades. Very unexpectedly, Fourth-grade was turning out to be a smooth sailing breeze, and I guess it was all due to the new atmosphere of fresh air I was breathing in. And I was digging this brand-new experience of being bussed to the West side of Cleveland to my learning facility called Milford Elementary. This is the time when I actually started meeting white people and Puerto Ricans, which was pretty cool. My first girlfriend was Puerto Rican. Her name was Amelia, and she was a very pretty girl. I used to give her $.25 of my lunch money, and she would go to the pay phone every evening with her white girlfriend and give me a call. At Milford Elementary, they were still practicing capital punishment by ways of the wooden paddle. And with my buffoonery, I had no choice but to become a casualty.

I was still keeping up and advancing in my trickery while entering into the fourth grade, and once again, the teacher was not fond of me. These were the days when the expression "a hard head makes a soft butt" was truly exercised. One day, a few of my classmates and I were inside of the classroom coat area rustling and acting silly.

When we came out, the assistant principal was standing in the doorway. He had everyone who was inside of the coat room meet him in his office. I never agreed with the decoration of his office because it did not match his demeanor. This guy had Mickey Mouse all over the place. Not only a Mickey Mouse pen holder, but every day, he wore a different Mickey Mouse tie and a Mickey Mouse wrist watch, and who knows what type of underwear he really wore underneath them trousers of his. As he closed the door behind him, he explained to us why he was about to exercise the school's rights to engage in "capital punishment." He went into the closet and pulled out his Mickey Mouse paddle with holes going through it, then introduced Mickey's white glove to our rear ends. No matter how hard he hit me, it didn't tarnish the way I felt about Mickey Mouse, but that MF Mouse was really teaching my backside a lesson. This was my first reality of the "color divided statues" because other than the white boy that he did not make come with us, even though he was a part of the group, he let us darker pigment skinned people know, that him and Mickey had it in for the arrest of us porch monkeys. And I Praise the Almighty that within that same week the school buses had stopped running due to Labor Union issues! :)

A lot happened in my life during the bus strike. As the days came and went, most children really didn't have too much to do, but we always found something to mess up. My dad was loving the big company he worked for, which always put one of us children in first place when it came to school candy sales. This particular year belonged to my sister. My dad took turns with us. When that day came for my mom and dad to pick up the candy, our living room had the appearance of a full-fledged candy warehouse. With my mom and father arguing all the time, my little brother and I used that toward our advantage. We ate over $300 of chocolate peanut butter cups. And we paid for it with our butts. Maybe the bus strike wasn't such a good idea after all!

One afternoon, while enjoying the absent of school with more than a few of the neighborhood children at a friend's house, that was right around the corner from where I live, you could see boys and girls everywhere! We were shouting, we were running and we were definitely playing hard! You could even see boys and girls wrestling one another! Because we knew there will be no school tomorrow, we was carrying on like it would never be any school days again! But something odd was transpiring on the front laws of one of the houses. It appeared to be three or four boys jumping on one guy, so I decided to help the poor kid. As I ran over there to join in on the fun, I noticed that that wasn't laughter but screaming coming from the kid that was being jumped on. What I thought was going on was not going on at all, because underneath that group of boys was a girl! And that little girl stayed right across the Street from me and we were pretty good friends. I noticed that that particular group of boys were squeezing on her, and she was screaming, "Get off of me!" That's when I sprung into action. As I was pulling on some of the guys to get them off her, they just got up and ran away laughing. So my brother, the girl, and I walked to my house. When we got there, my mom was gone, and my father was asleep as usual. He worked a lot of hours, so he was just shooting his regular sleeping.

About two or three days go by, and I hadn't heard anything from the girl from across the street, which I found to be very strange because we saw each other just about every day. My brother and I were upstairs when we started hearing some shouting. Like most children, our curiosity sends us on a path where we do not belong on; and due to our neglected walk into adolescence, which included lack of understanding, but wanting more adult information, we were very quick to pursue that curiosity. So off I went down the stairs. I tiptoed very softly through the kitchen. They were so deep into this conversation that they were having. The grown-ups were too busy to even pay me any attention. Finally, it was safe for me to poke my head around the corner, so I could get a sneak peek of what was going on. My curiosity caught me a good one this time.

The first thing my eyeballs landed on, to my surprise, was the mother of the girl from across the street. As I shifted my eyes farther to the right, I saw that sitting in my living room was the mother's boyfriend. I did not know what to make of this because our parents never did anything together.

But there they were, sitting in my living room, all four adults wearing the expression "I'm about to explode and do something that I know God don't want me to do!" Linda's poker face expression read, "Whoever makes a move that I don't like is going to catch one." The girl's mother's expression read, "I need some answers. Something's not right. I'm mad, confused, but I'm not here to fight, but I will if I have to." As I shifted my eyes over to the boyfriend, that's when I started to get nervous. Because I was becoming a master at reading body language! Man oh man! My curiosity gets on my nerves! But this boyfriend's whole body language was expressing attack! This man's facial expression revealed so much anger and by him being such a dark shade of a man only made his visual scarier! I watched as this chocolate mousse colored man face turned Burgundy and was struggling hard trying to hold back the bright red that truly wanted to show his true colors of what he was feeling and what he was willing to do about this ongoing saga between the four adults. The more I watched this guy, the fear I was experiencing was starting to subside as I was strongly wondering about the comparison my mind was doing. I've spent enough hours watching Bugs Bunny cartoons that every episode I now watch, is an episode that I've seen before. As I continued playing the Stealth bomber in the kitchen trying to get an understanding of their conversation, my curiosity continued trying to urge me to open the refrigerator door and throw a raw egg at this man's face! Just to see if the egg would really start to cook?

My father was standing there, looking mad and confused, and stated, "What the fuck are y'all talking about? I don't touch no fucking kids!" Now my father was an old-school gangster. Before he met my mom, he had just spent three years inside the old Mansfield Prison for hitting a man upside the head with an "alley red." For those of you who do not know what an alley red is, it's a square block of concrete. It's about eight inches long and three inches wide or something like that. It's red in color from the concrete mixture and will bust your head wide open if you are struck correctly with it. My dad was from the neighborhood of Quincy Avenue. So he was a little rough because guys from Quincy did not play games. My dad just stood there staring at them, and before I knew it, the Quincy gangster came out of him. With a loud roar, he shouted, "Get the fuck out of here!" and he turned his back to escort them out of the front door.

I found this to be a pretty odd gesture on my father's part because one thing he was always telling me and my brothers was, "Watch your backs, and don't take any wooden nickels." But he went against his own advice by absentmindedly turning his back. The now red-faced boyfriend tackled him from behind. They both went flying through my mom's living room glass table. Just as fast as the glass was flying everywhere, the red-faced man jumped up and ran straight out of our front door.

I was never the one to be afraid of anything due to all the butt-kickings Ike was given me. So I came out of my little hiding place and ran straight to the door behind Red Face. I was trying to see which way he went so I could tell my father because I knew, and Red Face knew, that my father was going to kill him! But to my surprise, the "Defensive End" didn't even run that far away? I guess it was due to his age, because he was doing his damnedest to catch his own breath, as he was standing in front of our house on the sidewalk.

When he saw me, he spoke very calmly. He said, "Young man, can you tell my wife to come out of there?" I did what he asked and never saw the two of them again, until in the courtroom. Within the next couple of days, two white men were knocking on our front door. Both were wearing long light-brown trench coats. They asked my dad to take a ride with them downtown. I watched my dad get into the backseat of their car and continued eyeballing them as they pulled out of the driveway and headed down our street.

Over the next month, my brother and I were either taken to or visited by detectives. They were asking way too many questions for a fourth- and second- grader, to comprehend. But I guess this was very necessary due to the seriousness of the allegations. When my dad returned home from his so-called vacation (at least that's where Ike is resting at), more than a few weeks had come and gone; and just as soon as we started seeing my father's face around the house again, my brother and I were putting on suits and heading downtown for court.

This was a brand-new experience for us. We truly had no idea what was going on. My dad's lawyer kept telling my brother and myself, "Just tell the jury exactly what happened that day when the other boys were jumping on your female friend." As he finished his statement, to which I heard hundreds of times over and over, I stood and wondered, in this hallway with people walking back and forth and wearing their Sunday's best, *Who in the hell is this person named Jury?* And right at that very moment, I found out who Jury was.

The bailiff came and got me and walked me over to a man sitting high up in the air with his black bathrobe on. Across from us were about twelve people sitting next to one another (they reminded me of smelly sardines), just staring at me, but not one time did I feel uncomfortable. I just went along with the program. Our lawyer started asking me questions about that very day. When he finished, the man that was sitting at the other table across from my dad's lawyer started asking me questions. This went on longer than I'd hoped for, but I really couldn't complain because I didn't have to go to school.

I take it everything went according to my dad's lawyer's expectations because as we were leaving the courthouse, my dad was smiling, my mom was smiling, and the lawyer kept repeating, "This should have never gone this far! I'm so embarrassed about the whole situation!"

At home, everything was back to usual. Linda and Ike were fighting every other day, and I was trying to find something to do while the school buses were still on strike.

CHAPTER 10

THE STRIKE IS OVER!

With so much time on my hands due to the lack of school, some days, I would get really creative! Like the one day when we had a very heavy snowfall. It was the good snow, the kind that sticks together and allows you to make a perfect snowball! When we were allowed to go outside and play, all the neighborhood kids were in their front yards, rolling up snow that had blanketed their grass, smiling while making Christmas snowmen to stand tall!

My brother and I decided to play snowball fight instead of being copycats. The next day, when we went outside, everyone's snowman had been pushed back down to the grass it came from! Little boys and girls alike were either crying or upset about their Christmas creation. I just got creative and told my little brother to help me build a snowman, and this will be a special snowman, and it will be the biggest, baddest snowman of all! And it's going to really be special because it will be filled with cream filling! We packed the inside of our adorable snowman with so much doggie poop from all the neighbors' backyards that you would've thought that our snowman had migrated from Africa! When we finished, my little brother and I got some snacks and took shifts at the window, just waiting patiently, which was not a hard job because we both are very good when it comes to being patient. Sure enough, just as the daylight started winding down, we saw three to four boys coming to tackle our snowman, and they succeeded in making sure that our snowman didn't make a touchdown. And in this fair exchange situation, our stinky snowman made sure that they will never forget that ill legal tackle that they put down on his poor self! And our wise guy snowman definitely may sure that they would never forget the strong sour stench that he delivered to them! Ha! Ha! >:)

The next day, it was time for something different, so I would stand next to the Stop sign at the end of my street and wait for a car to pull up and stop. Before they would pull off again, I would get behind their car and hold on to their bumper. As they pulled away, they would be dragging me down the street on top of the snow, and that was something to me at that time that would give any amusement Park ride a run for its money. For those of you that are not from the hood, we call this *boo–hoppin'*. And as always, I continued to show my little brother negative things to do.

One day, I decided to teach my brother Slim the techniques of boo-hoppin'. My brother, a couple of friends from the neighborhood, and I went hunting for cars to jump on. I explained the whole procedure to my loyal brother, and he was ready. A guy pulled up to the Stop sign. He was well aware of what we were about to attempt. He even waited to make sure everyone was on the back of his bumper, then he punched the gas pedal, and that vehicle took off like it was a bat freed from hell! I ate so much dirty snow and inhaled so much carbon monoxide that I thought I was going to pass out from this toxic martini. As he swerved his car from the left to the right, we all flew off the bumper. All I could hear was my brother saying, "I don't have my glove." We all turned our head toward the man's car. Slim's glove was stuck on the back of his bumper. Unfortunately, the man was driving too fast for his glove to be recovered. And it was funny! Because at the speed the car was moving, it allowed my brother's glove to be transformed into an animated apparatus and that's when we all started laughing very hard! Because this comical glove was now waving goodbye in our direction. All of our stomachs were hurting like something bad from laughing so hard! It was as if we all were participating in a stomach crunching marathon! Because we couldn't believe that my brother's glove was actually waving goodbye to all of us! As we were all working very hard at trying to get control over our oxygen intake in order to stop the giggling, we notice that even Slim had to laugh at this one even though one of his hands will be freezing from freeballing back to the house!

I can still remember the day that I did this one boo-hoopin' stunt, and sure enough it backfired on me. I waited and watched until I finally saw a car pulling up, and just like a hungry lion going after its meal, I jumped straight on the back of this lady's bumper. As she started dragging me up the street, the damn thing came apart and hit the ground along with my chin. I jumped up and ran as fast as I could, but I didn't get away scot-free with this "goofy & dumb" caper, because Earl's friend witness this jackass move entirely and he had no problems whatsoever snitching on me. And to be honest I guess I deserved it because it was all my fault for jumping on such a raggedy car!

With the bus strike not coming to an end as the weeks and months went by, boredom and curiosity have now taken full control over my soul. My dad was at work, and Linda said she had to make a run. Earl was in charge, which meant we were basically on our own. Slim and I went outside to play in the yard. And that's when we spotted a group of Jehovah Witnesses coming down the street and stopping at each neighbor's house with the hopes of recruiting them to their way of thinking. Quickly! I snatched Slim by the hand and said, "Come on, we have to hurry up before they get to our house." My mom and dad always had a thing for arts, and in our living room and dining room, there were artifacts from different countries: swords and shields from England and bamboo sticks and masks from Africa. We stripped our walls of the artworks and just waited.

After assembling ourselves into this new weird outfit, we ran as fast as we could and made it to the backyard of our house. I slowly came from behind our hiding place and started peeking out until I finally saw them walking up our driveway. I waited until I could see the white of their eyes from this "disturbing you before breakfast group". Finally I watched as the last person in tow foot step landed on our porch and use their pointing finger to press the button to the doorbell. As soon as we heard the bell, we sprung into action! We were screaming and hollering at them like we were zombies with super confusing energy! After about four seconds, we ran and jumped our neighbor's fence. We lived on that street for over sixteen years, and not one time did we ever get another visit from the Jehovah Witnesses. :)

Finally, the bus strike was over, which was a very good thing. Unfortunately, due to my absence from school, I was held back in the same grade with the rest of my friends whose parents didn't take them to school during the strike. So I was doing my second dance for the fourth grade, and my teacher didn't care too much for my dance moves. Once again, I was being the class clown. Once again, the class got quiet. Once again, I looked toward the classroom door. And once again, Mom was standing there staring at me. MF! I'm busted again!

My teacher got up from his desk, smiling at me while making his way over to greet Linda. For some reason, my mom never entered the classroom. I guess she didn't have the time to offer a speech to my classmates, but knowing Linda, I knew she definitely had something else up her sleeve. After a brief minute of the two adults talking, I was asked to come out into the hallway. I stepped out, and the teacher closed the classroom door to keep whatever was about to occur private. The only people occupying the hallway were me, Linda, and my smiley-face teacher. My mom was holding her purse in an awkward position and eyeballing me very hard. She knew that I knew who was sitting in her purse, that darn Roscoe!

His name was Roscoe. It took me a while to find out who Roscoe was, but eventually, my curiosity allowed me to find out. Whenever my mom would leave the house, my dad would ask her, "Do you have Roscoe with you?" And she would always reply yeah. I would think to myself, *What/who is this Roscoe? And why is it always with my mom every time she leaves?*

Then one day, they slipped up and revealed the whereabouts of this Roscoe. I watched as my mom was leaving to make a store run. She replied to my father, "Yeah, it's in my purse." Right then and there, the cat was out of the bag. Now it was time to play cat and mouse. I was the curious cat, and Roscoe was the mouse, and I was working very hard at playing detective. I believe that "Batman" would've admired my "Sherlock Holmes" snooping around techniques. And boy oh boy was I determined to find out who or what it was. As the days went by, I watched my mom very closely. Even at a young age, I truly never had an issue with patience because I could always savor the moment of satisfying the victory over my curiosity. So the more I watched her, the more I became familiar with her habits at home.

Her schedule went something like this: between 3:00 a.m. and 4:00 a.m. during the weekday, she would take my father to the rapid transit station so he can start making his way to work, and of course that road trip wasn't doing me any justice because Roscoe would be right with them just riding along. Then, I finally got it down to an understandable pattern. Linda is someone we can honestly call a "mini lottery miracle worker". Because from my observation of her, she had it all! The lottery magical potions, the lottery voodoo books, past lottery newspapers, etc. And boy did she know how to work those numbers, which meant a lot of time at the kitchen table for her trying to catch something that will put money in her pockets, which, in turn, meant a lot of time for me trying to catch Roscoe. So as I brought my personal surveillance to an end, I pretty much had narrowed down mom's movements to a science. Opportunity finally presented itself! As I watched my mom walk out of her bedroom into the kitchen with her bag of number goodies, I gave her a good ten minutes to get herself settled. I was at the dining room table, waiting patiently, and as soon as I heard her talking to her sister on the phone, I did a little peep around the wall. As soon as she picked up her pencil, I started making my way into her bedroom.

There it was, my mom's famous purse that Roscoe lived in. I was very slow and steady as I unzipped my mom's handbag. The lights were off in her room, so looking inside the purse would not do. I slid my left hand down into the bag and began feeling around. There were a lot of coins and little long pieces of metal. Just as I slid my hand to the back of the handbag, I felt something cold and very hard. As I started to bring it up to the surface of the bag, my imagination started playing tricks on me!

I thought I heard Linda walking toward the bedroom door. I dropped the cold metal, zipped the handbag back up, and headed back toward the living room. So once again, it was back to the drawing board. I was back on the case playing cat and mouse again. Just waiting until the "golden opportunity" was nice enough to present me with a second chance, and sure enough it showed up at my doorsteps. Ike had pissed Mom off, so doing numbers was like some type of soothing medication to help her cope with her husband. I watched to make sure my mom was losing herself into her numbers. I was back in their bedroom! I slid the cold metal out of the handbag. The dim light that was protruding through the shaded window gave me just enough so I could barely visualize, but it was enough light for glory to come into place! I was looking at Roscoe face-to-face!

Roscoe was a .38 special Smith & Wesson revolver handgun. As I stood there holding it and staring at it, I received a flashback. This was the same gun my mom had when she shot my dad inside of the car in front of me! Wow! I've always been a fast thinker, so I checked to be sure that Roscoe was empty. I quickly put my hand back down into the purse and found the long pieces of metal, which were the food for Roscoe. I pulled out some hollow points and some type of bullets that had blue plastic tips on them filled with little BBs. I quickly filled up Roscoe's belly. I aimed at the pillows on Ike's side of the bed, then at his baseball caps. Then I quickly turned to the left and was pointing at the TV. I did a 180-degree turn to the right and was pointing at the window. Satisfied with my achievement, I made Roscoe cough up its meal and placed the bullets back down into my mom's purse, and Roscoe quickly followed behind them. I did this little act more than a few times than was necessary, but at the end of the day, I met Roscoe and Roscoe met me.

Snapping back into the world of my realities, the three of us stood in the middle of the school's hallway, just allowing this situation to marinate for a couple of seconds while we all stared at one another in silence and the only reason we were quiet, was due to the fact that my mom's body language was doing all of the talking, and that was not good for me, because unlike my fourth grade teacher I could understand the "alien language" that was being spoken! And boy oh boy was her body language cussing me out for being such a top notch "Nincompoop". Me and Linda just stood there staring at one another "eye to eye" with the depth of a black hole, while allowing the seconds- hand of the good old clock to do its thing before this party started. But my teacher had no idea what was going on between the two of us, but his body language was now displaying that his nervous system was on "high alert"! He looked to his left at Linda and all he saw was that she was staring straight at me. He looked to his right, and all he saw was me staring straight at my mom. I believe we made him feel very uncomfortable because his wide grin had faded away and transformed into a look of concern for the both of us. You could clearly see that this teacher did not know anything about disturbed black families! Linda was standing there like a car with the bright headlights on, and I just followed suit, except I was the deer stuck in her darn headlights. As if my teacher had just developed a nervous condition accommodated with his fake smiling, with a lightly shaking body, he decided on becoming the icebreaker in this mother and son modern day standoff, softly he began to speak with caution, "Brian is a very bright child! [Too late to help me out now, you cowardly little man! Do you not see that stare that's going?] But once he finishes his class work, the clown always comes out. I spoke to him numerous times, but the fella just won't catch on."

I could see the anger gaining more power inside of Linda's eyes. That's when I also noticed that her jaws and her teeth along with her lips were moving in motion, finally she spoke to me while gritting her teeth. (Thank you Mr. Ike! For doing that evil dumb shit so much to my mom that now she's freaking brainwashed!) That's when I knew that all of the anger she was displaying wasn't necessarily generated towards me. She was thinking about Ike because her expression was just too vicious to be dedicated to a simple noddy schoolchild. With a tone that I did not recognize because it was softer and sweeter than my grandmother's voice, my Mom said, "What did I tell you, Brian? Didn't I tell you that, not one teacher 'in the rest of your childhood life span' better not ever call me up to another school about you and your clowning?"

Okay, I thought to myself, *I see where this is going because she is just talking to MF friendly for my taste.* And this had me scared! Because I really didn't want to be on the short end of the stick that was really masterminded and intentionally dedicated to Mr. Ike!

Mom watched my eyes very closely because she's the superior Queen B when it comes to reading body language. I glanced over at the stairwell and shifted my feet toward that direction. And that dumb gesture of mine sent Linda straight into action! With her purse hanging from her shoulder with that extra long strap for accurate movement, she gently unzipped the bag's zipper and placed her left hand inside and spoke to me with a very friendly tone but mixed with a very visible wicked grin, "Run, I dare you to run. I'll shoot you in your leg." My teacher couldn't believe what he had just heard. I could. And I didn't move! And my teacher should be thankful to us for bringing him into reality, because Dr. Huxtable's TV family truly don't exist! He just had a glimpse into a real black family from the hood for free. :(

When I got home later that day from school, Mom was too busy fighting and arguing with my father to pay me any attention. I just walked past them and went upstairs to see what my brothers were doing. They were sitting down watching a Bruce Lee movie together, so I joined in. When the movie went off, all three of us thought we were Bruce Lee and started imitating him. We started kung fu fighting! I ducked one of Earl's kung fu kicks and went straight for Slim. As I ran toward him at full speed, he got scared and protected himself! Slim fell down to the ground and stuck his leg out. My face ran straight into the heel of his foot. His toenail scratched my eye, and his heel busted my lips. The next day in school, my classmates were laughing at me because I had the looks of a child who had just stepped into the boxing ring with George Foreman! And from the evidence that was left behind on me, everyone knew that George Foreman walked away with all of his Champion boxing belts. My teacher looked at me with some serious concern, but after what he just witnessed the day before in the hallway with me and Linda, he didn't dare question me about any of my fresh facial tattoos because now after viewing me he really didn't know how serious or not Linda was about given me a reason to be limping while I walk. So he decided against calling home to my parents, I guess he figured "today a busted lip and a bruise eye, tomorrow a broken leg or a casket". And he was not trying to be a witness to either! So in return, I never gave him a reason to call my mom again and passed his class with flying colors.

CHAPTER 11

WHY ME?

As the new school year was off to a running start, it was pretty hard for me to concentrate within that fifth grade "eye opening" miserable year. My father seem to be drunk or high off something every single day. The screaming and fighting between my parents was an ongoing saga. My mother was doing everything she could to find a way to defend herself. At least once or twice a week, we had to go over to my grandmother's house. This would occur at any hour of the day, whether it was 3:00 p.m. or 3:00 a.m. We all had to jump into my mom's car and flee because he wanted to jump on her and didn't care that our young eyes were witnesses to this BS. With my mom trying to add a "positive into the negative" inside of the continuous situation that she had going on with her husband, Linda ate more food in order to insert more calories into her diet for more added body weight! So it will be more of a task for her husband to toss her around like a "raggedy ragdoll" on any given day. She even got a job being an undercover store security guard so she could always worked over time, just so she didn't have to come home and deal with his madness. She really had it rough.

I still remember vividly the day my mom sat at the living room table and my dad stormed in from outside through the front door grinding his teeth like some type wild animal with rabies. He headed straight toward my mother and spoke with an angry voice, "Give me some fucking money!"

"The only money I have is for the mortgage, Ike," my mother replied in a reasonable tone, making sure not to make this animal's anger transform into a serious rage. With my mom denying him his thirsty wish, he instantly started gritting his teeth very harshly. With his nose flared so wide, if his brain was not intact, it could've slipped straight through. I watched my mom brace herself. She didn't know what was coming next—will it be a choke around the neck, a glob of saliva flying from his mouth and directed at her face, or being called some of the various rude words that he loved to exercise so much. But to my surprise, none of those things occurred. Instead, he picked up the phone receiver and hit her dead bang in the eye with it.

I watched my mom's beautiful face transform from a beautiful black model into looking like she was just in a fight with a Cleveland Indians baseball bat! I was so small at the time :(I watched with tears as my supposed to be father stormed out the front door heading back outside to his wilderness. I wondered why my mother didn't shoot him. Then I just figured it was probably too hard for her to hit a "piece of shit" of a moving target with just one eye. (But in reality, so many black women continue to love and stay with the black man that put their hands on them illegally. Then these women of all races take into consideration that the person who just disrespected them move their lips to say, "I'm sorry, you know I love you" and then turn around and do the same dance number over and over on them again. I just don't understand. There are laws to protect these women, but they refused to utilize them! And we all know the two main factors: either it's because of the children or the financial stability. Wait a minute I just made a mistake. It is three main factors! How could I ever forget about the brainwashing?) Earl just so happen to be home at the time, as Linda stood up with a body that was angrily shaking she didn't say anything direct to anyone. But she did manage to release a very sorrowful "Why Me?" Into the deaf ears of the listening air. And I noticed that she didn't even have tears pouring out, but her facial expressions couldn't hold back the pain and hurt that her eye and her heart was sharing. She just got up, got in her car, and drove herself to the hospital. At such a young age, it was very hard for me to understand. Why do they kiss? Why do they hug? Why do they sleep in the same bed? Why do we have happy family outings? Why does he spit on her? Why did she shoot him? Why do they cuss each other out? Why? Why? Why? I just don't get it! Is this what individuals are referring to when they use the phrase "tough love"? Whatever it was, I knew in my heart that a woman would never receive that type of love from me!

My father did have his good ways, but nonetheless, it didn't account for his bad ones. And he displayed his good nature in a very unorthodox sort of manner, or should I say in a hood fashion? For instance, he used to always show me how to hold my hands in a fight, or how to throw a proper punch in order to open up your opponent's eye with a special twists, so I don't break or injure my wrists, and how to duck & block. But then he'll kicked my ass later on that day or somewhere within that week just for general-purpose or just for that "tough love" BS. He also started teaching me how to drive at a young age. He would say, "Brian, you want to ride with me to the store?" As soon as he would come walking out with a fifth of wine, he would get in on the passenger side of the vehicle. As he got in, he'd push me over to the driver side after sitting there for just a brief second while he drowned a fifth of "Wild Irish Rose" into his esophagus which assisted in creating an angry "Little Lake of Misery" in the bottomless pit of his sour stomach. And this would be accomplished with only five to six gulps, and the bottle would be empty. Without getting out of the car, he would toss the bottle into the trash can in front of the store, and he never missed a shot. "Now it's time to roll," he would say without even a burp. He would slide closer to me to bring his left leg over so that his feet could reach the gas and brake pedals. Once he was comfortable and sure that he could perform his one-leg acrobatics, he would look at me and say, "Let's ride."

Even though he did all these great things, he never made me feel like I was his son. He didn't offer the affection of little fatherly things to me that he offered to Slim and my little sister. Every now and then, when he was drunk, he'd say, "Brian, come here. I have something to tell you."

As soon as I was close enough to him, Linda would come out of nowhere and say, "Don't tell him nothing. Brian, get upstairs!"

He would start crying like he did so often while drunk. Then, the day finally came when I found out a few things. One, I found out why he used to always tell me that I look like my mother while gritting his teeth in my face. Two, I found out why he never treated me like my little brother and sister. Three, I found out why he liked to hit me so much.

CHAPTER 12

THE PROGNOSIS

It was a regular day of school, except for the rain outside. The bus ride home was pretty cool, and I was happy! I knocked on the door to our house and was surprised to see that my father was the one who unlocked the door. I stepped in and could see he was the only one that was home, and my happiness was quickly tarnished. He went back into his bedroom and got in the bed and just nodded off. I went upstairs to my bedroom because I didn't really like being around this guy by myself.

A few minutes later, I heard a knock at the front door. I started to unwind the handle to open the upstairs window. I looked down, and it was three of my neighborhood friends. "We about to go to the store. Can you go?" one of them asked. I went downstairs to open up the refrigerator and see if my dad brought home some candy bars or pies home from work. I didn't see anything, so I went to his room and asked him, "Can I go to the store." He said yes and told me to grab $.50 from off the top of his dresser.

I then headed out the door. From my house to the store was about a block-long walk, so the time span was two blocks, which, in time zone standards, should only accumulate to about ten to fifteen minutes depending on the pace of one's footsteps, and my friends and I were very fast walkers. As my friends and I were walking up my driveway back from the store, they asked me to ask my father if I could come outside and play. They didn't know it, but I didn't like asking him too much of anything. I just played my nonchalant role and said, "I'll ask him, but that don't mean I'll be coming back out to play."

When I entered the house, he quickly jumped out of the bed and met me at the top of the stairs. He was just standing there gritting his teeth. His eyes were low, and the only thing his nostril was missing was smoke. I felt like a young fawn smothered in Ray's baby back barbecue sauce, and he was the hungry nigga bear! I just stood there, scared, waiting to see what this evil bear was about to do to me. I was so nervous that I couldn't even brace myself like I watched my mom do in one of these terrible situations with this guy. "Who told you to go outside?" Due to the experience of hearing his rude comments and visualizing negative physical escapades between this guy and my mom when it came to giving an answer to one of his million-dollar questions, I learned to be a very quick thinker.

It's sometimes scary how well I can read a person, body language seriously explains a lot of things to me, and I could tell by the tone and pitch of an individual's conversation as to which bullshit angle they were going to try to deliver. So when this nigga bear started to drool, I just stood there, thinking, *Aw, man! Here comes some serious bullshit.* And just as I finished my prognosis, what I determined to be his inner bear personality going into preattack mode, it became evident that my judgment call was totally wrong! It turned out that he wasn't in his bear form at all! He actually transformed into an eagle with teeth! All I could do was brace myself. Standing there gritting his teeth even louder, he spoke, "You look just like your mother! Who told you to go outside?" By this time, he had hit me so many times in the past that I thought I was used to it. So I readied myself to take the overdose of medicine he was about to give me, and then my miserable home life will go on as usual.

I never asked myself why I was never comfortable with calling him dad, so I just spoke to him as usual. "Ike, you told me I could go outside to the store and to come right back. You also told me to grab $.50 off your dresser."

He was so very quick and eager to respond, "You look just like your mother, and you're a habitual liar."

I just stood there, thinking, *Well, this is different. He never called me a bitch before, and he just told me I look like my mother twice in a row. Aw, man, this is really bad!*

I must have put my head down while I was thinking because I never even saw it coming. The eagle snatched me off my feet with his talons wrapped around my little neck and slammed me against the hallway wall. This grown fucker attacking a little kid was pretty strong. He had my back pressed against the wall while suspending me in the air with his hands around my throat! My feet weren't even touching the darn floor! He had me face-to-face with him. I didn't see hatred, but he had a lot of anger in his eyes. I could hear and see that he had really mastered the gritting of teeth technique. But I couldn't believe that he had gone this far on me! When he released his hands from around my throat, I fell straight to the floor and on my knees. I was very thankful that my lungs were receiving oxygen again. As soon as I got my first breath, I took off running up the stairs!

I was trying so hard to make it to my bedroom, so I could crawl under my bed and wait for my mother to get home. I had two flights of stairs to clear before heading to my destination. Just as I made it to the top of the first landing of stairs, the eagle had his hands around my ankle. With one leg free (and thank the heavenly clouds I still had on my tennis shoes), I started kicking as hard as I could. I was trying my best to respond to his ankle grabbing. But, of course, I was no match for this persistent baldheaded eagle because while I was kicking at this guy, this was my first time noticing that he had a very clear ball spot in the middle at the very tippy top of his head. As he grabbed the leg I was defending myself with, he easily turned over my entire body until I was facing him. With one quick tug, he was dragging me right back down them damn stairs!

The back of my head and my back could feel every punch that was delivered to me as my body glided over each step. As soon as I was close enough to him, he wrapped his hands around my neck again. As we were face-to-face, I waited for him to tell me I looked like my mother again or to grit his teeth, but he did neither one. This baldheaded eagle was running out of gas. I threw a kick at him because I felt his grip loosening. That also gave me the opportunity to turn my body back around and allowing my tennis shoes to gain some traction, so I shot right back up the stairs, and he didn't give chase. I ran straight into my bedroom and flew under my bed. The adrenaline I had going on didn't let me realize how sore and hurt my body was, but like most traumatic situations, evidence will be left behind.

Even though I lost the battle with the eagle, I still found a reason to smile. We had a window that was between the first floor and the second floor, and my friends could hear everything that was transpiring. I could hear them shouting, "Leave him alone!" Just hearing that someone was concerned was enough to bring a smile to my teary-eyed face as I rested my sore body and drifted off to sleep. But before my eyes close for the night, I had just one last pleasant thought. One of the guys that was with my friends was doing the most pleading, shouting at the top of his lungs begging the bald Eagle to release its prey! I didn't even know the kid. He just so happened to be traveling along with the guys that I knew. But after hearing his loud replies of concerns for stranger was enough to help me sleep easier. A very short time into the future I found out that his name was Smiley.

As I slowly awoke, I did not know what time it was, but the sun was up. I figured it was safe to slide from under the bed. As soon as I stood up, I started to realize how much pain my body was in. I could remember both of my brothers asking me in my sleep, "Why are you under the bed?" And the only thing I could muster up was, "The Eagle". And they knew exactly what that meant, so they let me be. My mom never came to check on me that night. I didn't hold it against her because I already knew. As soon as she returned home from work and entered through the same doors I came through, it probably was another bout in the ring for her as well.

As I slowly made my way into the bathroom, I stood in front of the mirror. This was no ordinary mirror. It was the length of the entire bathroom wall. While standing in front of it, you could see everything. As I twisted my body toward the right and toward the left, I could see that I resembled the first stages of a roadmap. Due to the fact that I had lighter skin, I had purple, blue, and black lines and circles running everywhere, and all of this was very visible.

I was running late, and I knew the school bus would be pulling off soon. I didn't know if the eagle flew to work or not this morning, so I didn't bother to tell my mother about the cage match. My body was way too sore for me to wash up. I just left the same clothes on and ran down the stairs! I yelled to my mom that I was leaving for school and made it to the bus stop before the transportation pulled away. Fortunately enough for me, I was able to make it through the entire school day without raising anyone's suspicion or concerns.

Either by coincidence or purpose, my grandmother's street was part of the school bus route. As we were coming closer to that stop on her street, my train of thought started talking to me, "Brian, get off the bus now and go tell your grandmother what happened yesterday." So I did exactly what my mind told me to do. As soon as I exited the bus, the other children were quick to say, "Hey, this not your stop!"

I just responded with a shrug and started walking toward my grandmother's house. (This was the second time a soul was running.)

Finally, I made it to my grandmother's house and started walking up the driveway. I stood there a few seconds, knocking at the door. My grandfather was the one who answered, "Foots, why you get off the school bus?"

"I was scared to go home, Granddad."

He let me into their home, and I went straight to the back room where the grandchildren would hang out. My grandma came to see me instantly. "Brian, why did you get off your school bus?" she asked with a very curious look.

In a very meek voice, I replied, "Grandma, Ike jumped on me last night, and I am scared to go home."

"What do you mean he jumped on you?" my grandma asked. You could tell by the expression on her face that she was getting mad because her two eyebrows were starting to form into one.

I just said, "I'll show you," and I started taking my shirt off.

At that very moment, she called my grandfather to join us. She wanted him to see my father's artistic masterpiece that he left on the canvas of my body. "Look at him! Ike did that to him!"

My grandfather looked me straight in the face and asked me, "Why did he do it?" I explained the situation. My granddad walked straight out the room and headed directly to the phone to call my mother and father.

My grandmother kept telling me to turn in circles while she examined my body. She couldn't hold it in any longer. "He had no business doing this to you. You are a child, and you're not his child. Your father's name is Charlie!"

There it was, right smack in my face! My grandmother just gave me the answer as to why he always treated me different than the other two children. My grandma continued to give me cookies and cake until my mother and my stepfather arrived.

My granddad told me not to say anything about what my grandma revealed to me. The rest of my elementary years went on with minimal to medium difficulty. I was still getting choked out by my stepfather, my mother and older brother were still receiving the same treatment, and my little brother and sister were given only a "percentage pinch" of what we received.

CHAPTER 13

ME AND MY SHOES

As the seasons changed, so did people's mental demeanors. There was so much terrible news going on in the neighborhood. "Shocking News at 11" was becoming a household name in the city of Cleveland.

One summer, I was watching my neighbor who lived across the street from our house as he was walking toward his home coming from the direction of the corner store. (I truly respected my neighbor. He was always giving me reasons to look up to him. Whether it was teaching me how to shoot a BB gun or trying to explain to me how to handle my troubles at home, my neighbor was always willing to help me out.) I continue to watch my neighbor walking "because being nosy was not hazardous to your health at the time" as a car followed him with three men occupying the vehicle. My neighbor shouted at them, "Leave me alone! I have nothing to talk about!"

But the guys in the car wouldn't listen and continued to follow and taunt him. As my neighbor started walking up his driveway, the men in the vehicle stopped right in front of his house where his wife and his newborn baby girl were sleeping in their beds. The men continued to shout very rude remarks, and their words were getting more violent. My neighbor said, "Okay, that's what you going to do to me? Wait right there, my man!"

And they did wait like some stubborn jackasses displaying no worries on their faces. My neighbor came out of his house with a twelve-gauge shotgun and let one blast off toward the vehicle that the men occupied. The guys in the car never saw that one coming! You could see the buckshot hit the car as the glass shattered, and the rest of the buckshot that missed the vehicle went into our house. I watched the car hesitate for far too many seconds before the occupants realized that it would be best to speed off. I watched my neighbor go back inside of his house, and I didn't see him again until I was grown.

It was over twenty years later when I just so happened to run into my neighbor at the local gas station. We gave nigga hugs and talked, and then we started laughing as he explained that the last time he saw me was years ago when he was watching TV in his prison cell, and I made a guest appearance on the *Just in at 11 News* while wearing a black dress. As we both looked at each other crazy, we both started laughing again. I followed him to his house, and he gave me a newspaper clipping, and I couldn't believe how young I was on this old piece of paper. My neighbor looked me straight in my eye and said, "I heard all the stories about you, Brian. I even heard about you getting shot, and I was hoping you pulled through that! Boy, the way you was living life, a lot a guys in the joint didn't think you was going to make it out there. But I knew I would see you again. That's why I kept this newspaper clipping of you, and now I want you to have it."

After telling my neighbor thank you, I began to get in my car when my neighbor yelled at me, "Brian, when you make it, we walking straight to Harley-Davidson." I just smiled and gave a thumbs-up because once again, my neighbor was giving me reasons to look up to him. He knew that I wouldn't quit until I completely accomplished what I set out to do—flat out.

The very next night after watching my neighbor transforming that car into a "cheese grater", was not without its excitement! Each night that followed after that was truly testing one another for its run of the money. But it will be pretty hard for the rest of these nights to compete with me actually seeing that blast from the shotgun, "at least that's what I was thinking". But sure enough, it was truly getting to the point that each crazy day was living up to the next one. My neighbor, who lived to the left of me, was kind of upset about what happened the previous night to his friend. Even though they belong to different motorcycle clubs, they would still find time to ride together. I used to love watching my neighbor get on his motorcycle and fly up and down the street. The night before must've really weighed heavy on his heart. As he started up his motorcycle and poured out into the street, I could hear the thunder of his motor breaking through the the silence of the night air. He rolled past at a fast pace. As he entered the intersection on 131st., he did not slow down, and he didn't make a left or right turn, which were his only options. Instead, he just went flying through the middle of the intersection and crashed into the hardware store. A couple weeks after that, there was a story all over the news. They found a female body on Barlette Street. Barlette was just one street over from where I lived. Yes, my elementary years were ending in the wrong direction. My neighborhood was getting very crazy right before my eyes, and no one really knew why at the time and the reason will become an epidemic. Crack was in the hood.

The year was 1985, and I was starting my first year in junior high school. I attended Alexander Hamilton Junior High. It was a new experience for me, totally different from elementary. We were actually changing classes. There was no more sitting in one room all day with one teacher who had time to focus to either like you or not and vice versa. I knew instantly the first day of school that I needed to start making some money. The other children were dressed in the newest fashion, and I was wearing shoes from Payless, and it didn't go unnoticed. :(

The Lakers were really doing their thing around that time, and Converse had given a Lakers teammate his own shoe called the Weapons. So I went home, and I told my mom, "I need some tennis shoes. They have these tennis shoes called the Weapons. They're the same color of the Lakers team." A few weeks went by, and then one day, my mom called me downstairs. She had a shoebox. I rushed to open it, and to my surprise, she had brought me home the all mighty Weapons! I could see all the colors of the Lakers team in my face. I was so happy to be looking at all the purple, white, and yellow, but I should have inspect the shoes more thoroughly. :)

I went back upstairs and went straight to sleep, I couldn't wait for the next day at school. Finally, the day came. I took off and ran straight out the door. I wasn't going to mess these bad boys up before I got to school, so I didn't even put them on my feet until I got to school. I was there early; most of the children hadn't arrived yet. I made my way to the restroom and darted into the first free stall I saw. I pulled them bad boys out of that box, laced them up with the fat strings, and started stepping with my head raised high. Every class that I went to, all the children were talking, "He got the Weapons!" The word got around the whole school about the kid with the fancy shoes. So when the fashionable children got word of it, they posted up in the school's hallways looking for me in order to make this official. Class had just let out. I was walking toward the restroom when I spotted about seven or eight fashion kids standing there, and you know they were waiting for me because none of them had the Weapons on their feet yet.

One of the taller boys pulled away from the group. He was like, "Wow! You really got the new Weapons!" As he was staring at them, I could see when his brain was like "Hold on a second here, guy" because I watched his eyebrows starting to arch automatically. He circled me a couple of times with his eyes, staring dead point like an infrared laser on my fancy shoes. He stopped on the side of me with a powerful smirk going on. He bent over and reached down with lightning speed and pulled up my pants leg. As loud as he could shout, he was like, "Those not Weapons. This nigga wearing Eagles from Payless!" One *baaaaahaha* was released from a female student, and everyone started laughing.

I just stood there thinking, *Mother fucker!*

Then, he was like, "They still some cool shoes."

I said thanks while I was thinking, "Nigga, you just ruined my entire life!"

The next day at school, you could tell that the word traveled like wildfire. Everyone was staring at my feet, and last night, my mom and dad were fighting and arguing like cats and dogs. So I just wasn't up to today's school festivities or shenanigans, so I decided to play hooky from school for the first time. I heard that a lot of children were doing it, but I didn't know how it was done. So I went with what I thought would be the first stepping stone. I started stepping and went straight out of the side school door. I had no idea where I was going. I knew I was in the wrong for leaving, but I didn't care! I just knew that I didn't want to get caught.

I really had to watch my steps, and just as I was thinking about being careful, the security guard to our school was late for work. I could see her red Chrysler coupe coming down the street toward me. The only thing I was thinking was *Shit!* Because if she saw me, I was surely going to be in trouble. When I saw her car, I was standing right in front of Charles Dickens Elementary School. Charles Dickens had a big black fence around it, so I couldn't run across the grass in that direction. As I turned my head to the left and right so I could find somewhere to duck into. I spotted an apartment building. My Weapons and I ran as fast as we could to the door and darted safely inside.

As soon as I entered the building, there was a guy there about my age looking a little nervous. It only took me a half second to realize that I knew this jackass. It was Mr. Fashionable Kid, Mr. Pull Up My Pants Leg in front Everybody," right here in the flesh! He realized who I was just as quickly, and the first thing that came out of his mouth was, "I think I just saw the security guard coming down the street in her car?"

I was like "Yeah, I don't believe she saw me come in here." With both of us standing there looking like pure dumb asses, he asked me the same question I was just about to ask him. So just like a naive teenager, I asked him the question which was obvious since we both were standing in the same location hiding from the school security guard. "You cutting school?"

And with him being just as naive, he answered my question right back with, "Yeah, you cutting too?" So we stood there, waiting for her car to go pass. We slowly opened up the door, and just like a scene from the *Three Stooges*, we both stuck our heads out at the same time to make sure she was gone.

We waited until we saw her pull into the school's parking lot. Now we felt secure enough to continue walking down 131st Street. Then, he asked me where I was going. I responded back, "I really don't know. This is my first time cutting school." Then I asked him was it his first time, he said, "Hell naw, I do this shit all the time. My mom should be gone to work. It's a few other people from school that's coming over. You can hang if you want to." So I accepted the life-altering invitation.

We didn't go straight to his house. We had to go around the corner from his house to make sure that his mom was gone. Seeing her car missing gave us the green light to proceed forward. As he opened the door, he told me to hold on for a second. He had to put Woofey up until I was in the house, so his dog could hear my voice. Finally, I was upstairs. After a few minutes of talking, he decided that Woofey could come out. This dog was a grown sheep dog that liked to jump up on people. Twenty minutes later, there was a knock at the door.

It was a couple of guys from our school whose faces looked familiar, but I didn't know them personally. Two other guys that were a few years older than us were at the door as well. They were in high school.

After introducing ourselves, one of the older kids pulled out a forty-ounce bottle of beer, and the other older kid looked at me and said, "Do you have some papers?" I was like, "No, shit, I don't even have any books. I just walked straight out the school building. I didn't even have a chance to go to my locker." All the guys started laughing. That's when Fashionable Kid spoke up for me. He was like, "I don't think B smokes." That's when the older kid got a wicked grin across his face and shouted with a singing tone, "He going to learn today!" And they all started laughing, me as well, not even knowing what the hell we all was laughing about.

Fashionable Kid left the room for a hot second and came back with a brown thin little pack that had a capital *E* and a *Z* written on it. As the older kid picked the seeds out of the leaves (his name was Fly Guy), the other older kid (his name was Skeleton) was passing the forty ounces of beer around and making sure that everyone got a pretty good swallow. It was as if the two older kids liked to see the younger ones drunk and high. They honestly did it for their own personal enjoyment. As the beer started making its way into my system, I started to feel a little unbalanced. Now it was time to hit the joint, and I didn't have the slightest idea how to make this happen. I knew it had to be something like cigarettes, but I never smoked them either. But I had seen numerous people smoking. So I thought to myself, *I'll just imitate the smokers. Just suck it in and let it out through my nostrils.*

My first inhale went down the drain pretty smoothly. All the other guys were just staring at me and smirking. As I sat there with all this smoke in my lungs, because they kept telling me to swallow it, I thought I was a true master, but that's when my lungs alerted me that I wasn't a professional anything. I tried to let the smoke exhale through my nostrils, when a gigantic cough escaped through my chest, and the smoke simultaneously hit my throat, my nostrils, and my eyes. All at once, my body lost total control. It was as if I was trying to cough my heart out. I dehydrated myself with all this coughing, along with the tears that were flowing through my eyelids. This three-ring circus act that I had going on took about ninety seconds to stop. But when it was over, boy oh boy did I feel like I was floating with the clouds.

Although the school year was off to a negative start, Fashionable Kid and I had become pretty cool. We weren't the best of friends because my home life made me truly a Lone Wolf. So I did keep him at a distance and because he was always into something. Like the one day he came to school and said some people rode past and shot at him, and the bullet hit him in the head. But the reality was he was cutting school over one of the older kids house, and they was playing with a gun. And he caught the short end of that deal.

As the school days went on, I was still thinking of a way to get some money in my pockets. I was born a true hustler truly cut from a different cloth. At the age of nine, I was borrowing the neighbor's grass cutter and going door to door asking people if I could cut their front grass for five dollars. At the age of ten, I was walking around the neighborhood collecting cans, and then, I would walk about twenty miles to put the cans that I'd collected into this machine that sat outside of a shopping center and wait for it to spit this punk ass change out! Then I would walk twenty miles back home, stopping at a store called Lawson's, so I could pick me up a party pizza and some potato chips and dip. But here I was, twelve years old in junior high school, where the fashionable kids ruled with their Guess jeans and Nike Cortez and British Knights tennis shoes. So I needed to figure something out fast!

One day, it just fell in my lap. All the older kids in the neighborhood were getting jobs downtown at the Cleveland Indians and

Cleveland Brown's Stadium, and I wanted to be a part of that money train! So I turned my focus on and started plotting, but I had a tremendous situation! I wasn't old enough, and the minimum requirement was sixteen with a work permit! So I had to figure something out. One thing that I came to realize was that I was pretty good at figuring out just about any situation (whether it works for me or not is always left to be determined). My oldest brother fortunately had me by four years, so that put him at sixteen, and he had an ID. So that put his ID in my pocket, and I was on my way downtown Cleveland Brown! Woo who! When I got to the stadium, there was a long line of people trying to get a job there. But that didn't discourage me. Shoot, I was over thirty days late for my own birth, so I was going to try to turn this into a cakewalk. If people could just read my mind, they would truly see how grateful I am to God for my common sense and my "bushy tail squirrel" personality.

As I was standing in line, I was asked over and over by a not-too-great-looking midtwenty-something female, "Hey, kid, how old are you?" And I could see why she was asking me this question because just about everyone else was twenty years of age or older. I wasn't going to let that little bump in the road stop me. So I got the application, and upon completion, I headed over to the interviewer line. As soon as the lady looked up, the first thing she asked me was how old I was. I looked her straight in her face and said, "Sixteen is on the application, but I feel like twenty-one. Why, you single?" She smiled and honored my brother's ID without a work permit. I will never forget my first day on the job! It still touches my feelings somewhat till this very day. But I must look at the bright side of the ordeal? Because now I truly believe that certain people are "placed on the same path for a positive reason". And sometimes when that reason is first given, it can be interpreted as some "pure embarrassing bullshit!" But even though as the mockery of this day is tattooed on my brain "probably until my casket day", it did push me forward into the "grind of learning" more education about myself. So thumbs up to you "Cleveland Brown Football Lady" with the nine crackerjack eaten little bastards. "You guys really taught me a lesson!" Yes! This is a "very personal monkey" on my back! Because every time I walk inside of a Super Walmart, I stick a middle finger up to the section of crackerjack boxes that's always there to greet me. LOL! >:)

The supervisors were handing me a worker's ball cap and a black apron to work in, along with a referee look-alike shirt. I was wondering what they were going to give me to sell. There were so many choices. You had your soda pop and hot dogs. You had your big balls of cotton candy, along with boxes of Cracker Jack popcorn, and what would any ball game be without bags of peanuts. And not too many adults would truly enjoy a game without a tall cup of beer to spill on everyone in the bleachers. Well, I knew beer was out of the question because I wasn't old enough to sell it. I was hoping that I didn't get the soda pop either because it is pure common sense. If you carry liquid, you're going to get wet; and in this case, you will be wet and sticky, and there was plenty of bees around to keep you company if you fell into that category. There was not one time that I went to the stadium and didn't see a bumblebee hovering over someone sharpening its stinger. Someone up above must have truly been looking down and wanted to play a joke on me because the supervisors gave me a case of the old Cracker Jack popcorn that was $.75 a box. And the results of me cutting class were about to shine upon my dum dum self! This day, I would truly honor the word *stupidity* and give it a true reason to be in the dictionary with a photo of my dumb ass as a reference.

I was off and running, looking to track down and attack my first customer with my stash of famous caramel corn. Now a lot of fans were looking at me, but no one would approach me. If I was standing next to another person selling Cracker Jacks, the fans would go straight to him or her. I guess I just looked a little too young for them to bother me with their business. But the adolescent look did not stop this one lady with her nine silly ass children. I appreciated that she was willing to give me her business! At least that's what I thought until the transaction came into play. :(She approached me and said, "Let me have nine boxes." Very simple request, I thought, so I gave everyone their box of Cracker Jacks. Some of the children were even older than me and was offering me their I-don't-like-you expression. But I wasn't going to let these little brats turn my blue clouds gray! I continued my focus and kept my professional persona in position, letting them know that I was about being a young businessman. Then she handed me a twenty-dollar bill. That's when my professional persona face left the office! Running behind him was the young businessman that dwelled in me. And who took over the ship? You guessed it right! Mr. Nincompoop, who decided to continue dwelling inside of me after third grade! Mr. Nincompoop make it a habit to always show up at the wrong time, and Mr. Jackass that live inside of my vessel as well, was always teaming up with him. Yes! The two of them was in charge of this ship now and with them teaming up together just made me double stupid! Because neither one of these clowning personalities "that decided to make me their home" paid enough attention in school to be "Commander and Chief" of commanding anything that needed guidance!

I was standing there with this dumbfounded look on my face and this stranger's twenty-dollar bill in my hand. She didn't hesitate; she went straight into action. She played me like I was one of her nine. She said, "What, are you stupid? You don't know how much change I'm supposed to get back?" I just was standing there, thinking, *MF!* We started looking eye to eye at one another; then, she turned her head for a quick second because she could see and hear that her children were starting to laugh at me, even the little ones. That's when she softened up, and said, "Come here, baby. Let me show you." And she helped me count my way through my lack of education. As she and her giggly mean little bastards went to find their seats or looked for another vendor to victimize. My eyeballs shot straight to the ceiling! I was so embarrassed! I was standing there, thinking, *Whoever is up there that is looking down on me really has a sense of humor!*

And I was never the one to appreciate failure. I don't let failure linger in my life. I make it relinquish itself at all costs, so the next day at the stadium, I was ready!

I was walking in, ready to see what they were going to give me to sell. I tightened my ball hat, put my apron around my neck, and tightened the string around my back after tucking in my referee shirt. I slid my right hand into my apron pocket to make sure my calculator was armed and ready. My professional persona face was back in the building, the young businessman was holding steady, and as soon as I was next in line to receive my goods, they handed me a case of one-dollar soda pops. I don't know if word got back to them about what happened the day before, but the adolescent in me joined the party with the businessman and the professional persona face because this was easy counting. All together now, we shouted, "Soda pop here! Get your dollar soda pop here!" I was in my tough zone for real now! So bring on those nine giggly children, Ms. Teacher Lady, and stand back while I count!

Everything was starting to fall in place. I didn't make a lot of money because we were paid on commission, and they took half that, but for a twelve-year-old child, this was a lot to me. I didn't work every day. Because some games ran too late, and the buses would stop running. But things were truly looking up. Good-bye Lee jeans! I was now attending school with a fresh pair of Nike Cortez and a pair of Guess jeans of my own, and I wore them bad boys twice a week or more if given the reason. But so what! Because I was feeling good! Because I earned these clothes on my own, I even started doing school work.

CHAPTER 14

THE GRID

My mother and father tried to do the best for us as far as financial needs were concerned, but they did everything on a budget—not that they had to—but Ike always disappeared, losing money in some unknown place. So the budget gig really didn't work out on my behalf. So I really needed and appreciated my job at the stadium. It allowed me to finally say good-bye to the old Lee jeans that were just a little too tightfitting. In seventh grade, that's when I learned the true meaning of what a boner was wearing them darn Lee jeans. I mean, I heard the stories, but I had never experienced it until one day in science class.

Science class at Alexander Hamilton, that was one class I truly loved going to and respected throughout the year. Even if I have decided to play hooky from school, I would be sure to make it back just in time for science class and as soon as the bell rang for the end of the session, I will be running right back out of the school doors with no true destination, I just didn't want to be in school because my book smarts was not equal to my common sense. My science teacher knew that I loved his class just as well as he knew that I didn't go to my other classes. He was a skinny frail white guy with big glasses. His eyes had the appearance as though he was looking through fish tanks, but he was cool. The only thing that really bothered me about this guy was that every time he talked, little white lines of thick spit would always fling from his mouth. He always knew that I had the correct answers to most of the questions he asked. Even if I didn't raise my hand up, he would call on me anyway. "Mr. Dixon, come up to the blackboard and fill in the answer," he would say. I guess I was one of the few students that made him feel good about his job.

But on this one particular day, it was not the day to call me up to the chalkboard! After being introduced to beer and dry funny-smelling grass wrapped in the big *E* and *Z* paper that we put on fire, I think the combination of them both was thinning my blood. I was not having sex just yet, but after that first day of cutting class and partaking in the older kids activities, I was starting to have freaking boners. I was sitting in class with these tight-ass turquoise Lee jeans on that my mom made me wear when my cool bug-eyed science teacher called me up to the blackboard. I sat there for a second, ignoring his requests, trying to come up with a plan. Then I was like, "I don't know the answer today," and he said, "Yes, you do, now come on up here." All I was thinking was, *Mother fucker!*

As I started to rise up out of my chair, I could feel that my boner was hard as ever; and with the panic of having to walk to the blackboard, it was like all four elements were working against me at one time. The beer, the dry funny-smelling burning grass, and the excitement my body was receiving from these tight-ass turquoise Lee jeans rubbing back and forth against my boner. Most black men from Ohio are born with game about themselves. It's like we come out the womb with a quart of oil coating our lives and helping us slip through tight situations. So as I was sliding up from my desk to begin my journey to the chalkboard, I started sliding my notebook off the desk and placed it in front of me. As I started taking steps on the plank to eventually jump in the shark-infested water, I started thinking, *This is not good, and why the hell is everybody in science today? Any other day, these silly fuckers would be cutting this class*. My main issue wasn't just the boner itself. It was the fact that I was only twelve years old, and I was giving an average-sized boner of a grown man a serious run for his money. So if you were to look down there while my boner was excited, my boner made his presence and appearance very well known. >:)

Finally, I made it to the blackboard and was doing very well with my notebook playoff, which was short-lived because just as I grabbed the chalk and started filling in the correct answer, Mr. Fish-Tank Eyes Science Teacher came over and separated me and my notebook. This sucker just took my shield! He was like, "You don't need that. I'll give it back when you're done." I guess he was wondering what was so important inside my notebook that I just had to bring it up to the front of the class with me. As I watched him and his glasses and my notebook get acquainted, I was thinking, *Fuck! This spitty-mouthed bastard really just took my bodyguard.*

As I completed answering the question, I knew it was time for me to walk the plank once more, and the only pirate to help save my life was just confiscated by the teacher, and after viewing the content, I knew he wasn't going to give it right back. So all I could do was hold my breath, grit my teeth, and flair my nose. The professional persona face was back in the office. One thought did crossed my mind: Maybe I should put my hands in front of me and just cover him up. But I quickly dismissed that thought because an image popped in my head of Marilyn Monroe standing on the sidewalk with both of her hands in front of her crotch, trying to stop her dress from flying up above her waist and exposing her panties. So I just turned around and started stepping! Just as I was coming out of my third step, about four girls were pointing and screaming! And I noticed three were smiling.

So I fell in love with my Guess jeans because they could conceal Mr. Boner due to their baggie design. Other than my home life, everything was floating along pretty cool for the moment. But just as everything was feeling good, my stadium job came to an abrupt ending due to my thieving neighborhood buddies. On the last day of work, I wished that someone would've gave me a heads-up. All I was thinking was, *Easy come, easy go.* The job was going smoothly, just like any other game day, except this day more money was going to be made. I do believe we were in the playoffs or some type of Cleveland Browns–Pittsburgh Steelers game rivalry. There was so many people at the stadium this day, and this was the first time that I'd seen so many vendors from my neighborhood working. I was shooting my regular. I had to stay focused. Nothing was going to throw me off balance because I had to make this money! I was shouting to advertise my dollar soda pops at the top of my lungs! The hours were passing away along with the scream of the crowd, and it would be time to leave soon, so I headed off toward the rest room so I could wash the sticky soda from off my hands and prepare to leave and ready myself for tomorrow. As soon as I entered the rest room, I noticed all of the stalls had black aprons in them. I just shook my head, went to turn in the remaining sodas and cash that I made. I never went back to the stadium again, at least not as a vendor. I just didn't feel like being questioned about the "Great Stadium Vendor's Robbery Heist".

The rest of the school year was still going pretty steady, I just wasn't making money any longer, which was pretty cool because after being classified by the Fashionable Kids that I was meeting their standards, I met a lot of new people that didn't care about my clothes, and with each group of new people, there was something different to offer. So I still found ways to make a little extra cash, rather it be delivering turkeys to the families in need or passing out flyers for the neighborhood churches. These jobs didn't pay much, but it was okay with me because I was helping people. Yes, I can truly say seventh-grade was full of experiences for me. I was now favored by most of the neighborhood groups that had voluntarily separated themselves from one another, in order to only hang with the ones whom was only classified as who they were. Even groups that didn't get along with each other was in favor of me. And no one had any issues with me being friends with the gang-bangers that wears the different colors of the crayon box, that pretends to hate each other so much even though while looking at the outside of their skin, they looked exactly the same. But all in all, I felt pretty honored to be able to travel through all the neighborhoods. I was friends with the nerds. I was friends with the churchgoing kids, just as well as the drug-using kids. So I was getting pretty familiar and known from all ends, which I thought was pretty cool. Little did I know that I would benefit from this in the near future.

I would never forget this one school night. I was in the house doing nothing, and Linda asked me to go and get the family some chicken. It was a restaurant on 131st and Corlett called Hot and Juicy. They had some of the better chicken around the neighborhood at that time. I grabbed the few dollars that my mom laid out for me and headed straight out the door. There was a school across the street from the restaurant called Corlett Elementary. As I walked past Corlett, I counted over twenty to thirty children on the playground, and of course, this was not within school hours. I tried to take a better look to see if I could make out a few faces that I knew. That's when I started hearing my name being called. It was Fashionable Kid, so I made my way over to him, and as I got closer, I could see that everyone was up here. The nerds, the gangbangers, the church kids, and so on. There was really a lot of people. So I asked Fashionable Kid, "What's going on up here?"

He was like, "The grid."

So I asked, "What the hell is the grid?"

He was like," Dude, you haven't seen the movie the *Warriors*?"

I was like, "Nope." So he explained.

The grid is a human-made tunnel. With a line of people on the left and a line of people on the right, an individual would start at one end of the tunnel and make his way to the other end while being hit with sticks and punches and kicks all the way through. If you made it through the very-crafty-put-together "human meat tunnel" that was created by the jackasses of the older children, you'll have the status of being called 131. All the children was forming an alliance, and there will be no more separate-labeled individual groups from the various parts of the hood.

The older kids Fly and Skeleton saw me and Fashionable Kid standing there talking. They both decided to come over and with that very eager look in their eyes, as if they want to see me take a sip out of everyone's beer! And then turn around and have a few puffs off of everyone's burning grass.

"Wassup, pretty boy?" Fly said to me.

And before I could answer, Skeleton was like, "You got to go through the grid."

I was like, "Why?"

"Because you from 131ˢᵗ, little nigga," Skeleton said, looking at me, angry for no reason. (As if I just offended his mother!) Then he punches me in my chest as if he was my daddy! I just said okay because I'd rather go through this so-called "grid", before having to deal with this high-strung asshole, so I mentally prepared myself and entered the "Stupid Ass" human meat tunnel. I truly haven't figured out what it is about me yet, but as I was walking towards the beginning of the tunnel, I started getting a little nervous! Because all these guys' facial expressions change and they were looking pretty mean. I continue to watch as people tighten up their leather gloves, picking back up their sticks, and a couple of assholes with the likeness of Skeleton were taking their belts off. Fly stood at the front of the line. He was to give the 1, 2, 3 countdown, and as soon as he said 1, I was thinking, *Fuck!* He shouted 3, and I ran for the border, making my way through the grid. While I was going through it, I kept twisting and turning and sometimes revolving my body into a 360° circle, easily making my way towards the end of this dumb nonsense. And finally when I exited, Skeleton came straight over to me, popped me upside my head, and was like, "You did good. You don't even have a scratch on you." Looking into his eyes, I could tell that Skeleton was satisfied and disappointed at the same time. "I didn't know you had it in you, but you do, and you did better than everybody out here." (Common sense, if you watch football, the more you twist and turn, the harder it is to get tackled.)

And right then and there! My common sense didn't even allow a "half of a second" to go by before it was focus on Skeleton's mentioning's of, "Everybody out here!" And I didn't like the sound of that for some reason. I just knew it was going to be some bullshit behind that statement when Fly and Skeleton turned their backs and went for a short walk talking to one another. Then, both bullies walked back up to me! "You have to go through the grid again," Skeleton and Fly said simultaneously as if they just found out that they were biological twins.

"Why?" I asked. "Nobody else went through twice!"

"Because I said so, little nigga" was Fly's reply. So I did it all over again and made my way through to the end with the same results as before. But as I was coming out of the grid this time, someone tripped me and made me fall. Skeleton ran over and punched the kid in the face while Fly picked me up. "Now you 131," Fly said while smiling at me.

Becoming 131 did have its benefits. One of the benefits was that I got to hang with kids that were a few years older than me, but without being judged or beat up on. So now I was meeting even more people around the neighborhood. The older kids had this one house they all used to frequent, and I was invited to come over. The word of me going through the grid twice really did held some type of weight in our "neck of woods" because people were really treating me different. (I felt somewhat respected.) As I was getting closer to "The House" that everyone talks about, I noticed that there were two families that lived there, and both families were related. The grandmother was downstairs, and her daughter lived upstairs, and there were about five children there as well. This *house* was where I met Smooth and Smiley. Smooth and Smiley were brothers. Smooth was the oldest by a couple of years or what not, and Smiley was just a couple months older than me. Their house turned out to be the party house that I'd been hearing stories about.

So this is it, I thought to myself. *So this is where all the house parties be at.* I'd heard all the stories about Smooth and Smiley's house parties that usually ended with the help of the Fourth District Police Department. Stories of people high off some drug called wet. This drug would make some of them so high that they would take all their clothes off. I heard stories of people getting butt naked and thinking they were monkeys to the point that they were actually jumping up on the water pipes in the basement and hanging from them until they yanked it down and flooded the whole party, DJ equipment and all.

I was entering the basement from the backyard, and instantly, I started smelling the aroma of marijuana smoke. Coming in from behind me was an older man and some lady with a keg full of beer. Finally, at the bottom of the steps, I could see everyone's face in the dim light. The majority of the guys were people that I'd met at the grid. It was about eight people in all, and they were passing a joint around, so I just stood in place waiting for it to hit me so I could hit it! The joint came, I puffed, and then, I passed. This recycled gesture carried on for a few minutes. My participation this day at The House, had me very high and very tipsy, and I was getting hungry, and my stomach was starting to argue with me about filling it up.

Just as I was about to give the notification that I was leaving, the guys started cracking jokes.

That's when Smiley was like, "B, you still a virgin?" And I guess he could tell by my expression that he was right on the money. I was too intoxicated to focus on a fast lie to throw back at him. Then Smooth slid in on the conversation. "Come on, y'all. Let's take "B" to the "Honer Hoe House". I just stood there, naively listening to these over intoxicated jokesters.

"You about to get some today, B," Smooth said with a big grin on his face.

Now Smooth and Smiley were always up to something as well. I could remember the one time Smooth had a fly that he had removed the wings from it and some dead roaches marinating inside of some "Red Rose" wine. He took the nonbreathing insects out of the swimming pool of drunken death, dried them with a paper towel, then Smiley produced a pack of "E & Z" cigarette rolling papers and handed them over to Smooth. And the rest of us just stood there and watched as Smooth started laughing hysterically while he was rolling up the insects inside of the smoking papers and making sure to use the fly as the head of this "evil & weedless insect joint". He really didn't bother adding nothing else to it at all! I mean not even a pinch of tobacco or marijuana was in this "Trick A Nigga" devious invention of his. It was just "sadly funny" some roaches and a drunk fly to him. With an evil smiling grin now planted on his face, Smooth was like, "Let's go over to Hillbilly house and watch him fire it up." Right after Smooth's senseless speech, right on cue Smiley couldn't help himself and started laughing hysterically! That's when my common sense told me that these two have done this before? But without hesitation, we were on our way to Hillbilly's house. It wasn't far at all, only about a two-block walk, the same distance from the store to my house where the bald eagle flew around his nest. >:(While Smiley and I were standing in Hillbilly's yard laughing, Smooth called up to his window, telling him to come down so he can smoke this joint. He told him that he had something new called skunk weed. Now Hillbilly liked to smoke, but he really wasn't from our neighborhood. He came down those stairs very fast. Smooth passed him the joint and a lighter, telling him to fire it up.

I couldn't hold my laughter in any longer. I was like, "Hillbilly, I need to use the bathroom. Is it cool if I go over there by that tree?" Hillbilly wasn't paying me any attention. He was too concerned about getting that joint on fire. He tried over and over, but he just couldn't get it to light up, and when he finally got it lit somewhat, he would blow out a little, thin white smoke that he inhaled, but it wouldn't stay lit. I don't care if he had a blowtorch! Smooth's evil ass invention was not going to catch fire, "if anything" the only thing that was going on inside of that contraction, was that the insects was being roasted due to the marinating of the wine sauce? But nevertheless Hillbilly just continued trying and trying, and didn't show any signs of giving up. All the while he continued blowing out little white thin clouds of marijuana free smoke. Hillbilly was like, "It won't stay lit." That's when Smiley ran out the yard, and I was right on his heels. The word spread around fast, and it eventually got back to Hillbilly, and he was out for vengeance. Girls always liked me for some reason and were always trying to protect me if given a chance. A couple of days later, I was coming out of the corner store, and I heard someone calling my name. It turned out to be Hillbilly's girlfriend. She was like, "Whenever you go over to Hillbilly's house, don't drink no water. He said whenever one of y'all come over, he was going to give you some water out of the toilet." I just burst out laughing! For the next few weeks, I used to go over to Hillbilly house and play Atari with him. I would ask for a glass of water, pick it up twice, and bring it very close to my lips but never drink it. :)

So the five of us had decided to make our way over to the house on Horner Avenue. It was about a thirty-minute walk and with every step that I had taken I couldn't help but wondered to myself "What in the hell is going on? Where in hell are we going? Man, I'm high! I'm sure am hungry!" When we finally got to the street, the house that they were referring too (took me by surprise because I always bypassed this place every time while on a chicken run for my mom) just had to be the first house on the corner. Smooth walked up the stairs and knocked on the door. A tall, slender woman answered. She was like, "How many of you is it?"

"Five" was his reply. And she told us to come in. As soon as we entered the house, the tall, slender woman ushered us to this bedroom on the left. Apparently, everyone had been here before except for my "fresh meat," tag-along self. The tall, slender woman closed the connecting bedroom bathroom door and said, "Get undressed fellas. I'll be right in." And all the guys started taking their clothes off. I was still standing there, thinking, *What the fuck is going on in here!*

Then Smiley spoke to me, "Take your clothes off, nigga, did you hear what she just said? Because you going first Virgin Boy!" (I was standing here listening to the same guy that was screaming and hollering for the ball Eagle to stop beating on me. Now he's telling me to take my clothes off inside some stranger's bedroom?) So I nervously took my pants off, and while I was pulling my shirt over my head, I could see a woman exiting from the bathroom. As I continued to pull the shirt all the way off, to my very unexpected expectations, and to my surprise, the woman that was climbing up on the bed wasn't the same woman that opened the house door. I was so high that I only could stand there while guessing what was transpiring? It was so apparent that I wasn't catching the whole conversation. This woman had dark-brown skin and a little heavier on the body weight. Once she arrived in the middle of the bed, she began to take her T-shirt and bra off. I can still remember till this day, seeing her full breasts just fall down like heavy boulders sliding down a bumpy hill until they were close enough to her belly button. Then, they just hung there like rocks in a sock. She looked at all the guys in the room as if she was a "wolf counting her sheep". Then she spoke in a very light voice while removing her bifocals from off of her big face. "Whose first please?"

And that's when someone volunteered me with a push, and I landed right in front where her face was at. She showed no signs of emotions that she was anywhere near shy. She was very straight-forward in a strangely but very polite "massage therapists" way. She reached out and hungrily grabbed my hips, so she could bring me closer to the head of the bed. She grabbed my semi-harden and extended "purple-headed warrior" and introduced it into her mouth, and the two begun to tango! I can definitely say it was a very weird feeling, no doubt. I don't even know if I was liking it or not, but I stayed on course as she kept pursuing her personal goal, and she actually reached it! Because my purple-headed warrior head turned to stone! At this point, I believe she could have given Medusa a tight run for her money. Then, she gave me directions to where she wanted me to be position on the bed.

I had seen movies, but this was the real deal. I was climbing up on this grown woman and lying between her legs, and she knew it was my first time, so she made sure to have me in the right position. Once I was settled in, I began to sway my hips back and forth, not really knowing if I was doing the right thing or not, and I didn't care because the feeling felt right. But the way the wetness was covering my freshly harden stone, I figured I was doing something right. But I was only 12 years old, and she was in her thirties, so we definitely weren't on the same page. Nonetheless, I was trying to strike gold, so I could gush all over her. As I was rocking as if I was on the best wooden horse ever made, she started shouting in a medium tone, "Hold my legs, please. Hold my legs, please."

Smooth and Smiley jumped straight into action. They moved so quick that you knew they have been here before. Smooth ran over to the top left of the bed, and Smiley was on the right side of the bed just as fast. Simultaneously, they both grabbed one of her ankles and brought them up forward toward her head until she was folded like an extra dough human pretzel. Then, everyone in the world shouted at me in a simultaneous chant, "Jump up and down, B! Jump, nigga, jump!"

So I did what I was told, and I jumped. >:)

CHAPTER 15

THE CASE AGAINST THE HORNER HOUSE

After that day, I became close friends with Smooth and Smiley, which I would benefit from as time moved forward. (But a couple of days later I did manage to get the both of them a little upset with me. I was in their hallway with a lady who was sitting down on the staircase, while I was standing in front of her face, and watching as her mouth was doing the same tango like the lady on Horner Ave. initiated. And right when I was really getting into it, Smiley and Smooth's grandmother must've been wondering what were the strange noises coming from the other side of her door. So just like any other person in the world with curiosity, she opened it and I was caught in the act! She quickly slammed that door back in my "super shock" face! Now I was hearing noises coming from the other side of that door and she was screaming, "oh my lord, oh my lord" Smiley! And now here it is, some "thirty something" years later, and Smiley still continues to enlighten me on this very embarrassing situation. But he do be laughing when he bring up the story. Because he knew good in well that he and his brother introduced me to this.) As the weeks went on,

I didn't go back over to the "Horner House" with them. Whenever someone suggested it, I would just go home and play Pac-Man on the black and white TV set with the good old Atari system. I wasn't really ready for that type of atmosphere to be incorporated into my young life. It's already bad enough that my first sex partner (well, other than my right hand and left hand) was probably more than twenty freaking years older than me, which makes for pure balderdash for a preteen. Yuck! For some reasons, I know the view of this woman is going to become and hunt my darkest memories later on in life. (And just my luck many years later into the future while sitting in church, the pastor confirmed my suspicions when he stated, "The very first person that you have sexual acts with, will always be your first husband or WIFE". Double Yuck!) As the school quarter was pushing winter out of the door and letting spring in, Fashionable Kid kept trying to get my attention while we were sitting in science class. As he walked toward the teacher's desk pretending to go to the trashcan, he passed me a note. I opened it up and read it. It was explained to me that one of the girls in our class was the Horner house daughter. And when he pointed at her, it was no mystery at all because she was a younger version of her mother, bifocals and all. So this girl everybody's been spending time with was a freak just like her mom. She didn't mind cutting class and performing sexual activities. That's around the time oral sex and French kissing was the new thing in junior high. After performing her oral acrobatics next to the cafeteria and almost getting caught, she decided to wait for the school day to end so she could indulge in some more mouth-watering gymnastics.

We were walking home from school, and Fashionable Kid asked her if she performs like her mother does, and the answer was yes. So as we continue to walk, Fashionable Kid and the future "Street Olympic Oral All Star" started separating from the group with quicker steps. We followed as they made a left and began walking up the driveway of an abandoned storefront. Two of the guys and

I followed them. Instantly, when the two other guys and I stepped foot inside the abandoned storefront, about four or five of the children from school came running up the driveway. Boys and girls were just rushing to see what was going on. As they were running up the driveway, no one noticed that the security guard was parked at the light and was watching everything that was going on. As soon all the other children made it into the driveway, the Olympics was cancelled indefinitely, and everyone placed their gears in reverse. When we all exited the driveway, the security guard asked the future Olympic candidate what she was doing in there. The girl told her nothing and was placed inside the security guard car, and we watched as they drove away and didn't think anything of it. Unfortunately, it was just a regular occurrence in our neighborhood.

The next day at school seemed like a regular day. That was until they started calling our names over the school PA system. It screamed, "Fashionable Kid, Gruff, Cuba, and Brian, report to the auditorium." As I entered the auditorium, there were about five Cleveland police officers there, along with a couple of detectives. They asked me my name, I gave it to them, and in return, they gave me a pair of handcuffs to wear and accommodated that with a free ride to Loserville. So the four of us were on our way downtown to the juvenile detention center.

For the first three days in the detention center, I didn't even know what was going on, but I knew it had something to do with the girl coming out of the building. When my mom came to visit me, she didn't say hi or anything. She just asked me one question: "Brian, did you do it?"

"Did I do what?"

"Did you try to make that girl perform any sex on you?"

"No, I did not! Not even while we were in school inside the cafeteria! I was just the lookout man! Me and her never even touched each other, Ever"!

She only asked me that one time, and that's what I love about Linda. She knows if one of her children is lying to her. She just looked at me straight in my eyes for a few seconds, and then, she stood up and said, "I'm getting you a lawyer, and I will not be back down here looking at you locked up."

Days were passing as I sat in the detention center, and due to the circumstances of the case, we weren't allowed to go home on any type of monitoring system. After about two weeks, we finally had our day in court. As we entered the courtroom, the judge just stared at us as each of us went to sit in front of the table that was in front of our parents. The judge just sat there, staring at us. Then, he started shaking his head, displaying confusion in the matter. Finally, he spoke to us, "I really don't understand what's going on. The security guard said you four gentlemen tried to make a girl perform oral sex. But the girl never gave a statement, the other children that were witnesses said you guys didn't have time to do it, and now the girl nor her parents are nowhere to be found. The only person that is saying something is the school security guard for Alexander Hamilton Junior High. So I must ask you guys for the record, did any of you guys try to make any girl perform oral sex?" The judge looked at Fashionable Kid first for an answer.

"I didn't make her, but I asked her to, Your Honor, because she be doing it anyway" was his reply.

Next was Cuba. "She did me before, Your Honor, upstairs in the school cafeteria."

Next was Gruff. "She never gave me oral sex, Your Honor, but we had sex in school."

Now the judge was looking at me. "I was going to let her do me at that building when it was my turn, Your Honor."

The judge just sat there and stared at us in disbelief. Then, he just started shaking his head from our responses. A few minutes went by. Then, he spoke, "I don't have anything to charge you guys with.

It's unfortunate you guys had to stay in here for two weeks before we got to this point, so I'm going to release you." And before he could even finish his sentence, Fashionable Kid sprang into action! With the energy of the energizer rabbit, he stood straight up, with his right hand raised in the air as if he was in class and had to use the restroom really bad. That's when he shouted, "Your Honor, can I tell you something?" He definitely had the judge's full attention as well as the rest of the courtroom! So the judge allowed him to speak, and Fashionable Kid went straight to work like the best little army ant! And boy oh boy did he open up a whole new door that was going to release a "massive swarm of worms!"

"Your Honor," he said without a hint of being embarrassed and displaying some relief as if the biggest monkey had just leaped off of his bony chest! "I be having sex with her mother! A lot of us do! Like the whole neighborhood, Your Honor!" The judge could see what he was hearing but he could not believe his ears. He proceeded in a slow motion pushing his large black leather chair away from his beautiful overlarge wooden desks and looked over at the bailiff. The bailiff just look back at the judge with a half-smile, half frown, and half of a smirk all mixed together in disbelief. Finally he offer a shrug of his shoulders that was connected to his eyes being opened very wide with a shocking appearance to them, and the bailiff's eyebrows were doing their best impression of the aftermath, when an eyeliner pencil make circus clowns look very "SURPRISED". The bailiff didn't see this coming just as the rest of the courtroom didn't, but a least he didn't have his mouth open so wide that something with wings could land on his tongue like everyone else was doing! Anyone walking into that courtroom at that particular time would've thought the judge had just ordered everybody to participate in a game of "Simon Says" and round one was to catch a fly without using your hands. Then, the judge slowly glanced at every parent until his eyes rested on Cuba. "Okay," he said, and the okay was very drawn out. His facial expression offered nothing but eagerness for information as he exhaled from the heavy breath he had taken in. He really wanted to know just what was going on on this day in his courtroom. This already strange case that landed on his doorsteps that just couldn't get any stranger just transformed into something alien!

"Cuba, did you have sexual relations with the mother?"

"Yes, Your Honor," Cuba answered back with a muttering tone.

"Gruff, did you have sexual relations with the mother?"

"Yes, Your Honor," he answered with a straight face. The guys were at least a year older than me, so their parents may have dealt with them being in trouble with the courts before because their parents (except for having their mouths wide open) didn't show too much expression of being surprised as to what was going on in their child's life. But this was my first time, and sitting behind me was not only my mother, but my mother's mother as well. Yes, I said it; my grandmother was in the house. My grandma was a beautiful, God-fearing woman, and when it came to Grandma being on a loved one's team, she was always there going beyond the call of grandparent duty.

I remember the time my grandfather and my grandmother were driving in his Cadillac when they got pulled over and the cops found his gun. My grandma took the case for him. It was a little small town they were traveling through, and at that time, individuals who displayed racism weren't looked at as if they were doing anything wrong, so on that beautiful day the color of my grandma and grandpa was like "skin was not their friend". >:(When we would go visit her, she would have to stand the entire visit behind a steel wall, looking at us through a window that was the size of a tiled kitchen floor square. And she rode that case through for him with no complaints. And every time we showed up at her doorstep at 3:00 a.m., because the bald eagle was restless, she never complained. She would give us a light snack of cookies and milk, tuck us into bed, and right before she cut off the light, she'd whisper, "Everything's going to be okay." :)

Now this sweet woman that I admire was sitting in this courtroom, showing her support and taking in all this sour information. I was starting to get really nervous because I knew the judge was about to ask me the million-dollar question next. And there was no way out of it. "Brian, did you have sexual relations with the mother?" Before he even opened up his mouth to ask me the question, I was already holding my breath; and as light as my skin is, I'm pretty sure my face was a flushed, fresh-smacked-white-baby-butt-cheek red. As the judge was waiting for me to answer, I just sat there, holding my breath and thinking to myself, *Fuck, this is way more embarrassing than that one time in science class and getting busted by my friend grandma.*

As I exhaled, I slowly turned to look at my grandmother and my mom sitting right behind me. As I started turning back around to face the judge, my mind was racing. I had to give an answer right here right now, and there's nowhere for me to skedaddle. And just before I was about to answer the million-dollar question, I played copycat and pulled a Fashionable Kid move. I stood straight up like dog ears and raised my hand at the same time as if I was in class. I made one quick turn to look at my mother and my grandmother once more. And my grandmother's face held the expression of "I hope your answer is no." But I was not about to lie, and I was not about to tell the truth. I turned around to face the judge for my last embarrassing moment with him and shouted, "Your Honor, do I have to answer that question?"

I could hear my grandmother whisper, "Oh my god."

The judge was sitting there with his eyebrows raised to the air and said, "No, Brian, you don't have to answer, and we are done here. Everyone is free to go."

As we were being escorted out of the courtroom, I heard the judge ask the bailiff, "So where's the mother and that child at?"

As the days followed, we found out through the police investigation that the mother took off, and she was never seen in the neighborhood again, nor was her daughter ever seen at school. And later, we found out that her husband was always in the front room with the daughter watching TV while we were in the house group banging his freaky nympho of a wife. I don't know what his full condition was mentally or physically, but one was being impotent, and he didn't care when his wife and daughter left. He continued to live there.

CHAPTER 16

WILL THE CHAMPION PLEASE STAND UP

Being back in school was no different than we left for the nonsense. Everybody still treated us the same. As my seventh-grade school year was shortly coming to an end, I found ways to occupy myself so I could stay out of trouble. I joined the school swim team and softball team. Being on the swim team created a lifelong impression on me, which I still carry till this day. (And today is Sunday morning, July 28, 2013.)

Toward the end of the school year, Alexander Hamilton Junior High had a swim meet at Martin Luther King Junior High. This day will mark the grand finale of the school swimming meets until next year tryouts begin. On this special day either you win and take it all, or go home with water leaking from your eye lids. Now if my mother was to explain the earlier years of my history, she would describe me as "always active, self-motivated, and that I never like to lose at anything that I was willing to put my hard earned energy into." Now I was never a sore loser I just didn't like accepting a loss, but I will not allow, being less than number one prevent me from being the very bendable and smiling person that others enjoyed. If you won a challenge that we had going on, I would give you your respect and hoped you would give me a chance sometime in the near future to take the title back. I was not a shark in the water, but I did have the ability to play the part of a big fish. I was so ready for this swim meet, I couldn't backstroke, but I could definitely butterfly, and I could freestyle with the best of them. The first meet was up and ready to go. I just sat on the bench, waiting with anticipation. As the whistle blew, the second meet was over, and we were still in place for the win. The third meet was all mine. As the whistle blew, I pushed off the swimming pool wall with all the force that I had inside my legs, and I was off and running. As I streamlined down the pool, there was no way to tell what place I was actually in. As I came up for air and to a stop, because I had reached the other end of the pool, the announcer announced that I was in second place, and I was very satisfied with that because I did understand that in life, you cannot always be first or win them all—not even when you put your all into it. So I mastered how to allow disappointment to linger within my life without being affected by the results of it.

We were entering into the last meet of the day, and for the rest of the year, we were doing pretty well, but the other schools were following suit. There weren't any losers yet. This last meet would determine which school gets to take home the big trophy. When we first arrived at this competition, I noticed that a guy was missing from our squad, but what I didn't realize was how much of a problem that was going to be for me. As they were preparing for the last meet, the coach walked over toward me and said, "Brian, you have to swim this one," and I was very cool and calm with that because I'm always full of energy. So I stood up, tightened my goggles, and proceeded toward the top of the pool. As I was mentally preparing myself for this last chance of being a school "superstar", my focus was broken from the sounds of splashing water. That's when I had realize that the other swimmers was already in the pool and they were all turned around backwards! And that's when I performed a maneuver as if I had just got struck by lightning because I went straight into action! I performed a superfast about-face as if I was in the military and started walking away from the pool of death. And now that I think about it, I wasn't walking at all it was more of a horses "giddy up and go". And my swim coach must have gotten struck by lightning also, because she was right on my heels as I was running for the border.

As soon as we were face- to- face, I didn't give her a chance to talk because I already knew she was going to be on some, "coach encouraging the fleeing student BS" and I really wasn't trying to hear a conversation that's meant for the toilet at this particular time. So I blurted out, "You know I can't swim backwards, I can't even roller skate backwards. Why are you doing this to me, Coach!"

She said, "We are here to have fun. It's not always about winning Mr. Fish! It's about believing in yourself and giving your all and respecting whatever the outcome may be regardless of the fact because we are all winners at the end of the day. I know you can do this Brian, now get your ass in the water." She was a very serious and outspoken coach. I truly admire her spirit and had loved her technique of persuading me into something that I didn't want to do. Fair exchange is no robbery. So I would love to be in the position to put her PPC (pushy persuading compelling) ass into something that she didn't want to do! >:)

With my coach's stamp of approval sneaking its way into my heart to strengthen me up and with her threatening, gouging eyeballs, along with my thought of, *This is America, where anything is possible!* I started walking toward the top of the pool. I didn't have the slightest idea that I was actually walking the plank and that my coach was really Mrs. Captain Hook doing her best impression of imitating her wicked husband. As I entered into the water, strangely, I didn't have a sense of fear. For some reason, I was ready to go! Once again, I checked my goggles to make sure they were tight, pulled up my Speedos to make sure they were fitting properly. Now all I needed was to hear that great whistle blow. I did not want to jump the gun, but it seemed as if it was taking eons for that whistle to send me fish-tailing down the pool. Just as I was about to open my eyes and break my concentration for the takeoff, I heard the triumph horn blowing, and I was off and swimming! I pushed off the pool wall with more force and determination than I had my first round. I started throwing my hands behind me with what I thought was focus precision and brought them back up out of the water. I could feel the water rushing over my body as if I was a great whale prancing in the beautiful ocean. I could hear the loud screams from the spectators rushing into my ears, and that's when I started shouting at myself mentally, "Go, big fish, go. Go, big fish, go. Go, big fish, go!" I had the rhythm of the "Little Engine That Could" chanting inside my head as if it was tackling the hardest uphill climb to victory, "I know I can, I know I can!" All of these "marvelous mental encouragements" had me pushing forward for a win! I had no way of knowing if I swam myself into the slot of first -second- or third place as I rapidly moved down the pool, but I just knew that I had a chance at winning this thing. I could hear the energetic screams of my personal spectators getting louder and I knew the reason was because of the powerful movement of my fishtailing! That's when the whistle blew for what would be the last blow for the year.

I had all that action going on! But they weren't honoring my "big fish" self-proclaimed title. Their reactions was more of the likes intended for a freaking mascot! In my mind, I was truly giving the best game of Rock 'Em Sock 'Em a run for its money, but when I stopped and proceeded to rise out of the water, everyone was looking at me, everyone was pointing at me, and everyone wasn't cheering me on. Instead, they were laughing at me!

That's when my eyebrows formed a unibrow because it didn't take a rocket scientist to figure this simple equation out! As I was pulling myself out of the water, I realized that I was the only one coming out of the water, and I was still at the top of the pool where it all started. The other swimmers were down at the other end of the pool, trying to focus in on what the spectators was so amused about.

I didn't go anywhere! With all my thoughts of "big fish in the water!" With all my thoughts of "toot toot, little engine that could." But in reality, my nonbackward swimming self literally didn't go anywhere! All the water that I kicked, and splashed, did not amount to anything except a good show-and-tell for others to enjoy. And to add extra insult to my mental anguish, at the end of the school year, they actually gave me a small swimming trophy in the shape of a little gold man diving into an imaginary pool.

Even till this day, which is August 2, 2013, my mom always tells me that she has my trophy put up for me. >:(That swimming meet has always been a gorilla on my back. At the beginning of this year, I hit my beautiful fortieth birthday, thank God! I was deciding if I should go for my lifeguard license to smooth my pain. LOL :)

CHAPTER 17

SUMMER SCHOOL

The school year was over, at least for the children who had done what they were supposed to be doing in class. As for us knuckleheads, school was starting right back up because everyone who didn't do the right thing in class had to go to summer school. That really sucked because all year long, we were always fighting with another junior high school called Nathan Hale. They were placing all of us into one high school for the summer, and that battleground would be called John Adams. (And years into the future haven't too much really changed at that John Adams High school! And now that expensive freshly built restructured schoolhouse is even worse than when I was attending! And with today's social media mixed in with today's technology, make it very easy for students to post what goes on within the walls of a building that was constructed for learning. For one reason or another I found myself looking at the daily news or surfing through Facebook and YouTube, as I was taking a break from writing this autobiography you're reading now. And I couldn't believe the footage that was taken by student cell phones, rather it be students committing a black on black crime or even going as far to committing a crime on a teacher! I know it's like I'm calling the kettle black, but hey, we all can use a little walk on the "positive side of life" in order to respect and embrace some positive change. :)

The first day of summer school, I experienced my first black eye that wasn't delivered by the bald Eagle. I also felt breezing air from my first bullets flying past my head that wasn't coming from Linda. We made sure that the police, firefighters, and the news coverage personalities had a summer job. Summer was walking into its fourth week, and I was always looking for ways to skip school because people was seriously getting hurt, and I didn't plan on visiting any hospitals any time soon!

One morning, my little brother and his friend Shortstop came to answer my beckoning call (which turned out to be a very bad first time driving experience for all three of us). It was early in the morning, and I was getting dressed for summer school. I made sure that I had one of Linda's steak knives, a pair of brass knuckles, and two ninja stars that was a combo to a pair of nunchakus from the Chinese store located in downtown Cleveland. I even had the black gum bottom ninja shoes to match. I would've preferred to put on my Michael Jackson thriller jacket or slick my hair back like Prince, but this summer school didn't allow you to look beautiful. So my chosen costume was pure unrated ninja!

Just before I was about to make my way down the stairs to walk out of the house while mentally preparing myself for the school battlegrounds, I could hear my little brother and his friend calling me from outside. I went over to the window and started to unwind it, so it would open. "What do y'all want?" I asked him in a somewhat irritated voice because they didn't have to go to summer school, and I was jealous.

"We need you to come start this truck up for us," he said.

"What truck?" I asked.

"Midnight just stole a black Cherokee, and he got it parked on the side of his house."

There was no need for me to question them any further. Summer school would definitely have to wait. "Here I come," I said, and we were on our way to Midnight's house to steal the truck that he had just stolen.

Let us not forget that I was only a preteen at the time, and my brother Slim and his buddy Shortstop were a couple years younger. We didn't know how to steal cars; we only knew how to drive them (our father always took us go car racing, which gave us a little advantage), but I did know how to pull the pin in the steering column and make the vehicle's motor turnover. That was only due to me cutting summer school one day. This older kid that frequented Smooth and Smiley's house was waiting for the RTA in front of the Boys and Girls Club, and when I walked past him, he asked me, "What you doing?"

I told him, "Trying to find somewhere to cut school." He told me to come with him, and he paid for my bus fare. We landed in downtown Cleveland. As soon as we got off the RTA bus, I followed him to a busy parking lot, and he walked straight up to a Chevy Camaro. You would've thought his screwdriver was a key to the ignition. He jumped in, popped the lock on the door, so I could become an accomplice, and I watched in shock because I had never actually seen this done before. Just a couple of seconds slower than an owner probably turns the motor over with the authorized key, he had popped the steering column off and was pulling the starting pin. We were on our way back to the neighborhood in a matter of seconds. A few years later, he was murdered in Detroit. Rest in peace, my friend. (F)

Midnight's house wasn't too far away, and with the anticipation of driving a Jeep Grand Cherokee, we had no issues with the walk at all. Finally, the truck was in view, and it was a new truck. It was meant for me to drive it, I thought, because it was my favorite color, Triple Black on black on black! Once the three of us were inside, I didn't hesitate to put us in motion. I'd driven a few cars already due to the fact that all my friends were car thieves and flat-out crooks, but none of the past vehicles came close to this Grand Cherokee. Even though it was a truck, it had the steering of a car. It rolled with the smoothness of my grandfather's Cadillac. We bent a couple of corners, and that's when a thought came to me, so I spoke on it. "Hey, let's take this truck down to Bessemer Street so we can punch the gas pedal and see how fast it will go?"

Of course everyone was on board with this dumb ass decision I just conjured up. We sat at the light waiting for the red light to go green, right on the corner next to John Adams High School (where my stupid self was supposed to be in class but duh!). As we sat still waiting for the light to change, a Cleveland police cruiser pulled up behind me. My first thought was, *MF!* I did not want to make any certain moves to alert them of anything, but I had to say something to Shortstop because he was in the backseat rambling through everything, hoping to score something of value that he could keep.

Very casually, I was like, "Shortstop, slow down a little, and don't move. The police just pulled up behind us. Do not turn around and look at them." And just like the pro car thief that he wasn't, Shortstop turned his goofy self around and looked at the police straight in their faces. I would bet my last dollar that when he turned around and the protect and serve crew saw the surprised look on his look-officer-my-mouth-is-wide-open face, they knew right then and there that it was time for them to punch the time clock. Immediately, I was like, "I just told your dumb butt not to look at them. Get ready to run because they're going to get on us." I continued nervously waiting for the light to turn green. Not once did I look in my rearview mirror, or any other mirror for that matter. Finally, the light hit the green, and I hit the gas pedal very lightly, just as any normal car would do if the police were behind them. The second we came from under the light, the police cruiser started flashing me to pull over.

John Adams had an alley that ran between the high school and the school's mighty Rebels football field. The alley was a block long, and the pavement was made up of millions of little white and gray rocks, which, in turn, made for a very unstable fast getaway. As I was slowing the vehicle and turning on my right hand signal (because I didn't want to be ticketed for improper signal usage), I told my brother and Shortstop to put on their seat belts. As I was pulling into the school driveway, I made sure that I had that Jeep Grand Cherokee pointed neatly in the middle of the alley, so that it was prepared to shoot for a straight shot. In a matter seconds, their loudspeaker spoke. "Put your vehicle in park, turn the motor off, and take your foot off the brake," was the first command from the Cleveland police cruiser, and I did exactly what they asked. I just did it my way. This was a brand-new truck. You could not tell if the motor was on or off unless you were laying right next to it under the hood. So I put the vehicle in neutral, and then, I took my foot off the brake pedal in order for the tail lights to cut off.

As I was watching the officers through my driver's mirror, I started practicing breathing slower so I could get some type of control over the high-strung feeling that my body was experiencing because I had already planned out in my mind exactly what I was about to do. I watched as both officers exited the police cruiser and started walking toward my escape capsule with wheels. They both stopped at the rear of the vehicle and were discussing the fake license plate that was taped to the back window. One officer stayed at the rear of the vehicle and started calling the plate in to headquarters, and the driver of the cruiser started approaching my window. As he was coming up on my window, he started talking to me.

The officer said, "The reason I'm pulling you over is because the license plate is not registered to this vehicle." As soon as he got to my window and got a good look at me, the officer was like, "How old are you?" We were looking at each other eye to eye for only a super brief second. While he was getting his disbelief on, I politely slid the transmission to Drive, and then I stomped the gas pedal, and boy oh boy did that V8 come to life! As we were being slingshot forward, I could only imagine what type of dusty rock storm was being delivered on top of the peace officers from the four wheels spinning. It wasn't my intention to sandblast the poor bastards, but we all know that sometimes shit just happens on the job. That V8 in that Grand Cherokee was very powerful! It never did lose grip on all those rocks, and I never lost total control as we were speeding down that gravel-laid alley that really sucked for what I needed it for, but oh well, at least we were making tracks into our get away. So after bouncing off and scraping a few school concrete walls and their chain-link football field fence, we were on our way and coming up to the end of the alley, which let out into a residential avenue, and my only choice was either left or right.

If I made a right, I would be entering Martin Luther King Boulevard, which definitely meant for heavy traffic and surely 80 percent chance of an accident. Or I could make a left and would be driving deeper into the hood. And if I could accommodate a couple of corners and jump out this bad boy fast enough, I can hit a few fences and be right back at home and non-oblivious to the entire ordeal. So I smashed the brake pedal, and slid about twenty feet on the gravel, and hurried to cut that steering wheel as hard as my young muscles would allow me to and made a hard left. Then, I smashed the gas pedal once more. You know the old saying that's been passed down to generation to churchgoing generation: "God knows what's going to happen before it happens" or "God saves children and jackasses." And I was surely owning up to my end of the donkey.

As I cleared that first left turn, I started shooting up the street like I was just released from one of the world's best circus cannons. That V8 in that darn Grand Cherokee was not playing. It was gaining speed very rapidly, and as I was heading toward the street's four-way intersection, I decided to make another hard left. I was doing over fifty miles per hour when I decided to make that left-hand turn. Once again, I tell you, God saves children and jackasses. As I was coming up on the intersection at an uncontrollable speed, I remembered how Michael Knight would slow Kitt down a little bit before he made his turn. But before I could play copycat to the famous *Knight Rider*, God knew I wasn't ready for this Hollywood stunt just yet, and the steering wheel and breaks locked up on me. So instead of making a left turn, I slid and crashed into the corner of a sidewalk. No one was hurt, so we did not hesitate.

I told my brother and Shortstop, "Y'all better run and don't get caught!" I jumped out, and when my feet hit the pavement, the police cruiser was flying straight toward me with no holds barred. I was truly a deer stuck in bright lights for real this time! Within one foot from them running me over, the cruiser made a lifesaving hard left and missed me literally by inches! As soon as I realized that I wasn't on my way to meet my maker, the head lights and deer moment had turned completely off, and I took off as well, running for my life! One of the police officers took off with me, and boy oh boy was he determined! I could tell by all the noise he was making running after me. I continued to keep looking behind my shoulder to see how close he was, and the two or three times that I looked back, this sucker was getting closer to me. This white man could seriously run!

"Fuck, he's fast!" was my only thought of him. I had placed myself in some real balderdash with this track star trying to pass his handcuffs on to me like a baton, knowing darn well we were playing cops and robbers, and I was not his teammate! So I had to create some evasive action, like right then and there, because this white man meant business and he surely displayed that he was not playing! That's when I realized exactly what was going on in his mind. I'm sure he was thinking, "You little black fucker! Think you're going to sandblast me and get away with it! I think not! And I didn't appreciate the taste of them darn rocks you fuck! And as soon as I get my hands around your throat smart guy! You're not going to like the taste of my flashlight little buddy! Damn this kid is fucking fast!" You could just tell by his whole physical demeanor that he was going for the gold! So I started running toward the football fence, and once I entered, I ran as fast as I could to the bleacher section. I ran up the first flight of stairs and waited. I was hoping that my second wind would kick in on time and aid me in some help and give my getaway a much-needed boost.

As I was rapidly taking in and releasing air out of my lungs, right on cue, the officer appeared in the bleachers with me. Before he could mutter one word of any type of command, I jumped right over the balcony and landed on the football field's running track. The only thing I was missing was the "sound off shot" from a starting pistol and someone handing me the baton! :) As soon as I hit that track, you would've thought I was the one going for the gold. My second wind and fear of his handcuffs around my wrist had incorporated themselves into my lungs, and I started running like the Cherokee's V8! As I made it to the end of the track and wiggled my way through the exit fence, I took a brief second to look behind me. This was a true classic game of cops and robbers, and I had to measure just how far away this "law dog" was from this "young cat." To my surprise, he decided against jumping over the balcony because I did not see him anywhere. The doughnuts must've gotten the best of him, no doubt. :) I ran for another two blocks and made it to a street called Gay.

My street was about three blocks of a distance before I could actually scream, "Free at last! Thank God oh mighty, I'm free at last!" The surrounding area was starting to get congested with more police cars than I could muster! I looked to my left, I looked to my right, and then, I started casually walking up the driveway of someone's home. I kicked the wood out from up under their front porch, crawled under it, replaced the wood to its proper position, then laid in a small ditch that looked like it was created by a dog. I watched about seven police cruisers slowly cruise back and forth. My thumbs mentally went up like the Fonz on *Happy Days* because for the moment, I was cool and safe. (That was the third time *when a soul started running*.)

I stayed under that porch, lying in dirt for at least two hours. After dusting off, I started making my way back home. As soon as I walked through the door, Linda and Ike were rushing out of the house. When my mom saw me, the first thing she said was, "Brian, you know anything about your brother inside a stolen car?"

"Not really," was all I could conjure up without being totally dishonest because she said car, not truck. In my book, a half of a question can only receive a half of an answer. I was asleep by the time they returned home with my brother and was awakened by the shouts coming from downstairs. Ike was trying to get my brother to tell him who was driving the truck, and his method for getting answers was always chastising.

Smash! I could hear my brother being thrown against the wall as my father shouted, "Who was driving the darn truck!" But my brother would not tell. It took three or four more smashes into the wall before he finally broke. "I'm going to ask you one more time!" my father was saying to him as he finally decided on gritting his teeth, and that's something I've never seen the eagle do to my little brother.

"Brian was."

My mother and father shouted for me to come downstairs. "You were driving that darn truck," my mother said, and it wasn't a question that my mother was asking. It was more of an automatic conviction. But they both were too exhausted from going to work on my brother to even take on the challenge of disciplining me right then and there. So I was told to go back upstairs. My brother and Shortstop both were given probation from the court, but I guess he was too young to really understand probation, so he kept messing up and received six months at the juvenile detention center in Hudson.

With my brother gone and the summer coming to an end, I decided to start going back over to Smokey and Smiley's house. The first day back over to their house was a whole new experience with drugs. As I entered the basement, there was about five or six older guys already there. They were passing a joint around. The next person to hit the joint spotted me and passed it to me so I could hit it. There was already a different smell in the air coming from that joint, but I paid it no attention because every week, someone had some type of new weed. Whether it was monkey paw, funky skunk, or some newly developed backyard boogie. I really didn't care. It was free, and the older guys liked seeing us getting high.

As soon as he passed it to me, I took my two puffs and passed it to the next person. As I exhaled the smoke, I noticed that it went down really smooth. But my lips had no feeling in them; they were totally numb. I asked the person who passed me the joint if his lips were numb. He just burst out laughing. Then, I started laughing. When I finally caught my breath, I noticed that I was looking over in Smokey's direction. "Well, that's something you don't see every day," was my train of thought.

Smokey was standing in the middle of the basement under a light bulb that hung down. In one hand, he had a spoon, and in the other hand, he held a lighter under the spoon and was cooking or burning whatever was inside of the spoon. As I stood there staring at him, my whole face went totally numb! Smokey took a wire coat hanger and started to stir it around inside of the spoon. He pulled the mixture off the spoon by allowing it to stick on the hanger. I could see some type of milk-colored mucus liquid on the end of it. He dipped his fingers into some ice water, then allowed the water from his fingers to drip on top of the mucus, and the mucus instantly started turning white and had hardened up. He grabbed a white glass plate and a butter knife and started scraping the hardened white substance off the hanger. He then took some of what he had scraped off and started putting it inside of some joints. I asked Smokey what was that stuff, and he was like, "It makes the weed taste better." I could agree with that. >:(

CHAPTER 18

WELCOME TO THE GAME

As the days followed, I always made my way over to Smokey and Smiley's house to get my face frozen. The new school year was starting up, and I was entering into the eighth grade. The first day of school went along just as casual as a school day could. As the bell rang, it was time for me to roll out. I proceeded on my way home as usual, but as soon as I crossed the street, Skeleton was standing there.

"Where you think you going, little dude?" I saw the *bullshit* written all over his black ass face.

"I'm on my way home." And you could hear a little bit of nervousness coming from my vocal cords.

"Why you not making money, little nigga?" Skeleton asked with a serious, threatening tone.

"What do you mean making money?" the nervousness in my tone was starting to subside.

My businessman persona just took over the ship. I continued to keep my eyes on him as he was talking because I knew he wasn't playing or trying to be threatening. He was talking business, a side that I'd never seen before, and he knew he had my complete attention. "Follow me," he said. So I started following the asshole.

Where there is one, there's always two! He had me follow him over to Fly's house. As soon as Fly saw me, he started smiling. "You ready to start making some money, little dude? We've been waiting to run into you!"

"Sure," I answered Fly right back. (He was the lesser end of the dynamic dual jackass team). I did not know how I was going to make money with these guys, but I liked to work so I was up for any job within context. He had me wait in the backyard of his house. He returned pretty fast and handed me a piece of aluminum foil that was folded. What type of trickery shit is this they're trying to pull? was all I was thinking! But as I opened up the aluminum foil, I saw five odd-shaped white little balls in it, and knowing these two, I knew it wasn't a joke.

"What are these?" I asked with confusion written all over my face.

"Go over to Smokey house. Smokey will tell you what to do with them. You owe me $60, and you keep $40 for yourself."

"Okay," I said with a shrug of shoulders and started making my way over to Smokey and Smiley's house. I wasn't concerned about going home because they were probably fighting any freaking way. >:(

As I was walking up Smiley's driveway, Smokey already had been alerted that I was coming because he was waiting at the screen door holding it open for me. "Hold on a second, B. Let me grab a jacket." When he got his jacket, we started walking toward the corner of his street. Once we got there, Smiley was already posted up but he didn't say anything, he just continued to turn his head from left to right as if he's on a stakeout. The three of us were just standing there. After a few minutes, a car pulled up, and a man got out. "This one yours, B. See what he wants."

The man walked over to me and said, "Let me get a ten piece." I didn't know what in the world a ten piece was but my common sense knew it has to do with this aluminum foil, so Smokey assisted me. He took one of the little white balls out of my aluminum foil and broke it in half. He told me to give one half to the man and take his $10, so I did what I was told. As soon as I took the man's money, two more cars were pulling up.

The transactions went pretty fast, and I was out of white little balls within seconds on the hour, and I had $100 in my pocket.

I was like, "I'll catch you later. I have to take Fly his money."

Smokey was like, "No, no, no, don't take him his money yet. First, you gotta double up!"

"Double up?" I didn't have the slightest idea what the fuck he was talking about! And I knew his illiterate life-living self didn't speak two languages! "What's a double up, nigga? I'm not about to play with Fly's money." But Smokey promised me that everything will be safe. He even gave me a $100 out of his pocket for insurance.

That's when I started thinking that just maybe, "Smokey not as literate as I think he is. Now I was very curious about this move he calls a double up."

Smokey called another guy and told him that I had $100. I gave that guy the hundred dollars, and he gave me a corner of a plastic bag full of powder. I was a little nervous because I didn't want to mess up the money that I owed Fly. And Fly gave me little white balls, not no fucking baby powder! I was nervous now about this transaction, as I watched the seconds on the clock ticking by. I actually went from nervous to flat-out scared. So I doubled tapped my pocket to make sure that the paper hundred dollars was securely in place. Smokey took the powder, poured it inside of a baby bottle, mixed some baking soda with it, and placed the baby bottle inside another pan with boiling water. Within a few seconds, he was shaking the baby bottle; and as I continue my spectating, I noticed the baby powder formed into a little white ball. He then grabbed a coat hanger to break the ball while it was inside of the baby bottle. That's when it dawned on me. This is the same white stuff that this douchebag be putting inside the marijuana! Dirty motherfuckers!

When he finished chopping everything up with a razor blade, I had $240 worth of little white balls. I quickly made back all the money that I owed to Fly, and I had plenty left over for myself. I was now officially introduced into the dope game! My nose was now open to a whole new world, and I didn't take it for granted. Well, not in the beginning. It didn't take long before I was thinking, *If we are selling this stuff to people to get high, but we smoke it inside our joints, that's defeating the purpose.*

Smiley, Smokey, and just about everyone who frequented their house were smoking little white balls mixed with their ganja. I knew right then and there that in order to be successful, it was time to change the game. That's when a true Hustler was born.

Pulling away couldn't have come at a better time. As I was distancing myself from Smiley and Smokey, I had ran into Fashionable Kid. He was already into the dope game as well, so he said he was going to introduce me to his guys and I could start hanging on their block, which was called Durkee. I said okay, and we were going to meet up the next day. As we departed, I started to make my way over to Fly's house. Little did I know this would be the last time that I associated myself with him just as well. Walking up his driveway, I could see Fly and Skeleton sitting inside a new fancy car, and somehow, he had a fifth wheel applied to the truck that made his car look extra special. He was one of the first ones in our neighborhood showing the results from the little white balls payouts. Skeleton got out and sat in the back seat, so I took over the passenger side next to Fly. I handed him his money and noticed a smile forming on his face as he handed me a bigger piece of aluminum foil with even more little white balls in it. When I started reaching for the car handle so I could exit and get back to the block, Fly told me to hold on for a second. He pulled out a cigarette and a little glass bottle with some liquid in it. He dipped the cigarette inside the liquid and put a lighter to it. He puffed it a couple of times, then tried to pass it to me. When I didn't take it, Skeleton punched me in the back of my head and said, "Take a few puffs, little dude!"

"I don't smoke cigarettes!" I said with the toughest voice I could conjure up.

"This is not no regular cigarette. Now hit it!"

"I just told y'all I don't smoke cigarettes!" My irritation struck a chord with Skeleton, and he punched me in the back of my head again but time with more force applied to it this time around.

"Fuck! I'm really starting not to like these two bullyin'-ass niggas," were my thoughts as I was reaching for the cigarette because I didn't want this jackass punching me in the back of my head no more.

Fly was telling the truth when he said this was no ordinary cigarette because it reeked of a smell that I'd never encountered before and the odor was very strong. Even stronger than the juices that be running out of a garbage truck on a hot summer day, and yes it was definitely stronger than the radiator steamy pissy smells from the boys urinating on it in the school's restroom. As I put the cigarette to my lips and took my first two puffs, Fly and Skeleton started laughing like a couple goofy hyenas. I exhaled the smoke, and for some reason, I was not choking. In all reality, the smoke was going down and coming out pretty smooth. That's when I took two hard puffs, and Fly quickly intervened, "Hold on, little dude. You can't be hitting that shit hard like that!"

I was just sitting there, thinking, *First, these two jackasses make me smoke a cigarette. Now the lesser jackass is telling me not to smoke it like he's concerned about my health policy premium that he's financially contributing to.* So I stopped and passed it back to Fly. As we were sitting inside the car, I didn't feel any different from when I entered the vehicle. Fly was like, "Come on, let's get out." The instant my feet touched the pavement and I was standing straight up, the whole wide world and everything in it started spinning out of control! And I mean spinning like something "very awfully rapidly!" If I turned my head to the left, the whole world started spinning to the right! If I turned my head to the right, the whole world started spinning to the left! When I closed both of my eyes, I just felt like throwing up because my whole body felt like it was spinning! I did not know what to do. Every single little thing around me was incoherent! I knew where I was. I knew where I needed to be going, which was home, but I had no sense of direction when it came to moving my legs. My inner compass was totally off the Richter scale. I could hear Skeleton telling Fly, "Man, this little dude is messed up!"

Fly was like, "Yeah, I can see that, stupid. We can't let him leave just yet. He might get himself killed. Come on, little dude, you got to go upstairs and sit down for a while."

I focused the best I could as Fly and Skeleton started walking toward the doorway of the house. I tried my best to follow them, but my brain would not connect to my legs. My brain had me thinking that I was walking, but my legs were not budging. Fly looked back at me and was like, "Little dude, stuck on, stupid. Lift your legs up, man!" I tried to follow orders, but with every step I took, it was as if I was stepping over a fence, trying not to hit my kahunas on the barb wire. That day, I truly respected and understood the meaning of FUBAR (fucked up beyond all recognition)! I got the hang of my robot walk with the "artificial compassion" help from the two ass-holes, who happily got me into this terrible dilemma! I finally made it into the house and followed them up the stairs. Fly told his sister, who was around my age, to come get me, and she grabbed my hand and pulled me toward her bedroom. Fly told me to stay there until I was able to walk, and that turned into me watching his sister play Super Mario Brothers hour after hour. Finally, after drinking a gallon of milk, I was well enough to go home. But just think, I got out of school at 2:30 p.m., and I didn't arrive home until around 8:30 at night.

I walked into my stepdad's house after knocking on the door (because I was never given a key), and my mom was sitting at the kitchen table doing her numbers as usual.

"Where you been?" she asked.

"I don't know."

My mom had enough issues dealing with her husband, so she really didn't have the time to pay me too much attention. She asked me if I was okay, and I just nodded and went upstairs, got in the bed, and let the whole wide world continue to play the spinning head game on me. (A few years later, while I was in prison, I heard Skeleton's stepfather had fatally stabbed him. You gave me a lesson in life. Rest in peace, my friend.) (S)

As the morning came to light, I was finally able to pull myself together. Instead of going to school, I met up with Fashionable Kid, and we were on our way to Durkee! When we first got there, I realized that I knew just about everyone, so I knew this would be an easy transition from me going over to Smokey and Smiley's house to make money. Being on Durkee, I started moving up in the drug game ranks pretty fast. Within a couple of months, I went from buying double ups of little white balls, to buying pure larger amounts of powder cocaine. My name was ringing bells everywhere, and that was due to the fact that I was respectable and smart in them streets. Not only did I follow the rules, I made up my own rules to the game as well. I never joined any gangs like most of my classmates were doing. So that allowed me to travel to different neighborhoods. Whether you were a Folk or Vice Lord, whether you strolled with Bloods or rolled with Crips, whether you were from up the way or down the way, I showed my respect to all, and in turn, they showed me love back.

Some of the hard core guys used to say that I was too sweet for the hustle because some of my rules included morals that they deem "very stupid and unnecessary!" (But I beg to differ) Because at my young age I had a strong respect for human life! Of course I'm not no angel, but I'm damn sure not trying to walk in the shoes of the devil "by no means necessary"! And to me living life do not consists of the favorite quote that's mostly utilized by broke people! (Money makes the world go round!) No, No, No! That statement is pure BS in my book. I believe "respecting others to a certain degree, and how you carry yourself" is what (make the world go around! But people pride most of the time do not allow them to take this very simple route). So, when it came down to me being a "Hustler" in them streets, I let my conscience intervene most of the time when it came to guiding my movements! So, I would not sell drugs to any pregnant women, (I viewed doing that as putting a gun to my head and playing Russian roulette), I wouldn't sell drugs to any children under my age if they were users, (I viewed that as just plain old stupid, I wasn't going be the reason why someone my age or younger didn't finish school). And I darn sure wouldn't sell drugs to anybody who seem like they were mentally disabled, (because if you couldn't explain to me clearly how much dope you wanted to buy, you clearly wasn't going to get it from me). So yes, my conscience had me miss out on a lot of money, but that was very cool with me because I wasn't the type of "early bird that would eat any type of bread" (Flat out). And if I went to some-one's home to sell them drugs and there were children in the house, before I would leave, I would look inside their refrigerator. If I felt that there wasn't enough food in there for the children, I would take the money that the parent just spent and go buy food to put in their house. My rules were my rules, and I welcomed the title "too sweet for the hustle" with arms wide open.

I was financially floating in the dope game, while others turned into concrete statues and just couldn't move further up the food chain. Some even crumble worst than stale coffee cake. I was making very good money, but at the same time, I was terribly disrespecting my much-needed school values and myself by not attending like I was supposed to. I knew I had to stay away from the block and get my butt back in class and back on track. But you know what they say about Pisces and our ability to bring our imagination to reality. So I created a plan to where I could go to school and still make money. I came across a guy who needed a double up from the Kinsman area. I made sure that I straightened his hand up enough so he would strike up a conversation, so after placing in his hand what he was paying for, I slipped in my own little special bonus. "You doing like this? You need to come check me out up on Kinsman."

So one day in school when it was time for lunch, I went out the side door that led me straight to the Kinsman Road, and I found the guy that extended me the invitation. He started introducing me to everyone up there on that block. Everyone seemed to like me. So they gave me a pass to make money on their block. So I was allowed to circulate within their circle without any problems.

CHAPTER 19

STICK UP KIDS

The Folks and the Muslims had Kinsman on lockdown. I used to love seeing everyone united, even though everyone had different views. I used to post up inside Burger King and make a killing filling up my pocket with them greenery dead president's. Then like the "A" student I was not, I would go right back to class to finish out the rest of the day as if I was really interested. Little did I know, the Muslims were really paying (little old) me some attention. I can still remember the day when I knew I was really getting deep into the game because I bought my first gun. I took that gun everywhere with me because it was my lifeline. But I never took it to school because I had my own life rules. My rules and my morals really kept me in line while living this corrupted life that I was venturing off into. One day down on Durkee, a customer came to me and said he wanted something. So I gave him what he asked for. He took it, put it in his mouth to make sure it was real, then he just stood there, looking at me.

Finally, he said, "I don't have no money, so what you going to do?"

I just looked at him for a hot second. "I'm not going to do nothing, but give you three more for free, and I hope you come back and see me with some money in your hands."

Then my gun and I just walked away from that gentleman and still sold to him the very next day. Word got out that guys on Durkee were making a lot of money, so people started coming from other blocks to rob us, but that's just all part of the game. At least, that's what we always say until we become a victim of our self-created circumstances.

Sometimes, I would be up on Durkee by myself. Even though I was cool with everyone, I was always pretty much a loner. One night, the guys from the other blocks got me. It had to be somewhere between twelve midnight and 1:00 a.m. I was patrolling the block on my beach cruiser. I always left my gun in the bushes, just in case the police pulled up on me, but kept it close enough just in case I saw danger lurking my way. As I was sitting on my cruiser on Durkee's corner, I saw three guys walking toward me. I sort of knew one of them, and the other two faces were somewhat familiar, but I truly didn't know these guys personally. "Okay, it's cool. These guys are from Miles." As I was looking at the one that I was more familiar with, he was silently telling me to run, but I didn't catch on quick enough because I wasn't expecting anything negative. As they walked up on me, the bigger one out the group put a gun into my side and was like, "Give me all of your money, pretty boy." (I never forget a face! January, 2015, years and years later from when the bigger guy put that gun into my side, I had seen him inside a store in "Maple Heights Ohio". He didn't know who I was at the time, but I knew exactly who he was. But I let "bygones be bygones" and just left it alone. 30 days later, I ran into him again as I was leaving the juvenile courthouse building, "I was in the mist of fighting for my daughter" when I spotted him, I just stood in front of the courthouse so I can see which vehicle he would be climbing into. After I verify what he was driving, I ran to my car as fast as I could and hastily tried to play catch-up. After making it through the pay toll I got a heavy on my lead foot while semi-mashing down my gas pedal. Finally I caught up to the guy at a red light and position myself on the left side of his vehicle. I let my passenger-side window down and started honking my horn to get his attention. When he raised his window down I asked him, "do you remember me?" His response was," yeah, you look familiar" I said," do you believe in God?" He said," yeah, man I changed my whole life around, I seen you down at the juvenile courts a few minutes ago, I was thinking that you looked familiar" I said, "yeah, I believe in God too! Hey my man, didn't you used to hang with Blackmen?" He said, "yeah" (as this conversation was going on between the two of us, a line of cars were honking their horns at us because we had stopped traffic from moving) so I responded with, "See, that's exactly why I don't hold things against people. Because I'm that guy, that you and your two homeboys did that robbery on years ago up on Durkee" He responded with, "It wasn't me! Shoot, I was the one selling all the birds in the neighborhood! (For those of you who do not know, birds = kilos of cocaine. And he's telling me this while driving a very raggedy Van. So he's prime proof that crime does not always pay) Blackman was the one to get down like that!" I counterattacked with a, "No, it was you Playboy! I don't forget a face my man, maybe this will help you remember. I was the one, that y'all took the beach cruiser from, you know, the one with the Dayton rims on it. And the scars left behind on my right shoulder from you hitting me with the butt of your gun have turned into keloids and I hate when they start to itch sometimes. I know exactly who you are, but it's beautiful to see you fighting for your child my man. It's a good thing God changed our lives around, take care my man and be bless Homeboy." Then I politely applied a little pressure to the gas pedal on my 2015 triple black on black and smoothly floated down the Street. Now life has a funny way of bringing things around in a circle in order for certain situations to be resolve so everyone can continue fighting for a happier life. Because 30 days after the conversation at that stop light, I had moved into a beauty salon, so I could start utilizing my nail technician license, and as I was sitting down applying some gel product to one of my clients, the guy who put the gun in my side came walking through the door! We just started staring at one another, when the salon owner came over and introduced us. Her conversation went like this,"Sincere Nails", this is my cousin "gun toting guy", he the one that be cleaning my shop at night. "Gun toting guy" this is "Sincere Nails", he's our new managing nail tech." Me and him just looked at each other and started laughing. We had a brief conversation talking about life and fighting hard to be in God's favor. The very next day I packed out all of my belongings and never returned back to the beauty salon. Not out of fear, not because I thought he was going to come after me, I just know how to play chess with the game of life. And besides I would've been leaving the salon anyway, because in the next couple of days my "publication coordinator" email me an artillery about the editing process that we needed to get start on, so I can get "When A Soul Stops Running" ready for the open market).

"Dogg! I don't have any money."

After a quick search, he said, "I'm taking your bike, so get off of it."

Since I didn't move fast enough, he took the butt of his semi-automatic and blasted me twice in my right shoulder. With the pain shooting through my body, I got off "his" bike! :) Laugh out loud! I was watching my beach cruiser being walked away and getting ready to be put in the trunk of a car that had just pulled up, when my morals and my rules subsided for one second, and I shouted, "Put the gun down. Fight me one-on-one!"

The "thinner and darker complexion goon" of the three pointed his gun directly in my face and spoke to me in a very evil manner, "You just said that you want to die over a bike, pretty boy?"

"Nope!" And that was that. I just waited for the morning to kick in and went and bought another cruiser.

It was really getting rough on the streets because the very next night, when I was approaching Durkee, I went into the bushes to hide some of my stash. While I was in the bushes, I could hear voices, so I peeped through. I could see the same three guys that took my bike robbing two of the guys that would be on the block with me. They had them in a field with their hands raised high. I just sat there watching until I saw the three guys walking toward their vehicle. Then I ran out of the bushes and let off two shots right before they got inside their car. Then I turned around and ran back into the bushes. They jumped in the car and burned rubber out of there. I knew for a fact that I didn't hit anyone because I aimed straight at the car, not at them. Ike always told me, "Whenever you have to shoot at somebody, always aim for their legs. That way, you won't catch an instant murder case." And I did my best not to mess up that theory.

When the coast was clear, I came back out of the bushes smiling, because I already knew what they were going to ask me and sure enough Birdie said exactly what I thought one of them was going to say. Birdie was like, "Why you only let off two shots, B?"

I replied, "Because I only had two bullets." We laughed and went and made some more money. Birdie wasn't originally from Durkee, and I really did not know him that well, but our paths crossed again later on in life. Durkee was rapidly becoming known for being a hot moneymaking block. There was a lot going on there, and people were coming from all necks of the woods to try to catch someone off their game so they could have a nice payday.

Word got out that a customer by the name of Mac Truck was going around robbing people on all the blocks in and out of our neighborhood. One day, he tried his luck on Durkee, which also turned out to be his last free meal off someone from our area! We turned him back into a regular-buying customer. One early and bright sunny morning, I had just arrived on the block. No one was up there except for Simpson. As Simpson walked toward me, I noticed that he didn't have any shoes on, and I could see the anger in his eyes. He wanted to do something to somebody. "B! Mac Truck just caught me slipping, and he just robbed me!"

"Where he at now?" I asked.

"He somewhere around here." As Simpson went to the corner of Waterson, I went to the bushes, got my gun, and started running so I could catch up with him. Simpson was standing on the corner next to a brick building, but he wasn't moving. With the experience that I had gained from the street thus far, I knew that something was very wrong! Because Simpson's body language was very odd. When I was about six feet away from Simpson, I started walking up to him very slowly. I could hear a voice coming from around the other side of the building. In broad daylight, I uploaded a bullet into the sliding gear on my pistol. I measured the view at which Simpson was looking. I watched his eyes, and I raised my pistol up to Simpson's head level. I let the tip of my pistol follow the neck line down and up to the direction where Simpson's eyes were pointing as my arm was coming around him looking for point-blank range.

As I came around the corner and my pistol came around the right side of Simpson's head, I had my firearm lined up, dead, point, bang, with the middle of Truck's forehead. Truck was standing there with a gun wrapped up in a brown paper bag. Before Truck could blink twice, I spoke in a serious but quiet manner, imitating my mother, "Drop your gun right now, MF, or I'm going to blow your face off."

Everyone in my neighborhood knew that I carried a gun, but no one had ever really seen it because the only way you see my gun is if I was going to use it. And for some reason, this Truck character truly understood whatever he heard in my voice and read in my eyes because I didn't have to tell him twice (Linda's evil side was revealing itself inside me). Immediately, he started screaming, "Don't shoot! Don't shoot! Don't shoot!" and he released the brown paper bag with his pistol in it.

We watched as the bag fell toward the ground. As soon as it hit the dirt, Simpson and I were surprised because this clown didn't have a pistol at all. The whole time, the only thing Mac Truck had pointed at Simpson's stomach was a double deuce beer bottle. Simpson did not hesitate. The moment he heard the glass bottle break, he threw a punch with all his anger and connected it to Truck's jaw. That's when I pointed straight up in the air and let off one shot for notification. I knew that even though it was early in the morning, more of our guys were around. They probably were sitting up inside one of the trap houses that we occupied. Sure enough, within sixty seconds, it was like seven of us up there, and half of them Truck had already robbed at one time or another.

They were very thankful to me for this opportunity that I just provided them, which added to my street credibility. Quickly, everyone started hitting Truck. You could tell that Mac Truck's eighteen-wheeler of a body was totally numb from all the cocaine he had stolen and smoked up. But as cracked out as he was, this guy was still a guerrilla. He took hit after hit and would not fall down, and with blood coating him from head to toe, he fought his way into a garage and came out swinging a four by four piece of wood. I admired Truck's energy because of the fact that he never left his feet. It concluded in a truce because we knew his family.

CHAPTER 20

MEET THE VICE

I left before the show was over because I knew the police were on their way. We were really making a name for Durkee. We made Durkee go from hot to being on fire. Now with the drugs and with all the people hanging around twenty-four hours a day on the corners, we knew the police were going to start targeting us. What really put us on the map with the Cleveland police and made them turn their radar on was the day that they saw a crime happen right before their eyes, and they could not do anything about it.

It was another nice sunny day on the corner of Durkee. One of our guys was arguing with his pregnant girlfriend again for whatever reason. He had his Monte Carlo parked in the middle of the street. I do not know what she had done, but she had this guy very mad at her. As they were in the middle of the street arguing, this guy reached into his car and pulled out a revolver. Just as soon as he pulled it out, a police cruiser pulled up behind him. A few of the other guys and I were watching and shaking our heads because we knew he was going down one way or another. Whether it was on the pavement from gunshot wounds, or everything went smoothly, and they just took him down to the police station unharmed. But neither one of those choices would have the opportunity to present itself. And I wasn't too surprised by what actually went down because just about everyone from off of Durkee street that was in the dope game was a little off the hook mentally and some of us were even crazy enough to risk walking off the edge of life. So his actions weren't too far from the norm.

This guy of ours was always known for being a fast driver, and the boy could drive! (A little later in life, I had a Trans Am with a crossfire engine, and I was sitting at a light on Kinsman. He pulled up beside me with his girlfriend riding shotgun inside the same Monte Carlo from the Durkee incident. It was raining pretty hard outside, but as soon as the light turned green, we both punched our gas pedals. We were doing between 60 and 70 mph on a regular city street in the rain. As we passed through the next three lights, we slowed down and made a right onto the next street and lined our cars up nose to nose. Then, we stumped the gas pedal and were racing again. Immediately, I let up off my gas because we were on a brick street, and I got afraid because I was not experienced enough to drive this fast on wet brick streets just yet, but this guy was flying. Him, his car, and his girlfriend disappeared before my very eyes.) As the officers got out of the car with their service pistols drawn on our guy, they ordered him to drop his weapon. Not one time did he look back at the officers or drop his weapon. Instead, he jumped in the driver's seat of his car, put it in Drive, stumped the gas pedal, and poof! This guy was gone! By the time the officers even had a chance to get back inside of their cruiser, he was already at the end of the street and bending into the corner. By the time the police cruiser made it to the corner that he had just bent, we could hear his motor opening up on another street. Then, there was silence because he made it home and parked his car behind his house.

Just a few days after that incident was the first time that we saw the Cleveland's finest drug task force! We started calling them the vice! And boy did they catch us off guard. These fuckers traveled in unmarked cars, wore tennis shoes, blue jeans, and T-shirts just like us. Even though Durkee was a money tree, I did not like making money inside the frying pan. Three incidents happened that made me realize that I had to find a new home to hustle. Incident number 1, one of my guys from the block and I had sold out our product. I was just hanging around the block, waiting for my connect to contact me. As we headed toward the store on the corner, there was another guy standing there. Now this guy was from the neighborhood, but he wasn't from our block. I didn't have any issues with it because I was out there to make money, not enemies, from cats that shared the same hood. As we got closer to him, a black and white cruiser pulled up on us. My guy and I didn't run because we didn't have anything on us. After a quick search, they placed the three of us inside the police cruiser. As soon as the officers returned to the front seat of their cruiser, the officer on the passenger side started counting.

The officer spoke clear and calm, "Three for you, three for you, and three for you, but there's one left over, so which one of you is going to take number four?"

He was referring to the ten pieces of crack cocaine that he got off the ground, exactly where the three of us were standing. The officer turned around in his seat and looked at us. Then he focused his attention on me. "You look like you can handle four," he said, smiling and staring at me with the got-you expression.

I looked Officer Smiley Face straight back in his eyes and stated, "I'm not taking any of them shits. I already sold out. Y'all already know I would've ran if I was hot, and you know that! I just ran from y'all yesterday"

"Where you got your guns at?" he asked, still smiling.

"I think mine's inside that potato chip bag on the big ass rock," I responded, laughing.

As both officers exited the vehicle to look for more evidence, I turned my attention to the guy from the other block. "Dogg, I'm not taking no case for your rocks!"

"B! Them not my rocks." But before he could even put the *s* on his *rocks*, I head-butted him and started choking him in the back of the cruiser because I had a warrant and the officers had pretty much given me a green light that my warrant was going to have some crack rocks added to it.

Just as fast as it happened, the police snatched me out of the car and slammed me down on the concrete and put me in handcuffs. "Now you going down for disorderly conduct and obstruction of justice as well," the officer was saying to me as he made sure his handcuffs were locked.

"I'll take the disorderly conduct, but don't put them rocks on me. I told you that I sold out! You already know I would've ran if I had something on me," I said to him once again as I was huffing and puffing to catch my breath.

Even though I was a juvenile, they drove the three of us down to the Fourth District Police Station. They stopped the car and removed me from the backseat. The officer took the handcuffs off my wrists and told me to walk home, and as I started walking, he was like, "And don't get on the bus. You keep walking straight till you get to 130th and Kinsman. Then you keep walking straight down 131st Street until you get home." I did what I was told, and they didn't put a case on the other two guys either because they knew they would see us again and were in hopes to catch us for something more serious. And that freaking time came sooner than I expected.

Incident number 2. It had gotten to the point that I really didn't want to hang around on the corners because the police were coming around too frequently for my taste. So I decided to take a pay cut. I decided to ride around on a scooter and sell double ups to the guys who hung around on the corners. I would have a freezer storage bag full of rocks. I would pull up real fast to the guys who waved me down, ask them how much money they had, and put it in my pocket without even counting. I would pull a handful of rocks out of my storage bag and just pour rocks in their palms like a slot machine and be back on my way.

As I was pulling away from one guy, a police cruiser pulled up right behind me and flashed me to pull over. They asked me my name, and I gave my little brother's name. I was thankful that I had just sold out. With a quick search, they placed me into the backseat of the police car and called my mother. As soon as my mother arrived, her eyebrows formed a unibrow because she saw who was in the backseat of the police car. I knew her anger was trying to tip the scales, but she stayed in control of her emotions and didn't slip up and gave them my real name. She just told me to get in the car. She didn't even holler at me. She just said, "They said you can't have the scooter back because it's stolen." Linda didn't holler at me because she didn't care. She just didn't feel like killing me that day. Plus I knew she had to save her strength because who knew what type of mood Ike was going to be in by the time we got home.

Incident number 3. A nice number of us had gathered at Corlett Elementary School, and a good 95 percent of us were the same ones that went through the Grid. About nine to ten guys were shooting dice right in front of the main door to the school, and the rest of us were just scattered around talking, drinking, and smoking marijuana. That's when one guy shouted, "One time!" And as I looked up, it was too late. The vice had the whole playground surrounded. These fuckers had to have been sitting back, planning this raid because there was nowhere to run! But they really wanted us to run because if they caught you, they were going to definitely attempt to break your legs allowing their team to gain a personal award for the hunt and capture of an untamed "wild street animal". As they were ushering us together like cattle, they started asking for IDs and checked to see how much money we had in our pocket. If they felt that we had too much money, they automatically put a gambling charge on us. Just my luck, I had too much money. They asked me for my ID, but I couldn't provide one, so I gave them my name and waited to be put in the paddy wagon.

When the officer was done asking me questions that he would never get a real answer to, he told me and Fashionable Kid to have a seat on the concrete. I sat next to a guy that I didn't know that well, but he was from my neighborhood. We were very familiar with the uniformed police officer's routine, but vice played a whole different ballgame. The guy next to me found out just how hard they liked to "hit the ball." For no reason at all, this guy started laughing. And right on cue, I started talking to him under my breath and said, "Don't be stupid, goofy. You better chill out." But it was too late because like lightning, one of the vice officers squeezed his own fingers together as hard as he could into the form of a karate chop. He walked straight over to the guy and smacked him so hard I was sure his thoughts went flying right out of the ballpark! After his head was done connecting to mine, because we were sitting so close, I watched as, right on cue, the young guy started to cry. So many tears leaked from his eyeballs. I knew it wouldn't be long before dehydration presented itself. It took every single ounce of my mental capacity to control my muscles in order for me not to burst out laughing! There was no way in the world I was going to let this evil vice officer hit a home run off me in front of all these people! LOL! :)

Finally, we pulled up to the Fourth District. As they opened up the paddy wagon door, they put the adults on one side and the juveniles on the other side. They told all the juveniles to walk straight down Kinsman and keep walking down 131st until we got home. As soon as we got back to the neighborhood, there was a lot of commotion going on. We found out that one of our big homeboys West Side had just died! The story was he was being chased by the police and decided to swallow seven grams of crack cocaine to avoid a drug charge, and the plastic bag burst open inside his stomach. Some argued that that wasn't the true story, that it was way deeper than the information people was actually offering. And to add fuel to the fire, three people had just gotten murdered on 131st and Harvard at a gas station which was only a couple of blocks away from Durkee. Yes, it was time for me to truly find somewhere else to make money. (Never in a million years would I have thought that I would get shot at the same location just a few years into the future.) >:(

PART II

CHAPTER 21

FROM A BABY TO AN ADULT

Life was going on as usual. Making money, Mom and Dad fighting, and me not getting to know my little sister because whenever I went home, I would just give her some money and head right back to the streets. I never saw her grow up, I never saw her first boyfriend, and I didn't get to see her graduate from school. (I wish I knew then that she would die at such a young age because all the time I was running the streets, I missed my chance at being her big brother) :'(

As the eighth grade came to an end, my pockets were full with a capital *F*, and my report card was full of capital *F*s as well. Failing school grades was becoming a part of my life, so I was looking forward to repeating the eighth grade if that was my faith. With all my extra-curricular activities going on, my report card was becoming a thing of the past as far as an importance to my life. The staff at Alexander Hamilton Junior High School was sick of us terrible children. They couldn't believe that so many nincompoops dwelled under the same school roof. If they could help it, there was no way they were going to have us in the eighth grade for the second time around.

At the end of the school year, I was called to the principal's office, but she was out. Then I was escorted to the auditorium. When I walked through the door, I started laughing because everyone from off the block was called out of class and escorted to the auditorium, girls as well. As the principal walked over to the podium and grabbed the microphone, she made her message very clear. "Everyone who's seated inside this auditorium will be passed on to the ninth grade, as long as you don't show up for graduation."

So we started clapping and shouting, "Touché! Touché!"

Then, the principal called my name and told me to go directly back to her office. I wasn't familiar with this principal because I really didn't have any trouble in school other than having an *A* for absence. I just didn't go to all my classes, but I had straight attendance and good grades in the ones that I actually liked, which was only about two or three, and one of those included lunch. Finally, the principal entered her office, but she didn't say anything to me right off. Instead, she sat behind her desk and just stared at me for like thirty seconds as if she was trying to make up her mind about what she wanted to say to me and what measure of approach should be taken. She took a deep breath and started venting, "Mr. Dixon, I really don't understand you. You're not a student that causes trouble, and the classes that you do decide to attend, you ace the class, and your teachers like you. Even the teachers that only see you once or twice a month. You have a good record for school attendance, but you do not go to 70 percent of your classes. Mr. Dixon, you have a talent. You can actually cook and bake. So we are not sending you to a high school where all of your friends are going to be. We are sending you to Jane Addams, where you will be enrolled into a hospitality program. Mr. Dixon," the principal said, while she was exhaling, "try to do something with your life. Now get out of my office." I just started smiling and did what I was told.

Finally, I was done with middle school! I moved on to the next chapter of my life, high school. The summer came in and went right back out the door. Some people from my neighborhood lived and made it through the summer. Some people died. And one of those people that died, or to be more truthful, one of the people that got murdered was my friend, "Looney Tunes". I really looked up to this guy! Because he was one of the best dice shooters, and the funny part about his dice game was that he talked a lot of shit by rolling them bad boys into a 7-Eleven, just about every single time! And the saddest thing about "Looney Tunes'" last day? Is the person who took his life away was from our neighborhood. This is one of the first example of the neighborhood turning on its self. It seemed before you can stop talking about one person that was gone, within a couple of weeks you'll be talking about someone else. (Looney Tunes, McGruff, Little Turtle, Light skin little Dave, Buddha. RIP my friends). Some made money all summer long. Some moneymakers turned into their very own best customer. Some went to prison for a very long time or if they were "goofy enough", for the rest of their natural lives. Some were coming home, and us youngsters were starting school. Even though I was starting ninth grade a year or so behind, I was still grateful that I even made it to high school. As I walked into my homeroom class, I noticed instantly that every single student in this room was either my age or older.

Okay I get it! I thought to myself. My homeroom classroom was like in the basement of the school, totally hidden away from normal homeroom classes. So it was understood that this was a program to help students that still have a chance at opportunities to graduate with our dumb asses. I didn't do too much self-changing at all. Even though this was a new school and a new school year, I was still the same old me. So I only went to the classes that I liked. Hospitality was my favorite class. I was never late to this class, and I never missed a day. My instructors loved me, mainly because of my cooking skills and witty comments. I went from being a regular student helping to prepare meals for our restaurant that was located inside of Jane Adams to being the main chef. There was another guy in my class that was also a top contender in the cooking field, but his specialty was baking. His name was Slow Motion.

Now Slow Motion was a real cool and laid-back guy, and even though we had our own spotlights for the kitchen, we started becoming a team. If he figured out a way how to make a special type of bread, I would figure out what type of meal I believed should go along with its taste. Me being of the self-proclaimed "lone wolf" fraternity, I had plenty of guys that would put in work for me, but they weren't real friends. They were more like hired guns. But Slow Motion seemed to be a real dude in heart, so we started hanging. After a month or so, I even let him know where I lived, and he would come pick me up for school and drop me off back at home. I've always been fast paced for the most part of my life. I keep that energy going within myself, just like that damn rabbit with that battery stuck in his back! And for me to truly pair up with someone, they must have that same level of energy! But Slow Motion, who truly moved about life in slow motion, was given a green light because he displayed a real heart. One day, I questioned him about his slow movements, and he revealed to me that he was a diabetic. (A few years into the future, Slow Motion passed away. Rest in peace, my friend! Slow or not, your personality outshined a lot of things.) (P)

So far, school was great, but my pockets were at a standstill because I wasn't going over to Durkee any longer. But I always devised a plan to make money, and I had done one of the dumbest things that you can ever do in the dope game. I was selling drugs where my family laid their heads. I am very thankful to God that through my years living in such a negative light, no one never showed up at my home with a gun, looking for me (except for the FBI, Fugitive Task Force, Cleveland Police, United States Marshals, bounty hunters, and other proper authority figures with the correct paperwork for the government law offices later on in my future).

I wasn't flat broke; I just wasn't as productive as I was supposed to be. I was really missing Durkee Street. But I still was maintaining a profit every night, and I did this right underneath my mother's nose. I had a happy meal pale from McDonald's, and it was shaped like a pumpkin. In fact, it was a pumpkin, only it was made out of plastic. It was orange with the triangle black eyes and a black handle to carry it. McDonald's had given them out one year during the Halloween season as people would call it. And boy oh boy did I put that plastic bucket to work! There were just a handful of people that I sold double ups to at the time that were actually allowed to come over to my house. This was an all-night thing, and there was no way my mother was going to allow me to keep running in and out of the house at all times of night. So I hired my pumpkin bucket to work for me, and I'm surprised that my mother never caught on to us because in a sense, we were literally working right in front of her face. Between the hours of three and four in the morning, my mom would be sitting at the kitchen table, doing a rundown on her lottery numbers. She would be in total concentration while her magical candles was burning to aid her in some luck. This was the time that my dad would be gone to work, and all the children were supposed to be sleep. But not wide-eyed "hustling boy" me, of course!

As my mom sat at the kitchen table figuring out a way to make money from hitting a miracle number, I was right over her head making money without the miracle, and the only candle that I had burning was the imaginary light bulb that hung over my head. My bedroom was right over the kitchen. Because of the two windows being in line with one another, I was truly taking the risks; but in my heart, I believe it was well worth it! And I've never been afraid of taking chances when it came to trying to meet new dead presidents and pocket them. I used to keep a handful of pebbles at the corner of my driveway, and I instructed my few remaining loyal customers to toss a pebble up at my window, so I could open shop. I instructed them to throw as many as they possibly could until I came to the window because sometimes, I'd be sleeping. As soon as I heard the *clink clink* of the window, I would spring straight into action, which was a very simple strategy that I conjured up. I had gray duct tape wrapped around the handle of my pumpkin pal. I would remove the screen from the window sill and lower my pumpkin down to the concrete, my loyal customer would place his money inside of the bucket, and I would slowly but smoothly raise the bucket back up to my window right past my mother's view. I'd count the cash and place in the bucket what I thought was fair for the price and lower it right back down.

Not one time was I ever afraid of my mother finding out what I was doing. One reason is because she always believed in the spirits and the ghosts. A couple of times while my mom would be talking on the phone, she would mention that she believed something was always flying back and forth across the window, but she never looked deep into it. This little job I created was fine and dandy, but I needed more money, and that's when Slow Motion came to my beckoning call. Surprisingly, and by a very unintentional but very profitable coincidental conversation, Slow Motion and I started seeing eye to eye. (And with our very brief talk, I knew it would be a while before I saw moneymaking Durkee Street or Fashionable Kid again. It was actually a couple of years before I met back up with him, and when we did see one another again, it was not on Durkee Street. Instead, we were in a car together, with two other guys from our block, and everyone had a pistol on them, except the guy with the semiautomatic rifle. Because he didn't like pistols, he would always tell us that they don't hold enough bullets. We were all riding toward a little date that we had with some wannabe gangsters.)

One day, inside the Adams room restaurant, Slow Motion, the rest of the students, and I were finishing up our chores because we were just shutting down the available lunch menu. Slow Motion and

I didn't know each other well enough at the time to ask one another personal questions, but that didn't stop Slow Motion from inquiring into my personal life. As I was taking a quick breather at one of the dining tables, he came and sat across from me with a smirk on his face and jumped straight to the point. "Let me ask you something, B."

I responded with a, "Shoot, my nigga. I'm listening."

"Okay, so what all are you into, B?" he asked me very quietly so that my ears were the only ones that took notice. Slow Motion could tell by my not-surprised-at-all expression that he was barking up the right tree.

Even though I was eager for this conversation, because Durkee was too hot with police and the Jack boys shooting people on site, I really needed somewhere else to plant my feet so I could get back to being lucrative. Fortunately just about everything I do in life, I do it with a steady hand, so I still had to be careful with this guy. I looked him straight in his face, and I told him, "I do the same thing you do. So what do you do?"

Slow Motion looked me straight back in my face and was like, "I get that money."

My last response to him on that conversation was very vivid. I looked him straight back in his eyes as hard as I could, and with a frowning smile taking over my face, mixed with a serious voice but in a polite manner, I said, "I want some of that money."

The very next day, Slow Motion told me that he wanted me to meet some of his people. So right after cooking class, we jumped into his old school Nova, and we were on our way to his neighborhood. That would be on E. 102 Avenue, right off of Union Street. He parked his car in his yard and grabbed a bag of crack rocks and told me to come on. After a short distance of a walk, we came to a building that was a mixture of an apartment building and a house, and it was an ugly place. Once inside the unattractive building, we headed up two flights of stairs. I could hear voices coming from behind the door. When we entered, I was a little shocked because before Slow Motion could introduce me to anyone, I already knew two of the guys who were there. One of the guys who was there was the older kid from Smoke and Smiley's house that took me with him to steal a car from downtown. Somehow, this guy had a kilo of cocaine delivered to his house by mistake, and once he got it, he didn't look back. The other guy was Birdie. He and I were on good terms from being on Durkee together.

With me already knowing these two guys, I was accepted with open arms. As we all sat down at a long table that occupied more than half of the room, the other two guys introduced themselves to me. One guy called himself Doughnut, and he fit the part. The other guy's name was Snake, and he fit and played that part well. He never did anything wrong to me, but others that crossed his path weren't so fortunate. He was the younger of the two, because Snake and Doughnut were brothers. They weren't that much older than me, and there were no parents who stayed at this place. It was their house. Now that everyone was familiar with each other's names, it was time to discuss the house rules. It was no mystery when Doughnut and the older kid from Smoke and Smiley's house started laying down the rules. It was truly recognized that these two were in charge of this here bullshit fine as wine establishment. Actually, both of them lived there as well. (Never sell drugs where you lay your head. Duh!) So I found me a spot to sit and took note on what they had to offer.

Rule number 1, no one was allowed inside of the house but us. Rule number 2, everyone must pay $25 a day in order to stay inside of the house. Rule number 3, once a week, we will do unannounced vice drills. Everyone must make up their own escape route for when the vice hits us because we are going to get hit sooner or later. (Even though I felt that there should have been more rules, I was satisfied with the three I just entertained. But as the weeks and months went on, rule number 1 fell off. Rule number 2 never did really get into focus because we were making too much money. We would spend $25 on McDonald's per person due to the fact that we always ordered while we were high. Rule number 3, that's the only rule we really did follow. On certain days, out of the blue, Doughnut or one of us inside the house would holler very loudly "Vice!" and people would start running! One of the older kids would actually jump out of a window, land on top of a garage, and be gone with the wind. Now all of this was fine and dandy, but eventually, the vice came knocking on the door. And even though we all had practiced the drill quite often, this day proved that all practice doesn't make perfect!) Transferring from Durkee Street down to E.102 Street in Union was a totally different experience for me! But one thing that always kept me going forward is the fact that no matter where I went, my personality always shined to others and allowed me to have my way most of the time.

Now these Union Street guys were just a little deeper in the dope game. They had more connections than we did on Durkee because they lived closer to the projects than us "up the way guys." These guys had access to all the government public housing, like Longwood, Morris Black, Kent Kennedy, Garden Valley, Fortieth, and Thirtieth projects. So they never ran out of places to reup, and their price tag was always cheaper than us "up the way guys." For some reason or another, Slow Motion never did make any money at the house he introduced me to. He was too scared to go inside or either too smart. But he would always find a good connect to cop from. The first time I was ready to cop, he introduced me to a not too tall and very fat man named Box Car. When I first met Box Car, he was laughing and joking around with his family and friends from Milwaukee. The first thing that came to my mind was jolly when I looked in his direction. But this man was not jolly at all. He was very vicious! But for some reason, he never showed me that side of him, not even when he lightweight robbed me. He just sat me down, had a little conversation with me, and when he was finished talking, I was even more focused on the drug game. As I shook Box Car's hand for the first time, he asked me if I was Crazy B from off Durkee Street. I nodded my head as if I was saying yes, and he just smiled. Then he said, "Little dude, I heard stories about you. You got a gun on you right now?" I just nodded my head in the yes position again. Box Car laughed very heavy. He looked at Slow Motion and said, "You stay here. B, you come with me."

I followed him to one of the rooms in the house. We both sat down at a table. I was never scared when it came to making a transaction because only one of two things was going to happen. Either it was going to go the right way, or it was going to go the wrong way. But as long as I didn't get killed in whichever way it went, I would be satisfied. (He who walks or runs away lives to try something different another day.)

As me and Box Car were sitting at his table, the first thing that came out of his mouth was, "B, how old are you?"

"Under eighteen."

Box Car just smiled and laughed and shook his head. Then, he asked me how much I wanted to spend. I told him I wanted four and a juvenile. He just looked at me and smiled and was like," I got you." He disappeared for a hot second and came back with nine grown adults and pushed them over to me.

I looked at him with my eyebrows forming into a unibrow and said, "I didn't bring the fare for that there, my man."

Box Car's facial expression turned very serious, and with a serious tone, he spoke to me, "That's all you, little man, and you don't owe me anything but a thank you, and I don't owe you anything but a thank you."

I grabbed my nine adults and said thank you, and for some reason, he made me feel comfortable enough to turn my back on him and walk out of the room. He didn't get up; he just told me to tell Slow Motion it was his time.

Slow Motion dropped me off at my house, and I went straight to sleep. I woke up the next day like a child anticipating Christmas day. I went down to my parents' basement and started taking the clothes off my "adults," which was a lot of layers of clothing. I started to realize halfway through the dress rehearsal why they were over-dressed. The more plastic I removed, the more I started smelling gasoline, and my train of thought was, *MF!* I undressed the remainder of my "adults," and every last one of them was struck with the same sickening gasoline smell. But I didn't get upset because either the situation was going to get fixed, or it wasn't.

When Slow Motion made it over to my house that morning ready for us to go to school, I quickly ushered him down to the basement and showed him what I was working with. He looked at my nine "adults" with disbelief and said, "So that's why he gave you a triple up because he didn't give me that."

"I guess he didn't, and I'm not going to school today, and neither are you. Take me over to his house right now."

Slow Motion looked at me with a very serious and nervous frightening expression and said, "I don't know if you should do that. You might have to chalk this one up as a loss and just make back what you can. Then just cop from somebody else. I know you heard the stories about him." Now that would've been understandable if I didn't spend so much money. But I had nine adults dripping in gasoline. That means by the time I was finished with them, I would be known as the fuel pump man, and no one would be coming back to get their tank filled up with this balderdash. Respect is respect, and business is business, so I just looked at him and said, "Come on, scary, take me over to his spot!"

Slow Motion could probably tell by my body language that this was not a request. And just before we got inside of his car, my common sense took over my train of thoughts. I decided to go discuss this matter naked. So I left my nine adults and my gun behind. Besides, I was very aware of this guy's reputation, his arsenal, and his don't-give-a-flying-fuck goon squad. But street respect is pure street respect, so I knew I would be safe. Even if I left empty handed.

As we pulled up to Box Car's house, Slow Motion said, "I'm going to stay in the car and wait for you, just in case you come back running!"

I just said, "Okay, scary."

As I walked up the stairs to knock on his door, I knew he didn't know I was coming because I never notified him of any type of problem. Before I could even raise my fist to knock on the door, Box Car was pulling the door open and telling me to step inside and sit on the sofa. He was being cool. He even sat a can of Pepsi in front of me, opened it, and was like, "Caffeine is good for you in the morning, and by the time I finish talking to you, that Pepsi can better be empty."

I just nodded my head in the okay position, and I still hadn't said one word because we both knew why I was over there that early in the freaking morning.

"Young blood, the game can treat you good, or it can treat you bad. It can be your lover or your killer. It's all about how you play it, and what measures you are willing to take in order to survive and safely get ahead. Do you remember the first thing I told you when I asked you your name?"

I just nodded my head yes.

"Okay, little man, you have a future in this game. I knew who you were before you even came over here. That's why I gave you what I gave you. Now it's time that you utilize your thinking. Just think about it. You know how much you spent, and you know I more than tripled that. One thing about this game, little man, you have to become more than one person. This game requires acknowledgment of different types of occupations. I want you to get out of my house, take what I gave you, step out of your street clothes, put on your lab coat, and just do some thinking. You won't be shit in this game if you do not think properly!"

He extended his hand for me to shake it. I stood up, downed the rest of my Pepsi, and shook his hand. I left this man's house without ever saying a word but with a lot of respect for him. (Little did I know that would be the last time I would see Box Car. One way or another, he was associated with some guys from Milwaukee, which associated him with the Ohio prison system for the years to come.)

As soon as Slow Motion backed out of my driveway, I rushed into my parents' basement and put on my lab coat. It took me about two hours and a midget of my product to finally figure out the equation to which Box Car knew I would put together. I took what he gave me, dropped it in some water, and boiled it down. I watched the gasoline separate itself, poured out the garbage, and replaced it with fresh baking soda, which resulted in a pure white concrete hard rock. And I went straight to work! I was moving full steam ahead! I wasn't going to school too often, and I was barely going home. Every time I took a break from work, I was closing my eyes and going to sleep inside a crack house.

CHAPTER 22

WHEN THE CAT IS AWAY, THE MOUSE WILL PLAY

I had so much money that I didn't know what to do with it. I wish I had a mentor or someone who cared enough to show me how to use it toward a good future, but the game doesn't usually work that way. When it was time for me to cop again, I went through a few disappointments before I hit pay dirt. The first disappointment was from the fortieth projects. I received some product with something called B-12 mixed in it from some visiting Jamaicans, and that B-12 really did suck. You hold it in your hand for two minutes, and it starts melting, just like when Dorothy threw the bucket of water on that crazy ass witch of Oz! No magical M&M candy coating on these bad boys! >:(

My second disappointment was from a guy from California. I loved this guy. The only problem that I had with him was that every time I went to cop from him, he would always put a .45 semiautomatic into my rib cage while we made the transaction. (After a few months of making thousands from messing with this California cat, he disappeared. He either got caught up in a murder case or already had one in California. All I knew was that the guy was in prison for murder). But before he vanished, I copped something real nice from Mr. Pistol in my rib cage, and it couldn't have happened at a better time!

One early morning, all the guys in the house were on their way to Kings Island amusement park, which was located in Cincinnati, Ohio. We stayed in Cleveland, Ohio, so that spot was like four hours away. At that moment, my common sense told me that an opportunity was knocking, and I had no problem opening up any door for Mr. or Mrs. Opportunity!

The year was 1989, and I was sixteen. I was really grooming myself into becoming a businessman to be reckoned with. I just wish I knew how to invest. But still, I was operating on the wrong side of the law, so any type of investment was more than likely to become a downfall. And just as a famous rapper quoted, "All good things don't last," I would later become a casualty of that famous quote. The summer was getting on its way. School had ended, my pockets were big and steady getting bigger, and this was the opening day of Kings Island. It was early in the morning, and I could see Doughnut speeding toward the building in his five-door Ford Escort. He pulled up and asked me if I was going to Kings Island with them. I just shook my head no. Then, he said, "Well, since you're not going with us, the building is closed. So nobody will be selling anything over here today." I just nodded my head, like okay. I got up and started walking across the street. There was a girl that lived across the street from Doughnut's building named Shorty Cakes. Slow Motion had introduced me to her, and for some reason, Shorty and her mother took straight to me. Once again, I was an instant hit. They told me that I was allowed to come over to their house at any time, twenty-four hours a day. I believe her mother really wanted me to become a boyfriend to her daughter because we were around the same age. Shorty's mother did not like her current boyfriend. He was much older and very deep in the drug world. It was said that he had ties to the Mafia, which no one doubted.

When I got to Shorty's house, her mother was gone to work, but I was still allowed to enter. Shorty said, "Why you coming over here so early in the morning? I thought you'd be across the street."

"I was, but Doughnut and the older kid said that nobody could be over there right now because they're going to the amusement park. So I'm just going to wait until everybody is gone. Then, I am going right back over there. I'm not thinking about Doughnut's fragile house rules today!"

Before I could say another word, Shorty grabbed me by my hand and was like, "Come on, play me in some Super Mario Brothers until you decide to go."

One way or another, Shorty and I went from playing Super Mario Brothers to playing doctor with each other's body parts. By the time we finished, which was a very short time, I looked out of her window over at the building and saw that the coast was clear. I gave Shorty a kiss on her forehead, and I was on my way. (Little did I know that in the near future, Shorty Cakes would be shot and murdered while sitting in her car with her children. Right around the corner from her mother's home. Rest in peace, Shorty. You were always cool with me.) (N)

As soon as I got to the building, I grabbed the three crates that I had taken from a nearby store and put them under the window and let myself in. I went to the side door of the building and opened it. Just as soon as I opened the door, which was a secret signal that we were open for business, the line started forming quickly, and I was the only fortunate store clerk! (Well, me and this 9-mm. Glock that I got from one of them Folks members. I gave him some product and a couple of dollars with a clip and a .25 nickel plated. And he gave me a little story about the gun that I was very uncomfortable with. He told me that they got into a fight with a couple of security guards and took their guns. Now I don't know if that story was true or not. For all I know, that was his way of telling me that he shot somebody with that particular pistol. Either way it went, I wasn't going to hold on to it for too long anyway because I didn't believe in receiving guns from gangbangers that were not brand-new and coming from out of the original box. I just knew how to turn a quick profit. And the event that happened at this building this day moved me to sell it faster than I wanted to.)

The way I was working that side door, you would've swore I was a government employee passing out powdered milk, dry egg mix, and that delicious block of government box cheese. I truly worked that door from morning till about eleven o'clock that night. I had already passed the $10,000 mark around 9:00 p.m. Now I was starting to get tired until this prostitute showed up at the door who usually came over for Doughnut. I broke the rule and let her in. She was between twenty and twenty-three years of age, and she had a very cool personality.

The next couple of hours passed, and I couldn't take it anymore. I really needed a bed, but I had enough common sense not to fall asleep inside this building! As she sat on the stairs telling me jokes, I started feeling the tiredness that my body was enduring because her jokes started to sound like a confused mumbo jumbo. That's when I knew it was time for me to go. As I was preparing myself to leave, I pulled my gun out and slid the action back so I could put a bullet in the chamber. As I was sliding it, the sliding action jammed. I really didn't need this shit to be happening right now. I had too much money on me, a long way to go, and I had no one to call to come get me at this time of night. When the prostitute noticed that the gun had jammed, she started laughing, but her laughter quickly turned into a loud scream. Just as soon as the gun had jammed, with just a quick couple of pulls of the sliding action, it quickly unjammed itself and let off a shot during the process. The slug went right between the prostitute's legs and straight into the stairs. Then I started laughing, and she popped me in the back of my head. I ran around the house and found some brown paper grocery bags and filled them with other brown paper bags. Then, I paid the prostitute to walk with me carrying the bags as if we were a couple on our way home for about thirty blocks. I stayed away from the building for a couple of days because I needed to find a car, and that I did. I came across a jet-black four-door Chevy Caprice Classic from down south, with a black leather top and maroon guts. After the passing days went by, I was pulling up to the building on 102nd, and everyone was outside in front. When they saw that, I was the one behind the steering wheel, they all started smiling and hollering.

Birdie was the first one to walk over to me. He said, "I see you rolling now! And you should, I know you made a million that night we were gone!" Then Birdie started laughing and punched me in my chest. He jumped in his Iroc Z 28 and burned rubber while he was leaving.

One thing that I couldn't help but notice was that everyone was in front of the building, but their vehicles were nowhere in sight. That's when Doughnut walked up to me and said, "I told you that it was shut down."

I just looked him straight in his face and said, "All I did is what you would've done, true or false?"

He looked at me for about two more seconds and started laughing and shaking his head. I did not notice what he had in his hand, but then, he shocked me with his stun gun. As soon as I hit the ground, he picked me right back up and said, "You're right, but next time, don't be so hardheaded. I didn't tell you to stay away so you couldn't make any money, B. I told you to stay away because I didn't want anything bad to happen to you. Brian, you have to really understand something. You a young cat, and your name is ringing in the streets like us big dogs."

(Just a few days prior, I realized just how true Doughnut's statement was. My father, the eagle, told me that when he was on the number 15 bus coming home from work, there were a lot of children in the back of the bus arguing over who had the most money in the neighborhood. A guy and a girl was like, "Ya'll not Hip to B yet."

"B who?" they asked.

"Light skin cool B, from junior high school. He got all the money." My father said all he could do was shake his head.)

So I truly understood where Doughnut was coming from, and it was a good feeling knowing that he cared about me, but that still did not mean that I was going to obey him. As he started walking away from me, I said, "Hey, where y'all cars at?"

"Everybody put their cars in the shop. So you the taxi." And for some reason, I already knew that before he even said it. I was the youngest out of the bunch, so I always got the beautiful award of doing everyone's dirty laundry.

For the next few weeks, everything was going good, and everyone at the house was eating. Even if you were just a person we knew from the neighborhood and you were stopping by just to say hi, you made money just by saying hi because that building was a true revolving door for cash. As the summer went about its business, I wasn't spending as much time at the building as I used to. Because like the saying goes, "All good things don't last forever." So I started traveling to different neighborhoods so I could regroup some of my loyal customers and, at the same time, gain some new ones. Also, I had a girlfriend that I could see more often now. I met her in school. She was one of the girls that used to work inside of the Adams Room Restaurant at Jane Adams with me. She and I had started dating before I had a car, and her family was cool with me from day one. Her mother treated me as if I were a son, and her mother's live-in boyfriend treated me as if I was his younger brother, and her little brother looked at me as if I was his big brother. Her little brother was a cool kid. He was the barber around his neighborhood off Ninety-Third, and his neighborhood was gang controlled. I met more than a few of the gangbangers, and one of their respected members, D, was one of my best friends when we were going to Milford Elementary. We both shared that lovely day of the paddle form Mr. Mickey Mouse Man.

Even though I was originally from a Vice Lord neighborhood, D knew that I didn't gangbang, so I had a pass every time I went over to my girlfriend's house. (If only I had known that later in the future, her little brother would be gunned down while sitting in his mother's driveway. After being shot up, he made his way to his mother's porch. Rest in peace, my young friend.) (B)

So far, the year of 1989 was being real nice to me. We were in our last month of the summer. I was driving down Union Street heading toward the building when I saw a lot of bright colors. I was too far down the street to understand what was going on, but as I got closer, I could see exactly what all the commotion was about. Now I was the one that was smiling and hollering! (But with all of our glory, 1989 also was the turning point of our downfall. Just as bees are to pollen so they can continue to produce honey, police are to candy painted cars so they can continue to produce a cleaner, drug-free neighborhood).

I parked my car across the street from the building in someone else's driveway. Boy oh boy, these guys were not playing! The first car I walked over to was a four-door Ford station wagon, which was candy blue. I looked in the inside, and the whole backseat was missing. In its place sat four eighteen-inch woofer speakers. I slid over to the next vehicle, which was a Trans Am with the Testarossa Ferrari kit on it, the color of cotton candy pink, like the Barbie car. When I looked inside, the backseat was missing, and in its place sat six twelve-inch woofer speakers. Then I slowly walked over to the other vehicle, and I couldn't believe my eyes. Sitting there right in front of my face was a pickup truck, with a full-bodied Ferrari kit on it. It was dropped so low to the ground that a child couldn't even get under it. The color was a beautiful candy Brandy-wine red. When the owner chirped the alarm, the doors went straight up into the air as if it were a Lamborghini Dragon just waiting to fly away. As my appetite of anticipation was building to see what was on the inside, and I received a full-course meal because the inside of this "turned-out" pickup truck was the home of twenty-two twelve-inch woofer speakers.

After looking at the vehicles, I looked across the street at my plane Jane Chevy and was like "Fuck!" Now that the building had a new light show display going on, with all the new candy colors, business tripled. And for one reason or another, everything was running smoothly, but I still kept a distance away from the building and made money elsewhere.

CHAPTER 23

"NEW CONNECTIONS"

As the fall season was preparing others for hibernation, the first winter mist was set in place with a thin coat of ice on the ground and light snow flurries. I was sitting in my mom and dad's driveway a little before midnight. I was indulging on some beautiful-smelling cannabis and listening to NWA. That's when Birdie pulled up. He left his car sitting in the middle of the street and walked over to my driver's side window.

"What you about to do, B? Because I need a serious favor," he asked me with the anxiousness of a person who was watching the lottery numbers being called off on TV.

"I'm about to go in the house and get some sleep."

"B! I need you! I'm on my way to the Holiday Inn. I'm about to hit this female, but I don't have time to take her friend home. Shoot her to the house for me, and I owe you one!"

Now Birdie and I had gotten kind of close. I could even put the title *friend* on his label, so of course, I was going to do what he asked even though I was dog tired.

I watched as the female I was set to escort was exiting his car and walking toward my vehicle. I could see that she was very nice.

She was definitely full circle desirable with two thumbs-up. The first thing that I asked her was, "Are you in a rush?"

"No, I'm not in a rush. I guess I have a few minutes, but I do need to be getting home," she replied.

We sat in my driveway for about two hours, and with all the cannabis we smoked and the hot sex that she provided, I didn't have the energy to take her home. But I knew I had to, so I started up my engine. (If I only knew what was going to go down a few minutes after I left my driveway, I would've called this beautiful cannabis-hogging girl a cab).

I made a right out of my driveway and was heading down Melzer Avenue toward East 131st Street. I made it to the corner and made a right. So far so good, even though my eyelids were heavy. I was sitting on East 130th and Kinsman, waiting to make a left, and that's when I heard a car horn blowing. I had dozed off and didn't even recognize it, and her pothead self was asleep too! Not really being disturbed by the other motorists honking at me, I made a left and continued down Kinsman Road. I was struggling making my way across town because she stayed about an hour and some change away. I pulled up to the red light that sat on the corner of the famous Fourth District Police Station and the Shell gas station set right across the street from them. As soon as the light turned green, I lightly pressed down on my gas pedal and proceeded forward. Either before I went up under the light or right after I came from under it, I had dozed off. I was awakened because the car had jumped the curb, and when my eyes popped open, I was driving on the sidewalk right next to the gas station heading straight toward a big red fire hydrant! Even till this day, I've been blessed to be a very quick thinker, and my reflexes are just as superior! I cut my steering wheel to the left and quickly smashed down on my brake pedal. With the speed of a person's eyeballs blinking, I cut my steering wheel to the right, then I released my foot off the brake pedal and quickly punched the gas while cutting back to the left! I could feel the vehicle responding to my actions, and a smirk formed across my lips. As the front of my car started clearing away from the fire hydrant, with the help of the ice on the ground, my quarter panel wasn't as lucky. My rear end nipped the fire hydrant, and my vehicle was in serious need of plastic surgery! Needless to say, the rest of the way to her house, we both were wide-awake! The next morning, I called Doughnut, and we escorted my poor car to the same shop at which his vehicle had an operation.

As the summer of 1990 was coming into full bloom, I was seventeen years old, and I was shining around the neighborhood like the rest of the big boys! My Caprice classic came out of surgery on the fair end of the stick, and everyone was loving the new makeover! My vehicle now was a sunset red with the black leather top aiding in maintaining its originality. I had a black race car fin placed onto the trunk, and I had all my door handles removed so no one could carjack me! With one push of my remote, my driver's door would fly open for me. I was riding on some hurricanes triple chrome from KMC custom wheels. The inside of my trunk was the home of four fifteen-inch woofer speakers, and a 1,000-watt Zeus amp that was connected to an epic center. Having that much bass in your trunk was good for the ladies and showing off but not for the police.

As I was riding down 131st Street, I saw a guy that I knew that had just gotten out of prison. I stopped so he could get in. I started pulling off and turned the volume up. I barely drove one block when I noticed the vice car that was coming down the street on the opposite side of me. I saw when they made a U-turn and sped up behind me. We had nicknames for these two officers. The one that came over to my driver's side window was Sinbad. He was a really tall, big, light-skinned guy. He advised me to lower my window, and when I did, the first thing he said was, "How old are you?"

I stated that I was twenty-one. Because I didn't have a driver license, I always used my big brother's name and Social Security number. But he wasn't trying to go for it. He reached down inside my car and opened my door and said, "You are not twenty-one! I don't even think you old enough to be driving!" Then, he grabbed the back of my pants belt buckle and lifted me straight up in the air and walked me over to his police cruiser. He carried me like a rag doll, embarrassing me in front of the passing-by motorists with his "Magnet to Metal" technique that he had pretty much perfected. After a thorough search of my car and a clean Social Security number, I was released with a major noise pollution ticket and a promise from him that he'd be seeing me later.

The year 1990 was proceeding into the future just like the prophecies of the last couple years. Some people were making money, some people were getting robbed, some people were breathing, and some people were suffocating. Some became permanent daisy pushers in the cemetery. Some people got out of the game, and more people got into it. One nice sunny day, Slow Motion had given me a call. He was inquiring as to what I had planned for the day. I told him plain and simple that I was looking for another connect. He said, "Cool, I have someone I can introduce you to." I'm not a person that hesitates unless I feel negative energy, and Slow Motion gave me no reason to think otherwise. He had shown me enough of himself by now that I trusted his judgment call to a certain extent. So I jumped in my car and started making my way toward Slow Motion. As I was pulling up in his driveway, there was a gold four-door Mercedes parked in front of me. So I pulled out the driveway and parked on the street. Finally, I was meeting this much-needed new connect. He told me his name was Turtle, and he damn sure looked like one of them karate fighting fucks. He was also the guy that Shorty Cake's mother was referring to.

As the summer was going smoothly about its business, I started to get to know Turtle, and Turtle was not nice. Instead of being called Turtle, Monster would've been a better title for this different kind of a mule. He was quite the character. The first time he came to pick me up to ride with him, I guess he felt he had a point to prove to me or to set some type of standard in my brain. Even though he heard stories about me, I guess he still wanted me to really fear him in some type of way or another. As soon as I sat down in the passenger seat of his car, he told me to reach in the back and grab any bag that I wanted. As I turned around to see what I was reaching for, I noticed a tech nine semiautomatic. I believe the revolver was a .38 or .40 caliber, and I was positive that was a .45 semiautomatic handgun because it looked exactly like one of the ones I sold. I didn't say anything. I just grabbed one of the brown bags and took it into my house. As soon as I went into my basement, he was honking his horn. I went outside to see why this kung fu kicker was still sitting in my driveway, and I just knew it was going to be something stupid because my gut don't never be too far off from the truth. He told me to get in because he wanted me to take a ride with him. We drove a little ways and parked in front of someone's home. He told me to get out and go knock on the door. I knocked on the door twice and an older man stepped outside. That's when Turtle jumped out of his car lightning fast, with gun in hand, and walked briskly up the driveway.

"Where your son at?"

The older gentleman said, "I don't know, I haven't seen him in a few days."

Turtle just said okay and shot the man in his thigh. As soon as the boom sound was over, the man's son ran out of the house and stood in front of his father, looking very frightened.

"I just don't have it yet. Please just give me a couple of weeks."

Turtle just said, "Okay, I'll find you in a couple of weeks. Let's ride, little dude." I was thankful that this crazy Turtle didn't say my name.

We pulled into another driveway. Turtle had taken his last two puffs of his angel dust–soaked joint and made a phone call. A guy that looked to be in his midtwenties got into the backseat of the car and picked him a brown paper bag and went back into the house. The next driveway we pulled in was Slow Motion's. Before he alerted Slow Motion that we were there, he made a quick phone call. The conversation went like this:

"Hey, I just left so-and-so's house. Go over there with a couple of guys and take what I just gave him." Then, he looked at me with a wicked grin on his face and a wink of the old eye. "Go tell Slow Motion to come here, and come here right now! I don't care if he don't have shoes on."

I went and knocked on the door, and Slow Motion let me in. I said, "Your boy Turtle is off the hook. Do y'all have a negative situation going on? Because if y'all do, I suggest you jump out the window and run, nigga, because he's on that PCP, and he seems very touchy about you right about now."

"Everything's cool," replied Slow Motion, and we stepped outside.

As soon as Turtle saw us, he jumped out of his car with gun in hand, "Why your boy haven't paid me my money yet?" Turtle asked Slow Motion, and the funny part is, Turtle was referring to me!

"I don't know why that man haven't paid you your money."

I really couldn't tell if Slow Motion was going to add more to his sentence, but before his lips could even form another word, Turtle hit him in his right eyebrow with the butt of the revolver. I couldn't believe what I was seeing. I thought they were real cool. As Slow Motion was standing there leaking, Turtle told him to go grab a brown paper bag out the backseat of his car. I was standing there, looking at Slow Motion and Turtle in disbelief. The only thought I had was, "I guess Slow Motion don't believe in shooting people, but I do, if need be." And this was a much-needed *need be* for Slow Motion in my books!

As the months were going by, I was making a lot of money off this Turtle character. I had so many other connects that none of them were important to me. I had so much going on that I was starting to get nonchalant. And in the process, I forgot to pay Turtle his money. It wasn't that I didn't have it to give to him. I just really didn't plan on paying him, and I knew this was going to turn into an altercation with this guy. I'm a thinker, so I was really prepared for it whenever that day came to darken my doorstep. It was Friday when me and a couple of guys from the block were on our way to the shopping mall. I hadn't seen these guys in a while because I was always so busy. It was me, Simpson, and another guy that wasn't really in the game, but we used to hang at his house the first year we were in junior high cutting school. He's actually the guy that made up the story to confuse others about Fashionable Kid getting shot in the head. When we got to the mall, we fired up a joint and went shopping sky high. I was so high, and they were too that we forgot where we had parked the car. The parking lot was getting empty due to the fact that the mall would be closing soon, so we finally spotted my vehicle, and so did Turtle!

As I made a right out of the mall parking lot and started heading down Miles Road toward our neighborhood, I spotted some headlights coming up on me pretty fast, and my gun was in the trunk. As the speeding vehicle got closer to me, I noticed that it was a Chevy Blazer, and I had never seen it before. It quickly swerved from behind me and was riding on my left hand side right next to my driver's window. I still wasn't nervous. I was just waiting to see what actions I was going to have to take to ensure another day for everyone in my vehicle. I could see there were two people inside the other vehicle through the tinted windows. I could make out that the passenger was a female, but that didn't make matters any lighter because females can get just as crazy as a man or even worse. While I was staring at them, the Chevy Blazer window came down. I could see that it was Turtle. Now I was very nervous because I knew that this crazy clown had an advantage on me. I was more than positive that his gun was on his lap or on the lap of his female passenger. And from the looks of her, there was no doubt in my mind that she wouldn't have any issue whatsoever pointing and shooting out a hot conversation with me. He continued shouting and pointing for my vehicle to pull over towards the curve but I did the exact opposite after making sure my seatbelt was "locked tight"! Then I put the pedal to the metal," flat out"! As the gas was being punched by my heavy foot none of my guys in the car was nervous about my driving because this was not their first time playing "shotgun passenger" in a car with me. Turtle and I both were doing about 70 miles per hour on a 35 miles per hour speed limit city street. When I yanked up in my driveway, all the guys jumped out and ran. I popped my trunk and grabbed my weapon and walked down to the middle of my driveway. Turtle stopped in front of my house.

"Come here." He could see my gun in my hand because I wasn't trying to hide it. "What you running for, silly ass?"

"Because I owe you money."

He got out of the truck empty-handed and walked over to me. "B, you only owe me a couple grand, and I know you got it. Nigga, you own four cars!"

And he was right. At that time, I owned a Chevy Blazer, a Chevy Camaro, a Chevy Caprice classic, and a Pontiac Trans Am. "You better be getting my money to me before I take one of your cars!"

Instantly, my brain went to work. I didn't have a need for four vehicles, and I wasn't a big fan of my Trans Am. It had already given me two reasons to let it go! The first reason came when I was racing my boy from the hood down a rainy brick street and almost killed my stupid self. The second reason is what truly pushed me over the edge to get rid of this Pontiac! I was up on Kinsman Street, getting some gas when a canary yellow blazer with a black top and gold Dayton rims pulled up beside me. The truck was full of pretty girls, and I knew the driver. It was one of the Muslims that was running that part of the neighborhood. We had done a little business together. I considered him one of my coolest connects, and he had taken a liking to me as well. He would always tell me that I reminded him of his little cousin, who unfortunately became a victim of the game. (Rest in peace. You are truly missed. M) :(

Muslim said, "Drive to your house and jump in with us. We about to go Go-Kart racing." I was all for that. As I was pulling out of the gas station, I wanted to show off in front of the pretty girls; so as soon as I got in the middle of the main street, I started to smoke my tires, and my vehicle started fishtailing as it was gaining speed. And when I glanced in my rearview mirror to see how much smoke I was making, I could see red and blue lights coming through the grayish white thicken mist that I had stupidly created. And I knew right then and there that they were not on their way to a call from their dispatch! Because in their eyes I had just turned myself into public enemy number one, so the flashing light show was turned on only for my goofy self. But just like any other situation that gives my nerves a scare, "my mind went straight to work"! "Brian, we are going to make a left at the oncoming cross street, then we are going to make another left at the next intersection, then you're going to cut the wheel as hard as you can and make a hard right, we're going to proceed at 50 miles per an hour for two blocks, then you're going to make another left and hide your car behind your mother's house. And your final escape will be going Go-Kart racing with all of the pretty girls". But! God felt that there was something wrong with my plan. He knew that I was headed in a direction that maybe would've brought me to Him a little too sooner than what He had planned me for. Before I could even get my police chase going good, my tie rod broke, my driver side tire folded in, and that fast car wasn't going anywhere fast at all, and neither was I. So I forfeited my Go-Kart trip and was taken downtown "Cleveland", for a misdemeanor warrant.

(It would be a few months before I would see Muslim again, and when we did see each other again, I moved in with him). But in all, the Trans Am had to go!

I was pondering, and before Turtle could mutter another word, I said, "I'll be right back!" I ran into the house. He probably thought I was going to give him some money, but instead, I came out with the title to the Trans Am and gave it to him. He didn't say anything. He told his female passenger to drive his truck, and I watched both vehicles pull away from my home.

I never saw Turtle again. The last I heard of him was about a robbery that went bad. Story goes he was on PCP and robbing a gambling house in Akron. As he cut on a light in one of the rooms filled with mirrors, he saw his own image with the gun in hand and let off a few shots. The police were right around the corner.

CHAPTER 24

THE BEGINNING OF A DOWNFALL

The year 1990 was gone and left the door wide open for 1991. That's when everything in my life started falling apart like most relationships when the love is lost. As the saying goes, "You cannot continue to throw stones at the penitentiary, and not expect to ever break a window." From New Year's Eve of 1990 till the summer of 1991, I saw the most money I had ever seen flow through the building that sat on the corner of 102nd and Union Street. We were very well-known from the projects of Cleveland and throughout the suburbs. This is the same year the movie *New Jack City* came to life. This movie is one of the greatest movies of all the drug-related movies in the black movie culture, others may disagree. It's really just my personal take on the movie, because to me I viewed it as a cartoon that was just played out with human bodies. And the only reason I had this view is because I was really living that life. The movie portrays a New York hustler that takes over an apartment complex and turns it into a place of business for illegal activity. As soon as *New Jack City* hit the movie theaters, we all decided to go see it. We jumped inside of our candy-coated cars, with all speakers turned up and all chrome rims sparkling like diamonds. We formed a line of handsome-looking vehicles (all purchased from drug money, of course), and we made our way to the movie theater with such a skilled formation. One car would stop under a green or red light and allowed the rest of our group to pass. We would block off traffic throughout the city while making our way to the final destination.

As we pulled up into the movie theater and parked our vehicles, there were a lot of people standing outside in line waiting to get their tickets. One person with all the connections throughout Ohio from our group started walking straight towards the ticket box, and bypassing everyone that was standing in line. I don't know how his conversation went with the ticket bearer, but within a couple of seconds, he was waving us to come on. As we were walking past the crowd that was standing outside, we could hear a lot of voices saying, "Now they got it going on!" We were officially on the hood street map. And we also were officially placed on the Narcotics Police Division street map as well. Even though Doughnut's building was seeing more money than ever, I still didn't go over there as much as I used to because that building had been up and running illegally for a couple of years without any interference from the police. That had me a little more than nervous because I never heard anyone in the house talking about paying the police off, so that meant the building was totally unprotected.

It was a nice day, and I had been out hustling since the break of dawn. I was tired, and my body was winding down, so I went to Linda and Ike's house, took a nice shower, and put on some fresh clothes. I went into the basement to roll two small joints, and then, I was off to pick up my girlfriend so we could go to the hotel and spend some quiet time together. Her house was a few blocks around the corner from Doughnut's building, so I decided to stop over there and smoke one of my joints before going about my way. When I got to the building and got inside, it was sort of a full house. Doughnut was there, as well as his two younger brothers, and the Older Kid was there with his girlfriend. One of Doughnut's brother's friends was there with his friends, two crackheads, and here I came to add to this crowd of people. I was in the building for about five minutes when a customer came to purchase something from Doughnut. "I've never seen that person before, not even when I used to be over there during all of the 24 hour time frames. But standing there purchasing some product was a 'Perfect Stranger' to me." But it was apparent that Older Kid and Doughnut was not concerned about this fresh faced guy, because they both was on the magnificent heels of the "Paper Chase". And they were going to do whatever was needed to be done, in order to collect every single dollar from whatever hand that was turned over waiting for something to be dropped in its palm, before the magical re-up clock struck 12, and all illegal activity turns into a spoil pumpkin. (True to the game, drug dealers do not like or accept spoil pumpkins if it can be avoided.) But due to my absence from the building I never thought twice about the stranger. (Probably just a new guy since I've been away). So I just figured it was business as usual, none of my concern. And boy oh boy was that a "Big azz mistake" on my thinking. :(

As we were cracking jokes on each other like we had our own personal hood celebrity roast going on, Doughnut walked over to one of the windows looking for more customers and yelled, "Vice, vice, vice!" Everyone thought he was playing, and no one followed protocol! But I could see from his body language that this wasn't a fucking drill!

I ran over to the window to look out, and I couldn't believe what I saw! Four agents were already at the side door downstairs, trying to gain access. I don't know how many cars were out there, but with a quick glance, I counted seven cars, and they all were empty! So following protocol or not was useless because the building was definitely already surrounded! This situation called for improvising. The darkness of the night that surrounded our building due to the streetlamps always being shot out was gaining some brightness from all the flashlights pointing at every single window of the fine as wine establishment that was about to be demoted to sugarless grape juice! I just stood there thinking I needed a plan, quick, quick, quick! Everyone was running around, creating their own chaos because of their uncontrollable fear. I was just like "Fuck! Need a plan! I need a freaking plan!"

Reality hit me quick. I knew not a single one of us was getting out of this building without coming into some type of police contact! I could tell by the formation of their cars outside they did their homework before they decided to kick the door down. I wanted to find somewhere to hide, even though I knew this was a useless idea. I should've just laid down on the floor and pretend to be passed out from a drunken slumber.

While people were finding hiding places, I saw a couple people going toward the stairway that led to the front of the building, so I followed. We were all standing on the stairs, and I don't believe any of us were breathing. We could hear the officers had caught a few people and were shouting at them upstairs. The hall stairwell where we hid was very dark. An officer came over to where we were and stuck his head into the stairway but didn't see anything. He called to another officer to bring him a flashlight. But before the other officer could even make it to him so he could brighten up our day, he heard the sounds of plastic pill bottles filled crack cocaine being released by these jackasses that my dumb ass decided to follow! As each fully filled bottle hit the uncarpeted stairs, is when we all should have had a fork stuck into us, because we were done cooking! As the bottles continued to roll down the stairs creating a specific tone, I knew exactly what the bottles and stairs working together was transmitting to the officers, "The fat lady is singing! It's time for the cows to come home! So come and get it! The fiddles are right here in the stairwell, with their dumb-ass." As the sounds continued to just get louder, I was wondering with all of the money they were making, why in the world they never took the time to get some carpet on the stairs? But my common sense quickly pushed that idea to the side, because if the stairs had carpet on it, we would never hear the footsteps of the robbers. So with or without carpet it wouldn't have made any difference, because this was a no-win situation. So I just accepted the "truth of life" that we all were in a very fucked up predicament and at any second now the storm is about to be in our mist and lightning is going to strike us with vengeance. >:(

When the officer heard all of that freaking noise we were making he started calling to his fellow officers like he was the police precinct number one "Cockatoo"! "They're in the stairwell! Squawk squawk squawk! They're hiding in the stairwell! Squawwwk!" At that very moment I would have given anything if I could've gave Polly a cracker to shut his tell-a-tale beak!

As the other officers rushed to help their fellow brother, they were shouting, "Be sure that the front entrance is covered!" And covered it was! Because as we went down the stairs and made it to the front of the door, there were bright lights and officers everywhere, and they had already started the process of pulling our security door away from the house hinges! Right then and there all possibilities of escape were diminished! "Now where is that big ass fork at?" Because the way things were looking were beyond regular cooked! Because this situation had just transformed us into a Cajun entrée! Damn! "After Throwing So Many Stones At The Penitentiary, A Window Has Finally Been Broken".

The officer who first located us in the stairwell was standing at the top of the stairs pointing his service twelve-gauge at us. They continued to keep the flashlights shining in our faces so we couldn't see anything, which turned out to be very effective. As we walked through the stairwell doorway to join the rest of the captured crew, our lips were greeted with a slightly powerful backhand that wore a leather glove. Then we were turned around with a mug from the back of our heads to land our faces meeting with a head butt from the wall that it was smashed into. After our face date with the leather glove and the drywall, they placed our hands behind our back and secured us with the black plastic straps around our wrists like handcuffs, and we were ushered over to the window landing and placed down on our knees and you better believe that they did not put us down on our knees so we can start praying. No! It was way too late for that! As my knees were starting to flare up from the circulation of blood being cut off because of the position they had us in, I decided to turn my head just a little bit to see what was going on and I noticed that most of the officers were wearing a ski mask or some type of apparatus to shield their identity, and some of the angry officers had a riot helmet strapped on so tight, I just knew it was going to leave an impression under their chin like tight ass tube socks does the legs. These officers really had a plan together because not a single one of us got away, and they had no sympathy for the girl that was there either because she was on her knees right next to me.

It didn't take long to figure out what they were going to do next because it was initiated very rapidly when one of the officers started speaking, "I'm only going to ask this once! Who is going to own up to the sawed-off shotgun?" No one on our losing team offered a single game play to him. And the officer didn't ask again just as he promised. Instead, we heard a loud thump! It came from the officer's helmet introducing itself to the back of the female's skull. Then, there was another thump and another thump and another thump, and after each thump, you would hear a new person crying out loud. Now it was my turn, and even though I couldn't see him, I could feel the energy and excitement of the officer standing behind me preparing to play pool.

Then, the thumb was initiated, and my lips and nose went smashing into the wooden window landing! Instantly I released blood over everything that was in front of my face! As the officer thumped the last person in line, he smoothly glided back down to the beginning of the line once more to start his illegal interrogation all over again. "Who had the shotgun?" the officer asked the unlucky person at the top of the line that was down on their knees.

"I don't know" was the reply, and that's when the officer went back to work with his riot helmet for answers. You could tell that this officer was getting frustrated because his hits were getting harder. He was making his way back to me, but this time, I would be prepared. One of my morals in life is "Get me once, shame on you. Get me twice, shame on me." While the officer was playing pool and using his helmet as the cue ball, I was getting my game plan together. As the blood was running from my nose and out of my lips, I started sucking up all the liquid that I could and held it in my mouth. Once more, I could feel the energy from the officer while he was standing behind me. "Who had the shotgun?" he asked.

That's when I spat everything out my mouth onto the window landing in front of me. I started shaking my head from side to side, making sure that I got all that bloody saliva all over the front of my face while my left-to-right head shake gave off a desperate impression of "Damn, damn, damn, I can't take no more of this abuse. I give up! Now let me show you my white flag." I started shouting and crying, "I had it, I had it, I had the shotgun!"

Right after I screamed shotgun, I experienced a hard sharp pain to my butt bone that was created by his steel toe boot stuck in my ass! Then he put a hand on my shoulder and harshly pulled me backward, and I landed on my back with my legs in the air looking like something to be roasted over a big fire in Hawaii. With so much going on, I didn't even realize that I had black plastic strips wrapped around my ankles, which really made me look like a pig-on-a-pole.

As soon as the officer saw my face, he asked me how old I was, and I told him sixteen.

He looked at his partner and said, "I'm not going down for this." And his partner's reply was, "Me neither." They asked me if I had any ID on me and I told them no. I told them I thought I had to be eighteen in order to apply for a state ID. They picked me up off the floor, cut the black plastic straps from my hands and ankles, and sat me down on one of the sofas. A white officer that wasn't hiding his face came over to me. He just had a ball cap on and a badge dangling on a chain around his neck. He started to search my pockets and found my joint. Then, he asked me my name and address. Of course, I gave him my real name with my real address. He told me they would let me go, but if I told anyone about what happened here today, they would find me and kill me. I knew it was only a scare tactic, but I was more than satisfied with that. I just wanted out. They had the two crackheads come over and sit with me. One of the crackheads was acting as if he were beaten to death. He was acting as if he could barely walk or talk or understand anything that was going on, and I couldn't help but respect his acting skills! As the detective asked the crackheads their names, the other officer placed everything they found in the house on top of a table within our view. That's when I saw something that I had never seen before in this building. It was a strongbox, and it was locked.

"Whose strongbox is this?" the officer started asking. No one would answer. Before they opened the strongbox, they made sure to collect every fingerprint from it first. When they finally got it open, we knew it was all over for that apartment building.

Finally, they released me and the two crackheads. As soon as we got outside, both of them started running down the street as if they were being chased by a pit bull. I got inside my car and drove back to my parents' home. When I finally staggered into the house, my mom was sitting inside of her favorite red chair in the living room looking like she just finish a boxing bout. I got down on the floor next to her and laid my head on her lap. She started rubbing my head and asked me what happened, and I just muttered nothing. The money I used to receive from Union Street was totally dead now. My pocket was truly going to suffer a bit.

After my episode with the police, I was staying closer to home. Now, Muslim stayed in my neighborhood, and he was a pretty cool guy. Every time he saw me, he would pull over, and we would talk for second. He was pretty much like a big brother figure. We got much closer after the streets murdered his cousin. But even before his cousin left us, Muslim used to always tell me that I reminded him of the fallen soldier. One day, we were taking care of some business. He was aware of my little family problem, so he decided to ask me a personal question. Ever since we were in a car accident together, we had gotten much tighter while attending therapy. He said, "It's apparent that you're making money, but where you sleeping at? Because I don't ever see your car in your driveway."

All I could do was shrug my shoulders as I replied to his question. "Most the time at the hotel or whatever dope spot I'm hustling at."

"I kind of figured that. Get whatever you need because from now on. You stay with me."

I just started smiling because it felt good knowing somebody cared.

Living with Muslim was pretty cool. He taught me more about the game and which guns should be used for which situation. As soon as I moved in with him, he gave me a brand-new 380 with seventeen shots. Being around him really matured my street knowledge. It was with him that I touched my first kilo. We had so many cereal boxes full of cash that it was ridiculous. Till this day, every time I see a box of frosted flakes, I just start laughing or smiling. But our time together was very short because the DEA had already started an investigation on him and his entire family a year beforehand.

One morning, Muslim said, "B, let somebody else make some money. Dogg, don't hustle today. Chill out some. Get yo girl and go have some fun. Don't miss out on life because all you see is green." I pondered what he said for a few minutes, and then I decided to take his advice. But I wasn't going to get my girl because we weren't together any longer, but I did have a lot of female buddies. I got dressed and left the house, not knowing that I would never be returning to it again.

We never saw it coming. But 1991 was the year that the DEA and the vice squads started making very organized and accurate plotted raids. It was about midday when I started circling the blocks to see what was going on, and to my surprise, all the corners were empty. I called a couple of people, and they both said the same thing. People were hesitant to be on the streets right now because the Feds were in full force rounding people up that was already marked. So I decided to start making my way back to Muslim's apartment, and that's when I got a call from one of his people.

She said, "B, don't go back over to Muslim's house. We didn't know if you were in there or not. That's why I'm calling. The Feds got everyone! I'm talking about everyone! And not only in Ohio!" What she said was so true because when I drove past Muslim's spot, it was boarded up with a drug-free stamp on it. Not one time did he sell drugs from his apartment. Well, at least not to my knowledge. I didn't know what to do. In my eyes, things were just so wrong. I didn't take the time to try to understand that God was trying to send me a message. At that time, I wasn't mature enough in my spiritual walk to catch it.

I was riding around in my car thinking about everything I had just lost. Muslim was gone, all my jewelry was gone, and all my money that was in the apartment was gone. I was really getting tired of the ups and downs of the fabulous so-called street life. I was back staying at my mom's. I started walking more and kept the car parked. Some days, I would think about Muslim and wonder how he was doing. I heard he was looking at twenty-five years for conspiracy and money laundering.

In 2013, I ran into Muslim. The guy is doing good! He has a wife and children, and he still consider himself my big brother. I got love for you (J). :)

With so much being taken away from me, I started to understand that one saying people used in a balderdash situation like mine because I truly didn't have a "pot to piss in!" So now, I had to return back to Durkee and start looking for a new connect.

CHAPTER 25

RETRACING STEPS

As I made my way back to the block, I saw Brown riding around on his bike. "I heard what happened. You cool?"

"Not really," I responded. "I need a new connect."

That's when Brown introduced me to this guy named Quito. He wasn't from our neighborhood, but with his personality and the deals that he gave people, everyone from the block welcomed him with open arms. The first time Quito and I met, it was like we had known each other for years. He was only a year older than me. We became really close when he introduced me to his girlfriend, and she introduced me to her sister, and we started dating. Just like me, when you first look at Quito, you would think that he was just another laid-back guy that takes care of his business, which he was, but at the same time, due to the fact that we grew up a little too fast, we both had this little boy inside us that liked to play. Sometimes, when he came to pick me up for our transaction activities, I would find myself with him doing sixty miles an hour down a back street and jumping over railroad tracks, just so we could fly in the air for couple of seconds. During this time, I fell in love with his girl's sister. We all were spending a lot of time together and getting to know one another.

One day, Quito and I truly solidified our friendship for the moment. I cut up some crack rocks, wrapped them in plastic, put them in my mouth, and started making my way to Durkee. When I got there, Melvin and Brown were the only ones on the block. We gave each other some respect and started circling the corners together. As the three of us were walking past the houses, I heard a voice coming from a female telling me hello. I turned my head to see where it was coming from and noticed it was a girl from the Catholic school where me and my boys used go in junior high to try to pick up girls. After I responded to her, her guy on the porch started staring at me with a very mean look on his face. He had a mean, challenging face that continued to taunt me as I walked away. I didn't mind a fair fight. Win or lose, a good fight can help someone release stress. I've always been known to be somewhat on the sarcastic side when need be, so I shouted to the girl, "Your boyfriend must like me more than you because he keeps staring at me like he probably looks at you!"

It was very apparent that the guy on her porch really didn't like what I said because he stood up and shouted, "What you want to do, nigga?" As soon as he said that, it was like music to my ears because I was still working through the mental and physical emotions of losing everything! So now, I could focus on him since he was offering the opportunity to help me release some very unwanted stress because I was seriously going through some life-hurtling obstacles. So yes, a fight right now would be good for the soul. But there was a flipside to that coin because there was no reason for that guy to be looking at me so meanly. He could've just lost everything or something more and was also looking for a good fight to release some type of stress. At the end of day, I figured this would be therapeutic for the both of us.

I spat all my crack rocks out of my mouth and gave them to Melvin to hold for me. I told Melvin and Brown I'd be right back, and they just started laughing. As I started walking toward the girl's house, the guy came walking down the stairs really casually. The mean look he was wearing on his face was gone. He simply took his right hand and put it behind his back, and when he swung his hand back up from around his back, it was holding a nickel-plated revolver. He didn't hesitate; he simply pointed at me and squeezed the trigger. It happened so fast that I was stuck on stupid for a quick second. I was totally caught off guard by this powerful move he displayed on the chessboard of life! Because he wasted no time going after the king! He waved the gun around, while still pointing it at me, and started shouting the name of the gang he was claiming. He continued to repeat over and over how crazy he was, how he don't care about killing nothing that sucks in air.

But I refused to be put in checkmate in such a tasteless manner! That's when my brain went straight to work, so I decided to start agreeing with him. While standing there with my hands raised high above my head as if I was asking God to pull me up, I shouted, "You're right! You are crazy." I didn't give this guy any time to think or feel threatened by me any longer. While he was still waving his gun around in the air and bragging about his unstable mental capabilities that could probably take the whole wide world out, I smoothly did an about-face with my hands still reaching for God to pull me up if worst came to worst. Then, I just started walking away. Brown and Melvin were still standing where I left them with their mouth doing the fly-catcher dance. When I made it to Brown and Melvin, I turned around to see what the guy was doing, but he was no longer visible.

Brown and I jogged down to his car on the corner, and Brown handed me a 9mm semiautomatic. As soon as I felt that cold blue steel in my hand, I sprinted back toward the girl's house where I had unfinished street business. When I made it to the driveway, I slowed my pace and observed the area with some serious caution. Everything looked safe, so I made my way up the stairs and knocked on the door. As I was knocking, I was very careful not to stand directly in front of the path of the porch door, so I wouldn't automatically be turning myself into a target for a bull's-eye, just in case the self-proclaimed crazy guy decided to shoot through it. No one answered my knock, so I decided to peek through the wire screen. The fact that they didn't close the main door made it easy for me to visualize the inside surroundings. I could see the crazy gun-waving guy sitting on the sofa. When the girl saw me peeking through the screen, she shouted at me, "Brian! Please just go home!" She was right, so I decided to obey her commands and go home. Right after I punched my hand through the screen door and let off two shots.

I reminisced a split second on what Ike laid down on me before I squeezed the trigger. "Unless it is extremely necessary, never shoot anyone above the waist because you might catch an instant murder case," he had said. With that in mind, I targeted his left and right leg, resulting in two bull's-eyes. I took off as fast as I could. I was moving faster than a drug-induced Armstrong pedaling as fast as he could for the gold and made my way back to Melvin and Brown. They were sitting in the car with the motor running waiting for me. I jumped in and told them to take me home. When we made the right-hand turn onto my street, my common sense kicked in. I couldn't go home because the girl knew where I lived. Instead, I went across the street from my house.

The house across the street always had a lot of girls over there, and Quito's girlfriend and her sister were friends of these girls. I would always see Quito over there, but I never knew who he was until recently. I knocked on the girls' door, and they let me straight in. My girlfriend was there looking at me strangely, and her sister's eyes was following suit. The eyeballs of the friend who actually stayed there were riding the bandwagon. They knew right away from my whole demeanor that something was definitely wrong, so I revealed to them in very brief details the last few minutes. Just as my version of the truth was rolling off my tongue, we listened as we heard police sirens coming from every direction.

We all briskly walked over to the living room window to see what was going on. What we saw was very bad! The police had Linda, Ike, and my little sister in the same position that the crazy gun guy had me in. All three of them were reaching for the sky simultaneously with the officers' service weapons drawn on them. With superfast reflexes, my brain started going to work because I figured it would only be a matter of minutes before they figured out I was right across the street. And just when my brain started devising a plan, Quito and one of his friends walked through the door. Quito was looking at me, laughing. He was like, "You cool? It's all over 131st! You shot old boy in his legs, and the girl gave the police his gun. The police looking for you not only for shooting him, but they also think you got shot."

"I don't know how he missed me, but he did," I replied.

"You know we have to get you out of here right now."

"I know." I knew I just couldn't walk straight out of their front door. Then, I looked at all the girls in the house. (In junior high, all the girls showed me favoritism over the other guys. After school one day, I was walking with about five females. One of the girls asked if she could give me a kiss as it was time for me to turn down my street. She was cute, so I figured why not. We were face-to-face when I noticed she was looking at me sort of puzzled. Then out of nowhere, she said, "If you were a girl, you'd be cute. Hey y'all! Wouldn't Brian be cute if he was a girl?" And they all started laughing and screaming yup!) That's when my brain started directing me to exactly what I was going to do. "I'm going to walk straight out that front door right now!"

I guess it's safe to say that my mom was the acting wardrobe director when me and my childhood friends were younger. For one reason or another, my mom would always dress us up like old women for Halloween. Without a word to anyone, I shot straight to their friend's bedroom and made a quick observation of everything that was available for me to recreate my mother's masterpieces, and there was plenty at my disposal! I had no complaints of the articles to be used! I hurriedly went straight to work. As I was removing all my clothing, I noticed that the shorts I had on, which were my little brother's, had a burn hole through them. The shape of the hole resembled a cigarette burn right where a man's sack of walnuts hang! (That crazy guy came very close to blowing my nuts off!) I quickly dismounted that thought and continued with my escape plan. Finally, I had stripped down to my birthday suit and started pulling up the best choice mini skirt around my waist. I quickly slid a halter top over my head and placed one of her best wigs on top of my scalp. I put on a pair of her best Mary J. rhinestone sunglasses and squeezed my big feet into her grandmother's best Sunday heels. (This worked out because her grandmother and I were about the same darn height.) Then, I decided on the cherry-red lipstick while stuffing socks into the halter top, ensuring that I had some fluffy breasts. With a quick glance in the mirror, I was satisfied with the fast results. I rejoined the group and notified them that we needed to be on our way!

As we exited through the front door, Quito and his girlfriend were in front of me, Quito's friend and my girlfriend were on the right of me, and the girl that lived in the house was on my left. We made our way to Quito's little white Ford hatchback looking like clowns at a circus as we all loaded in. I had no worries while we were leaving because I knew we presented the imagery of teenagers going out to party. As we gained a small amount of speed pulling away from the scene, I could see that my family's hands were down. They weren't reaching for the sky any longer, and I knew my mom was going to kill me. Not because I shot the guy, but because she was probably doing her lottery numbers when the police arrived, and once again, it would be my fault that she missed her number. (That was the fourth time *when a soul started running*.)

Finally, we made it across town, and I stayed with Quito and his family for about two months. I got to know Quito and his family pretty well. Then, I was right back to the neighborhood. That also meant that I was right back to the domino effect of my life, and dominoes fall down, not up—unless you're some type of magician, and that I was not. I guess since the police got the guy with his gun and he discharged it in the city limits, and they probably found out what gang he belonged to (and who knows what trouble he was into before shooting at me), so I was never charged with that crime. But sure enough, after he made bond, him and his crew were waiting for me to come back to the neighborhood for some vengeance. Word traveled pretty fast so everyone knew I was back in the hood, including the crazy gun guy.

One night, I was circling the blocks on my bike, and out of nowhere, a car came speeding past and sideswiped me. They got me pretty good. They had gotten some ways up the street before screaming their gang's name. I guess after being shot, he must have been broken a little and was being very cautious and smart. Just as countries go to war, most nations attack from a distance. So that was his strategy as well, as they decided to let off some shots more than a block away from me. All I can say is fair exchange is no robbery; they got me back. I was just glad that they didn't do enough damage that would require major service at a hospital.

(Year 2014, as I smiled at the completion of my book and was now ready to send it to the publisher, I decided to go and get *When a Soul Stops Running* tattooed on my hand after giving the artist my idea for how I wanted it. I had to wait because he had someone he was working on, so I left for a quick lunch. After returning, I held open the door to the shop for a woman who was leaving, and as she passed by me, she said, "Hi, Brian" and kept going. When I entered the room with my artist, he was looking at me with a smirk on his face. Then, he said, "I'm going to be sure to do your tattoo to your exact specification because that woman that just left said you shot her boyfriend some years ago.") >:)

As the summer was coming to another ending, police were everywhere, and that was due to the fact that drugs were everywhere. Sometimes, you just had to leave the blocks so you don't get caught in somebody else's spider web. The vice were just making too many appearances for my taste. This was truly not my cup of tea.

With the last of the warm days ahead of us, Quito and I decided to go fishing. We grabbed our little girlfriends and one of his homeboys and made our way over to my grandparents' house. My grandfather loved fishing and used to always say to me, "Foots, when are you going to go fishing with me again?" And I would just say, "I don't know, Grandpa." And I truly didn't know because I was traumatized the last time we went when I was younger.

(My grandparents and I were making our way back from Lake Erie with a bucket full of Lake Erie's finest dirty water catfish. As I sat on the concrete stairs watching my grandfather lay newspaper on the ground before us, he quickly grabbed one of the catfish out of the bucket and politely laid it on top of the daily news. Before I could get a good look at this fish's lips moving in a unique formation, he was bust upside the head with a hammer. My grandfather took a good look at the fish and questioned, "He still not dead, Foots?" And that's when the catfish received a second blow, but the results were the same. The fish was still moving its lips, and now it was wiggling its tail fin. One, two, three, four upside the head again got the job done. With fish head parts all over the newspaper, the lifeless remains were joined by another catfish from the bucket. But this time, my grandfather decided to use his cutting knife and started cutting away with no mercy in sight. I watched everything that made up this poor fish's insides come sprawling out on the daily news. My grandfather said, "See, Foots, that's why that fish wouldn't give up so easy. This is his girlfriend, and those are her eggs. Always remember, Foots, never easily give up on your family.")

I appreciated and respected the little life lesson, but I made sure that me and grandpa's fishing trips would always remain in limbo. :)

As I parked in the driveway of my grandparents' home, I got out of the vehicle that I rented from a crackhead and walked toward my grandfather's garage. As usual, I tried to sneak up on him, and just like any other time, he was prepared. He already had his switchblade drawn before my first step passed over the threshold of the doorway. We both laughed and hugged one another. He gave me enough fishing rods for everyone in the vehicle, and we were on our way to go fishing. (I never knew that would be the last time that I would ever see or talk to my cool grandfather again in our physical form. Our next meeting will be in a dream. I miss you, Grandpa. I love you. I still owe you some fishing rods! Rest in peace. (DD)" :'(

We decided to get out of the Cleveland area in order to go fishing, but that trip was cut short before we could get freely to the highway and get started on our journey. We had to pass through a predominantly white neighborhood, with the police squad called "Stickum" which was located in the upper numbers of Euclid, Ohio. We were waiting at the light to make a left on to the highway when a patrol car came past us on the opposite side of the road. He stared at the five young black faces in the vehicle across from him. As he passed, my eyes went straight to the rearview mirror. And sure enough, that police cruiser made a U-turn. As I let a few horses go from the engine as I approached the on-ramp, the police cruiser played tag-along. He didn't turn on any flashing lights, nor did I hear a siren screaming. He just tagged along. After about eight minutes, a helicopter decided to shine its bright light down on us, and the one police cruiser had multiplied by seven.

They had all five of us sprawled out on the highway in the beginning position of making snow angels. That's when we all traded off the fishing trip for a jail cell. The negative domino effect in my life was moving at a rapid pace, and it was all due to my poor decision making. How many people can actually say that they got arrested with their girlfriend going fishing? Only my dumb ass! Things were switching from bad to worse to unbelievable! It was time for a change, so I decided to solidify myself and stay away from the drug game. I started spending time in the library, focusing on a plan to recondition my life toward a positive walk. I went crawling on my knees to the board of education, and even though I was eighteen years old at the time, they still allowed me to reenter high school and I even joined the baseball team in order to give me more time to focus on staying away from the streets. But the relentless dominoes refused to stop falling in my direction. Those darn dominoes were truly working round the clock, calculating a path of destruction for me, and they had no issues with overtime.

CHAPTER 26

BLINDSIDED

For a few months, I lived the life as a regular teenager going to school. My days were very simple. Early in the morning, I would drive to class. After school straight to baseball practice, then I would spend the rest of the day with my girlfriend. I was even back at home where my mom and my dad were arguing much less. Ike and I were actually getting along, somewhat. I also had a point to prove to him because he kept telling me I would never get my diploma, and nothing lights my fire more than someone's personal doubt in me. But those self-improvement times were cut short because of my loyalty card that's connected to my heart. Sometimes, I can't help but live by my own life rules. For example, if someone put a foot forward and had my back, I would be in debt to them until I could put a foot forward for them as well; then, the contract is terminated.

By me staying away from the streets, I was really starting to get to know my girlfriend, and she was really a beautiful-hearted, laid-back individual. She was very happy that I wasn't running the streets any longer. We were really starting to get close. We even started calling each other pet names. We both loved Mickey and Minnie Mouse, and we loved their relationship even though it was built on fiction. But we managed to transform that same fiction into mental and physical solitude within our relationship. I didn't have money like I used to, but I was very happy. My girlfriend was starting to make me feel whole, so money was not a main priority any longer. We were still okay because I had just gotten the settlement check from when Muslim and I were in a car accident. The irony of the ordeal is we were actually hit by a Muslim company truck, so the payoff was helping me to keep my nose clean.

March of 1992 was when reality really hit home! That's when a reason to continue changing my life smacked me straight in my face like a monkey throwing the best of his rebirth meal at the zookeeper! LOL! I went into my mom and dad's basement looking for a stress-free atmosphere in order to aid me in clearing my mind on this new drug-selling-free life I was trying to grab, when something invisible kept tapping me on my shoulder as I was sitting on the bar stool. This invisible tapping was the same feeling you get when you're in a very crowded room, and out of nowhere, your instincts makes you quickly turn your head, and once your eyes focus on the direction to which your instincts made you turn, you notice that someone was staring at you. For some reason or another, we all can feel that "unseenable" vibe.

Slowly, I turned my barstool around, trying to figure out what was making the hairs on my body stand up straight and sliding me closer to the early stages of paranoia. But no one was there, but I knew something was wrong because my body would not release the goose bumps that were sticking with me like them darn things that be sticking to your socks when you're running through grass that's never cared for. So now, this cat must find a reason to satisfy this annoying curiosity! I stopped breathing for a second just to listen, but I didn't hear anything. But for some reason, my eyes continued to stare at the black door that had a very large sofa pulled in front of it. I walked over to this large sofa and pushed it out of my way so I could gain entry to this black door. Slowly, I turned the handle and braced myself for whatever was not in there because our minds do play tricks on us during our most vulnerable moments, and I was in the transition of trying to do good over bad. I quickly snatched the door open, and that's when tears started pouring from my eyes like the largest floodgates of Hurricane Katrina had just broken. >:(

Linda, my beautiful mother, was standing there in a cloud of cocaine smoke, and the first thing she told me was that it was my fault for her being trapped in the closet. (Yeah, she hit me with some pure bullshit). She told me that one day, I dropped a piece of crack. (I can still remember the day when Linda was sitting at the kitchen table doing her numbers, and she asked me how do people smoke crack cocaine. I explained to my mom that I really didn't know. I think they smoke it out of the glass pipe, but I've seen some people crush it up and place it at the tip of their cigarette!) And to add another permanent tattoo to my brain, later that day, I decided to fry a hamburger, and since the cat was out of the bag, my mom felt free to expand the notification of my earlier discovery. She came around the corner and peeped into the kitchen, then told me, "If you give me a piece, I'll finish frying your hamburger." (Later in the future, I would wonder, did my clash with Linda about some fried beef, have something to do with me visiting a Burger Restaurant carrying a shotgun with a black dress on?)

Karma may not come back exactly how you put something out. But it will definitely find an avenue to smack you in your freaking face!

I had just turned nineteen and was now truly living a normal life in a chaotic atmosphere, which was perfectly fine because it was the norm for me. But I was really fighting the "game of life" trying to stay on top of my footsteps as far as school was concerned. I continued to hold down a B-average, and I was working at Burger King inside the North Randall Park Mall. I went from keeping the tables and floor clean to frying the French fries. I hated this job, but my girlfriend was happy. She never wanted me to return to the streets.

But on this life-changing day, school let out early. And due to the recession of incoming funds in my pockets, my funds continued to remain on a diet, so I didn't have money to buy a car for the winter. Here it was the middle of March, and I was driving back and forth from school and work inside of a T top I-Roc Z28. But I didn't care because I was determined to do the right thing. As I parked my car in front of my mom and dad's house, I walked across the street (to the house where I put on the high heels and miniskirt for the getaway) to see if my girlfriend was there. She always came over to her friend's house after school. As I walked through the door, I was greeted by the grandmother of the house. Quito's brother was there as well and the mother of the girl who lived there. They all told me that my girlfriend called and left a message for me. I understood that she would be on her way in a little while after she left the library with her mother and sister.

With the tardiness in place, it resulted in an open window for my personal dominoes to go into overtime. Quito's brother said, "Brian, I need you to do me a favor."

"And what favor is that?" I inquired.

"I need you to shoot me over to Maple Heights. I need to run into a store over there next to the Maple Heights movie theater."

"I would if I could, but you know how my girlfriend feels if I'm not here when she arrives," I replied back with no hesitation.

Quito's brother was cool, but I really didn't know his motives that well. A few minutes went by, and Quito's brother brought me the phone. Quito was on the line. "B, do me that little favor. Shoot my brother over there for me right quick."

Now here's the guy that hid me from the police when I had just shot someone, so my loyalty took over my moral thinking. I was subjected to his requests, and I put my foot forward. I didn't want to drive my car because it was a little messy outside. So I walked across the street and asked my dad if I could use his vehicle and we were on our way. I wasn't worried about any foul play coming from these two brothers, because they both understood that I was walking a path to make my life better. But (Boy oh boy) I was wrong about these two heartless caring money hungry bastards!

As I pulled into the shopping center driveway, I headed toward the store next to the movie theater. Quito's brother said, "There's more parking spots in the back," so I headed toward the back of the shopping center. I parked right in front of the store, but Quito's brother didn't get out. He was on his cell phone asking someone where they were. I asked Quito's brother what's up. That's when I saw an inconspicuous black Suburban crossing in front of me, and Quito's brother said, "Hold on a second, Brian. That's my boy."

I decided to watch the Suburban, and as it was circling the parking lot, I noticed a few cars had people sitting in them, which was very odd. The oversized black truck parked behind me and one spot over. That meant Quito's brother had already given them a description of the car we were in. It also meant this was a freaking drug deal, and neither Quito nor his brother had given me a heads-up about this bullshit play! Because they knew I would have never agreed to this trip!

Just as soon as the Suburban stopped moving, a skinny little black guy jumped out and headed over toward my vehicle. Quito's brother offered him the backseat. And just as fast as the skinny guy closed the car door, Quito's brother was pulling out a brown paper bag from his underwear. I opened up my car door, stepped out, and stated, "Y'all on some bull crap!"

Quito's brother cried, "B, don't leave!"

The expression on my face revealed how disgusted I was! I wasn't angered because they were taking care of business. I was heated because I had no notification of what was going down. (I do not participate in other people's plans unless I have input on the blueprint and able to manipulate it to fit my thinking.) The skinny guy made an observation of what was in the bag, then said, "Okay, let me go to the car and get the money." I watched this skinny guy walk back toward the Suburban, and as he reached for the car door to get in, I waited for their dome light to come on inside the car. I spotted a white guy at the steering wheel, and around his neck, I could see a chain. That metal around his neck had the same twisted chemistry of the metal that the vice squad wears in Cleveland. I put my father's car in drive and shouted, "Dude, this is a set up for you, you jackass!"

Quito's brother was like, "No, it's not. What are you doing?"

I knew exactly what I was doing. I was punching the darn gas pedal so I could get the fuck out of there! If Quito's brother had any knowledge or common sense, he would've understood what I was doing. I was utilizing my own common sense and trying to separate myself from this dumb shit! As I punched the gas pedal and made a hard right turn, I looked into the rearview mirror, and every car that was occupied came to life. Somehow, the Suburban beat me to the exit and blocked my escape route. I was only nineteen, and my walnuts had no sense of fear in them, and my common sense was always on its A game. I knew this officer was inside his own personal vehicle trying to play the element of surprise tactic, so I continued straight toward him, and sure enough, he put his vehicle in reverse and got out of my way.

So far, so good, I was thinking, but I didn't know the area. With everything going so fast, I instantly made a hard right out of the parking lot, which turned out to be a dead-end street.

"Fuck!" I slammed the car in Park, left the keys in the ignition so I could report it stolen in a few minutes once I got away, and I started running for my life through the woods. (This was the fifth time, *when a soul started running.*)

It was very dark while I was running through these soaking wet woods, but I did not let that slow me down. What slowed me down was the deer wire I ran into. It tackled me down to the ground (just as fast as the young boys tackle my African snowman when I was younger. And at that very moment I knew I had fallen into some serious shit) and wrapped itself around me. I lay there for a few minutes until the officers finally caught up and were standing over me, looking down, laughing. As they were cutting the wire off, they said, "You move pretty fast, kid. If it wasn't for this wire, we probably would've had to catch you later on down the road."

But I was in their custody, and I didn't find anything funny, nor did I hold a grudge against the officers because they were just doing their job. And for one reason or another, every officer I've ran into always kept a pocketful of corny jokes, and they were having fun with me. I was truly upset that I was going to jail this day for somebody else's idiotic blueprint.

In the newspaper, Maple Heights portrayed that day as if they trapped some king penguins from the Arctic drug field. It's was totally understandable for such a small city, but if this same play was in Cleveland, it only would've had life by word of mouth. I spent a couple of nights in their city jail, and due to the fact that they considered this to be a first-degree felony, I was transferred to Cleveland's County Jail. A few weeks went by before Quito finally bonded me out. That was my first time actually sitting in a jail cell for a long period of time for something I didn't construct. When I got out, I was so happy, but I had no money in my pockets. After explaining my situation to the bus driver, he went into his pocket and paid my fee.

Once again, I thanked him as I was exiting the bus, but being very anxious and overly excited that I was about to see my beautiful caring girlfriend, that I wasn't thinking in a "look both ways before you cross manner" so as soon as my foot touched the pavement, I walked directly in front of the transit, so I could cross the street. I guess the bus driver's horn wasn't working because as I was crossing in front of the bus, my eyes caught the bus driver doing a lot of motioning. Unfortunately, it was too late, and my next step landed me on top of a woman's car's hood and over the top until I landed on the ground. When the woman exited her vehicle, she already had tears rolling from her eyes. She continued to repeat, "I'm sorry, I'm so sorry. Are you okay?" My blood was pumping too hard and fast for me to even notice that I had just gotten run over. I gave the woman a friendly hug and ensured her that I was okay and continued on my way while everyone else was left looking at me with their mouth doing the fly catcher dance in disbelief. My girlfriend was happy to be hugging her boyfriend with a very strong I-missed-you hug! And that hug was much tighter than usual. She started explaining to me that she wished she had gotten to the house earlier that day because she knew I would've never left. Not even to put a foot forward for the morals of loyalty because that situation truly wasn't worthy of opening up my personal loyalty door.

Once I was out of jail and waiting for trial, all the dominoes decided just to lay down and create a path for me to just start walking on a road leading to nowhere but my demise. Due to the lengthy time I spent in the Cleveland County Jail, I wasn't allowed to attend school any longer for my job. They had given me a chance, and I messed up. MF! There goes my diploma (maybe the eagle was right about me being a dummy). Even my car was feeling the heat of my negative domino walk. While the summer of 1992 was really showing off its hot face, I had crashed my car and was forced to put it in the shop for a facelift. After a couple of weeks, I received a call from the mechanic, and he told me that they were ready to start painting my vehicle, but I needed to come up there to see exactly which shade of black I wanted them to use. That's when I saw Simpson and asked him for a lift. Simpson and I walked into the shop, and I couldn't believe my eyes. The repair work they performed on my car was beautiful. I had totaled the whole front. The owner of the shop wasn't there, so I pleaded and used a little bargaining chip to con the painter into letting me take the car out for a spin before he applied the last process of finishing up the job.

Simpson and I made our way to the neighborhood so I could show off my car. He was sitting in my passenger seat lighting up a joint that was marinated with PCP.

Why not? I thought to myself. So I joined Simpson's party and had more than a few puffs of that super mind-altering device. Within a couple split seconds of exhaling the smoke, I was driving in a dream world where all my surroundings were very blurry, very vivid, very slow, and very fast all at the same freaking delusional time. I was the "Commander and Chief" of a 400hp motor while on PCP. Simpson and I were waiting for the same red light to go green in the same location where years earlier, the police were behind me when I was inside the stolen Cherokee. With my delusional state of mind going on, I was still coherent to a certain degree. Right before the light could change, Quito's brother pulled next to me inside of a white Trans Am he had just brought. He let me hear the roar of his King Kong gorilla engine, which actually sounded nice, but let's not forget, PCP amplifies everything. He could've been riding a bicycle with a soda pop can stuck in the forks to create a lot of noise, and I still would've heard the same sound.

The traffic light struck pay dirt, and I brought my Godzilla of a motor to life, and both vehicles were moving very fast. Halfway up the street, I noticed that Quito's brother started falling behind, but it wasn't due to the fact that Godzilla would probably beat King Kong in a fair fight. It was due to the RTA bus that was right in front of us. I was going too fast to utilize my brakes. That's when the PCP came to my rescue and told me (using the voice of Fly and Skeleton),

"Little dude, that's no problem for us, my man. Just slide over to the left lane with the oncoming traffic and beat them to the light."

Now where was that little white-haired woman from the movie *Poltergeist* when you needed her! Because I did not need to be going into the light. The speed limit was twenty-five miles an hour, and we were already doing sixty-five.

"Little dude," Skeleton's voice was reassuring me, "just apply a little more pressure to the gas pedal, then whip around the bus and continue winning the race. You are victorious!"

So I decided to follow the PCP's fantastic blueprint that was created specifically from an idiotic, stupid jackass like myself. I started initiating the movements that were going to leave me either victorious or paralyzed. Everything was smooth-sailing as I started to glide over into the oncoming traffic until an old school four-door Cadillac made out of real steel decided to pull out of line right in front of the little unibody sports car I was driving! Then both vehicles kissed really, really hard! It was a girl on the porch of the house where the accident occurred who just so happened to be one of the girls that experienced the first look of my boner in science class, and yes, she gave me up. (On 2014, that same girl became a Facebook pal, and we gave each other a call and just started laughing.)

The day was getting no better, so to make matters worse on my pathway of the notorious falling dominos, a couple of hours later, I was on the east side of town walking down the street with Quito and his friend. We were on our way to Quito's cousin's house to get out of the way because the block was too hot. As we were walking, there was a group of guys shooting dice next to a building and eating hot dogs. When they noticed us walking past, they started making lewd remarks because they knew we weren't from their neighborhood. The door was open for me to throw back a couple remarks of my own. After the brief back-and-forth, we continued on our way. When we arrived at Quito's cousin's house, we were told that he had just left.

We started retracing our steps back to our own neighborhood. As we were walking, there were two guys standing on the sidewalk, but none of them fit the description of the guys that were shooting dice. Quito and his friends started walking in the street to avoid them, but I decided to stay on the sidewalk after assessing that these were not the ones we just had the altercation with. As I was passing them, I was hit in my left eye with a glass bottle (and sadly, I still wear that scar today). As soon as I completed the spin the bottle spun me into, I noticed Quito and his friend were being attacked by multitudes of people. Just surveying the area with my watery eyes, I believed that it had to have been between ten to fifteen guys attacking them. Quito's friend started running and left us! At that moment, I started feeling the numerous punches that were connecting to my head and my body. Somehow, Quito was able to bring himself to my rescue, and we were back into the action! We were smart enough to get back to back, throwing punches for our lives. Quito saw an opening in this mess, yanked me by my T-shirt, and we ran away from those guys with the aftermath of their trophies left on us, which included me sitting in the hospital getting stitches, and Quito in the room right over from mine, trying to figure out how to get his tooth back into his gums. Unfortunately, Quito's procedure was unsuccessful.

I earned the award title "split left eyebrow," and Quito won the outstanding award of "losing teeth" that would require artificial replacement. We were very unhappy because we weren't worthy of those awards. But the guys who jumped on us were, so Quito and I decided to go back and present them with some trophies of our own. Fashionable Kid was more than happy to accompany us and another guy from our block as well.

As we got closer to their playing field, the other guy from our block decided to fire up a PCP joint. He was high instantly; he quickly turned "stony shit face"! He was so high that he started handling his fully automatic improperly and shot up the inside of the car we were riding in. So I terminated the whole ordeal because I wasn't out to kill anyone. I just wanted to shoot a couple people in their kneecaps, but my gut told me that it wasn't going to go down that way with PCP involved. So those hot dog–eating dice players were the winners. But I understand how life works. You win some; you lose more. It just is what it is. You just have to keep the mentality right in order to deal with it and "Just Embrace a Loss, Without Revengeful Thoughts" and I earned my master's in learning how to suck it all up, within reason!

CHAPTER 27

SEASONS COME, SEASONS GO

As the fall/winter of 1992 came into place, the summer had ended just like every other summer. Some people started selling drugs, more people started using, some people were still living while more people were dying, some people went to prison, and more people were just in the way. But this summer, there were more senseless killings because crack was taking over the world where we lived. For example, Smokey's little cousin and his best friend Stone Wall were tampering with a man's van, and somehow, the man ended up catching both of them at the same time. The man took his belt off and gave both of them whippings in front of everybody while searching their pockets for crack rocks. The very next day, Smokey's little cousin showed me a .357 Magnum. He couldn't have been any more than eleven years old at the time, but now, he's in jail for life on a murder case. A few years later, Stone Wall followed suit to the same dance, "Sentence to Life in Prison."

November was finally here, and I was prepared for whatever fate awaited me on sentencing day. The judge couldn't figure out if I had something to do with the case or not. My lawyer and the prosecutor kept trying to get me to snitch on Quito's brother, but my dad didn't raise me that way. So I was going down because I wouldn't play ball.

For some reason, the judge tried to give me the benefit of the doubt. I guess it was due to my clean record. I was standing in front of the judge with Quito's brother and with our families sitting behind us in this very quiet courtroom. The judge asked Quito's brother one simple question. He looked at Quito's brother and asked, "Did Mr. Dixon have anything to do with this case?"

All Quito's brother had to answer back was no, but instead, he didn't answer the question directly. He started mumbling how sorry he was and how he would never do it again and blah blah freaking blah. I just stood there wanting to head-butt him on the bridge of his nose and then trip him from behind his legs and watch him fall backward landing in his own DNA.

Quito's brother had more cases pending before he caught the one he welcomed me into, so he was given five to twenty-five years. After the prosecutor had a conversation with my mother, I was awarded three years instead of five in the state penitentiary. I really appreciated my mother pleading for mercy on my behalf because they had no issues with giving me five years for not telling. As we were being ushered to the door that lead to the walk of no return, I turned my head toward the courtroom, blew my girlfriend a kiss, and told everyone that I would see them later because I don't really like telling people good-bye that I hope to see again. Once behind the door, they put me and Quito's brother in the same cell. Without any thought of forgiveness, I balled up my fists and waited for the guard to walk away, so I could start giving Quito's brother his awards upside his head. Before I could initiate my beatdown, as soon as the officer closed the steel gate, he started making this little bitty noise that grew into something very large. It was the same type of noise that you hear when one of those weather alarms is starting to go off. This guy, right before my eyes, had actually turned himself into a "Human Severe Whether Alert System" and with all those tears that were leaking out of his eyelids, the noise he was making really did fit his personal little rainstorm. Watching his reality playing itself out in front of me put me in a position to have no other choice but to check myself because it's just not in me to be coldhearted. Besides, there was no way in the world the real man in me was going to allow the other me to harm this guy even though I was sitting in the cell with the same guy that put me in here for the next three years! So my soft side had me "smooth sailing" and put my fueling attitude at ease, and I just told the guy, "It's going to be okay. We'll both be home again." The more I started to ponder my new situation, the more that I started smiling. I looked at this way: In reality, I'm here for the next three years for something that I didn't do. But I would rather accept that than being in here for the things I did do. Sometimes, we must balance the scales of life even when we don't want to because our gut feeling just tells us it's the right thing to do! We must accept this as just another piece of the puzzle of life. So three years is fine and dandy with me.

I was now a true convicted felon and was standing in something that would remind you of a cat litter box while being sprayed down by a jail guard with some type of a human bug spray. The way this spray smelled, I believe it would've given any bedbug a run for its money! They were just being certain that my black self and the other felons didn't have lice to bring into the city jail, but I wonder why the spray had to be so freaking cold! It was as if they kept the shit in the refrigerator just for our stupid asses!

Once inside my orange prison gear, I was given a wool blanket that smelled like other people's musty bodies and corn chips. Then, I was placed inside a winter-cold cell that was giving that bug spray a run for its money. My feelings were nowhere. I was just taking stuff in because this was a whole new world for me. I wasn't sad or mad, happy or scared. I was just sitting in a cold cell with a very dim light with my body totally numb to emotions. I was working into my third night inside of the Cleveland County Jail when once again, I heard the jail guard's keys rattling at the door. I thought it was breakfast time, and I was waiting for the shoot to open so I could retrieve my food like the animal they thought I was. But that didn't happen. Instead, my cell door was opened, and the guard told me to pack up. It was time for me to go to the reception penitentiary located in Lorain, Ohio, so I could be classified to the main institution to where I would be living for the next 1095 days.

I was sitting on an ex-Greyhound bus that was transformed into an inmate relocator mobile unit, with steel bars welded over each window. This remade Greyhound gave me such an impression that it allowed me to utilize my imagination. I blinked my eyes a couple of times like Dorothy would have done with her ruby reds and removed my prisoner status. Even though my hands were shackled to my ankles, I felt more like I was an extra hired by a temporary movie service company. And this was the beginning footage of the Mad Max thriller franchise. Finally, I entered through the gates of the Lorain County Correctional Prison Facility. As I exited the bus, a prison guard helped me with my first step down. He looked me in the face and said, "How old are you?"

"Nineteen," I responded. He just shook his head, and told me that I looked like I was a big fourteen.

After taking mug shot pictures while holding different displays of inmate patent numbers and being fingerprinted multiple times, we were finally shuffled inside another cold cell. But this one was special. It was the notorious twenty-three-hour locked down cell block. But I managed to squeeze out of that solitude of an ordeal because I was listening to all the other inmates share their thoughts on this new living situation. I just decided not to think like them, and I moved toward thinking out of the box! Now, I just had to wait and see if opportunity presented itself, and it did.

One night, a female guard was walking, doing her cell checks, and I was standing inside the little window peering out. She placed her flashlight up to it and told me to move to the side, so she could complete her safety and number check. Then, she asked me for my name.

"Dixon," I responded.

"Well, how old are you, Mr. Dixon?"

"Nineteen and hungry."

"And what are you in here for, if you don't mind me asking?"

"Drug possession with intent to sale."

"You don't look any older than my son, and he's fifteen!"

I didn't know where she was going with these twenty-one questions, but I didn't mind at all. Then, she asked me if I were to work in the kitchen, would I behave myself. I placed my two hands in front of my face to symbolize that I was praying and saying please and nodding my head yes. She didn't say anything else. She just walked away, and I never saw her again. (Well, until a few years later when I had to serve my second prison number.)

The next day, I was relocated to the workers dorm and given a kitchen job. As I was walking the yard to make it to my destination, I actually ran into Quito. We didn't have much time to talk, so we exchanged prisons numbers so we could stay in touch. I didn't even know that he was locked up too. After a couple months or more, I was back on the Mad Max bus and headed towards my parent prison, which would be the Madison Correctional Institution. After being bug-sprayed and given my fancy penitentiary blues with my inmate identification number written across my chest, I was placed in a dorm to start working on those three years that needed a serious diet.

Being in the Madison Correctional Institution was pretty cool. It was like being at college without any females. It was not one of those hard-core prisons that you see on TV. So I started experiencing a lot right away due to the fear level being so low.

My first encounter with a seasoned prisoner was so funny. I was walking the yard by myself just thinking about my girlfriend that I was sure to lose, and I didn't want to be doing that. So I decided to go to the recreation dorm. I sat on the bench, watching two guys play pool when a prisoner walked over to me and told me that his name was Stars. He was as black as black can get on a dark night, and he didn't realize that I already knew who he was. He just couldn't remember me because I was too young. He used to be the football coach at the Boys and Girls Club. My father used to always say that he had sugar in his tank, and boy oh boy was that bald eagle right! So I didn't tell him who I was for the moment. I wanted to see what his conversation was going to be like first.

Stars was like, "I bet all the girls call you cute." I was laughing in the inside. While keeping a straight face I just answered back with a yup.

"I have a lot of connections. If you need anything, just let me know," he said with a smile revealing all of his teeth that made him look like a grand piano. That's when I couldn't take it anymore from this "Midnight Color Smooth Talker" and I burst out laughing. Then I called him by his government name and reminded him who my father and my oldest brother were. He stared at me for about fifteen seconds with a concentrating expression. Then, he started laughing and said, "Little Brian, boy you have really gotten big!" And instantly, his whole demeanor changed. The bass was back in his voice, and he put some lips over those smiling ass teeth of his. He transformed into the football coach again, but the way he had his prison outfit tailored, making his blue pants look like the "skinniest skinny jeans" was not working with the deep voice. I just continued laughing at this character! He still kept the offer on the table, but the morals of the offer had changed into a black man to a black man demeanor. That was cool and all, but Ike had already told me never to accept anything from anybody in prison. Ike gave me a rule to follow. He told me always to remember that "if you cannot get it on your own, that means you don't need it! Flat out!"

Stars told me to tell my dad hi, and we both went about our way. All in all, I would never have a chance to use that offer even if I wanted to because within the next couple of days, I didn't see him anymore. For one reason or another, he had beat a man close to death with a pool ball inside of a sock.

I had no choice but to be a winner when it came to disadvantages circulating around me, because I didn't belong to a gang or any type of prison organization and I had no plans on joining one. So I figured, I will have plenty of lightweight to medium problems for myself at my new temporary home. Every single day, I was wondering when someone was going to try me because I knew it was coming. I just couldn't determine when. And for the most part, everyone was pretty cool, which was kind of bothersome. However, this was a minimum-security facility where they sent older prisoners that had been down for a very long time that had managed to have their security status lowered. Everyone was pretty much on their best behavior because they didn't want to ride the Greyhound unit back to one of the more corrupt penitentiaries. Since I was so young, most of the older guys treated me and the other younger guys as if we were their nephews.

One morning, a domino just had to raise up and show itself, then took a dive right back down in my face just so I could walk on it. Due to the fact that I started selling drugs even before the legal age to drive, my body was accustomed to always getting up early in the morning, so I could beat everybody to the money. Everyone on the cell block knew that I got up early so I could go inside the TV room and watch the *Awesome Power Rangers*, as I was trying to rekindle a bit of my childhood! The guy that was assigned to keeping the TV room clean decided that since he had a softball game early that morning, he would clean the TV room during my Power Ranger hour. This would've been totally fine with me, but he didn't go about it in the right respectable manner.

I was sitting there, watching the Red Ranger morph into his character when the cleaning guy walked in, made a beeline straight to the TV, and cut it off in my face. Then he told me that I had to get out because he needed to clean. I didn't say anything. I politely stood up, walked over to the TV, cut it back on, and sat back down. He looked at me with a crazy puzzling expression, then started walking back toward the TV. I politely told him, "Don't touch it," and he roughly cut it off again while staring me down. I moved as fast as I could and got both of my hands around his throat and started slinging him into the aluminum chairs and for good measures because I knew I was going to the hole! I knew I also needed to take advantage of this opportunity and kill two birds with one stone. The first bird, I had to show him that he was wrong for what he was doing and hope that he never tried that ignorant move with any of the other inmates. The second bird, I had to create an image so the other inmates truly understood that I was very capable of taking care of business, if needed be. I smacked him a couple of times like I was the Red Power Ranger, and during the whole incident, I just kept laughing because his whole face had turned pink. I mean I had heard the stories, but this was the first time I was actually witnessing it on a white man! When the prison guard riot unit entered the building, I was standing next to the correction officer's desk, and they ran right past me and went straight to the hot mangled-up-pink-faced man, threw him on the ground, and put him in handcuffs. Then, they said, "Where's the guy he was fighting?" And the prison guard pointed at me. They looked at me with disbelief because I did not have one scratch on me.

Finally, after an unpleasant two-week stay in the hole, it was time to be interviewed by the internal corrections review board. They were trying to hold in their laughs but couldn't as they were reading my disciplinary charges. They told me "No more fighting over Power Rangers cartoons!" and released me from the hole. I was moved to a cell right next to a guy that was the same age as me. He was from the

St. Clair area, and the boy was wild. He stood about 6'4" and was a boxer and just as silly as me, but he had no morals. We became prison friends, and we were a good collaboration because he was the muscle, and I had a few brains. But this kid was always into something that was unhealthy for the prison life. He would always tell me, "Watch this!" During the daytime, he would catch prisoners sleeping in their beds and put matches between their toes, light them, and wait for the reaction. At night, he would put a bar of soap inside three socks, catch people sleeping, and bust them one good time in the head while they were trying to rest. And when he was really bored, he would break up that thick blue state soap that had OPI embedded on it and aim it at the prison officers while they were sitting at their desk, and he would hit his target.

One day, he went a little too far due to the fact that neither one of us had money support coming in from the outside. He started taking people's locker boxes to the bathroom and kicking the lock off so we could have something to eat. But one day, he kicked the wrong box, and I was the lookout while he was doing this. We made a terrible mistake by kicking the box of a guy that was a runner for the Aryan Brotherhood! We truly didn't realize how much trouble we were in until it showed up at our front door. It was the middle of the day, and everyone was out on the yard, except me and this St. Clair kid. We had decided staying in until the sun went down when we were approached by seven white guys. All of them were wearing a very serious expression on their mean-looking face, and I knew they meant business, and it was sort of scary. I got a little nervous because they were outnumbering us two by a lot, and I knew exactly what this little gathering was all about. The guy that was in charge said, "I am not going to ask you guys no questions. Just give me all of the stuff back."

St. Clair kid just looked at him and was like, "I don't know what you're talking about, buddy."

And in a cold voice that would give anyone's spine a shiver, the Aryan guy responded, "I'm not going to ask twice." And all his guys came off the wall and moved closer to us.

That's when we all heard a voice come from out of nowhere. "Hold on a second!" the voice shouted loudly from across the dorm. It was a very respected Muslim guy named Rapper from East Cleveland, and he was known to take care of his business and had a lot of followers. Tension was already high between the Muslims and the Aryan Brothers because both groups outnumbered all the other crews in the prison. So both organizations walked a very thin but also very respectable line toward one another. Rapper made his way from the other side of the dorm and stood in front of me and St. Clair kid and asked the Aryan guy if he saw us do it.

The Aryan guy said, "No, but someone told us that it was them."

"So you're not 100 percent positive?" Rapper asked them.

The Aryan guy didn't answer him. Instead, he looked at me and asked me how old I was, and I told him nineteen.

"This one time only," he said. "We're all going to forget about it." And I watched as his guys put their shanks back into their pockets and exited the dorm.

Now I was doing my Toni Braxton and breathing again as I slid my shank back into my pocket, and I promised myself that I would never again put myself in a situation like that because I was definitely scared! And by me not being affiliated with an organization, I was sure to get the short end of the stick if that situation would've continued to play forward. For everyone who reading this who does not know, the Aryan Brotherhood does not play games! I am very thankful to Rapper and the Brotherhood for that unique way of handling the situation. From the bottom of my heart, thank you both! (R) and (B)

Once they were gone, Rapper was staring at us very angrily and said, "Y'all think this is a game? It wouldn't be too cool to see one of y'all dead in here!" Then Rapper walked away without another word because we were all from the street so we knew exactly what he meant. A couple of weeks later, a young guy who was going home in the next few months was murdered over a porno magazine. (I never thought I would ever see Rapper outside of these prison walls because he had a few years to do. But I did! And it was in Hollywood, California, as I was standing on my last leg.) As the next few months went slowly by, St. Clair kid was still shooting his regular, but he was smart enough to pick nonthreatening targets.

One day, an old school cat pulled me to the side and said, "Look here, young brother, the way you been running around here with that clown is pure nonsense. I know you got another prison number in you. Trust me, you will be back. But I at least want to see you make it out of here alive. You too close to going home, little brother. Tell me something youngster, did you graduate high school?"

"No," I replied.

"Check this out, young blood. You have to cut your boy loose and trade that time in for school. You got less than a year left. I want to see you walk out of here with your GED. Can you promise me that?"

I didn't say a word. I just nodded my head yes and did what I was told. So I headed straight over to the counselor's office and signed up for school. Then I went and told the St. Clair kid that I had to pull back on our foolishness so I could focus on getting a GED. I even convinced him to join school as well. Then I decided to show him a picture of my girlfriend because getting my life together had a lot to do with her. We still called each other Mickey and Minnie in our letters. But the letters stopped coming in on their regular schedule. When St. Clair kid saw the photo, he was like, "Wow, dude, I know her. That's my homeboy's girlfriend. She just bought him a sweater this past Christmas." And I knew he was telling the truth.

As the next few months traveled at a turtle's pace, which was better than a snail race, I was asking other inmates how to go about getting a job. I fortunately landed a job in the kitchen and continued to study and stay in the gym lifting weights. During my last ninety days, I was given a furlough and moved to the going-home dorm. The month/year was June of 1994. I had about two and a half weeks to go before I left. As I sat up on my bunk bed and opened my eyes, I was not inside the prison walls. Instead, I was at a house with my grandfather. He was standing over me with two white lights that appeared to be in the form of humans. They were a little far back behind him with a very vivid bright glow to them. My grandfather bent his head down and kissed me on my forehead and told me, "It's okay, Foots, but it's time for me to go." I asked my grandfather where he was going. He just repeated, "It's okay, Foots. It's time for me to go." I lifted straight up in my bunk bed and opened my eyes and realized I was still in prison.

I sat there very impatiently because we had to wait until the guards allowed us to get off our beds in order to be on the floor. As soon as the time struck pay dirt, I walked as fast as humanly possible to the telephone room and made a collect call to my mother. When Linda answered the phone, I could hear it in her voice that something wasn't right. Slowly, she said, "Hey, Brian."

I didn't even say hi back. I just asked the question, "Did Granddaddy die last night?"

My mother replied, "Yes, your grandfather passed away yesterday. Wait a minute! How can you possibly know that?"

So I explained my dream to her. After hanging up the receiver, I went straight to the showers, so I could let the water run over my head because it wasn't too cool to shed tears around a lot of grown men who haven't had sex for eons.

Later that day, the GED scores were posted. Nervously, I walked over to the bulletin board to introduce myself to the results of the tests. But before I could see my score, I had to briefly slow my pursuit because St. Clair kid was walking toward me explaining that he didn't pass. So we both walked back over to the board to find my name. My results were the opposite, and I started smiling from ear to ear like a kid in a candy store. A lot of my smiling had to do with the bald eagle and the old school cat who told me to go to school. Ike told me I would never get it, so I couldn't wait to tell the neck-grabbing guy because I knew he would be proud. I also couldn't wait to tell the old school cat because I knew it would make him feel like he accomplished something in at least one of the young individuals that came to this place. So this day, everyone had an award! Even my grandfather because somehow I just believe he's in heaven. :)

As the month of June was coming to an ending, so was my precious prison learning experience. I never looked back as I was riding in the prison van on my way to the bus station. It was a long ride, and it give a young man a lot to think about. I was very grateful to my uncle because throughout the three years, (which was reduced to two years because of good time, because I only had one incident within two years of my stay and because of receiving my GED) him and his wife were my only visitors. I finally arrived at the Greyhound station and started making my way to the furlough house.

My first week at the furlough house, I was visited by Quito, his girlfriend, my girlfriend, and her mother. I pulled my girlfriend to the side and explained to her that I understood if she had someone else in her life. We could still remain friends, if she choose to. I had just opened the door for her to decide on what she needed to do while giving the option for us to remain friends is really priceless. She looked me straight in my eyes and told me that there was no one else. (She never did realize how good I can read body language.) My visit time was up, and it was time for them to go. Quito and I walked over to a corner in the hallway. I looked him straight in his eyes and said, "So what's up with her? She just told me that she doesn't have anyone else in her life."

Quito didn't say anything, but his facial expression had me on edge with curiosity! He just looked at me with a smirk on his face and said, "I'll be here to pick you up in the morning so you can go look for job." We all hugged, and they were on their way.

The next morning, I was very excited because the furlough house gave me a pass for three and a half hours to go job hunting. We weren't allowed to get into anyone's personal vehicle, so I would meet Quito in downtown Cleveland or right around the corner from the halfway house if the coast was clear. All my visitors that came to see me lived together. As I entered my girlfriend's bedroom, she was willing and waiting for me. As I passionately kissed her and started removing her clothing, the big Mickey and Minnie Mouse poster that was placed in glass hanging over her bed made a smile appear on my face as Mickey and Minnie watched us do the nasty. When we finished our lovemaking session, she told me that she wouldn't be here tomorrow because she had to leave early in order to make it over to her grandmother's house in time for family planning. All I could do was kiss her forehead and say okay.

The next day, when Quito came to pick me up, we decided to meet behind the furlough house. And boy oh boy was my homeboy in a rush. He didn't tell me anything. He was just driving with a "lead foot" and floating through some red lights. We were moving pretty fast in his drop top Corvette, and unfortunately since it had been three years since I was in a vehicle that was moving much faster than the speed limit, I just continued bracing myself every time he made a turn or touches the brake pedal, the whole way there. I was just trying to be prepared for when we hit something! When we "quickly" got to his house, he didn't say anything to me. As soon we walked in, he went straight to his bedroom and closed his door. I was standing in their living room just thinking, *This dude is really acting odd.*

For some reason or another, I was still a little tired. I didn't know what Quito was doing, I just figured he was getting dressed or whatever. So I decided to go to my girlfriend's bedroom and wait for him to finish up. I knew she wouldn't be home, but I didn't mind. I was satisfied with being in the presence of her personal things. But when I twisted the handle to allow myself in, it was locked! And I found this to be very odd due to the fact that her door can only be locked from the inside. That meant she hadn't left yet, which was great because now I can give her a good morning combo, which included a hug and a very passionate kiss. I knocked on her door a couple of times without getting an answer, so I decided on calling her name. Strangely enough, there still was no answer, so I put my ear up to her door like any other human being would do in such a puzzling situation, trying to imitate an inspector that I was not.

I was fortunate enough to hear some slight movement going on. That's when I shouted out to Quito just to see what he was going to say. "Quito! I am about to kick this door down!" He knew I didn't pretend when I said that I was going to do something, so I was not surprised when his reply came back with a "Okay, do what you have to do!"

I was already in position when he delivered his answer, and I didn't hesitate! I put that Air Max straight to work and kicked the door straight off the hinges. Just as fast as the door fell to the floor, so did my heart and the tears from my eyes. The guy that was inside the room with her was ready as well because just as fast as my heart and my tears fell, he ran passed me like a streak of lightning! I didn't even see what the guy looked like! My girlfriend was standing on the side of her bed, pulling up some black panties. I walked straight over to her and grabbed her by her hair and started shaking her head because I don't believe in hitting women unless in a life-threatening situation, and this wasn't a life-threatening matter. It was worse! This was a heartbreaker!

So I figured a good shaking was what the doctor ordered for this little heartbreaking lying rat! Because her Minnie Mouse license was instantly revoked right then and there! I'm sure my girlfriend was shaken drunk by the time her sister and Quito made it into the bedroom! Without noticing, I had added moans to my crying. Her sister grabbed my arm and said, "Brian! No! Look at me, Brian! You're better than that!" I released her hair from my grip, snatched something off her dresser, and threw it at the Mickey and Minnie Mouse encased in the glass that was hanging so beautifully on the wall over her bed. (Wow, she was doing the nasty right in front of all our love mascots with a different Mickey! MF!) As I listened and watched it all fall down from my mighty Red Ranger blasts of whatever I threw at it, a little smile formed across my lips, and the river of tears was drying! I just stood there, watching the glass shatter like my heart and fall toward the floor like my tears. That's when Quito came over and grabbed me, and my tears resurfaced with the force of a tsunami and landed on his shoulders.

Quito was my boy, so dropping tears in front of him was like dropping them in front of my brother. I took my place in the passenger seat of his vehicle, and that's when waterfalls was a part of my life all the way back to the furlough house. I was so in love with her that I couldn't get my demeanor together fast enough. I was a shaking watery eye rack! But I'm a Pisces, so it's totally understandable. (Just hit the Internet and read up on my zodiac, and it will aid you more in understanding my motives during the course of this book.) But due to me not being able to mend my broken heart back, the furlough house sent me back to the state prison to finish off my time. They couldn't take me sobbing anymore. I was given a couple more months for not complying after being placed back inside the penitentiary.

While occupying my days distraught from what transpired with my girlfriend, my release date finally hit the calendar. I was right back at the Greyhound station, waiting for my older brother to come pick me up. My brother stayed about forty minutes away from the station. I had talked to him earlier, and he said he was on his way, but that was three hours prior. I was sitting there, pondering my lost love when another prison van pulled up to release some more people. As we were all discussing our happiness about being set free, we decided to walk over to the store that sat directly across the street with the big "Liquor Here" sign that was posted very high in the air with all the bells and whistles blinking on and off, that sign has so much going on, that it would've made in recovering alcoholic break their promise to themselves. We formed a posse and headed over to see what they were offering. We all started sipping cheap corner store wine and guzzling beer, which was a very, very bad decision for a fresh out of prison, sensitive stomach.

When my brother finally arrived, I felt as if I was the drunkest I had ever been in my life. He had his family with him that I had never met before this day. His fiancée was in the passenger seat next to him, and there were two little girls in the backseat. During my drunken slumber, I managed to conjure up the best hello that I could muster. It went something like this, "Hello, everybody. I'm your uncle Brian. Don't you ever let me catch you drinking. It's bad for you." Then I hung my head out of the car window and released everything from out of my stomach that I could managed to push out, and left a sour liquor trail that any alcoholic Tracking Dog could've followed all the way to their house.

CHAPTER 28

CALL ME THE JOKER

My brother made me stay with him for a few months because he didn't want me going right back to the streets, and he was so far away from our neighborhood that I had no choice but to comply. But it was hard for me to find work on his side of town, so I moved back in with my mother and father. I knew it would be a short stay because they were now living in a two-bedroom apartment in the suburbs, and my little sister and brother were living there as well. I quickly landed a job doing die-casting for me and my little brother through a temporary work service. The work we did was worth much more than our paychecks, but it was honest slave money. It just didn't sit well with me that every time a white guy came in from that same temporary service, he was hired permanently within their thirty days of coming on board. I was truly putting my hard work in because I knew this job will keep me away from the streets, but the color of my skin always allowed me to be overlooked or not looked at all, I was only offered over- time on any given day of the week that I chose to have it. All in all, one month I had over one hundred hours a week for four weeks straight! That's four hundred fucking hours for twenty something working days! I was very exhausted and looking for a deserve promotion, but the only thing I got told was, "Brian, the foreman said you're going to have to stop working so many hours because is not policy or safe for the company." That's when I was starting to get tired and had enough of the colored- motivated favoritism! And I was darned sure tired of the notorious Ike and Linda shouting boxing bouts as well! Everything was just so negative in my small little world and my distress was starting to win the battle over my positive morals of life. >:(

Linda and Ike's arguments were at an all-time high. I was doing a lot of overtime and couldn't get the proper rest, and Ike was always telling me to get out of his house. Some nights, I would have to sleep at the bus stop since my mother and father had moved to the suburbs, and I didn't know anybody out there to let me into the building. They stayed inside of a secure building, and no one would ever answered the phone when I called to get in once I was off work! And that bus stop sleeping really sucked! >:(

Just like the law has a long arm, so do the streets. Night after night of sleeping at a bus stop, I decided not to do it anymore. I let my job go and returned back to my old stomping grounds. Being back on 131st was a totally different experience. Most of the guys that I knew were in prison for ten years or more, and there were a lot of new faces floating around the neighborhood. I tried to catch up with Quito, but he was on a different level of street game now. He had a lot of younger followers that all carried guns. Every time I ran into one of his followers so they could relay a message to him, he never would get back with me. So with the couple of checks that I managed to save, I started looking for a new connect, and I found one. I headed over to my neighborhood to meet this guy. I quickly hopped on the public transportation and started making my way.

As my stop was coming up, I saw about five to eight people fighting on the corner of 131st and Harvard. I recognized two of the younger guy's faces that were in the mix of things, and they were doing their best fighting two grown men. I jumped out of the bus window and quickly ran across the street as fast as I could, pushed Beans out of the way, and started throwing punches at his target. One solid punch to this older guy's chin and the guy's legs decided to put him down for the count. Then, I made my way over to Stone Wall and pushed him out the way. I tripped his target from behind his legs and mugged him backward at the same time. Instantly, he lost focus and balance and decided to lay on his back.

"That's enough," I figured, "they can handle the situation now." But as I started walking away, I noticed Stone picking up a rock that was at least thirty pounds. Stone walked over toward one of the guys that was down and out and was getting ready to drop that big rock on his head! That's when I sprinted into action.

I said, "Hold on, Dogg! We just beating these guys up. We not trying to catch a murder case, homeboy!" Stone had no choice but to respect that because I was considered an OG in the neighborhood, so he reluctantly relinquished the thirty-pound rock right next to the guy's head.

I got pretty cool with Beans and Stone after that incident, but I had to keep a thorough eyeball on Stone because he was young, and he was a live wire and couldn't care less about his actions. I liked Beans a lot because he was full of morals, but that was to be expected because he was Muslim. Stone was a totally different character! One night while over in Maple Heights, a few guys decided to shoot at me and run. Someone told me who they were and where they lived. So Chopper, Stone, and I drove out to North Randall to see if we could give these guys some awards. As we entered the parking lot where these guys were supposed to be hanging out, I grabbed a wooden baseball bat, Chopper grabbed the aluminum bat, and Stone pulled out a big ass 357 Magnum. While I was eyeballing him and that piece of hardware that he'd magically pulled from the thin air, my mouth formed a smile for a second because his piece of hardware would allow us to fight "fire with fire" if need be. But then I realized that I was looking at one of the "American Nightmares". I was just sitting in the vehicle staring at this young guy and even though I knew him somewhat, a very caution scary feeling started coming over me. I started doing some math because I had just completed some prison time for something that I did not do! But here I was again in another bullshit predicament and while the train of thought was carrying on within my thinking pattern, that's when I noticed a glare in his eyes and that glare was so familiar because it was the same glare he had while he was holding that big ass rock over that one guy's head. That's when I told Chopper to pull out before any door could be opened up on this "morally suicide" of a vehicle. My gut told me to call this whole mission off! Because I was only out here to hear the sounds of my baseball bat cracking a few kneecaps and nothing more. But Stone was out for much more! It was as if this young cat was a real-life vampire! And that little Nigga wanted to see some fresh blood! And I truly believed that by him jumping into the vehicle without him really being asked to come along for the ride, really didn't have anything to do with this young cat being loyal to our neighborhood. I think it was just his personal desire to transform someone into a permanent Daisy pusher in someone's graveyard for the hell of it. That was twice I voted against Stone's evil ass thought patterns. It's a sad story that I wasn't around for his third because I did care for the young cat. (Currently, 2014, Stone is doing a life sentence, and it was whispered in my ear that Quito was also on the case and turned out to be the main witness against Stone even though he was the puppet master. Only those two know the true story behind the madness. I really miss you, youngster. You were always good people to me. In my opinion, if it's not our Creator doing the pulling, certain strings shouldn't be pulled by regular man.)

After that incident, I decided that I needed to figure out a way to start staying away from the block. Things weren't even going in the right direction as far as the dope game was concerned either. All the connects that I knew were either locked up, turned into drug users, or laying 6 feet under some dirt or the worst thing of all and that's working for the federal government that consider them a partner to trap someone, in order for them to receive a lighter sentence or no prison sentence at all. Yes the dope game was definitely F.U.B.A.R.! With all the snitching going on, I truly had trust issues with everyone I came into contact with. There was a beauty salon on 131st that I started to hang out at because Quito's brother's baby mother worked there, so everyone in the salon got familiar with me very quickly. They told me day after day that I need to change my life around. After the owner saw that I was an automatic hit and favored by most of the female clients that came into her salon, she asked me to be a model in one of the Cleveland Ohio Beauty Hair Shows. I wasn't doing anything with my life at the time, so I agreed. I was still holding up the old structure of being fresh out of prison, as far as my body was concerned.

So the day of the hair show, I decided to peek through the curtains to see what I was up against. To my surprise, this was the first time that I'd ever seen so many beautiful black females under one roof. I had to make sure they would remember me over all the other male models, so I laid my prison structure body down on the floor and started doing sets of fifties with my push-up game. As it was getting closer to the time for me to walk the stage, I had managed to give my chest a nice muscular blow, but that wasn't enough! So I decided to enhance my appearance just a little bit more! I got to thinking, *I've always been different. Why should this day be any less? Shall I walk the stage like everyone else? I don't think so. I'm going to parade on stage!*

When they called for our beauty salon to show their workmanship, I was the last one through the curtains. All the women started screaming and clapping as I made my dramatic entrance because I came through the curtains stripped down to only my bottom underwear! It was an unforgettable night. The next week, the shop started receiving new clients that had seen us at the hair show. The beauticians were always talking about teaching me how to do hair or nails, and one day, I decided to take them up on their offer. Due to my living situation, one of the hairdressers moved me in with her. Now it was time for me to get some money together, so I could start going to nail technician school. Before I started school, my mind told me that I needed to get in some practice. I made my way over to Sally's beauty store and started buying all types of acrylic powders and liquids along with plastic nail tips and drying machines. Now it was time to find me some clients. I went to downtown Cleveland and had some business cards made. I also needed a nail tech name, so I started calling myself Joker and there it was.

Nails by Joker was conjured up into existence. The reason I chose that name is because I really liked that character! He was funny, and he wouldn't hesitate to take care of business if need be. The Joker always had a girlfriend that had his back, so he solidified my admiration for his character. Now transforming into my new identity was a cake walk. (Box Car said you have to become different individuals.) I started walking up and down the dope strip with a mouthful of crack cocaine and carrying a black briefcase full of nail products. When customers came to buy some little white balls, I would pass them one of my business cards, and I actually started receiving phone calls from the purchaser or someone that they passed my business card on to. I wasn't driving at the time, so clients used to come pick me up from the block and take me to their homes to perform my duties that I knew nothing about. Then, they would kindly drop me back off on the corner of 131st and Harvard to transform from a nail technician impostor to a real live part-time dope man. I never knew how many female hands I was truly messing up due to the fact that I had no experience at all, until one night, my brother and I decided to go to a nightclub and this nightclub was very known to just about everyone in the Cleveland area! It did make no difference if you were from up the way, down the way, or from the suburbs or whatever! Because "Vel's On The Spot" was the place to be every single weekend! (Just make sure you bring your gun) After ordering my drink I put my back to the barmaid just to turn around and have my eyes land on a very pretty girl that was looking in my direction, so I decided to move a little closer to her and asked her to hit the dance floor with me and she kindly agreed. So we started making our way to the dance floor so are bodies can began to sway together to the beat.

While we were on the dance floor massaging our bodies together, I asked her what she did for a living, and she told me that she was a nail tech. I responded with a very confident "Me as well," as I was slow-motioning my body to the left, then over to the right of her thigh with a very cool two step that I knew all too well and once my nose finished its travel up her neckline to have my lips land on her earlobe, the Casanova that be dormant but dwelling within my soul came to life as well as one of my deep voices that sent magical massaging whispers into her beautiful ear, I announce that I was Mr. Nails by Joker. Instantly, she stopped dancing with me and told me how bad I messed up her girlfriend's nails, and she left me standing on the dance floor. I was feeling good off my liquor, so I just continued to dance by myself, and I thanked the nail gods I wasn't embarrassed for long when two girls voluntarily offered themselves to party with me on the floor.

Within the next couple of days, I started searching for a beauty academy to attend, and I quickly found a school on Euclid Street in East Cleveland, Ohio. Everything was looking fine and dandy until the school notified me that there were no grants for nail technician's courses. I needed to come up with some cash before the day ended. That's when I got a very unexpected phone call on August 12, 1995. There was a girl that worked at the hamburger restaurant. She was cool people, and often, she let me practice on her body and her nails to enhance my skills. Practice really makes for perfect! She was very helpful in my perfecting a signature stroke on both of them avenues. >:)

Since she was already aware that I was a street person, she was curious if I knew anyone that did robberies because there was a lot of money in the safe that the manager did not pick up from the night before. That's when my imaginary light bulb turned on and started provoking me to make a very stupid decision. She continued to explain that the individual would have to hurry up and get there because the manager was on his way to pick up the loot for deposit. I took this as an opportunity to get my life on track. But the only problem was, I didn't know anything about robberies. My mind went to work anyway. First thing I needed was a disguise! There was a little thrift store up the street, so I went in and purchased a black dress, a flowery hat with some sunglasses, and a flower-patterned pocketbook. Now I needed transportation. Just my luck, a drug user was riding past me on a bike. I paid him to borrow the bike and quickly jumped on my new ride and started pedaling as fast as I could to my friend's house down the street from the hamburger restaurant. I was desperately trying to travel as fast as I could, with my thighs burning from all the hard pedaling I was putting in. I never believed in physically hurting people for financial gain, so I left my friend's house with a rusted out, nonworking shotgun. I wrapped some duct tape around it to make it look authentic, jumped back on the bike, and started pedaling as if my legs had transformed into a motorcycle motor.

As soon as I made it to the restaurant parking lot, I laid the bike down at the end of the establishment driveway and walked slowly toward the entrance door. I took a quick peek inside to make sure there were no older people in there because I truly wasn't trying to give anyone a heart attack. Plus, I knew older people liked to carry guns and are not shy about putting it to work. When I finished my amateur surveillance, I looked to the sky and asked God to please forgive me. Then I went inside. I came out just as quickly as I went in, got on my new ride, and started pedaling away. After opening up my purse and looking inside, I became very frustrated because the manager had beat me to it, but I did get enough to take to school for a down payment on the tuition. So far so good! I will be starting school!

Things were going sorta okay because I had a place to live, even though it was an awkward situation! Here's the problem: the hairdresser and her boyfriend were always trying to get me to have sex with them. This guy of hers always wanted to play tag team on his baby mother, like we were true super stars of the WWF! But the real funny part about his sexcapade thoughts was that the mother was in total cahoots with this goofy clown. And boy oh boy did they pull tricks out of the old gag bag! I anticipated sooner or later, that these two will really believe in their minds that they have actually found the imaginary key to my "Pandora's Box" of desirable temptation. I would never forget when these two freaky rabbits really attempted at turning that imaginary key after they must've been praying to their very own sex god. I could see it in their little gang-banging thirsty eyes that they wanted to jump me in, so I could automatically become a member of their little freaky dickey bedroom crew. They understood the fact that I was fresh out of prison, so naturally, they were assuming they had a very easy catch. But soon enough, they found out just how off course they were from catching this fish.

On this one particular night, they cast their fishing hooks, and I give them an F– for their dumb effort! I hadn't seen too many movies over the course of the last few years due to my imprisonment. It must have been a full moon in the night sky when I was in the room that she had given me, studying for my first upcoming exam. So I guess they figure it was time for me to pay rent with my boner. I heard a knock at the door, and it was him, the baby daddy!

(I really do give this clown a capital 'E' for effort, because this goofy guy was truly persistent in trying to engage his "Two-Man and One-Woman, Butt Booty Naked Rodeo Show" on me). After opening up my bedroom door and standing face-to-face with Mr. Cool Dude of a weirdo, he asked me if I had ever seen the movie *Friday* before, with Ice Cube in it. I responded no. He said it was a comedy, so I decided to catch a few minutes of it before I went back to studying. I could use a break with a little laughter in it. And boy oh boy did I get a laugh! When he put the movie inside of the VHS player, three people appeared on the screen, and not one of them was Ice Cube, Smokey, or that Big Perm! Instead, it was a man and a woman in a 69 position, with another man standing right behind the woman, doing the back-and-forth dance inside of her muddy cave. I turned my head to them, smiling and laughing, but they weren't smiling or laughing with me. And the thirsty expression pouring from their faces put my nerves on the "defensive side of life" pretty darn fast! Looking at these two with my eyebrows forming into a unibrow, they had the appearance of starving hyenas, and they just knew that I was their main course! Now I have heard of people giving a reference to an out-of-body experience, now here I was with something new! Because I started getting an out of character nervous experience! So I started thinking quick! Even though I knew I was shooting in the dark, I was going to try my best to break their concentration! But the more I stared at them, I knew darn well that they were beyond the breaking point, because they both were staring at me as if I was a gourmet-naked zebra, and they were honestly ready-to-eat.

Now the hairdresser didn't say anything. She just continued to let me see her mouth drooling with no signs of embarrassment! It was her weirdo baby father that did all the talking for both of them, so with all the back and forth serious eyeballing going on, he took a step forward to break the uncomfortable silence. I could tell by his body language that he was telling himself mentally to put aside his lust for a second and had placed a Superman symbol on his chest then he said, "We want you to try that with us."

Instantly I realized that that wasn't a question, it was a freaking demand! And I looked at that clown as nigga like he was crazy! So to make sure that we were all on the same page, I responded with a "Try what, playboy?" I already knew what this goofball was talking about, but I wanted to hear this freaked out weirdo say it out his own mouth.

"You know, what they doing on TV." That's when I turned my head toward their little son because I felt him eyeballing me, and he was right there in the playpen looking at all three of our dumb asses the entire time! He couldn't have been no older than two or three years old, but he sure did look like he knew what they were talking about, and his expression told me that this was not his first time seeing or hearing this type of conversation from his mommy and daddy.

I straightened my face up so my expression would resemble one my mother serious demeanors. I put my deer stare on full blast on both of the sex-craving animals, and I'm sure I had some very serious deer-stopping action protruding from my eyeballs. Then I spoke very clearly and loud enough so that I presented my statement as direct as I could muster up at the time, because the shit was so funny! I really had to gain control on my composure from laughing! I responded, "Y'all are out of y'all rabbit ass minds! You two silly MF need some serious carrots!" (After my experience at the Horner house! How dare they conjure up such a freaked out idea!)

With that being spoken, I went back to my bedroom, but there was no way I could go back to studying after that little incident. Instead, my thoughts were on figuring out a way to get some money so I could stop living in this circus.

I met a beautiful person, and I loved cherishing my new girl-friend, Keisha, but we had an awkward situation as well because I'm of the Christian faith, and she was of the Muslim belief. But all in all, she was one of the most beautiful and kindhearted people that I had met thus far since being home. She was pure with no ill manner or hidden agenda. Instantly, we fell in love. I was her rock, and she was truly my ground that holds me. And to keep the tension down under the circus tent, before I started sleeping with a water hose to protect myself from the "two live crew!" Keisha made it a point to come over every single day I was home. I felt a little bad for not being all the way truthful with Keisha because this beautiful person didn't know that I lived a double life. She had no indication whatsoever that her new boyfriend was a nail technician student by day and a low-level street pharmacists of little white balls and part-time robber by night.

After a few weeks went by, Keisha's presence started to fade due to her schoolwork and her job. That reopened the door to the hair-dresser and her weirdo child father, so casting hooks was back at work. A couple of days later, I was standing on the block, trying to sell a few cocaine rocks and waiting for someone to call me for a manicure when Chopper rode by and asked me to take a ride with him.(Chopper was one of my first childhood friends that I'd met when I moved to our new neighborhood. He stayed exactly across the street from me, and we were always cool, sort of like brothers.) During that ride, after I explained my living situation to him, he told me to pack my things up and move in with him and his grandmother who owned a mini mansion in Shaker Heights. While attending nail school, I met a gay guy that was a very decent individual and very funny at the same time. He became a good friend of mine. He knew I was down and out and trying to do the right thing with my life. He worked at a restaurant on the other side of town. He used to tell me and Chopper what time to come through, and he would pass us something to eat on the house. Then one morning, I messed it all up! Just like the cats in the movie Casino, I was eating good and let it all slip through my hands!

Chopper and I were keeping a regular weekday routine. We'd go to the restaurant to see my gay friend for breakfast, and then he'd drop me off at the bus stop so I could go to school. One morning, when we walked into the restaurant, I had no idea a new manager had taken over the establishment, so I didn't get into the regular line to conduct a playoff. Instead, I went to the counter where my gay friend worked. As soon as Chopper and I finished saying hi to our friend, I heard a sarcastic voice say, "You need to get from down there and go to the back of the line like everyone else!"

Instantly, my eyebrows formed a unibrow, and I walked down to the cash register where the new manager was. In a very polite voice, I said, "You didn't have to say it like that. I will jump over this counter and smack your face around." (The Red Power Ranger was starting to resurface.) Now this manager guy was not a little, skinny, scrawny of man at all. He was stocky and carried a very confident persona about himself, which I admired, even though his looks weren't holding up their end of his personality. I knew I would have my work cut out if we really got into a physical altercation. And just as that thought was crossing my mind, his retaliation for my provoking manner was a twist of his lips that stated, "Yeah right, I wish you would go for it." And with one swift jump, I swung my body over the counter. As my feet connected to the floor on the side where the fast-food workers made their living, my jaw was connected with a hard right punch from the manager, and my brain quickly registered the fighting proficiency of this guy. And he registered at a passing grade on my measuring scale! As this burger-and-fries manager guy and I were slugging it out, our punches were pretty much tit for tat. That was until the guy found some type of auxiliary power within himself and hit me in the left side of my head with a very hard punch, which turned my whole body around, and I was facing Chopper!

As Chopper was looking at me, I made sure that I put an expression on my face that said, "Nigga, why you just standing there? I can see that you're enjoying the show! But can I tag you in? I need help. MF! Chopper! Your dumbass can't read facial expression!"

I thought I had bit off more than I could chew! And in return, while he was standing there with his mouth catching flies, Chopper's expression told me, "Wow, B! I can't believe your stupid ass just jumped over a hamburger counter!"

And before I could read the rest of what his goofy expression was trying to tell me, I heard a female voice say, "The police are on their way!" That's when I realized I also had extra auxiliary power within myself. It's called "run, nigga, run"! So I spun my body back around, and the burger guy and I were face-to-face. Then, I quickly grabbed his pants pockets and spun his body around and stopped him in midspin with a sleeper choke hold. I guess he was already exhausted from swinging so many punches at me because he went to sleep in a matter of seconds. I don't believe in hurting a guy when they can't fight back, so I laid him down on the floor in front of the cash registers and told Chopper to close his mouth because it was time for us to leave like pronto!

The next day, I got a call from my gay buddy. He told me that I didn't have anything to worry about because the manager was so mean to all of the burger workers that when one of them saw the altercation getting ready to start, they went to his office and cut off all the cameras. It was very fortunate in my case to have a couple of unasked cheerleaders working on my behalf. The day after that, I was right back up there with a mask, collecting tuition for my nail school. But when I entered the place, the manager was inside the restaurant room, so I waited for him to come out.

Finally, he appeared from around the corner. I pointed my life like toy pistol at him, and I told him to open up the safe. He squinted his eyes, took a good look at my fake gun, and said, "You just going to have to shoot me because I don't have the keys to the safe or the registers in my pockets! So shoot me!" And while he was telling me he didn't have the keys, they were in his hand that he was holding over his head. (He was really an anal asshole because he told me a lie about the cash registers! I had just emptied them before he came from around the corner.)

But I had no time for argument. I'm not that kind of a robber anyway. Nor do I have any problems with taking a loss from anything that I can't legally control with the help of a lawyer. So I politely accepted my defeat and turned around without saying another word to Burgerman and exited the place with only half of the fortune that I needed for school. (Of course I had the full fair for my school tuition! Because I hit every single cash register in there including the freaking drive-through! But, within the next few minutes, I will have to share my loot with some very helpful "crooked strangers"). I made it to the corner where my getaway vehicle was waiting for me, and as I was getting closer to my escape capsule, I could see Chopper smiling. But within a blink of an eye, Chopper wasn't smiling any longer! His smiling was replaced with a very serious and nervous facial structure and he was shaking his head from left to right and pointing towards the distance, as if he was saying to me, "No, no, no." He threw the vehicle into the Drive gear and smashed the gas pedal, but he wasn't driving toward me to pick me up. He was driving toward me and pointing his finger forward as if he were telling me to look in the other direction.

As Chopper went flying past me, I quickly spun my entire body around, "and this time without the burger Manager's punch to my jaw helping me out", and less than three cars behind me was a Cleveland police cruiser. Instantly, my mind started turning and going to work. I started running toward the police cruiser, pulled my fake gun out to make sure that they could see it, and raised it up in the air over my head and started shaking it like that crazy guy in my neighborhood who made me shoot him. These officers were making me do the same dance with my arms raised high that I had just had the manager doing a few seconds ago!

Ironic, I say to you, just freaking ironic.

So I was now running down the street with my hand in the air and waving it as if I was in a classroom waiting for the teacher to pick me to answer the question. Quickly, the cruiser made a U-turn and was coming up rapidly on my heels. I was just about to cross the intersection when I threw the toy gun as hard as I possibly could because I knew they would have to stop their pursuit for a hot second and go retrieve some evidence. And just as I thought I had done something very creative, I could hear another patrol car in the distance coming to aid in the pursuit, and they were closing in very fast. I was running with every horsepower that I could produce inside my legs because I was not ready to go back to jail! Especially on a robbery charge! Besides, I figure I had too many hours in nail school already accomplished, and I was not about to let those hard earned hours go anywhere! I wanted my license! I wanted to do something right in life! As that thinking process was going on in my head, I heard the roar of the police cruiser motor right behind me, but then, it started to fade away, so I turned around to take a quick look to see what was going on. The patrol car was going in reverse because I had ran between some concrete barriers that their cruiser couldn't fit through. I made it to a house where two females were sitting on the porch and spoke, "Hey, I just robbed a restaurant, and I didn't hurt nobody. I didn't have a weapon. All them police sirens is for me! I didn't hurt anyone. I only took the money because I'm trying to continue paying tuition at nail school, and I'm willing to split it fifty-fifty right here, right now. So the three of us went into their basement and started dividing the pocket change that I just risked my life and my freedom for like a dumb ass. (That made number six when a soul started running.)

It was an early Monday morning so my school was closed, which in turn gave me more time to come up with some type of opportunity to get my tuition together. Because come Tuesday, the school would have its hand out looking for payment. I looked over at Chopper, and he was passed out, but it was time for him to get up so I could get busy. We jumped in his car and just started riding around. He was doing the driving while I was doing all the thinking. As I was riding shotgun, trying to conjure up a plan out of thin air, I looked to my right, and there was a police station there, but I really didn't pay it any mind. Across from the police station was a very well-known food chain. I looked at Chopper, and he knew what was on my mind. He said, "Are you serious? What are you going do if the police is sitting in there having breakfast?"

I responded with, "There are no police in there having breakfast because they don't sell doughnuts in there, duh!" We both started laughing. :)

"Okay, but how are you going to scare them? The police already got one of your fake guns, remember? Duh!" And we both started laughing again. :)

He let me out the vehicle a little ways down the street from the restaurant, just as I was about to go in there with nothing hoping to still come out unharmed and with an unauthorized loan. I spotted an oil rag and a very short stick lying on the ground.

Okay, I thought, *I'll scare them with this.* I walked in, and thirty or less seconds later, I walked back out, jumped back in the car with Chopper, and we drove back to his home.

When I finished counting, I had enough money to pay Chopper, put a little food in the house, and make the down payment for my school tuition. Tuesday morning, I was just as happy as a happy person could be. Because I was on my way to school gracefully taking a ride on the public transportation, and then I noticed everyone was looking at me with a puzzled and confused look written on their faces that ended with their glare not being for sure. But I really didn't pay close attention to it. I figured they were looking at me because I was a man wearing a beautician apron and carrying a nail kit case that had the beautician's school pink logo on it. I never cared what people thought about me because when it's time to go, it will only be me. So I truly didn't pay any mind to all the puzzling, gawking eyeballs. I was more concentrating on trying to get my life right. When I got to school, it was pretty much empty; majority of the students hadn't arrived yet. While I was at my locker placing my nail kit inside, one of the female students walked up to me. She was wearing the same expression on her face that the people were wearing on the bus I just got off. She was like, "Joker, do you know it's a picture of you posted on the front of the newspaper?"

Before I could think or blink, my whole body went numb, and my heart started beating very rapidly as if I just stuck my nose in the best power cocaine in the whole wide world! "And what did it say?" I asked, trying to pretend that I wasn't as scared as a mouse hand-feeding a starving cat.

"You robbed the restaurant on Kinsman, with a woman's dress on, duh!"

I asked her if she had told anyone else or if any of the students had seen the newspaper as well. She answered, "None that I know of." I told her she could have everything inside my locker. She gave me a hug and a kiss on my cheek, and tears just started running from her eyes. She told me to take care of myself. The only thought I had was bye-bye to my nail technician license. :'(

As I was exiting the building, I knew that would be my last day of nail school. I needed time to think and to get a hold of my conscience before my thoughts tried to run wild. I needed somewhere to go, but I didn't know where to go first because I was sure that all my avenues were on fire. With a ball cap pulled all the way down over my head, I got on a bus and headed toward downtown Cleveland. The first stop I made was at a newsstand that sat on the corner. And there I was, on the freaking front page, and right up under my photo was Stone. We're always told that no sin is bigger than the next, but Stone was in much more trouble. The newspaper stated that he was wanted for murder, and they had caught him and placed him inside the juvenile detention center, but he somehow managed to escape. I knew for sure that I couldn't go back to my neighborhood now! Here we were, two people from the same area that's already hotter than a frying pan at such a very young age. One wanted for armed robbery, the other wanted for murder, and who knows which one of our other partners from the block was committing some high crime at that very moment just to add something to the fire! So going to the neighborhood was a very big no-no. I didn't have a next move. I needed to soak all this in. I needed time to think and allow my common sense room for creativity! I really needed somewhere safe to go, so I called the one person I could truly trust and count on. My man, Beans! So I jumped on the rapid train and started making my way over to his house, and I had a good feeling because I knew as soon as I darken his doorway, he would be welcoming me with open arms. :)

As soon as I paid my fare, there was a female train conductor sitting on the front seat that was purposely invented for handicapped passengers. She started staring at me, so I told her that if she keep on staring like that she would have to give me her phone number, and that's when the beautiful smile mix with some semi-laughter appeared across her face. Somewhere during the ride, I had dozed off and completely missed my stop. And in my deep sleep, I kept hearing someone saying, "Excuse me, excuse me, hey, phone number guy."

As I slowly opened my eyelids and took a stretch, I noticed that it was the train conductor. She said, "This is the end of the line, and I'm pretty sure that you've missed your stop."

I responded, "Well, you're looking at me again, so are you going to give me a phone number?" She started smiling and wrote it down. As I placed the paper inside my pocket, I glanced at it so I could see her name. It read Diamond, which was fine with me because at that point in my life, anything with a sparkle of light to it was very welcome. We started a conversation, and I never left the train until it was time for her to get off work. I had her drop me off a few blocks away from Bean's house just in case she was one of them people who read the newspaper as soon as they walk through their front door after work.

It was a little late, but Beans was still quick to answer the door. The first thing he said was, "Wow, you and Stone got the block hot, people scared to go outside to make money! What you plan on doing, B man? You know you have to get out of Ohio!"

I said, "I know, but first, I have to come up with some money!"

"You need to rob a bank and find out where Stone is hiding out at and take him with you because at this point, you two don't have nothing to lose. But Stone really don't have nothing to lose!" I was in agreement with Beans. But first, I would have to have a talk with Stone one-on-one to make sure his head was together under this extreme pressure we were already carrying and with much more ahead! I couldn't have the knucklehead off his game! I didn't want anyone dying on my watch! So as long as Stone's body language was not releasing negative vibes within my conversation to him, I will go against all my morality grains and take him with me. Beans asked me if I've ever seen the movie *Heat* with Robert De Niro and Al Pacino. I said no, so he placed the VHS tape inside of the recorder. After watching that movie three times back-to-back, I knew right then I would never rob another restaurant again.

The next day, I got in contact with my big brother. He had moved deeper into the west side of Cleveland. He knew what was going on, but his wife didn't, so he told me to come stay with him until I could figure out what I planned on doing. After strongly imagining that I was a suitcase, Beans closed the trunk of his car. I had a very bumpy ride to my brother's house, but I had no real issue with the ride because it was all for the cause. For the next couple of days, my brother and his wife were very happy that I was there because I was instantly put into a butler's position, to which I didn't mind at all. My brother and his wife didn't have to rush in the morning any longer, making their way to work because I would get my two little nieces ready for school and spend the remaining hours babysitting my newborn nephew. (2015. As I'm sitting here going over the editing part of "When a Soul Stops Running" all I can do is shake my head and wonder. I wonder if I wasn't the person that I was back then, while I was babysitting my nephew, could I've really had a positive influence on his life, if my life was going in the right direction? Because I just received a phone call from my big brother that his son and three others "two females and one male" was just picked up for murder in Cartersville, Georgia. All I can do is pray to God that this is an identity mix up! :("Damn nephew? You only 20 years old. You have a whole life ahead of you! I pray that you are INNOCENT") I had talked to Diamond earlier that day, and she said she would be by as soon as she got off work. This would only be our second time seeing one another. And boy oh boy did I leave an impression on Diamond for the rest of her life. (You are the best "R" and from my heart, thank you for everything.)

The summer of 1995 was gone, and Autumn was in its early stages to take a backseat to the oncoming rough Ohio winter, but fortunately enough, we still had some nice weeks of seasonal days left. For some reason, mosquitoes were at an all-time high, and I didn't know what it was about me, but they were very attracted to my scent. Maybe it's because I ate so much fruit, and they could smell it. :) At least that was my dumb thinking. Going into another day, everyone was absent from the house, and I was just sitting inside my brother's home with a hungry stomach. There was plenty of food, but I'm a very picky person when it comes to a food intake. A Long John Silver's commercial continued to repeat itself every time *The Price is Right* went into commercial break, which was making that commercial seem hypnotic to me. That's when I knew that I was just too comfortable with my criminal situation because I headed out the door and walked up to Long John Silver's for some of that delicious, crunchy fish accommodated with some tasteful Hush Puppies during the lunch hour. I continued to keep my ball cap pulled down on my head, being very sure not to expose too much of my face. Being over here where my brother lived now, I truly didn't put too much emphasis on my disguise because my brother and his wife moved into a majority white neighborhood, and I was always told they believed us black folks all look alike.

After my belly was full and my taste buds satisfied, I started making my way back to the house wearing a smile. My brother's home was a two-family house that sat right next to the fire station, and I never knew anyone lived downstairs until I started walking up the stairs. Just as I reached to turn the handle on the outside screen door, it opened by itself, and a white male that stood exactly my height was face-to-face with me. We both smile and offered a warm hello and went our separate ways.

Later that night, I was staring out of the upstairs window when I saw Diamond's car pulling into the driveway. She came in and met my brother, his wife, and the children. As the two ladies were sitting there talking in front of the TV, I gave my big brother a nod to meet me in the kitchen. Then I started explaining to him how I had ran into his neighbor from downstairs.

He said, "Don't worry about it. I'm sure he didn't recognize you. Shoot, he probably thought you were me." Then, we started laughing! But before I could whisper another word my brother told me don't worry about it, so I threw the rest of that conversation on the back burner. For the remainder of our time, all of us adults were busy laughing and smiling from the reminiscing of me and my brother's past childhood stories, so going into the evening hours was running pretty smoothly. Me and Earl had separated from the group to engage in some man-to man private conversation, when out of nowhere comes a loud voice! My brother's wife started screaming in a low tone that eventually grew louder by seconds, "Oh my god, oh my god, Brian! They have a picture of you on TV!" My brother and I moved quickly and made it over to see what she was talking about, and there it was! A very vivid photo of me was on the right hand corner of the TV screen, and the rest of the screen was showing the robbery footage. The news cameraman was interviewing a civilian that said he had seen it all. As the civilian was snitching on me, he was looking dead blank into the TV camera. And since I was sitting right in front of the TV, it was as if me and the guy telling the story were looking directly into each other's eyes.

He was telling all the viewers that were watching news at 11, his bullshit story (which was pretty much authentic) that was allowing him to gain his couple of minutes of "Neighborhood Fame". I just continued to watch his lips when they started saying, "I know the guy. He used to sell them darn crack rocks around here. I probably wouldn't have known who he was if the stupid guy would've took the time to shave his beard off! I just don't understand why he didn't!" And as I was watching this guy talk, it dawned on me that he still owed me $60 for some crack rocks.

Now that the cat was out of the bag, it was time for me to explain everything to Diamond and my brother's wife. Diamond said that I wasn't the type, she instantly felt sorry for me and continued to whisper over and over with disbelief that they must have the wrong guy, even as the news put in America's face that I was "definitely that damn type". It was much later into the night, that even though I had all the odds pointed against me, Diamond wasn't so quick to turn her back on me. And even though she barely knew me, this beautiful person decided to stay over and whether this storm with me. One thing I learned that night was that this woman that I had truly just met, is something of a natural good, and that is something that is not easily found. You have a better chance at finding a needle in a haystack or finding a woman that was born in the 90s that actually knows how to cook a man a very decent meal. The one thing for sure and even till this day as I'm writing this story, "I truly appreciate Diamond for transforming herself into my protector. That night she became my Superwoman". The news was over and the early morning mist was making itself present into the 12 o'clock hour and as much trouble I was facing, I was still trying to be sexy! So while we were laying on the floor, I pulled my shirt off and put it under her head to use as a pillow. (Yes ladies and gentlemen, Casanova was doing his thing!) I did not know when we both fell asleep from the warmth of our bodies touching, but I was awakened by my brother's wife lightly kicking me in my ribs and whispering, "Brian, the police are outside, and they're knocking at the door!"

I jumped straight to my feet and put my Air Max's on. I didn't have time to grab a shirt because as soon as I tied up my last laces, the police had gained entrance through the back of the house and were knocking on the door that stood between me and them. As my brother was walking toward the door, asking, "Who is it," I was making my way toward the stairwell that led to the front of the house.

The officers behind the door responded very quick, "It's the police, and what is your name?" My brother gave them his first name, and the officer started addressing him by it. "You have one chance to open up this door right now, or we're knocking it down!"

My brother said, "Okay, okay," then turned and looked at me. I gave him the okay nod, and then, I headed down the stairwell. The officers in front of the house couldn't see me because the door had curtains up, but their flashlights were coming straight through the curtains at the bottom of the stairs and shining right in my face, reminding me of the time at the "Drug Building" when the police officer introduced his boot to my backside.

With my adrenaline going into full swing, I swore that I could actually feel the heat streamlining from their 10 D battery holding flashlights that probably had my name on it! I heard some commotion coming from upstairs. As soon as my brother opened the door, the police officers thought he was me because we looked so much alike to them. So I guess the saying is true because me and my brother do not look alike, but we do have the same skin tone. I could hear the officers' walkie-talkies going off on the other side of the door that I was standing in front of. "We got him. We got him. The suspect is in custody."

As the officers started running toward the back of the house, I darted out of the front door, and boy oh boy was I moving. I sprinted as fast as I could across the main street and ended up in the backyard of a used car dealership, and a couple of the officers weren't too far behind me. I was back there on my hands and knees like a baby, crawling around with all of the sirens and lights and voices shouting. I just knew officers were quickly coming from every darn direction possible! Trying to grab the title "I Got Him! I Made the Catch! He's Gonna Eat my Flashlight First".

There was so many uniformed bodies running around that the only thing missing was some bodies with badges dropping down out of the night sky with parachutes attached to them. Hiding in this car lot was becoming old really fast I wanted to jump up and start running, but I didn't know which way to go! I wasn't familiar with this territory at all. I was at such a horrible disadvantage. And to add more hardship on top of my situation, I finally realized that I wasn't wearing a shirt, and all these lights had awakened a mob of freaking mosquitoes.

I had to slow down moving and making noise because two or three officers had made their way to my exact location, but a few yards away. I started sliding around cars as slowly as I could. The beam of their flashlights hovering over my head in a synchronized crisscross fashion sort of reminded me of the beginning of a 20th Century Fox movie. I lay belly flat on the pavement as if I was a painted handicap symbol, so I could look underneath the cars to see exactly where they were at. When I squinted my eyes, I noticed that their feet was pointed toward the other direction, so I slid over and crawled inside some bushes. I still felt as if I wasn't covered enough, so I grabbed a handful of the bushes (which was the home of hundreds of little blood deprived mosquitoes) with my left and right hand and folded them over me like a sports jacket.

After a couple of seconds of squatting down in the bushes, I realized that I was inside somebody's home, and they were not offering a helping hand because these fucks had wings! I had just awakened one of the biggest family reunions of mosquitoes that anyone could ever think of! And boy oh boy were they happy to have me over for dinner. Due to me trying to be sexy earlier with Diamond, and due to me being very nervous and running like I was Flo Jo, I was sweating terribly with my top half naked like boiling chicken. There were so many mosquitoes charging in that I could actually hear the sounds of their wings moving back and forth in my ear, but I could not move because I knew there was 100 percent chance that I would be apprehended!

As the beam of the officers' flashlights continued to cross over my direction thus agitating the mosquitoes, I could actually make out the pattern of the swarm of these little bastards. With so much going on, it gave my mind the fuel to start playing tricks on me. The sounds of their wings was flickering back and forth so close to my ears that they started to sound like one voice that continued to repeat itself over and over while taunting me! And by the language of their wings, I could tell that these fucks came from down south! It was as if they were saying, "Feast, feast, feast! We about to eat your black ass Mr.! And we loves us some sweet dark meat! By the way, Brian, did you eat any fruit today, baby! Because you smell awfully fruity and sweet! Yeah! We're more than certain your very delicious and nigga, so your ass is grass pretty boy!" (The little needle nose fucks, reminding me of Fly and Skeleton)

And that's exactly what those greedy little bastards started to do! They were hungry, and tonight's events turned me into a gourmet meal for these suckers! I started experiencing bites all over my torso. Next, they were starting on my neck, and then they were sticking their little needle nose asses in my lips. I experience so many stabs to my nipples that it felt like a woman was sucking on them! They were truly abusing me! This was very unacceptable being eaten alive and molested by insects all at the same time! They were truly taking more than what they needed! Greedy little fuckers! (They continued to play me, like people were trying to play the system with their EBT food stamp cards in the year 2013 when the system shut down and the computers couldn't read the dollar amount on the card! People display a no-holds-barred while loading up their food carts with much more than their EBT spending limit allowed! Shoot, some individuals were still shopping and standing in line to checkout when the system started raining on their parade and came back online! The fat lady was sure singing, and the show was over! I was watching the news as people just left their food carts in the middle of the supermarket aisles.) And that's exactly how I pulled the carpet out from under those greedy little mosquitoes and left them in the bushes because I couldn't take it anymore! My DNA was at stake and it was losing ground fast! I would rather risk getting chased by every officer in Ohio than to fill up another Southerner mosquito freaking belly.

I jumped up and made a dash like a hot streak of fresh lightning, and thanks to the unwanted motivation from my Down South pointing nose friends, my Air Max got me out of that jam as if each shoe was fitted with a little nitro inside of the air sole. The officers didn't see me as I came flying out of the bushes and made it to the building where more expensive cars were stored. As I started scaling the side of the dealership structure, I managed to do something so goofy that I wish I truly didn't do. I tripped the alarm and turned this dealership building into one of the world's biggest snitches! Now I had more alarms and flashing lights to add to what the police already had gone on! And all I could do is accept my blunder, because goofy-is- what-goofy-does! With all the blue, red and white lights flashing back and forth you would've thought it was the great Independence Day going on outside. And this one police cruiser was touching me personally, because it had the nerve to only have red and white lights blinking on and off, constantly reminded me of the little red button and that hot flash of my mom's camera that I shouldn't have touch! I paused for a quick second and gave a middle finger to all the sirens and flashing lights for disrupting my transparent mobility! Because now everybody could see everybody, so I just took off running. They weren't too far behind me as I doubled back to crossing the main street again, but this time, I wasn't heading right back toward my brother's house. I ran into the backyard of the fire station. As I was looking around, I didn't see anywhere to go, and the police had made it to the driveway just as fast! I was peeping around the corner of the firehouse and watched as they started walking slowly in my direction, being sure to be cautious, which meant I could get shot fast. But in the midst of their hesitation, it allowed me a couple of seconds to catch my breath and think! Finally, my second wind took control of my lungs. As the light of their flashlights were getting closer, I spotted a tall wooden picket fence, and I just knew that they couldn't make it over it with all the hardware they were toting around.

I started reciting to myself, "Wait for it, wait for it. Go!" As soon as I heard the officers say, "Don't move!" I took off and jumped the fence, but it was taller than I expected, so my acrobatics didn't allow me to maneuver over it the proper way. As I was coming down on the other side too fast, the fence had a nail sticking out of it, and it sliced me right in the middle of my chest. You can still see the permanent tattoo that darn wooden fence gave me today. I guess that was the fence's special little way of letting me know whose team it was really on! :)

After being chased for the last few minutes, I sorta figured out the strategy and patterns they were utilizing trying to figure me out. I made it to a parking lot of a convenience store and laid face flat down on the ground in a parking space. After a couple of minutes, my second wind was fully charged again, and I came out into the open with my hands raised high above my head. When they spotted me, all I was thinking was, *Wait for it, wait for it. Go!*

As they started walking closer to me, I kept taking steps back, making sure that I continued holding my hands in the air so they could see that I had no weapon. As I was just about face-to-face with fifteen officers or more, I ran up a driveway and jumped on top of a fence and onto a garage. I continued ducking in and out of people's backyards, making short special appearances to be sure that they could see me! I had this act going for about two miles in the opposite direction of my brother's house. Then I lost them and ran back to my future savior, Diamond.

As soon as I tapped the door because I was afraid to knock, my brother opened up very fast as if he was already waiting for me. He looked at me smiling and was like, "I told y'all he'd be back!" And we both started laughing! Diamond was just staring at me, her facial expression was saying, "Who are you? Should I be afraid?" But once she moved toward me and gave me a hug, her body language was telling me, "I got your back! I'm going to help you figure this out."

I gave my brother a hug and focused on becoming car baggage once more. I laid down in the trunk of Diamond's car, and we were on our way to her house. Once we were sitting in her living room, I explained to her that I had a girlfriend, and she decided to understand my position and get along with Keisha for my sake. (That was number seven when a soul started running.)

CHAPTER 29

THE FACADE

When I woke up the next morning, Diamond was gone to work, and there was an older woman sitting in front of me, just staring at her new visitor. Although, the expression she displayed on her face didn't make me feel uncomfortable because her body language was at ease, the only thing I could sensed was curiosity. The older woman turned out to be Diamond's mom, so it was time for a much-needed conversation between the two of us. I'm not into just flat-out lying to anyone, so I gave her a conversation as to why I was becoming her new roommate, sprinkled with a version of the truth. I was very thankful that Diamond's mom worked so much that she never took time to read a newspaper or watch the news.

After a couple of days, I figured it was safe enough, so I decided to finally go outside and inspect my new temporary neighborhood. That's when a thought invaded my thinking pattern because I think out of the box, and that's out of the box, that's looking at both boxes when need be. So before I stepped foot out to begin my tennis-shoe expedition, I started thinking about the guy on the news who owed me $60. Reminiscing on his conversation to the news camera, the guy said if I would've cut my beard off, he wouldn't have known who I was. Therefore, I had no choice but to play detective, and I started looking through the cabinets and found some fresh new razors and proceeded to remove my beard just like he suggested. When I was done, I washed my face, then took a quick look in the mirror. I honestly didn't recognize the much younger reflection that was looking back at me. I had the appearance of a sixteen-year-old.

Their house was located at the end of the street, so I started walking in the opposite direction where it seemed to have more activity going on. When I finally made it to the main street a couple of blocks down, I didn't know where I had relocated too! I walked over to take a glance at the street sign, and it read "St. Clair." Right then a comical smirk appeared across my lips, because even though I had just escaped from a rough neighborhood, I only accomplished to reappear in a neighborhood that was rougher than mine. (Slide over, smoking hot frying pan! And hello Active Volcano.) Due to all my prior Street activities, I turned out to be pretty good at improvising many situations, so now it was time for me to go to work and see what was going on around here. I'd heard the stories about this side of town, and one thing for sure. It was money on this side, and all I had to do was find it!

There was a small shopping plaza on the corner of Seventy-Sixth Street, so I decided that I needed some potato chips. As I was coming out of the store, I noticed a bus stop that the younger crowd in this particular neighborhood were using as a hangout. I decided to walk over there to be nosy and begin my investigation of learning about my surroundings so I can find a connect. But instead of going in the bus stop with them, I stood on the outside like I was waiting for the bus so I could eavesdrop on the spoken conversations. After a brief few minutes, I could tell this group was safe, so I gave them one of my mental green lights for being cool people. Pulling a joint out of my pocket and smoking it in front of them was a natural occurrence for this group. One of the girls came over to me and asked me if she could hit it. The guys didn't say anything to me, nor did they hide their suspicious expressions. I told the girl that she could have it and walked back to Diamond's house.

The next day, I repeated my same routine, this time leaving my joint with one of the guys that asked me what my name was. I responded, "Joker." This went on for a few days, and after about two weeks, everyone in that part of the neighborhood had accepted me. Now it was time for me to start making some money around here! Due to my laid-back personality and the fact that I had soft facial features, everyone sort of thought I was a nerd, (Box Car: "This game requires acknowledgment of different types of occupations" "You won't be shit in this game if you do not think properly") and I played my part very well. I knew when I started asking questions there would be no red flags detected in my demeanor, so they made it very easy for my true intentions to pass undetected.

One day, while we were all sitting at the bus stop getting high, one of the guys had just made a sale to a customer. I asked the guy, "Why is it that every time you go running over to someone, you always come back counting money in your hand?"

He responded, "I be hitting licks."

"Hitting licks? What in the world is that?"

I played "plumb dumb" to the knowledge of the dope game, and every last one of the guys and girls wanted to be my teacher. They wanted to see this new nerdy cool guy make some money, and after each one of them shared some of their street knowledge with me, they were surprised how I seemed to learn pretty darn fast. Within a month or so, I went from sitting at the bus stop serving to regular customers with them to actually becoming the supplier to my previous dope game teachers. Even the heavier hitters in that neighborhood were taking notice of my craftsmanship in their neck of the woods. But I remained respectable to the game, so from time to time, I would spend a couple of thousand with the "heavy hitters of St. Clair" because a brother in my position did not need any new unwanted problems!

The only time I would go to the bus stop now was just to sell them a package so they could double their money. One day, I was running low on product, so I went back to my own neighborhood to find me a connect and see some familiar faces. When I got there, I ran into Beans and a couple of the other younger guys from the neighborhood. The four of them looked a little upset, so I asked him what was going on. He explained to me that there were some older guys that moved into the neighborhood and they were selling drugs on their corner and totally disrespecting the turf. I just shook my head at these younger guys and told them to go get me a gun. One of them walked behind the house we were standing in front of and brought me a twelve-gauge shotgun. I placed the shotgun up under my arm and started walking down 131st toward the house where the new guys were, which just so happened to be the same house where I stopped Stone from dropping that big ass brick on old boy head.

As I got closer, I could see a few of the new people sitting on the porch. I walked up toward their stairs and asked them who was holding something. I told them I had $20. When I was close enough, I lifted up the shotgun and told them to slowly remove themselves from the porch. This resulted in about five of them standing in front of me. I started explaining to them that they had to move and find somewhere else to set up shop. Little did I know, one of their crew members was on his way back from the gas station across the street, the same gas station where three people just got murdered not too long ago, when a previous drug transaction went very wrong and the ones on the short end of the stick were thirsty and seeking vengeance for blood like them darn mosquitoes. While I was standing there with the shotgun trained on them, I was hit in the back of my head very hard. I lost all the feelings in my legs and fell to the ground, but just as fast as I hit the ground, I was right back up and on my feet because my adrenaline was super high like I just had a cup of Starbucks heavy on the espresso shots. Unfortunately, it was too late because the same guy who hit me in the back of my head now had my twelve-gauge pointed right back at me. You could tell that the guy was very nervous, which in turn had me a little nervous because I didn't doubt he would pull the trigger. As I stood there with my hands in the air wishing God would pull me up, he said, "Somebody call the police! And don't you dare move, Mr. Dixon!"

Okay, I thought to myself. *I see what's going on. This lame dude is thinking about some reward money.* I could see what the front newspaper would read in the morning: EXTRA EXTRA, READ ALL ABOUT IT. CURRENT DRUG DEALERS THAT TOOK OVER YOUNG GUY'S TURF CATCHES WANTED ROBBERY SUSPECT THAT DRESSES IN DRAG.

As I was staring down the barrel of the gun that this lame just stolen from me (which the real owner will not be getting back), the guy saw my feet shift. Immediately, he shouted at me with a mixture of fear and anxiety within the controls of his "unstable shaky actions", "Please don't run nigga!" As soon as he said don't run, a police car came speeding down Harvard and made a hard right onto 131st Street, exactly where we had our little standoff going on. When the guy looked away for a split second at the flashing cruiser, I turned my back and started running! This guy that was trying to make a citizen's arrest was less than twelve feet away from me, so when I turned to run, the blast he released from the shotgun had my ears ringing. I was running as fast as I could. As I was fleeing, I started running my hands all over my body, searching for a signs of blood. But my palms came up empty.

I quickly ran up a long steep driveway without an ounce of hesitation to slow me down! I was in the backyard of a storefront where we hang out and got rid of crack rocks, and this time, a little smirk appeared across my lips. Because this time, I actually had an advantage because this was my actual stomping grounds, unlike the unknown obstacles that I faced on the west side of Cleveland, at the "mosquitoes family picnic!" To my surprise and so very quickly, I could hear police everywhere, and I knew that they were looking for me because my Spidey sense toned in and said, "hey jackass! You better figure something out quick! Because the police are not just looking for a man that's running. They're trying to catch that "wanted street animal" Mr. Brian Dixon. Think nigga think!" So I anticipated on their search being very intense, which meant I had to intensify my creativity in order to see another jail-free day.

Once again, it was time for the *Tom and Jerry* cat-and-mouse show, costarring the very determined Keystone cops! I knew they were very determined because they were running me in the paper every week, turning me into a newspaper super star! And they were still showing the robbery footage on the news like it was one of the Superbowl coolest commercials. I'm a Pisces. I like a lot of pure good old affection, not negative promoted attention! But how dare I attempt to play a small violin when I'm the goofball that created this Frankenstein of a problem. I knew if they caught me tonight, I was going to get beat up, and the officers would become heroes. And I honestly wasn't trying to give them any awards, nor did I want any for myself for being plain old stupid!

I quickly surveyed the backyard to see what would make for the best option, and within my surveillance I heard the noises of fast running footsteps coming closer to my location so I quickly crawled under a camper that was sitting on some bricks. And that's when I spotted a little empty space that I was sure I could putty knife myself into, so I started shoving my body into that little hole while using an imaginary shovel, and it was not an easy job! Once I got settled in, I had to perform a Spiderman using my hands and feet to produce some pressure to keep me up in there. But there it was, I finally managed to lock myself into place and started my very short and quiet hibernation process. If all goes well within the next couple of seconds? I will be able to emerge from this cocoon with wings, and fly my stupid ass back down to St. Clair.

As my breathing was starting to slow down I didn't dare move! And just as soon as I gained total control over my very nervous and shaky bodily functions, two officers magically appeared from the thin air, And boy oh boy were they close! These two cats were so close to this mouse that if I was a snake, a hospital somewhere would be having two hard working gentleman that got hurt on the job arriving ASAP. Sometimes it's a sad story that I find just about everything funny, so it was a little hard holding my composure but I had no choice but to wait for these two very eager gun toting-silly rabbits to jump back into the hat from which they magically appeared from. With a lot of overuse energy floating between the three of us, mind tricks was at all time high!

One officer said to the other, "I know darn well he ran back here! I watched his ass run straight up into this driveway!" "Are you sure? I know that Boy was moving pretty fast."

When I heard them beautiful words, I allowed myself to enjoy a little undetectable chuckle within the seriousness of this situation. (And the only reason I allowed myself such a chuckle, is because the doctor said, "he would never run or jump like regular children") After their flashlights came up without a reason to proceed forward with their investigation in this backyard we all were sharing for a brief moment, the one officer whispered to his partner "shush! Listen. Do you hear that? He had to jump the fence! There's no other explanation." And just as quickly as they had come—*Abracadabra!*—them cats were off and running to catch that invisible mouse.

A few minutes after that, I heard someone whispering my name, and I was very familiar with the voice. It was my man, Beans, so I gave my inner Spiderman the rest of the night off and with a well-deserved thumbs up to him for a job well done. I released my grip and drop down from that tight little space that I truly cherished. When I stood up, we started laughing. He said, "Man, I saw the whole thing. We thought you got shot!"

I started laughing. "Me too, nigga! I don't know how he missed me. He probably wasn't pointing at me when he shot." I got into the car with Beans, and he drove me back to St. Clair. (That escalated into the eighth time when a soul started running.)

When I entered the house, no one was home, and thank God for that! Because with all the ruckus I just endured, my dirty clothing would've given any Bigfoot monster truck tires a run for its money! And what in the world could I have ever told her mother about my muddy clothing? I knew Diamond was at work because she had transferred over from driving the train to working the bus transit line. I was also happy that her mother wasn't home either, and it had nothing to do with the looks of my clothing.

(Diamond's mom was a cool, churchgoing lady. I even attended church with them a few times, but we all know how some church people truly are! LOL. Diamond's mom had developed some type of illness or determination to get what she wanted. Every time we were in the house alone, she would walk around with only her silky legless pajamas top on, and every time she came around me, for one reason or another, her shoulder strap would always fall down and expose one of her nipple-knee scraping, extra-extended boobs. All the while she'd be looking me straight in my face with a goofy "oops oops oops" followed by a nonshy "hey, boy, come over here quick and help me fix this shoulder strap" expression coming strongly and direct from her eyeballs).

After telling Beans I'd catch him later, I locked the door behind me, feeling super tired. And even though my clothing was muddy and my shoes were wet, I didn't even bother taking anything off. I was just so darn tired, as if some type of Kryptonite energy beam was draining me of all my Superman powers or, even worse, as if all them damn down south mosquitoes had did a Transformer move by connecting themselves together to form a Mega-Needle-Nose and started sucking my life force dry! I didn't want to dirty up anything in their home, due to my laziness of taking a shower, so I was thankful that their wooden floor didn't have any carpet on it. So I just laid down and close my heavy eyelids then proceeded to black out. I don't know how long I was laying there dead to the world, but I was awaken by Diamond lightly shaking me, and she had tears in her eyes! "Why are you bleeding? Look at all this blood! Where is it coming from?"

I tried to answer her questions, but for some reason, I could not speak any word at the time. And she didn't waste any time wondering about anything else (my protector). She helped me to my feet, and we walked to her car. I do not know how close or how far we were from the hospital, but she got there pretty quick and slammed her car in Park right in front of a fire hydrant and I watched as she disappeared through the emergency door, caring less about a ticket or a tow-away-truck. She ran in and a split second later, she was being followed by two nurses and a wheelchair. When the nurses reached into the back of the vehicle to help aiding me in my removal, they decided against using a wheelchair. They laid me on a gurney and pushed me straight to the emergency room. They wasted no time cutting my clothes away and preparing my arms for IVs. I still did not know what was going on, and I wasn't able to ask any questions. I was just so tired.

As I started slipping into unconsciousness, I remember being turned on my side and a voice saying, "We are going to have to break through his breastplate." I don't know how long I was out of service when I slowly started opening my eyes, but I did notice I was inside a different room. I looked to my right, and there stood a police officer in conversation with two doctors. I was very exhausted, but I still had enough strength to move my arms and my legs around. I noticed that I wasn't handcuffed to the bed, so that meant that they didn't know who I was just yet. But I knew right then and there that I better turned into my little brother because he was too young to have any warrants! With the absence of the handcuffs also meant Diamond dropped me off and left before anyone could ask her any questions. Smart girl! My protector! :)

I decided on playing possum and focused in on the police officer and the doctor's conversation. I overheard the doctor explaining to the policeman, "It's a miracle that he's still alive. The X-rays shows that he has a metal pellet that entered through his back, and it cannot be removed because its sitting right between his heart and his lungs. And his breathing was the most shallow I've ever experienced in this field of work. He literally wasn't getting any oxygen to his brain, but it's undetermined for how long. The CAT scan says he's fine. His lungs were so full of blood it's a wonder he didn't drown himself. But mysteriously enough, at the end of the day, he will be going home."

I tried to turn over a little on my side, so I could get a better look at them. That's when I let out a loud grunt. In the middle of my ribs, I was cut open, and I had two large plastic tubes sticking inside my body right up under my arm. That's when the doctor started walking toward me. He said, "Hold on a second, son. Try not to move so much. You have two tubes running through your breastplate. One is to drain the blood from your lungs, and the other one is to inflate them. I don't believe you have knowledge that you've been shot, son."

After a brief conversation with the doctor, he gave the okay for the officer to make his way over to me, but I wasn't worried about his questions. At this time, Cleveland was terrible with shootings. The first thing he asked was my name, so I offered him my little brother's name. The second thing he asked was where I lived. I told him thirtieth projects with my girlfriend and her four children and sometimes her baby daddies and her cousin come by and spend the night which is cool because we all know one another. That's when he gave me that expression that I was looking for! I knew I was in the clear. To him, I was just another statistic, which worked fine for me! The third thing he asked was where I was when I got shot and who was the woman who brought me to the hospital. I told him walking down St. Clair Street and that I don't have the slightest idea who she wa. He was satisfied and told me that they're going to try to find the shooter. And not one time did he ask me how old I was. If the officer or the doctor would've paid the mounted wall television some attention when they were in my recovery room conducting the lightweight interrogation with me, they would've notice me on the screen. As I watched the officer leave my room, I finished watching the news. Then, I couldn't help but back out.

After a day or so, the two tubes were removed from my body, and I was given a clean bill of health with precautions to be taken. Then I was released from the hospital. When I got back to Diamond's house, she wasn't home, but her mother was, and she told me it was time for me to go. I understood, and I knew part of it was due to the fact that she was hungry like the hairdresser and her weirdo baby daddy, and I wasn't feeding her. I asked her to tell Diamond that I said take care, and I'll see her later. She said she wasn't going to be able to do that because Diamond told her that she was going with me. After shaving my beard off once more, I made a few dollars on the block and purchased an apartment for the two of us. Diamond knew I needed to travel around, so I used to drop her off at her transit station, and she would leave her vehicle with me so I could take care of my business. I had a lot of respect for Diamond because even though Keisha didn't shy away from displaying her rejection of the situation, Diamond remained a beautiful-hearted person throughout the ordeal. :)

The first thing on my agenda was to get one of the drug users to put an electricity bill in their name. I needed more money, so I decided to drive to my neighborhood to re-up. I was sitting at a light on Miles road. (Right in front of a building where I will be hidden from the law in the very near future by a long lost friend. And Stone was hiding less than a block away from there on the same street.) When the light turned green, I started driving just as calm and casual as I could, and out of nowhere, I saw blue and red lights flashing in my rearview mirror. All I was thinking was, *Fuck! Here we go again! Cat and freaking mouse!*

So I pulled over to the side of the road and watched as the officer got out of his cruiser. I recognized him! He stayed right around the corner from me when I was a child. I was just going to wait until he arrived at my driver's window, like the officer did when I was in the Cherokee, and just punch the gas pedal on him. He was overweight and older, so I figured by the time he made it to his police cruiser to chase me or call it in, the starch from the donuts would've taking over to slow him down, and I'll be long gone. But surprisingly, when he got to my driver's window, he continued to walk past me. I didn't even notice that a car had pulled over ahead of me, which was this officer's true target. I turned on my left signal, lightly touched my gas pedal, made a right on the corner, then punched the gas pedal.

On my way back down to St. Clair, I gave Beans a call, explained my situation, and we both started laughing. Later that day, he brought me a small package that I could work with. A few hours later, one of the guys from the bus stop and I were walking up and down St. Clair, looking for customers so I could get my electricity turned on. Unfortunately, the only customer that fitted the criteria was the neighborhood bully. He loved his drug habit and knew how to maintain it. He lifted weights and ate well too. He's what we call a very functional crackhead. I never really dealt with the guy because I knew he was a problem, but the guy that was walking with me knew this clown. They must have been real cool because while they were talking, the crackhead playfully smacked the young guy I was with in his young face, and then he started walking toward me, smiling.

I explained the situation to the lame, so he told me his terms and conditions in a sort of ruthless tone. But I didn't mind because

I needed this chump. We loaded in the car and headed downtown to the Illuminating Company. I found a good parking spot right on the side of the company building. The bully crackhead told us to stay in the car while he went in and pulled some strings together. Then, he would come out and tell me how much money he needed. I could already sense that this clown was conjuring up some type of buffoonery, so I just had to make sure that I played my cards right with Mr. Bully.

Once the young guy and I were in the car alone, I asked him why he let that guy smack him like that. He just shrugged his shoulders, looking very embarrassed at the same time. Then the youngster spoke, "He be disrespecting a lot of guys around the hood. He used to be a gangster but then he started smoking crack." Now I understood exactly why this guy acted the way he be acting around the neighborhood. Because these cats around here still regarded him as an OG, just like we have regards for Mac Truck on my block. Now for the most part, individuals honestly view me as a really cool cat, but the dog inside of me is not cool at all when it comes to people being disrespectful, and the true story is, "I wasn't from their neighborhood! I'm just a semi-crazy-ass visitor!" Which made him just an OG crackhead to me! And I didn't respect this guy because of the way he carried himself! I only truly give respect where respect is due. So I kept my respect under control with this chump because I needed him, but that was only as long as he maintained himself. A few minutes had gone by, and the guy was walking back toward the car. He motioned for me to come inside the Illuminating Company, so the youngster and I both got out and followed him in.

Everything had checked out, and he was just waiting for some paperwork to come back. As we were sitting there, I decided to buy a bag of Cheetos from the hot dog vendor. (All the black people I know love Cheetos! LOL!) As soon as I opened up the bag, the young guy asked me if he could have some, so I poured him out a few. As soon as I held the Cheetos bag in the upright position, the crackhead put his thumb, index finger, and middle finger straight down inside my bag without asking, and he had no way of knowing that I just counted one strike, two strikes, three strikes! You're out! Now your ass is grass! And I'm about to stump through it!

As he was pulling up the stolen disrespected Cheetos, a few of them fell on the ground, and he just started laughing as if it was the funniest joke in the world. I didn't say anything. I just chimed in, laughing at his little joke with him, but I was laughing at him because he was going to meet the Joker as soon as we got back to the car. When I glanced over at the younger guy, he was wearing an expression on his face that stated, "I told you so!" I just gave the little cat a wink of the old eye.

After we concluded our business at the Illuminating Company, we made our way back to the car. One thing I do believe in and offer is my respect. I don't demand it, but I do respect it and really appreciate it when individuals utilize and offer theirs in return because it always brings a smile to my face. A simple hello or a good morning and even a small gesture of "How're you doing today?" means the world to some individuals because we know there are still people in this world that care about other people just for the sake of caring. And respect toward older people is something that I cherish. Even though this crackhead wasn't an old man, I still allowed him to ride in the front seat on our way downtown, especially for what he was about to do for the cause, so I had no issue playing the part of a chauffeur to this lame. But due to his actions, he now had to ride in the backseat, and for his sake, he's very fortunate that a child safety seat wasn't present because that would've been his seat on the way back.

As we neared the vehicle, I told the younger guy to sit shotgun in the front. As we all loaded into the car, I kept it simple, and my true angered intentions went undetected by both of these gentlemen.

I continued to act normal and thankful for what he had just done as I turned the ignition on and started checking all the mirrors and windows, making sure I didn't see any police cars around. I politely asked the tough ass bully to sit in the middle of the backseat so I could make sure there were no cars coming from behind me so I could pull out safely.

As soon as this guy was in position, I killed the engine and jumped like a black panther straight from the jungle! I went straight over my driver's seat and landed in this guy's lap. I quickly grabbed both of his arms and locked them underneath my knees. I then quickly slapped him, then backhanded him, then I slapped him again with the force of a Power Ranger for good measure.

"You see how it feels? Now apologize to the youngster for smacking him earlier. Now apologize to me for not asking me for some of my Cheetos." Then, I looked him straight in his eyes and told him, "I apologize for doing this, but you already know that you brought this on yourself. I do hope we can still be cool because I need you." I didn't wait for answer because if he would've opened up his mouth and said the wrong thing, my anger would've sure enough transformed into a pure evilness. I jumped back in the driver seat and asked the youngster if he would like to smack him a few times. He just shook his head no while he was laughing. I gave the guy in the backseat a high-five hoping to end this little altercation in a truce and to ensure that he completely understood what he was dealing with. (A true fucking nutcase with morals.) Then, I drove us all back to the neighborhood like we were a happy family. Fair exchange is never no robbery, people.

The next day, I could tell that the word had gotten around very quickly because everyone was looking at me with a shocked expression. They didn't think that I was capable of doing something like that. (Never totally judge a book by its cover!) So because of the way I carried myself, these guys on St. Clair figured I was cool and non-threatening. But because of my actions that I delivered to the OG, that little incident marked the beginning of my end on St. Clair Street. The newspaper was running articles on me again, and Mr. Cheetos snatcher was showing the article to everyone he could possibly find. Right then and there, I just walked away from the neighborhood. I was so fortunate to have a jumpstart! In 1995, down on St. Clair Street, the NOVFTF (Northern Ohio Violent Fugitive Task Force) ripped through the homes to which they thought I was hiding! They were really working that hit list of theirs! It would be a couple of months before I saw Diamond again.

A few hours after I left St. Clair, I decided to ride through just to be nosy, and the NOVFTF and Cleveland police were everywhere. I had gotten in contact with my little brother, and he took me to his friend's house over on Cedar Avenue. But that only lasted a few weeks because one day, when I went to the store, the NOVFTF and Cleveland police came kicking down that door. They were keeping me so busy running and moving to new locations that I wasn't getting my proper rest. But I had to keep moving because they were not playing. They were truly full steam ahead in their pursuit. People told me either they had just left, or they had gotten word that they were on their way whenever I was about to seek shelter. I must say they were really doing their homework. I was only escaping them by pure coincidence. My thoughts of calling them the Keystone cops had long faded away. I now had a newfound respect for the officers.

I never believed in luck, but my luck was running out, and my options was very far behind from my actual footsteps that was moving briskly. Fortunately enough, I was able to relocate to East Cleveland and started playing with little white balls out of a very well-known drug-infested apartment complex. But that only lasted a few weeks as well. This mouse maze that I was tripped in walls was getting to close for comfort! When my friend and I were walking up to the complex doors, one of the occupants stopped me and told me that the FBI and police had just left. My rope was getting very tight and short, and I knew that it was really time for me to leave Ohio. Now I needed time to ponder up a plan. I started riding the bus for the next couple of days. I was doing the transfer after transfer dace shuffle and always sitting in the back. I was trying to focus so I could devise a proper plan for my escape.

One day, on the back of the bus, a guy was like, "B, what's good!" It was a guy that I knew from my old neighborhood (who supposed to have moved to California some time ago, but here he was on the bus with me and he was familiar with my newfound situation) named Dewdrop. But besides all of that, I was just happy to see a familiar face that I positively knew wouldn't turn me in for some award money. He thought they had caught me, and I explained to him that I didn't have anywhere else to go for the moment, so he took me to Pastor's house. Pastor was happy to see me. He used to be one of the coordinators at the Boys and Girls Club, and he was more than happy to have me stay with him for a while because he could be his happy self around me. Pastor was gay, but I guess nobody knew it except for the guys he had engaged with at the Boys and Girls Club. He hid his secret life so well, and apparently, so did some of my younger childhood friends. I started wondering why he told me his secret but quickly put it behind me because I had bigger problems than discussing his sexual preferences. When Pastor was on the phone, you would've sworn he was a woman, and I was all new to this coming from him. Finally, he explained to me his reason for carrying on his feminine-like ways, and I respected it. It was cool being at Pastor's house for the weeks I was there, but I always remained on pins and needles because being there had me right back in the neighborhood, and I truly didn't know Pastor at all after he revealed his secret! For me to be considering him a friend was truly a no-no. Pastor stayed in a building on Miles Road right in front of where I pulled away from the police officer that lived around the corner from me.

Finally, I came up with a plan, but I wanted to see my big brother before I initiated it and left Ohio. My brother had moved back into the neighborhood, so I didn't have far to travel to see him. I knocked on his door, and he called everyone down the stairs to give me hugs. My brother looked me in my eyes and said, "Brian, they're swarming over this whole neighborhood looking for you and Stone. Little brother, you have to leave Ohio, or they might tighten up on you sooner or later, bro."

I replied, "I know." But it felt good coming from someone who truly cared about me. I grabbed him and gave him a big hug and a kiss on his cheek. This guy always had my back. I told him that I would see him in ten years, hoping I could last the time of the Ohio statutes of limitations. He asked me what I was going to do for money in order to leave. I politely told him that I was going to go rob a bank, and then I will be a memory to Cleveland. He just shook his head and told me to be careful. His answer was so subtle because he knew that I wasn't going to hurt anyone just as well as he knew that I was on my way to do it.

"Tell my mother I love her, and I will see all of you guys in the future. That statute of limitations should be over with when I come back around to get on her nerves again" We both started laughing as I started getting into my travel. As I was walking back to pastor's house, I ran into Keisha, and she started walking with me. She had been riding with me the whole time, well at least the best she could allow herself. She was in tow with me from the hairdresser's house, to Diamond's mother's house, to the apartment Diamond and I shared, to my brother's friend's house, to the apartment complex in East Cleveland, and was still with me while I was hiding at Pastor's house. She never left my side. We were truly in love, well, puppy love for that matter, and she had no issue displaying how she cared for me. As we got within about three blocks from Pastor's door, we ran into a quick conversation with a guy named Jews.

Jews from the neighborhood. He revealed to me where Stone was located, and surprisingly, his hideout was right down the street from my hideout. We followed Jews over to the expected location and waited in the front while Jews quickly made a phone call, and when the door opened, Stone was standing at the back wall with an assault rifle. I just started laughing and asked him if he was trying out for a part in the next Rambo movie. He was trying his best to bring forth a laugh while looking super nervous the whole time. There were three or four of us in this apartment that were wanted by the law, trying our best to avoid that long legal arm. Out of nowhere, there came a knock on the door that had us all on pins and needles and ready to shoot or run! (You know that feeling that we all get when somebody is standing behind you making the hairs on your body get all prickly?)

When the door opened, it was Beans, and we burst out laughing. He was dropping off the *Heat* movie that I asked him for. I needed to study it before the morning sun came up. I explained to Stone that I will be taking him with me, but he was definitely not allowed to bring any weapons with him whatsoever! Because anyone I gave a job to couldn't be into physically hurting anyone for financial gain or any other reason. I only used the element of surprise, and my blueprints always fall through. I knew Stone lived by a different rule because he was a hothead, but reluctantly, he agreed and wanted to stay with me that night, but I was totally against that lame ass ideal. We were both in enough hot water and separation was the best move for me and him. I asked him to chill on ice till the morning showed its face.

Finally making it back to Pastor's house me and Keisha "Made Beautiful Love Music" to one another which would be our last song. :(A couple of hours later I was walking Keisha back home and as we pause for brief second in front of her door, I politely gave this beautiful, kind-hearted-loving young woman a very passionate kiss, and she hugged me tightly. I loved that girl so much, but I knew it was time for me to let her go. She had played her part well, and I was thankful for her time she spent with me. I still remember the day that truly put us at forever odds. We already didn't share the same religious faith, but the day that she told me that she was with a child growing inside her and I had no other choice but to give her half on the annihilation of the fetus, a part of me in the inside died! :(And even though the thought can still bring a tear to my eye. I never held it against Keisha. I walked the rest of the way to Pastor's house alone, crying, just thinking about the times we spent together and the way she cared about me.

(One day, Diamond told me that Keisha had come by her house when I wasn't there, and they started a conversation. Keisha told Diamond that she appreciated how she was helping me and had my back, but don't ever forget that "he's mine." I just started laughing. I can truly understand Keisha's rudeness because even though I was living a reckless life, she had honestly stayed by my side, which automatically made her Queen B. Keisha had been there for me when no one else was, without ever complaining. I remember another time when I really understood that this girl was a team player. I had just bought a brand-new 9mm Glock and was walking up 131st. Birdie was driving and spotted me, so I got in the vehicle with him.

As soon as I closed the door, I alerted to him that I was packing. "So be sure to be smooth sailing with your driving. No speeding, Birdie, and don't run any red lights."

Now as long as I've been knowing Birdie, I've never known him to be high or overly intoxicated while having a drink. He was always conscious of his surroundings. But I do not know what was going through this deaf jackass's head that night! As soon as we made it to 131st and Harvard, he made a left through a red light. As soon as he cleared the illegal turn, there were red and blue lights right behind us. I just looked at him like he was crazy. Then I said, "Don't pull too close to the curb. I need room so I can jump out and run. Goofy!" But he was so busy trying to hide whatever he had on him that he pulled to the side of the curb that had my car door right in front of a fire hydrant! With the police right behind us, there was no way I could jump out fast enough and run without being shot, so I just had to let this ridiculous situation play itself out. The only thing I was thankful for was it was night time, so I just might have a chance. After seeing that our vehicle had come to a complete stop, we watched as the two officers got out of their cruisers with one officer on the side of my door with his gun pointed at me, and the other officer on Birdie with his gun pointed at him.

As we stepped out of the car, I did what I was told and placed my hands on the trunk. The first search from the officer went smoothly. He didn't feel the gun on me, and they were a little upset that they didn't find anything on us or inside of the car at that time of the night and even though they didn't know our names, they still knew exactly who we were. After our fictitious names came back clean, the officer said, "Thoroughly search them one more time."

As the officer was saying this, the gun had already changed positions in my backside, and he was sure to find it this time. As the officer started searching me again, I didn't give him the benefit of the doubt, and I told myself that I was not going to make any move unless he was going to discover the gun. But this second time around while he was searching me, he was gripping and squeezing every spot he touch. I knew this was the training technique. As he started getting closer to the gun, I kept telling myself, "Wait for it, wait for it. Run, nigga, run!"

That one last hard squeeze by my nut sack pulled my underwear an inch too much, and the gun slid down my leg, fell out the bottom of my pants, and I took off running! I've always been fast, and for the kid that the doctor said would never be able to run and play like regular children, I had some very powerful legs that would prove him very wrong. When I started running, I had some very good traction going on, but it was too much darn traction, and I wasn't gaining speed like I should! The reason being, when the officer was doing his last thorough search, he had placed his hand inside my coat pocket and was holding it. So the reason I was running with a lot of traction but no speed was because I was dragging the officer on the ground! And boy oh boy did I pay for it! But at the same time, I bless those officers' hearts because they didn't hit me nowhere near what I was expecting. The few blows that they did give me were very respectable due to the situation. I had no hard feelings. The main thing I didn't like about that night was when the officers were looking at my gun, while holding it in my face, they called it cheap. I had used an alias as I was sitting in another locked jail cell door. No one would sign for me to get out, I was too wild in them streets, so no one could trust me. Only beautiful Keisha had my back, and my mother had her back because she made sure Keisha could get around to get the proper paperwork for my release.

Keisha understood that me and Diamond weren't romantically involved, but we did have fun times together. I brought out Diamond's wild side that she never knew existed. October 31, 1995, Diamond accompanied Beans and me as we dressed up like the characters from the *Dead Presidents* movie for Halloween. We drove up to a haunted house on Lee Road and Harvard with our black and white makeup, looking like we just walked off the movie screen. We did our makeup so good that the guy who was running the haunted house asked if we could stay to participate as monsters. We quickly agreed, and boy oh boy did we give the people what they were and weren't looking for! As the people reached the mark that Beans and I decided on, we came out of the dark and tackled them down to the ground and dragged them on the floor, then disappeared into the dark. We only got it off a few times before the guy who ran the haunted house had too many complaints, so he decided to kick us out without giving us our agreed-upon paycheck. LOL!)

Finally, I reached Pastor's door and took a second to delete everything from my mind. Then, I took a few minutes in order to delete everything from my heart because I needed to be 100 percent focused. I took a deep breath and stepped into his home. I walked straight to the room that I was borrowing and placed the VHS movie *Heat* into the recorder. I watched the bank scene over forty times throughout the night, studying it, and becoming one with it. I looked for their flaws, I looked at their gear, I listened to the way they talked to the people in the bank, and I watched how they made their getaway. After soaking in everything, along with my own creativity, I had blueprinted a full-proof plan.

On April 18, 1996, I was up very early in the morning, eating a powerful energy-laced breakfast that wouldn't hold me down but add fuel to my legs because I knew in the next couple hours, I would be doing a lot of running because I devised this caper to take place without a vehicle being involved. As I started putting on my bank robbery gear, Pastor called me to the phone. It was Keisha, and she sounded a little frantic.

"Hurry," she said. "Turn on the news!" When the older model TV decided to finally come to life, I couldn't believe my eyes, but I knew it was real. The newscasters were reporting from right down the street from me! The news anchor was reporting that the fugitive task force had Stone trapped on top of the apartment building, negotiating with him to surrender. I just shook my head. I didn't feel bad that he would be getting arrested because a clean arrest was always cool, and he wouldn't be dying. One thing for sure, you just can't go around making senseless killings!

I was sad because I didn't have too much time to find someone as solid as him for the replacement. I truly needed three people in order for this to go smoothly, but the plan was still ago, and then there was a knock at the door. It was my man Dewdrop! (I really didn't have a choice in the matter of Dewdrop becoming a part of my plan, because he pretty much told me that he was going to be a part of it one way or another, because he said he trusted me. Then he told me the story about when he left Cleveland and moved to California trying to get his life together, but it turned out to be a harder "turn round of life" than he truly anticipated. After he got to the point of explaining to me that he left a newborn daughter behind in California and that he was trying to get back to her with some money in his pocket, that's when I stopped him from talking. I gave him a very personal green light to tag along with me. But what was truly ironic about this whole situation was that, the whole conversation between me and him was a reflection of me looking into a (Human- Mirror-At-Myself) because in the very near future, my own life, will become a "Parallel Twin" to the conversation me and him just entertained. "I definitely, will be leaving a daughter behind in California." :( ) As Dewdrop and I had just finished going over the plans, I gave Pastor a hug and told him thank you for everything, and he told me it was a pleasure having me over. And I knew he meant exactly what he said because when we pulled away from the nigga hug that I gave him, his freaking nipples was hard! All I could do is laugh! But he will always have my gratitude.

(In 2013, I ran into Pastor at a doughnut shop, and he told me that he was married to a woman, and I just couldn't believe my ears. But as he went on with the story, he was going through a divorce because he couldn't stop seeing his boyfriend, and the wife had finally gave up on him. Now I was believing my ears. Good for you, wife!)

Our first stop was the gas station that sat at the corner of Miles. I needed to get a forty-ounce bottle, so I could fill it with gasoline in order for Dewdrop to execute his part of the plan properly. He was waiting for me to go in and distract the cashier, so I had the cashier go grab all the batteries that they had to make sure that my scanner was on full charge. After illegally filling up the beer bottle, we boarded the transit bus and started making our way to St. Clair.

As we exited the bus, one of the younger guys from the St. Clair neighborhood (that I knew all too well, because his father was alcoholic and his mother was a pure crackhead, and the guys in the neighborhood never gave him any type of respect because of the way his family was living. And come to think of it? I never really seen him change his clothes) was just sitting there doing nothing. I asked him how old he was, and his answer put him at a juvenile level, which was great. I was thinking "Cool" because if he got caught, he didn't have to worry about adult prison. We sat at the bus stop for a couple of minutes, going over the plans one more time with the extra add-on guy; then, after synchronizing our watches, Dewdrop and I parted ways, and the add-on guy became my new Stone, which was wonderful for me because this young cat was nowhere near being a freaking murderer.

We were finally standing in front of the bank. I was steadily looking at my watch, walking out every second of the blueprint in my thoughts. I turned on the scanner to make sure Dewdrop was taking care of his business, and that's when I was given the green light. I calculated Dewdrop's radius from me, and the scanner just revealed that the paramedics, the fire fighters, and the police were on their way to his location.

(As I stated earlier in this book, I am not into physically hurting people for financial gain, nor am I into manipulating others into carrying out any type of serious violence toward another individual for personal reasons. I never wanted to be one of the statistics on the future television show *First 48*).

Dewdrop's mission was very simple, and I knew he would complete it with expertise because I planned for his heavy load to be carried out in a light fashion. All he had to do was go into the blueprinted establishment and make sure that all customers and workers was in the clear by yelling very loudly five times, "This is a robbery!" Then he had to give the workers enough time to press the alarm button. But he wasn't robbing anything. He just needed to make that statement very clear. Then, as soon as he realized everyone was paying attention, he was to light the fire on the forty-ounce bottle in front of everyone, walk outside of the establishment, and drop it on the ground. Then it was "run, nigga, run" to the chosen safe house.

As I cut the scanner off after receiving the notification that I was aiming for, I grabbed the hand of the guy from St. Clair and squeezed it sort of really hard, making sure that I had his full attention and to ensure he completely understood what I was about to say. "You do not come in here at all! Make sure you understand me, little nigga! The only thing you're doing is standing in the doorway to make sure that I don't get locked in." I then released his hand, and I tilted my head toward the sky and said, "God, I'm so sorry for what I'm about to do, but I don't know no other way to get out of Ohio right now. Please don't let anyone get hurt. Please don't let me get hurt. I just want to grab what I need (and right then and there it donned on me! I guess the guys was right about me being too soft for this type of game? Because here I am about to commit a bank robbery and praying to our Savior for everyone to be okay. Unlike most of the guys I know, I will only be going in there to acquire the exact amount to which I thought I needed. If I needed $10, but it was $110 for the easy taken. I would only be leaving with the $10. Because that is the amount that I told the Savior that I was actually going to retrieve. And I was not about to disrespect what I pray for. "Always Put Morals Before Greed") and leave. Amen." My body was now shaking like a dryer on spin cycle with a pair of tennis shoes in it, making it shake like super crazy off balance! Then I mentally transformed into the Robert DeNiro character and entered the bank.

As I went in, I didn't threaten anyone because I wasn't trying to add any type of verbal assault charge, nor did I ask anyone to move to a certain location because I did not want to add on a kidnapping charge to this dumb act I was committing. I simply told everyone, in my best DeNiro voice, "This is not your money. Your money is insured by the insurance company. No one is going to get hurt. This will be over very quickly."

I jumped over the counter and started placing money inside my book bag that was strapped to my chest. I didn't even allow the cashiers to aid me in this nonsense I had created, and rather I pocketed a dye pack or not, I was right back over the counter and headed out the door within forty seconds, and with all that money in my face, I didn't take what my outer greed wanted. And with all that money that I was viewing, I only relinquished the bank for what I thought I needed. It's a must that I continued to keep the blueprint very clean. The only mess I left behind may have been from the water inside my book bag for the dye pack passengers to take a swim, just in case I might have picked a few of them money color changing devices up, within my fast-paced-unauthorized-interest-free-bank-loan- self serve- requirement-maneuver. As my task was finally coming to a completion, I thank everyone for being such good team players and walked right back out the door.

While the guy from St. Clair and I were getting into our tennis shoe getaway, my breathing started getting heavy, and my lungs were short of oxygen. All types of mucus started running out of my nose, and my eyes were burning as if I had just stuck my fingers in a jar of jalapeno peppers and placed them on top of my nachos, then wiped my eyes right before I ate a chip. All this was due to the fact that in my haste, I misplaced one of the dye packs in my book bag. It didn't fall in the water, and my little mistake let me know exactly what my goofy self had done. But I did not let that stop me from moving. I was very scared! I was truly running for my life, and I was also running faster for a new life. Finally, we made it to the residential area, and we started creeping slowly behind every house, trying to get to our destination. For some strange reason, I started to get super nervous because while we were sliding from house to house. I did not hear one police car siren. This had my nerves on the very edge because it made it very hard for me to track them and be conscious of their whereabouts. I knew they were quietly searching for their suspects. And they we're doing their job well! They were making it very difficult for me to initiate the game of cat and mouse to work in my favor. I told the guy from St. Clair to slow down because the next street we had to cross was kind of wide, and he was truly running with no thought pattern other than "get away, nigga!" He made a chicken running around with its head cut off look like a very expensive GPS device! Most people do not know, but when you are put in a predicament to truly run away from something that might harm you, your running must include a strategy and common sense, or you're bound to get trapped if you're in unfamiliar territories.

I told him to wait on the side of a house that we somehow fortunately made it to. As he was catching his breath, I slowly walked down the driveway that had no covering for me; it had me wide open, and there was nothing I could do about it. We could only go forward, and there was not one single other option. I did my best to stick my head out and look down the street without being detected by anything or anyone. As soon as my eyes caught a clearing, I saw a police cruiser, and I quickly jumped back into place. I walked over to the guy from St. Clair and told him, "I believe they saw me! Because they're searching!"

And just as he finished saying "No, they didn't," that police cruiser motor came to life, and all notions of running strategies were instantly eliminated. It was time to move to protocol, and this called for separation and the old "run, nigga, run!" Super fast evacuation! This guy and I started running at top speed, and as fast as we were going, we did not repeat one of those movie scenes where someone trips and falls, and I'm sure that if anyone had seen how fast our legs were moving, we would've been mistaken for Scooby Doo and Shaggy without any doubts! We stopped at another house for a hot second to catch our breath. And due to the honest guy that I am, I don't let anything get in the way of me paying my workers for a job well done. I reached in the book bag and handed him some money. "It's time for us to separate, little brother," I said. "Just meet me at the safe house. Thanks for everything, my man. I'm out!" As he was standing there, concerned about stuffing his pockets, I was off and running!

I could hear police sirens all around me, which was good because now I could calculate their positions. I was not trying to come across any freaking cruisers if I could help it! I ran up another driveway and into the backyard. I tightened up the book bag and attempted to hop the fence that was before me, but as soon as I put my fingers and tennis shoe into the fence like cat claws, one of the biggest Rottweilers I've ever seen ran straight up toward my face. With this very thin, twisted metal dividing us, he barked once, then just stood there staring at me, growling. I was truly afraid of this dog! My fear level was back at an all-time high, because me and this monster of a dog was damn near touching nose to nose! We were so close that if anyone was looking at us, they would've swore we were Eskimo kissing! Now having to deal with this dog and being chased by the police gave me a special internal capability to utilize my senses at its full telepathic capacity. So I thought I was actually starting to hear this dog's thoughts, like with them damn mosquitoes! Woofy was saying to me, "I dare your thieving black butt to come over on my side of the fence! I double dog dare ya! I'm going to take the law into my own paws and fuck you up!"

I knew I was no match for this political correct ass licker, but just as I was about to run away from our confrontation, an older white lady appeared out of nowhere with gardening gloves on and said, "Don't mind him. He's just a big baby."

But I was thinking, *I definitely do mind him, lady! Shit! I just read his fucking mind! He wants to be a K9! And his evil self might be racist!*

"He don't bite, mister."

Maybe not you, lady, but I will bet my last dollar that he loves the taste of dark meat! was my only thought to her untrue statement.

This beautiful sweet lady started to study my facial expression, then said, "What's wrong, young man?"

I didn't want to straight out lie to her because I could tell she was a good-hearted person, so I gave her a version of the truth, with a hint of manipulation. I said, "I was over this woman's house that's older than me. I never knew she was married, and now her husband is chasing me because she gave me some of his money so I can pay for a school trip. She told me that I didn't have to pay it back. But he wants it back really bad. He's chasing me as if I took it from her."

She asked me if I needed to get through her yard, and I said yes. She said she was going into the house for only a few minutes, then she and her little Snoopy were coming back out. When she told the dog to go inside of the house, I noticed that his name was Ike. As soon as the happy couple cleared the way for me, I jumped her fence, ran through her yard, and jumped another fence. I landed in the backyard of yet another house but behind the garage. I knew she was going to release her dog in the next couple of minutes, so I knew to stay put because Ike was going to become my unwilling protector. When the police came up the driveway where I was hiding and saw the size of that dog, I knew Ike would send their search in a different direction.

When she released Cujo, he came straight over to where I was and starting growling. He stopped after a few minutes. He knew I was there, but I guess either he got familiar with my scent or maybe some of that tear gas seeping out of my book bag was reaching his sensitive nose, so he left me alone. A few seconds after that, some officers were walking in my vicinity. Before they even got close enough to me, Cujo went into action. Mr. "He Don't Bite, He's a Big Baby" was going crazy. You would've thought he had a bad experience with the police at one time or another. The officer stopped and decided to go in the opposite direction. I laid behind that garage for about five or six hours. When I finally emerged, I didn't go to the first safe house that we all had agreed upon. I went to my second safe house first because I had to catch the news. I wanted to see if anyone got caught, and sure enough, someone did. The newscaster explained that two suspects robbed a bank, and one of the two was in custody.

Okay, I thought. *Time for me to catch a Greyhound.* But first, I needed to make a couple of stops.

One-stop was in East Cleveland so I could hand over to Dewdrop what I owed him and so I could pick up a new ID and a Social Security card. From this moment on, I would be known as Mr. Devon Richfields. My second stop was to Diamond. I lay down in the backseat of her car, and we were on our way to pick up Keisha. Keisha was so happy to see me. She didn't want anything to happen to me that would ever have a reason to bring tears to her eyes. As we pulled up to the Greyhound station, the three of us started crying. We all gave hugs and kisses, then separated. I walked into the Greyhound station, pulled out my fresh, new ID, and purchased a one-way ticket to California! I wiped the last of the tears from my eyes and took a very deep breath before I boarded the bus with nothing except absolute curiosity running around in my head because I knew as soon as I step foot on this bus, I was saying farewell to everything and to everyone that I knew. And I was going to be trading all that in in order to become the starship USS *Enterprise* and start traveling to parts of America that I've never been to before. I wiped away my tears and slowly exhaled. Then I put my Air Max on the first step of the coach, and it was followed by my right foot. (This was the ninth time when a soul started running.)

PART III

CHAPTER 30

WELCOME TO HOLLYWOOD!

One of my first stops was in Chicago. I got to see the famous and notorious Nike Town. I must have spent about three hours in that store, and the workers were very friendly with me before they even knew if I was going to purchase anything or not. I brought lunch for everyone, and they gave me a nice discount. I left out of there with three to four pairs of Nike Air Max. My trip to California was pretty smooth, except for the close call in Texas. As we boarded and were getting ready to pull out of the very famous Longhorn state, some Texas marshals walked onto our bus and pointed at two bags that they had placed on the ground on the side of the coach. Then, they started asking everyone on the bus who owned the bags. I didn't even want to know anything else about their conversation, so I ignored the rest of the words that came out of their mouths and just started staring out of the bus window. Since they weren't getting any answers, they started randomly picking people to get off the bus to be searched and questioned, and you just know that I just had to be lucky number 7-11.

As the officers searched through my pockets, they asked me questions simultaneously without me even giving an answer: How much cash money do you have on you? Who are you traveling with?

Where are you coming from? Where are you going? Who else carrying those bags with you?

After he was finished playing cavity search and asking me 101 dumb dog stupid questions, they allowed me to return to my seat. As we entered California, I saw so much smog hovering in the air that it really took me by surprise! The whole darn sky looked gray, even though the sun was shining bright.

While I was on the bus, I suggested to myself to start acquiring any information that could help me out a little in my new home state. I asked people, "Where's the safest place to go?" I was told by some returning residents that Hollywood should be my first stay because Hollywood was neutral territory for the gangbangers. This turned out not to be entirely true, but that's where I went. Hollywood, California: home of the movie stars and wannabes, young runaways, and people trying to shake the long arm of the law.

Once I was settled into my hotel room, I grabbed a few hundred dollars that looked like red bills that came straight from the Monopoly board game, and this was due to the dye pack exploding on me when I was making my unlawful withdrawal. Now I needed to find some mom-and-pop stores because I needed to change this red paper into something with a little more "green thumb" about themselves. I guess Hollywood was accustomed to all different kinds of money flowing through its neck of the woods and from all of the various forms of life, here in this fast-paced city, because every time I handed over a pinkish looking dead president, other than holding it up to the light to make sure that it was official, I saw no other reason within their body language to become suspicious of my funny colored money, which was very fine and dandy with me.

The next day, all the fear of everything I left back in Ohio had finally made its way through my system like I drink the best Miralax cocktail ever! I was just feeling so free and alive like a human butterfly! As I walked to the street corner of my hotel, I looked down on the ground and realized I was standing on one of the Hollywood squares. I instantly put both of my hands in the air and balled them in a fist position, as if I were a boxing champion, then started jumping up and down, saying to myself, "I made it! I made it!"

That's also when reality set in, and I realized that I made it by myself. I was truly alone, which didn't make too much of a difference because that's the way I lived, Mr. Lone Wolf. I started making my way around to the stores, spending the red tattooed bills until they all looked like only one ethnic group. With no issues, they just held it up to the light, then handed me my change. The majority of the store owners didn't even bother to play detective. They were just satisfy to be turning a profit, which left me with a smile. For the next couple of days, I made my way around Hollywood as if I was a real life tourist on a vacation. But in reality, I needed to get familiar with my surroundings because this was no vacation. I was merely trying to get an understanding of my new stomping grounds. I observed and participated at the Mann's Chinese Theater, and then I went on to entertain myself with *Ripley's Believe It or Not* and all sorts of other new places like the Hamburger Hamlet and the famous Disney movie theater, along with Star Burger and the famous Jack's restaurants, and I couldn't believe how lifelike the figurines looked inside the Wax Museum! So far, I was really enjoying my vacation/new home investigation.

As time was moving too rapidly for my taste, I was starting to put a dent in my money fuel tank. I knew I had to slow down or even stop eating at some of the more expensive places. I was sitting on the stairs, feeling a little hungry at Capitol Records located on Vine and Hollywood Boulevard, when I decided to walk over to a place called Tommy Burgers where they actually put chili on top of the hamburger, something I've never heard of before. I will never forget the Popeye's Chicken I passed on my way to the burger joint because that's where the Hollywood pimps used to conduct their business.

After ordering me a quick snack, I decided to play a videogame while waiting for my order to be called. That's when I got a very unexpected tap on my shoulder. Thinking it's someone trying to tell me that my order was up, I simply said, "Just give me a second. I'm on my last, man."

That's when I heard a voice speaking in broken English saying, "Where you from, fool!"

I turned around to see a little Mexican guy, with big black pants pulled all the way up to his belly button and a black-and-gray checkered shirt, with all the buttons open except for the one that went around his neck. I couldn't help but to gave him a very confused look. I also looked confused at the six guys standing behind him who were dressed just as he was. They were traveling in different shape and sizes it made me want to run to the door to see what type of fancy clown car they all piled out of. The littlest guy asked me again with an angry expression on his face, "Where you from, fool?"

I answered "Cleveland" without any hint of confrontation being released from my vocal cords.

"Where, fool?"

"Cleveland, Ohio, man"

They all looked at one another and started laughing. Then, the little guy told me "It's okay, fool. You neutral, homey." I didn't know what the fuck he was talking about, but I was sure to make a mental note of this slightly confrontation circus act.

I watched as they all turned around with their big pants and waddled out of the restaurant looking like penguins from a National Geographic short film. (Little did I know, in the months to come, a few of them would be working for me and protecting me.) That night, I decided it was time for me to make a trip back up to Ohio because I left a few dollars up there with Keisha. Just in case I got caught, she could put some of the money on my books so I can eat behind bars and fully pay for an attorney. As I was thinking of a plan for my return to Cleveland, I stopped at a bar in Hollywood. I observed a few people standing out in front enjoying the ganja, and they shared with me. After soaking in some wise words from two of my respected rap artist, I passed the joint back to one of the brothers out there. Then I told Spice 1 and Vinny from NBN that they would hear from me again. Finally, after staggering halfway down the star-paved avenue from being so darn stoned, I turned the handle on my hotel door and fell straight to sleep somewhere in that room.

The next day, I loaded up my Air Max and headed toward the City of Angels, making my way to find a beauty salon because now it was time for me to go incognito. When I sat down in the beautician's chair, she asked me what I would like to have done. I told her that I wanted some extensions. I told her that I wanted to walk out of there looking exactly like a Jamaican, and just before I could open my mouth again, a Crip gang member bust through the door, telling his guys to come on because they were having a meeting at the park, supposedly negotiating a truce with their rival gang, the Bloods. As the next few hours went by, she was finally done. I walked out of that shop with twenty-inch dookie braids. The only thing missing was a gigantic marijuana stick protruding from my lips. When I started to board the bus, there was a white guy behind me very close within my age range or a few years older. We wound up being paired together in a seat. As we were making our way from state to state, we became pretty close in conversation because he revealed he was on the run too. He was making his way to New Hampshire where his mother lived to grab a couple of dollars. As I was getting off the bus in Cleveland, he gave me a phone number and the address to where he was going. I told him that I would be on my way the next day. I placed my suitcase inside one of the lockers at the Greyhound station, then jumped on the first Metro transit, and headed back towards my old neighborhood.

Once I arrived, I didn't call Keisha on the phone because I was pretty sure that the heat was still actively watching her because they were still running my photo in the newspaper. I just sat inside some bushes close to her home until someone I knew came past. That didn't take long because I spotted my childhood friend Zero coming down the street talking to himself. I didn't judge him because I knew this was some of the results from the PCP that he indulged in far too often. I sent him over to Keisha's house so he could notify her that I was there. When she saw me, she was totally shocked. She couldn't even tell it was me. We cried together, hugged, and kissed. When she handed me the rest of the bank money, I noticed that it was clean. I saw no red or pink at all. I asked her how she was able to manipulate all that dye in such a neatly fashion.

She said she just put it in some warm water with some dish detergent and let the two marinate for a few hours. That's when we both laughed because we realized simultaneously that that Dawn commercial was telling the truth about rinsing the grease off dirty plates. As I waved good-bye to Keisha, I stepped up on the bus, feeling I would never see her beautiful face again because I knew I had lost her. I knew we weren't meant to be. Just sometimes, situations between two individuals, only comes together for only a season. (The year of 2005, Beans had me and Keisha standing face-to-face. I will always love her.)

After a nice little bus ride, I was in New York City, the Big Apple, where people and pigeons never sleep. The way the white guy explained it to me on the bus, it was as if New Hampshire was just around the corner from New York City, so I traveled in a taxicab to his mom's house, and the meter read four hundred freaking dollars! I'm sure if I paid more attention in school, this could have been avoided. Once we reached the destination, I reluctantly paid my cab fair and went to knock on the door.

When his mom opened the door, I was greeted with open arms. These white folks acted as if they've never met a black person ever in life. And they were truly so cool! His mom was sweet and always showed a cheerful personality. His dad was laid-back and treated me as if I was one of his children. His sister acted as if we had known each other all our lives, and his younger brother was a very high-strung young man. For the few days I stayed with them, the young-ster continued trying to get me to smoke marijuana and do pushups and lift weights with him at all hours of the day. He was the captain of the football team at his school, which he had no problem showing why he held the title. I really liked that funny kid! As the days pass which amounted to a week or a couple of days less, I knew it was time to hit the road again.

After drinking and smoking as much weed as my body could handle, his mother drove us to the Greyhound station. When it was time for us to go, she waved while we boarded the bus. She yelled for me to take care of her son. I answered with a nod of my head. We sat in our seats and finally made our three-and-a-half-day travel back to California. When we got to Hollywood, we both agreed that we had different views on life. But we did manage to put a good show on for his mom. After arriving, we decided to start off by get-ting a hotel room together, then take each day as it came. We went searching around Hollywood, looking for something affordable, and fortunate enough we just so happen to stumble upon something that was within our budget.

"We found it!" we both shouted at the same time and was very thank for our search results. And this particular hotel was located right across to street from some type of "Mega" Gay and Lesbian supercenter. This turned out to be super cool for me because I had many nights with lesbian women that lived at that supercenter, who wasn't truly a lesbian. They just needed somewhere to stay. For about a week and a half, we stuck together like stepbrothers. I believe that was due to the fact that we both didn't know anyone, and neither of us truly felt safe in this new neck of the woods. As the next few days went by, we decided to venture off separately, but we would always meet back up at the hotel at whatever time we agreed upon to make sure that we both were okay.

One day, when he came back, he was happy-go-lucky with a super big smile on his face. He told me to pack my things because he had met some people who said we could move in with them rent-free and at that very moment if we wanted too. I asked him, "And where are these generous people at? Mr. goofy!"

That's when he informed me that they were downstairs waiting for us! I watched and waited until he was finished packing his things, while he continued to convince me to pack my things as well. Then I followed him outside to the awaiting carriage. When we got outside, there was a car sitting there with three drag queens in it, and the fourth one, my roommate that I didn't pick up on, started putting his things into the trunk. As he climbed into the vehicle with the rest of the lively crew, one of the manly women asked me if I was coming. I just shook my head no and started laughing when they pulled away. I just hoped my white friend remained safe. I never saw my ex-roommate again, and I'm sure if I did, I wouldn't recognize him anyway, especially if he was now into only displaying his true self like the former Michael Jenner. (2015: Two thumbs up to Caitlyn Jenner for her courage.)

As the next few weeks went by, I started to get to know some of the attendants in the hotel, and it all started by no choice on my part. I just have a habit of observing things when need be. I started noticing that there was a group of guys living here as well. Some of them were affiliated with the Crips because they carried blue flags. The one guy that seemed to be their controller carried a purple flag, which meant he was from Grape Street.

One day, I was sitting on the stairs in the building we occupied, and a Lamborghini came riding by. I'm a true car person, and this was the first time I had actually witnessed one of these in real-life time, so I jumped to my feet and shouted out, "That Lamborghini was cold-blooded!"

One of the guys that stayed inside that room with the rest of the gangbangers told me that I couldn't be saying that. I asked him why. And he just looked at me like he was growling and walked away. Later that night, I was sitting in my room, trying to come up with a plan to start making money because my pockets were starting to show the results of the unwanted diet it was on. A knock came at the door, I got up to open it, and nine to ten guys came inside my room with guns in their hands, and not all of them were carrying handguns. A couple of the trying-to-scare-me guys had some type of semiautomatics that I had never held before, but I've seen a few people from my neighborhood with them. But for some reason, I wasn't scared. If they were going to hurt me, it would've already been done because these California cats don't play when it comes to killing, so I knew I was safe for the moment. (I just figured by me not being afraid as soon as I saw them toting their guns, it was just the turning point in my life from all of the balderdash I've lived through, that had unfortunately really taken a toll on me and my nerves, so as long as they weren't pulling any triggers, this was just going to be another conversation that I had no choice but to take part in.) I just stood there and waited to see what was going to go on next.

The Grape Street guy asked me who I was, so I gave him my name. Then he asked me if I was gangbanging, and I told him no. He told me that I talked funny (I was thinking the same thing about his speech) and asked me where I was from with the same demeanor as the little penguin-walking Mexican. From that moment on, they started calling me Cleve. After our encounter, they started inviting me down to their room. These guys were not playing. In one corner,

I noticed two AK-47s and other assorted rifles. In the other corner was a white powdery substance sitting on top of a table with a scale to weigh it, and baking soda boxes all over the place. Sitting on the sofa and the floor were all types of women that would go out into the Hollywood night and make their money and bring it back to this group of guys.

Grape Street asked me "how I was surviving." My response was "not too much at all my man." He told me that I was a nice-looking guy and he knew I had what it took to be pimping in Hollywood. I started laughing, and he looked at me with the expression "I'm serious, playboy." I shrugged the thought of that off my shoulder and started buying little packages of powder cocaine from him. Once I learned how they did the sales of white balls in Hollywood, and due to so many people becoming familiar with me and liking the type of person that I was, I was given a pair of rollerblades by one of the Mexican penguins because him and his group was on their way to fight another gang somewhere in Los Angeles called Shadow Park. So while he was running past me he just gave them to me and said, "Here fool! I have to go Essay!" Now am no stranger when it comes to rollerskate, but I have never introduced a pair of rollerblades to my feet, so after falling down a few Hollywood hills trying to learn how to use them, I was gliding around the Hollywood Boulevard with ease and getting rid of my little white balls to anyone who wanted to smoke them! And during my rollerskate escapades I was fortunate enough to meet just about all of the pimps in Hollywood because I made that Popeyes chicken that sat in the middle of Hollywood Boulevard my place to take lunch breaks and give my legs and feet their much needed rest. And them chicken coop pimps had a lot of respect for this young guy that had come down to them from Cleveland, Ohio. They love how wild and very respectful I carried myself, so my personality allowed me to enter their place of building business and they allowed me to conduct my own illegal business to a certain degree.

One day, after packing my pockets, I was heading back to my hotel room but a domino had popped up there, because the vice had just left, and they were in the process of closing the hotel down! It all started because the Crips got into an altercation inside of the building and started shooting. And by this time I really wasn't in good favor with these guys anyway other than conducting business, because they used to get mad at me because I wouldn't just sit up in the room with them and get high all darn day. I would only knock on their door to buy my product, then I'll be right back out the door. I knew time was of the essence so I quickly grabbed my belongings and started walking down Hollywood Boulevard, pulling my suitcase in search of a new place to live. That's when I ran into one of my customers that was looking for me.

His name was Mexican. He was about ten years older than me, which placed him over thirty. He was a stocky American Mexican born in New York City with a very cool personality, and he was on the run from Chicago. He told me I could move in with him. I didn't mind at the time because Mexican was nowhere near totally strung out. He was a very functional addict for the time being. He always had money to spend, and I figured out why. That's because he had a moving job contracting with the truckers of Mayflower Blue-Chip out of Hollywood.

As soon as I moved in with him, he had me come up to his job. His boss liked my attitude and my motivation, so I was hired that day. My pockets started looking nice again since I was working for the moving company and still rollerblading up and down Hollywood Boulevard, making extra money whenever my time allowed me. Being roommates with Mexican was an added on bonus as well because he was a live-in customer! But after a while, things started to go sour because Mexican wasn't interested in cocaine any longer and started using crystal meth. So now when I looked at my going astray friend, he had a totally different look, so I would no longer be calling him by his first name because I have lost some respect for him. Now he's "The Mexican!"

CHAPTER 31

HOLLYWOOD HUSTLIN'

One day, he was going through one of his crystal meth episodes, which was no harm at all pointed in my direction. I just found it to be very irritating because he couldn't stop moving around! So instead of spending another night watching him go through his motions, I decided to leave the apartment because I didn't like seeing him that way, but I wasn't his daddy, so I went about my business. I had my Air Max on, so I was ready for just about anything if I had to run from it. I was walking and looking at the Hollywood stars that passed under my feet when I saw a guy running toward me.

He said, "Cleve, I need your help! This guy is trying to take one of my girls, and I know you can handle him! So come get him off my back for me!"

I didn't mind at all because the players at Popeye's Chicken had taken me in and taught me some good ropes about the ins and outs of the pimp game in their neck of the woods. When I walked inside the grease-popping skinless-bird establishment, I was taken by surprise by what I saw! There was a group of girls that were new to Hollywood. One in particular really stood out! She was a bright white and very, very pretty, one of the prettiest white girls I've ever seen. While the two pimps started an argument over which girl was going to go with whom, I walked over to the porcelain girl and asked her which one of the guys she was going with.

She shrugged her shoulders and said, "I don't know."

I told her, "Come on if you want to go with me."

As I exited the door and started walking, I should have only heard one set of footsteps behind me, but there were many. So when I turned around to see what was going on, five of the other girls had decided that they wanted to come with me as well. And the other players didn't get upset with me because they were the ones who taught me that a man can pick his woman as many times as he like! But if that woman haven't chosen you to be her man, you're only on borrowed time. So I was only doing what I was told, because they had chosen.

Everything was going smoothly for the most part. The Mexican and I were going to work, and the girls were going out, making money, and bringing it back home. I don't believe in making anyone do anything, but I did have my house rules. Rule #1: No one was allowed to sell sex after 9:00 p.m. (I figured the crazies come out at night in Holly Weird, just as soon as the streetlights pops on! And I needed everyone safe and sound to ensure that that rent money never comes from my personal pocket.) Rule #2: There's to be no harmful drug usage! If it's not weed or wine, it's not allowed in this house. Rule #3: We will not conduct any illegal activity on a Sunday. Instead, we would go around and look out for people that we thought could use our help. (We weren't doing any major sinning on Sunday. We would just take a few people to the Star Burger restaurant on Sunset Boulevard and La Brea and buy them a meal.) As the time went by quickly, I was starting to make a little name for myself in Hollywood. The pimps even gave me a nickname. They started calling me the Tennis Shoe Pimp. But I was no pimp at all. I was merely just the superintendent inside this guy's apartment. We all were just a group of misfits all working together, trying to survive, and hopefully find a silver lining within the black clouds that formed our lives. And I let everyone know, "You are welcome to leave this working environment at anytime you choose to do so! No prison system here, just house rules."

And just as all good things don't last, once more, the dominoes started falling. The shit started with "The Mexican!" He started using so much crystal meth that the girls found it uncomfortable being around him if I wasn't there because he was always trying to get one of them to play with his little man, even though I continually asked him not to do that. But the crystal meth continued to tell him not to embrace my words. Then some of the women started breaking house rules without a conscience! Since I decided not to become a guerrilla pimp, they looked at me like Mr. Rogers and started staying out past nine o'clock. Finally one by one, they stopped returning until they were gone. Everyone except for Julie, the trusted pretty white girl that stayed by my side. She and I couldn't take the Mexican's habits any longer. We tried to cope with it by amusing ourselves on his behalf! We started playing little harmless tricks on him. We would take all the food out of the refrigerator and cabinets and flip all the sofa seat cushions over on the floor. He would just put everything back without saying a word, then go back to looking for whatever he had lost, which was nothing at all, for the next few hours! So we packed our things up and moved. We couldn't get an apartment because Julie had no identification at the time, and she was on the run, and I wasn't ready to use my new paid-for illegal witness protection identity just yet. Because I wasn't for sure if the FBI knew what name I would be using. The federal government already knew I was in California so to be on the safe side, we just paid drug customers to rent us rooms around Hollywood until the owners saw us so frequently that we didn't need ID to rent rooms any longer. We just used our Benjamin Franklin identification cards.

We eventually started living like a young couple in love and making sure to live life and not let life live us. I would get up in the morning and go to work for the moving company, and she would go and take care of her walking street business. We both always agreed to return to the hotel rooms by six o'clock. Not only that, but I was starting to fall for her so much that I even invited her on a date to the movies. This was the first time she really displayed some emotions on her face. We sat inside of the Chinese theater, watching a movie called *Set It Off*, which was about four female bank robbers. It starred Queen Latifah and Jada Pickett, and when the movie came to the footage of Queen Latifah being shot up by the police, tears and soft sorrow started pouring out of me unknowingly because it was too close to home, and I was lost in my thoughts.

Thinking back to Cleveland, I knew at any given time while I was making my unlawful withdrawals that I could have been wearing them same shoes as the character she played but only in reality. As I continued to watch, a small smile started to form across my lips as the officer was watching Jada Pickett ride away on the Greyhound to freedom. When Jada was in the hotel room crying after she made it to her destination, I could truly and honestly feel the pain of the character she was playing! After the scene with Queen Latifah, Julie continued to hold my hand with a soft squeeze to it and wiped the tears away from my watery face. And the old saying fair exchange is no robbery was right around the corner.

It was really hot outside, so we decided to spend our time inside another air-conditioned movie theater. So after stuffing and hiding a 12 inch pepperoni pizza we had just ordered and a couple of marijuana joints inside of Julie's "Oversize Handbag", we were on our way. The feature film was called *A Time To Kill*, starring Samuel L. Jackson. Julie couldn't believe the horrible things being done to the little black girl! Tears started pouring out of Julie like a running faucet with extra pressure for the water to move faster than usual. As

I started to condone her in the same way she had done me, Julie couldn't take it anymore! She looked me straight in my face and said, "Let's go!"

That's when I realized that Julie haven't truly experienced racism until that day. One day, while I was at work, Julie didn't follow the rules we had. The only real rule she had to follow now that it was only me and her was only deal with men sixty and over that drove expensive cars. When I made it back to the hotel later that day, Julie was not there. As the next couple of hours went slowly by with a no-show, I decided to hit the streets to see what was going on. I walked up and down Hollywood Boulevard and didn't see her. I went to Popeye's Chicken to check with the older players to see if they had any information, but I came up very empty-handed. I walked up and down Sunset Boulevard, La Brea Boulevard, Melrose, and Fairfax, asking everyone questions, from the crackheads to the heroin users, from the punk rockers to the squatters, from the Sunset female prostitutes to the drag queens of Melrose, and no one had seen her. I retreated back to our hotel room, fearing the worst. One thing I would never forget is when the chicken players told me, "They are here to pay, not to stay." So with that train of thought floating in my head, I figured she must have ran off with a more qualified manager, which was fair game because we win some and we lose some. But my heart told me that this equation was not the reason here!

The next couple of days was bringing in the start of a new season, so my moving job slowed down a bit. Not only was this the slow season, but a new management company had taken over, and due to me being one of the newer guys, I wasn't needed as much as the guys that had been there for years. I spent more time on my roller blades, skating up and down Hollywood Boulevard, selling saliva-soaked cocaine out of my mouth because the money was coming so fast I didn't have time to wrap them in plastic too often. I was just chopping and selling.

One evening, after I had sold out, I went back to my hotel room and traded my skates in for my Air Max. Then I was off on a mission to find a connection. I saw an older guy with a head full of really big wavy curls that he was wearing for hair, and the first thing I noticed (because I always size new people up first) was that this old guy was in shape! As I walked past him, he asked me if I was looking for something, and I told him that he probably didn't have what I was looking for. In return, he told me, "I got whatever you're looking for, homeboy." Then, he showed me a freezer bag that had five to six ounces of crack cocaine chopped up in it. I pushed him behind the bushes and asked him if he was crazy. He told me no and that he had just gotten out of prison.

I explained to him that things had changed since he'd been gone. "You can't be doing it like that, my man!" I added. I purchased what I needed from him and went about my way.

So much time had gone by since I thought about the one girl I had falling for and my past Ohio life that I was now starting the process of elimination to cleanse my system mentally and physically because I was ready to start forgetting everything negative that had passed through my short life. It was time for me to start fighting for change within this vessel of mine. I was getting the feeling that it was time for me to relocate due to the fact that I was really known around Hollywood because I always gave the customer more drugs than the money they had to ensure that my face would be the first they looked for when needing their fix. And I was the only young black guy running around Hollywood with a pretty white girl. People were coming up to me, knowing my name without me ever meeting them. I was sitting in my hotel room, wondering where would be the best city for me to travel to so I can start my transformation for the better, when there was a knock at my door. I was fearing the worst when I nervously opened it after hearing the voice of a female.

I discovered it was Julie, and she looked bad! Very bad! And her new body weight was giving the skinniest toothpick a run for its money! She told me that one of the hotels that she went to in order for her to take care of her business was occupied by Grape Street and his crew. When she tried to leave, they snatched her into their room. Even though they knew she was my girl, they considered me to be an outsider because I wasn't from California. When she mentioned my name to these animals, it was only mud to them. But little did they know that I'm not your ordinary mud! I'm the type of mud that corrects the foundation of problems when things not right. >:)

Julie explained how they raped her repeatedly and shot her up with heroin while making her smoke crack cocaine. As she walked into our hotel room, she handed me a Grape Street gang handkerchief they told her to give it to me and that we better get out of California within the next couple of days. I understood their message, and fair exchange is no robbery, so it was a must that I responded with my own message. >:)

I put her inside some bathwater and made her something to eat. After she gave me the information on their location, I was on my way to give them a small award for all their hard work on Julie. As I walked through the hotel hallway, I listened to every door, waiting to hear signs of them. Finally, I noticed the voices from the room they were foolishly occupying. I took the handkerchief they gave her to give me out of the plastic sandwich bag I had just recently drowned in alcohol. I cut a hole in it and placed it on their door handle. Then I put fire to it, then ran back to Julie, and we called a cab to take us to the hospital. After thirty days, Julie was back on her feet and doing well. All her test results came back negative. We both smiled at her clean bill of health. :)

During this time, the older gentleman from the penitentiary and I became business associates, and he revealed to me that his name was Dodo Bird. (You know, like the bird that's considered extinct. You know, the bird that got the famous name that represents stupid or very naive? Boy oh boy! Only if the scientists knew that there was one still roaming around the planet Earth, and it had a perm hairdo and sold crack rocks!) As more time went by, we had become very familiar with one another to a certain extent, so familiar that he was my only connect. As things seemed like they were back on track, another domino fell in my life. I was walking down Sunset Boulevard, making my way to Fairfax so I could make some money for me and Julie when I heard someone shouted, "Cleve!"

As I turned my head, I could see that it was Grape Street standing on the balcony of his hotel room looking very angry at me. "That little move that you pulled can get you killed, Cleve!" he shouted.

"So?" I retorted. "Come kill me!"

As he started running down the stairs, I pulled my shirt off and studied him while he was running toward me. I was hoping to catch him on the chin like the burger manager caught me on mine! But I missed his chin, and my knuckles landed straight on his nose! With the leakage coming from his nostrils mixed with the swelling, this Grape Street guy face was transforming into a bruised plum. We were in the middle of the street on Sunset Boulevard fighting. It started off with just me and him, but within a couple of seconds, I was fighting three people, and I was not winning at all! The only language that my head and body understood at that time was purely "Kick A Nigga Ass While He's Down!" But for some reason during the course of the fight, (that I was praying to be able to walk away from without "Much Needed" medical attention) they started to pull away from me? And that's when I saw what had rapidly initiated their departure, a stream of fear invaded my privacy! One of his guys was standing in the hotel driveway pointing a gun at me. When he pulled the trigger, the gun didn't go off! He started hitting it to unjam the bullet, but before he could get that together, I was off and running. I didn't get too far because someone had called the police. A pedestrian in their car had seen everything and explained to the police what they had witnessed. The officers had me sit on the sidewalk until the paramedics came and checked me out because I had so much blood on me.

As the next few months passed, we had our own little war going on. I knew all of their spots where they sold drugs around the Hollywood streets. So every time I caught them slipping, I would take advantage of that opportunity. They had a favorite bench on the corner of Sunset and Highland, and I couldn't wait to see them working there. I used to hide in the bushes and wait until I could catch one of them off guard. Whoever was sitting on the bench would catch my balled-up fists hitting him as hard as I could in the right or left ear. Then, I would run in the middle of the street with my hands up like a boxer, telling them, "Come on, let's put some work in."

But every time one of them took a step toward me, I would take a step backward. They weren't fast enough to catch me, and I always ended up running with them shouting behind me, "We gonna kill you, Cleve! You better get out of California."

Yeah right! Y'all not no real goons, I was thinking to myself. Even if they really were killers, they just didn't understand that I didn't have anywhere to go. I was happy of the fact that they gave me something to do as far as retaliation was concerned because dealing with them helped me to stay on top of my game on a high level. A day or two later, I saw one of them at the school playground. He had just finished smoking some PCP. I walked up behind him, put him in a sleeper hold, and waited for him passed out. I started asking the customers who had a car. I put the sleeping guy in the front passenger seat, got in the back, and told the customer where to drive. Once we got to our destination, the PCP guy was wide-awake and not too happy because he noticed that I had just dropped him off in a rival gang territory. I told him to have a nice walk, and I didn't even punch him in his ear because I figured he was going to have enough troubles getting back to his neighborhood. >:)

Things were going okay for me and Julie again. She was taking care of her business, and I was steady rollerblading up and down Hollywood Boulevard. After one crazy night, we decided to get an apartment and take a break. The reason being was that one night, we were out later than we were supposed to be and found out the police were going to sweep our hotel. This message came back from the informants we knew. As Julie stood a little ways down the street, I saw a younger guy pressing her for a quick sexual encounter, so I quickly pulled up on the both of them and explained to the young guy that she's with me, she's not working.

He said okay and acted as if he had left. A minute or so later, Julie came running up to me with a black eye. The guy watched me from somewhere, and when he saw the opportunity, he ran up and punched Julie and took off running. A day or two later, we were walking down Santa Monica Boulevard, going back-and-forth about who was right about a movie we watched together. A good Samaritan driving by must have thought that we were arguing and called the police. As we were walking, four horses pulled up behind us with officers on them. They made me spread-eagle on a hot California-sun concrete wall, and then they pulled Julie to the side. They continued trying to get Julie to say that I was the one who gave her the black eye, but she wouldn't give in to them. One officer didn't even get off his horse. He actually had his horse pin me to the wall, and the horse continuously sneezed on the back of my neck. I told the officer that his horse got one more time to sneeze on me. The officer was so mad at my statement that he turned uncooked-sausage pink! That made me laugh hysterically, and then he started repeating himself over and over, "Hit my horse, I dare you! Come on, hit my horse. I dare you, little black man! You said you were going to hit my horse! Here it is! So hit my horse, I dare you!"

And since Julie wouldn't give them what they wanted, they called her stupid, told her that I was going to do it again and that they were not going to help her. Then they released us and sent us on our way. The four musketeers had us laughing all freaking day, I tell you! :)

We knew it was time for us to leave this area before the gig is up, and we found ourselves forever sleeping six feet deep. Fortunately, we located an apartment building to move into that was a few blocks away from Hollywood Boulevard. It was money all around there, and I started getting it. It didn't take long for my presence to be known in this neighborhood by the ones who really controlled it. While Julie and I were walking down the street one day, three Mexicans pulled up on us, and the leader told me that his name was Loco. Apparently, people had been telling him I was making money in his neighborhood. Once he understood that I wasn't in a gang, he told me that I had to pay a day fee and a night fee in order to work in his governing domain. I agreed with what he said, and once I had my pass, I started truly putting my work in. I even had his own gang members making money for me. I didn't have to leave the building to chase down a paycheck and the Mexican gang protected me to a certain extent.

The police were always wondering who this black guy was whom they let live amongst them so freely. Just as the dominoes loved to play their part as a stumbling block in my life, they continued falling. Julie and I had so many close encounters that it was becoming a regular routine.

One night, sort of on the late side of the evening, one of the Mexican protectors and I were walking to the store. He was a little younger than me, but the guy had a very good aim when we be at target practice. As we walked past the bar before we reached the store, there was a woman sitting on a bar stool in front of the entry door. She looked at my little buddy and told him it was too late for him to be outside.

I told her, "It's okay. He's with me."

Bluntly, she said, "Nigger, I didn't ask you to open your mouth!"

I don't know what type of night this pale-faced woman was having, but the BS that rolled off her lips was totally uncalled for! So I called her a silly heroin addict, and we continued on our way. As we were returning from the store and passing the bar once more, a really big Triple H wrestling looking guy came storming out in my direction with the silly heroin addict on his heels like a little kid that went and got her big brother. He stopped right in front of me and asked me if I had a problem.

I replied, "No, I don't have a problem. Do you have a problem?" Now the only reason I had this cocky attitude toward this individual who was much bigger than me! Is because I had seen about eight or ten of my gang protector guys coming down the street, and I knew they were going to protect me. So when the Triple H lookalike turned his head to watch them coming down, I balled up my fists and waited for him to turn back in my direction. As soon as he did, I hit him as hard as I could in his right ear, and he went down to one knee holding his head. As he started rising back up with this crazy stare, he looked me dead in my face and told me, "Now that's what I like!"

Now I was nervous! I started stepping back, and at the same time, I was wondering why these guys weren't willing to help me. In my heart, I knew I was about to get a beatdown by this semi-WWF monster. Then one of the Mexicans was like, "We know this fool, Cleve. He pay us rent. Stop running! You have to fight him heads up, fool."

I wasn't trying to hear what that goofy Mexican was talking about! Wrestler guy continued to chase me around the parked cars. I could tell he was getting tired, and I could feel my confidence starting to restore itself, trying its best to get my bravery to follow suit. Everyone was standing around, watching and shouting. I finally stopped in the middle of the street. I could tell as he walked closer to me that he caught his second wind, but that didn't steer me away.

Just when we both were about to attack one another, Julie was running down the street screaming, "Don't hit him! Don't hit him!" She ran right between the both of us, then turned around to look at the man straight in his face and said, "Don't hit him!"

The big wrestler guy said, "Why not?"

Julie screamed as loud as she could, "Because I love him!"

Everyone around us went from a serious expression to bent-over laughing out loud, which turned out to be the best thing for everyone. Some of the people was acting as if this was the funniest thing they ever heard in their boring lives. When I saw the wrestler guy laughing, I started laughing and also started stepping back from this second winded monster. He looked at Julie and said, "Okay, not tonight." Then, he looked at me and said, "I'm going to catch you later." And he gave me the old wink of the eye, so I knew I had to stay on my tippy toes at all times while going for a bag of chips. Any time a street person gives you a wink of an eye, that's an honest warning signal for danger, my friend. So if you allow yourself to get caught slipping, you couldn't be mad at the enemy, because you were prewarned.

A few days later, dominoes just started falling "back to back" and making my life just a little more miserable than it already was.

Domino #1. Julie came back to the apartment with tears in her eyes and it was not of sadness, it was because she was pissed off and frustrated! She explained to me while she was walking from the store, one of the newer pimps in the neighborhood said this to her, "why you with that young lame? You need to get with me and really become something". And there it was, someone disrespecting me in the neighborhood where I worked! If I didn't handle the situation as soon as possible, that the next time he sees her he may want to put his hands on her? (You, whoever reading this book. We know what time it is. "So I put on my Air Max!") Me and Julie quickly exited our apartment building and I was hoping that the guy haven't left yet because the situation had just occurred, and sure enough there he was, standing in the exact same spot where he decided to open up his mouth about me. He knew what was going down as me and Julie walked towards him, because he placed his paper bag down on the ground and planted his feet. But little did he know it didn't make no difference which way he planted his feet, because I was not going to let those toes of his grow any roots into the concrete beneath him. Julie and I stopped right in front of the man. He had about 2 1/2 inches on me and more body weight but I wasn't that worried about him, because I never received a threatening vibe from his body language. Instead I received an energy of concern flowing from this gentleman. I asked Julie, "is this the guy?" She responded," yup". I asked the gentleman, "Do you know me?" But before he could let one word loose from his loose lips, I grabbed the bottom of both of his pants legs (just like the way "Fashionable Kid" grabbed my pants leg when I was in junior high school and revealed my look-alike "WEAPONS" artificial-converse- tennis-shoes to the whole freaking school! Yes! Of course I still carry that "Monkey". LOL!). And lift him straight up in the air with a hit of my right shoulder to make sure he would fall backwards and landed on his back. I quickly turned my body around like the fastest "Red Power Ranger" and pulled both of his ankles toward his head, then I quickly sat on the back of his thighs. I was even shocked how fast I turned this particular shit talker into a human pretzel. I told Julie to come here, then I harshly told the man to apologize to her. He did what was asked of him, but I walked away with a sprained wrist.

Domino #2. A couple hours after that, I was right back in the same predicament but with totally reverse results! Dodo Bird had just told me that this one pimp that was notorious for beating up his "working women" was harassing my Julia! I went straight into action! And I came out of that with a bruised lip and a bruise eye socket, and he walked away with a tattoo neck from me choking him and a star on his forehead from my head-butt. So we ended in a truce and gained street respectful one another.

Domino #3. I had just traded one piece of my good cocaine rocks with one of the Mexican gangbangers because he wanted to smoke it and he didn't like the dope that he was selling. It was so small that I put it inside my little hip pocket on my jeans. As I was walking back toward the building where Julie and I were living, a drug user flagged me down and told me not to go into the building because the police were in there going through everyone's apartment. Before he could even finish his conversation, the Hollywood vice pulled up on us. As the officer searched me, he found what I had placed in my pocket. He was so very happy to find this little piece of nothing! Because he just knew there would more to find on me. He laid the little piece of nothing on the hood of their police cruiser and continued to squeeze and grab, hoping to discover the buried treasure, but I really didn't have anything else to offer. As he continued his cavity search, I continued to watch that little piece of nothing melt away on the hood of his cruiser. After he didn't find anything else, he asked the other officers who had the little piece that he found, but no one knew what he was talking about. They still insist on taking me to the police station anyway and making me walk back to the building.

Domino #4. Since Julie and I could no longer live at the apartment building we had really just started occupying, we moved in with a customer, and after about two weeks of being there, her two sons had moved in with her from her home state. Not only were Julie and I living there, Julie also had a girl that worked for her dwelling with us as well. One day after the son and I had just finished smoking some marijuana, he told me that me and my girls would have to leave the apartment forever. I could understand his reasons, and I was in agreement with him. I told him that I'd be gone in a week, but he said, "No, you're going to be going right now."

The next thing I knew, he got up and briskly walked toward the kitchen. He grabbed what he was looking for and started coming at me with a nice-sized turkey carving knife. One thing that's natural about me: I get a reverse effect from marijuana! I don't get sleepy or tired; I get very focused and hyper. One of my customers was there with me, and Julie's employee was there as well. The other customer wanted to intervene, but I told him to stay out of it because I didn't want him to throw my timing off. As the son continued to frantically wave the knife back and forth at me as if his mind was telling him that I was the biggest turkey of all, I continued to count his motions. "Wait for it. Wait for it. Go!"

I caught his wrists and twisted the knife out of his hand. Then, I quickly proceeded to put him in a sleeper hold and laid him down on the floor once his dozing off took effect. I told Julie's employee to start gathering our things. While we were upstairs taking care of our business, the customer that was with me had gotten scared and poured water on the son's face; and when his eyes popped open, he jumped up and went straight out the door. We were just about finished packing when I heard the fire alarm going off, but I didn't react to it because my total concentration was eliminating myself from this new terrible situation I've just created. After we had all our things gathered up, we headed out the door. As soon as I stepped foot out of the apartment door, I saw the police coming down the hallway, so I ran. I made it to a laundry room and crawled inside a dryer and shut the door. The reason the police and the fire department were there was because the son got on the elevator and pressed the emergency stop button. He told them as much about me as he possibly could, which was nothing at all.

Domino #5. With nowhere for us to live, Julie and I headed back to the hotels of Hollywood California in order to have a roof over our heads. Once again, everything was running pretty smooth because we stuck to our blueprint. Dodo Bird was still my connect, but he had really gotten the police hot in Hollywood. He was definitely looking at three strikes, so he took a break from the famous city of movie stars and fancy cars and had us take rides down Crenshaw Boulevard to meet up with him. Inglewood was the chosen destination to get our product, which just so happened to be a Bloods neighborhood, but fortunately, some bounty hunters I met in Hollywood had already given me a pass and got in touch with the Inglewood set, so we were safe when we traveled there. But we still had to be careful because we were riding the public transit and two incidents that occurred were not out of the ordinary once you live in Los Angeles California! Incident #1. Making our way from and back to Hollywood was always a health hazard, due to the different gang territory that you would have to travel through in order to get to your destination. Because you never know when a group of gang members is going to get on the bus and do a walked through just to see what colors the people have on, and this one particular day this one guy with his blue handkerchief was not so lucky as we watched them drag him off of the bus. And neither was the one guy with red handkerchief in the very near future of our bus rides. So me and Julie stayed in "safety gear" or in California, is what they call "neutral clothing". I will be in all "black with my black ass" and "Julie would be in all white with her white ass". We were making sure that we got back to Hollywood in one peace, and without any "blue bruises on our skin" or "any red blood on our clothing"! But not all the time is the craziness due to gang related activities, Los Angeles is just full of characters. Let me explain incident #2. Me and Julie was sitting on the back of the transit minding our own business just trying to get our packages of little white powder home safe, when a man came and sat down in a seat that I had my arms crossed over. Now there was plenty of seats on this bus, but this guy decided to favor the one I was next to, and as soon as he sat down, he told me to remove my arm from where it was resting. And he said it in a nasty way so I told him no! This guy took the books and everything else that he was carrying and threw them in the middle of the bus floor then told me, "Let's go!" So I acted on his threat, which almost turned me into a loser of that bout! After the quick tussle he had me pinned down in my seat while I was looking at Julia for help! And Julia was looking right back at me with her mouth close, but with both of her eyebrows raise high into the air like, "you know I got all of this powder on me, so you on your own buddy". And that's when the "Red Ranger" auxiliary power kicked into gear! I grabbed the pole that was protruding from the bus seat and connected to the ceiling of the transit unit and swung myself around with enough force that made the man fall back into the seat and now I was on top of him as my right hand transform into a sludge hammer and I started hitting him in his head as if I was trying to nail the coffin down forever! This continue for a few seconds until the transit driver pulled me off of the guy and made him get off the bus. All I can honestly say, is that that man was pretty strong.

It was a very exhausting Sunday for me and Julie! I had sold out the night before and didn't have anything left, and I was ready to sleep the entire day away. That's when Julie and I got a knock at the door. It was Dodo, so I told Julie to let him in. He explained that he had a room inside the same hotel. I said, "Cool, I'm going to sleep."

I do not know how much time went by, but Dodo was back knocking at my room door, and Julie let him in as I was sleeping. A couple minutes later, as I was lying there with my eyes closed, there was another very strong knock at the door! Dodo Bird came over to my bed and whispered, "Cleve, the police at your door!"

I didn't care because I didn't have anything illegal in our hotel room except for myself, so I had me covered. I told him to let them in. But when I told him to let them in, I was talking to myself because Dodo and Julie had ran into the bathroom. That's when my hotel door came crashing in! Before I could even focus on what was transpiring, I was picked up out of the bed by my belt buckle and slammed down to the floor face first. Then some hard plastic wraps were placed around my wrists and my ankles. As I sat there against the wall, hog-tied like a rodeo's favorite prize, my sleepy slumber started going away, and my vision was getting clearer. As I looked around my hotel room, I could not believe what I was looking at! I knew this wasn't a dream because the plastic strips were hurting my wrists! Everything was so bright and vivid, and the only thought that was traveling through my mind was, "Fuck!" As I was watching the officers picking up things off the floor and placing them on the table, I saw an electronic measuring scale, six or seven bags of powder cocaine, a box of baking soda, at least an ounce of hard crack cocaine, plastic sandwich bags, and IDs that didn't belong to anyone in this room. I just sat there, shaking my head because I knew it was going downhill and I was the snowball. One thing I started noticing was that not one of the officers came over to me and asked me if I was Brian Dixon. I was also wondering how long that was going to last once they got us downtown because we were definitely going downtown!

They placed me, Julie, and Dodo in the back of the same police cruiser. On our way down there, Dodo kept telling me and Julie not to say anything. He continued telling us that they didn't have anything on us, so there was no need for us to have any worries or to open our darn mouths. But I wasn't paying Dodo any attention because what he didn't know due to the fact that I looked so young was that I've already completed a three-year prison sentence so my outer shell was preserved, and I've been in the streets since the age of twelve! So I already know the rules to the game. My main concern was what in the world made the police come down to my room and kick my door in. And why didn't Julie's goofy self wake me up and give notification of the wonderful illegal gifts that he stashed in our damn room? And why didn't Dodo tell me that he had "pure prison time" things in my room when earlier he had just told me that he had a room at our same location?" Question after question continued to circulate around in my head as if I was on one of the best and fastest merry-go-rounds at the park!

By the time we pulled up to the Hollywood Division Police Station, I was still trying to process everything just before they begin to fingerprint me, take my mug shot, and start processing me. And I really had bigger problems now! Because there was a very good chance that they were going to find out just who I really was. They put all three of us in separate rooms for questioning when we arrived at the station. Once they concluded their interrogation, they said they were going to bring Julie to see me because they promised her they would let her see me before we went downtown. Already I knew what that meant when I saw one of the Hollywood horsemen that pulled us over not too long ago leaving from her direction. Julie had snitched, but I knew she would deny it to her dying day. When they finally allowed her to see me, she cried on my shoulders, and I released some tears on her forehead. We kissed for the first time very passionately, and then they threw us in different prisoner transport vehicles, and we were on our way to the Los Angeles County Jail.

After the photo shoot and being fingerprinted was completed, I was placed inside of the jail house's finest clothing. Then I was placed in a housing unit with individuals that hadn't been charged just yet. I truly didn't understand this procedure because in Cleveland, Ohio, they throw your butt in the tank along with everyone else! Guilty or not, you were viewed as a criminals first. One of the inmates told me that this unit was specially created for the detectives only and that I better hope that I receive a DA reject. He continued to explain that if you were placed in this unit, it meant that the detectives didn't know if they were going to charge you or not due to the lack of evidence.

Well, one thing that I knew for sure, charge my black ass or not, they had my freaking fingerprints, and I knew before they let me out there was going to be a worldwide search. That search would be conducted by their high-tech, super duper microscope searching fingerprint computer. After about two and a half weeks living day to day in mental fear, the jailer called my name and escorted me to the detective's interviewing room.

He looked me dead in my face, with a very serious expression. I already knew what he was about to say. This fucker was going to be like, "So, you're Mr. Big-n-Bad Dixon, Mr. On the Run who's wanted in Cleveland, Ohio! And you have the nerve to visit California? And the balls to come to my city! And the dumbness to continue on your crime spree here! In the Wild Wild West? You really are stupid! Am I correct, Mr. Jackass?"

But that's not what happened at all! I relaxed, then focused on reading his body language, and I concluded in my private unspoken interrogation that the seriousness on his face was due to the fact that he was getting tired of his job. I could tell by the way he handled the whole interview that he was ready for a different position within the police force. As we sat there, he placed a folder between us both. Then he said, "Mr. Fields, I'm looking over the case, and there is no way that the officers can connect you to the things that were found in your room. The report reads that the officers spotted Mr. Dodo conducting illegal street business. He even conducted some business on top of one of our unmarked cars. So when he came to the hotel, he was followed to your room. But the officers stated that they had never seen you or Julie with Mr. Dodo on that day in question nor was any of the fingerprints found on the evidence that was removed from your room connected to yours or Julie's. So I'm here to tell you that you have a DA reject. You guys are not being charged. You are free to go. You will be released a little later today. Consider yourself lucky, Mr. Fields. And if I were you, I would consider thinking about a better life." (Umm, maybe Julie didn't say a word.)

Finally, they called my alias name to be released. When I got to the bus stop, Julie was there waiting for me. We hugged one another so hard that I started to believe she was in love with me, and maybe I felt the same way. We didn't have any money. We lost everything in the hotel room that day. All we had was the clothing on our backs. We didn't even have bus fare, but the conductor had a kind heart and gave us a free ride back to Hollywood.

CHAPTER 32

MY SAVIOR

Once back in Hollywood, we retreated to a friend's house. Julie couldn't go to work because she was on her monthly girly thing, and I couldn't go to work because I didn't have any product, and I damn sure didn't like asking people for no handouts, and for one reason or another, neither my pride nor my creativity was going to let me down. I went into our friend's kitchen and got some flour and salt. I mixed the two together and added a little water, and then I placed the concoction into the microwave and nuked it until the flour started burning black in the middle. I then took it out and ran it under some water for a split second, sprinkled it with more salt, then nuked it again. The final result was a very bad-smelling house and some flour that looked like crack cocaine. I knew at first glance and taste that the customers wouldn't know the difference. Because once they bit into what they thought they were getting for their money, for a split second, they would think it was real due to the numbing effect that that microwave salt gives. And that's all I needed in order for me to have enough time to walk away with their money and then put my Nike Air Max to work over a fence. I didn't feel bad about the moves I was making because they shouldn't be doing drugs any darn ways. So after achieving a small goal from selling that bullshit to people that were not locals, I just jumped on the bus and headed toward the Shadow Park area of Los Angeles. That part of the city was saturated with all kinds of illegal activities that were mostly run by the Mexican gangs, and I was safe because I had a pass from the Mexicans in Hollywood, so I was sure to make some money because the connect will be right there at the park with me.

As the sun was starting to show itself, it was time for me to leave, and I was very satisfied with my short-term pharmaceutical gig. I was well over the $2,000 mark, so I figured it was time for me to get an apartment and re-up on my side of town. After thanking and paying the Mexicans their rent money for allowing me to hustle in there territory, I started making my way back to Hollywood.

(Now this is one "Domino" that really caught me slipping and it was my fault because now I was a customer of my own product :( ) After Julie and I finished shopping for some clothes and shoes to wear for that day, we went looking for somewhere to live. When I used to rollerblading up and down Hollywood Boulevard, I would always stop and talk to his big guy named Pay Check. Pay Check would always be walking the boulevard with his pit bull name Shadow. Shadow and Julie were an instant hit together, which was no surprise to me because Julie was a true animal lover, rather it be picking up the plastic can holding wrappers from off of the ground and tearing them to shreds so birds or some other type of animal couldn't get trapped in it, to becoming just an honest savior for animals. On a late-night, on our way home from the movies, Julie spotted a cat that was on its last leg of its nine lives, so she had me pick it up and brought it home. Even though we both knew that this cat will never be meowing again, she took care of it until it passed away. She once told me that as soon as we were able to get out of the life that we were trying to survive for the moment, she wanted to go to school and become a "Marine Biologist". One bright and beautiful California day, we bumped into him on our apartment search. He informed us that he had a two-bedroom apartment and we could move in with him with the agreement of paying half the rent, so we moved in. Now that we had somewhere to live, we also understood that Hollywood was way too hot for us to conduct any type of business without being noticed by some officer that had seen us one too many times, so we went looking for a car to rent so we can hit the road and make some money else.

As I was making my way back from Inglewood with more grams than what I actually needed to be taking on this road trip, Julie quickly grabbed a couple of working girls from Sunset Boulevard. Not knowing exactly where to go, I followed the advice from the notorious Hollywood Popeye pimps. And we were on our way to San Francisco for them to put in work and for me to hustle all over Market Street, and this street was known and respected for its illegal activities. So with Oakland being on the path of us making it to San Francisco, I was hoping to make my pockets bigger while passing through, and I guess with the thought of money on my mind, the money gods allowed us to participate in some business at Fisherman's Wharf. I loved those older guys with their dry fishing rods that were always looking and willing to pay for some real fishy action. >:)

After a few trips, time was really moving fast, and our pockets were finally back to where they were supposed to be. Throughout this course of being good or I can even say being great coworkers, Julie and I had gotten very close to one another, which made regular illegal routines feel so normal to us that I didn't even look at her as a working girl any longer. I started looking at her as a girlfriend. Some days it didn't even dawn on me that I was still running from the law because everything was smooth-sailing! So far, this crazy life I was living seemed nice. We were back in Hollywood, and we had just given Pay Check our rent money. We were preparing ourselves to take another trip to San Francisco when Julie gave me kiss on my cheek and told me that she was on her way to go shopping for a couple items before we left. Pay Check and I had just finished lunch, and he was on his way to work being a security guard. As I locked the door behind him, I hurried to my room so I could take a number two on my toilet. I loved the fact that we had separate restrooms connected to our sleeping areas.

But as soon as I sat down on the toilet and started relaxing my numb muscles from all the cocaine I was inhaling, there was more than a few very strong knocks at the apartment door. I heard Pay Check calling my name, and he was acting as if he was going to have a heart attack if I didn't open the door fast enough. Pay Check started shouting over and over, "I don't have my keys, Cleve," so I tightened up my butt cheeks, and since I knew it was him, I didn't bother to look out of the peephole, which was a very horrible mistake on my part.

As soon as I opened the door, Grape Street was standing there with four of his goons! And the overweight lame who tried to shoot me after the "burning handkerchief" incident was looking at me like I was Christmas candy! He made the nympho hairdresser and her freaked-out baby daddy look like kittens compared to the hyenas I thought they were! And when my eyes caught sight of these niggas that was about to do me in, I did not hesitate! I went straight into action and rushed Grape Street! As we both fell to the ground, I was getting punched and kicked from every direction. All I could do was put myself in the fetal position and accept the gifts that they were administering to me. Once they were out of energy, they put me on my knees and the one guy that I made walk home from the rival gang neighborhood snatched my braids and pulled them downward, so my face would tilt up toward God. Grape Street walked over to me and put his gun between my eyes and started pressing it real hard against the bridge of my nose. I was sure this was going to leave a mark even if he didn't shoot!

Then he asked me if I was scared. I said, "Yep, because I know y'all on some payback shit that y'all started."

He started laughing and said, "I should shoot you in your stomach for every time you hit one of us in the ear. Or maybe I should let Light Skin shoot for dropping him off in a Blood territory!"

With that being said, Light Skin decided to yank my hair down even harder! With all this going on, I couldn't help it any longer, so I started laughing a little because I was really catching them off guard at that bus stop and leaving at least one of them with a ringing ear. Light Skin looked at Grape Street and was like, "I told you, cuz, they said he crazy!"

Grape Street removed the gun from my face and decided to have a pep talk with me, like I was one of his flunkies, and stated, "The only reason I don't kill you, Cleve, is because your ass is a fighter. You got heart, cuz, and I respect that, but you have to get out of California, Cleve, before you seriously get hurt."

He allowed me to stand up, and I took off running. When I got to the end of the hall, I shouted back at them, "I can't leave you jackasses! I don't have nowhere to call home, cuz!" I watched them as they entered the apartment, and then I started walking really slowly down the hall because I didn't want any of the mess that I let loose in my underwear to start sliding down my leg. After they finished ransacking the room I was renting, I went back in and started packing my things. They took all my money that was out in the open, but they didn't get my secret stash. Pay Check came and looked in my room and said, "Man, they had a gun on me."

What I realized is that when he left for work, he put Shadow on the balcony, something he never did. (Later on in life, actually while I am sitting here writing this book, I see Pay Check has a lot of rap videos on the Internet, and someone was questioning him about being a fake Crip. As I view more of his videos, it seems that he was trying to pick fights with rappers like 40 Glock, and their phone conversation made it into the limelight. 40 asked him why he is trying to get himself famous by picking weak fights with him. I am not knocking Pay Check. He was only trying to make it happen like the rest of us. But he's very famous in my book because I'm more than positive that he set me up, and I am not mad about the un-trust situation between me and him, because God has pulled me through worse situations than that! And He allowed me to be able to write about it, so Pay Check's doings was merely another testimony of His works. "2014, Palmdale, CA./ Sheriff's homicide detectives responded just before 12:30 PM to a McDonald's restaurant where 15 people were inside at the time of the murder. {Witnesses say there was no altercation. The guy just walked through the door and shot, then left out another door.} It was sad for me to see this on the Internet, rest in peace Big Man.)

Once Julie and I had our belongings together, I asked Pay Check if I could buy Shadow from him because he already knew how crazy Julie was about that dog, and he was not capable of taken care of the canine anyway. He agreed, and Shadow and I were on our way around the corner to our new apartment I had just rented a few days beforehand. We were living right behind the Chinese theater, which was totally cool! Because one of my favorite movies was *Pretty Woman*, and I stayed right up the street from the hotel where they filmed Richard Gere climbing the fire escape with the rose in his mouth, conquering his fear of heights for true love. Julie was happy and smiling because she had a new dog and a swimming pool. We even met a gay couple that was pretty freaking cool! Julie and I, along with our new openly gay buddies and their gay friends, would all pack up and camp out behind the big famous Hollywood sign while smoking the best ganja we could get our greedy little hands on. And we always took Shadow for security! And we were very confident that our Shadow would handle his business especially since his previous owner was a security guard.

Things were going good until I started messing up big time! I was using cocaine at an all-time high, and it was getting the best of me, and the saddest part about it was that I could afford it! My magnetic personality mixed with the attitude of an Ohio hustler always caught the attention of someone up on the food chain in the street, and they would always be interested in me. I started getting involved with a crew from Cuba and one of the Mexican cartels and a very fast talking connect from the country of Panama, plus a guy from Hoover Crips, and let me not forget my guy from Bounty Hunters Bloods. I was in twine with all these suppliers at the same time. I needed help with the things I was doing, so I had a Mexican gang member and his wife, who was also from his set, move in with me and Julie. But my cocaine habit started running everyone away because I always stayed paranoid, always thinking the police were going to come and kick my door down. Or I thought everyone who lived with me was conspiring against me, and I could actually hear what they were thinking. Yeah, I was messed up! I had become my own customer who didn't have to pay for the product and was never out of it.

I remember when the police were going from door to door at our apartment complex conducting a routine search. I was scared, high, and I just knew that they were looking for me. I had a phony box spring mattress, and when the police came into our place, I hid under it. I can still remember the heat from their flashlights shining through the nylon box spring. I was tumbling downhill toward an actual pool of fire with nothing good coming out of it except for my destruction. One evening, after cussing everyone out for no reason whatsoever, I decided to go for a long walk. It was a late-night weekend when I was walking down Hollywood Boulevard crying. I was missing my mother, my grandmother, my sister, my brothers, my cousins, my auntie, and my friends. I was at the point where I started losing my mind and didn't care about finding it!

As I continued to walk with my head down looking at the Hollywood stars and wondering why I couldn't have made it like them. I heard someone yelling my name, "Dixon! Dixon!" When I turned my head and looked, I couldn't believe my eyes. It was Rapper! The guy who stopped the Aryan brothers from doing me in when we were doing prison time together! As soon as he got close enough, I grabbed his hand and gave him a real big hug! After I released him, he got a good look at my face and said, "Aww, man, what's wrong, dog? I already know you going through it, my brother! They still showing your face on TV back home and putting you in the newspaper!"

I looked him in his face and told him I didn't know what to do. Then I explained to him that I started using cocaine. Rapper just started laughing. He grabbed me by both of my shoulders and told me to look at him! He said, "Brian, I saw the way you carried yourself in prison, and when I came home, me and you had some of the same circle of friends and didn't even know it. Brian! Look at me! You are capable of a lot, my man! You're going to get past this! Just pull yourself together, and start praying! Trust me, you're going to be fine!"

As we were separating, he gave me his number. I tore it to shreds before I got to my apartment due to my paranoia, but what he said to me really weighed heavy on my heart because what were the odds of me running into Rapper in California, all the way on the other side of the United States? (The Lord truly works in mysterious ways. Thank you, my friend.) (R)

When I got back to the apartment, I already knew that I owed everyone in there an apology. Even the dog will receive a sympathetic plea. So I took a deep breath, inserted my key. Then, I started turning the doorknob as slowly as I could with embarrassment written all over me. When I stepped into the apartment, Shadow ran up to me as he always did no matter what. At that very moment, my gut told me exactly what was going on, and to make sure that my gut was headed in the right direction, I walked over to the closet, and bingo, the gang members' things were gone. As I opened up the bathroom door, it looked as if there had been a tiny storm. I ran out the door and searched Hollywood City from the rooter to the tooter. But there were no signs of Julie. When I returned to the apartment complex, Shadow was gone and Julie's cat!

I sat in that apartment for days, just staring at the door. I didn't know how long it had been since I'd eaten. I didn't know how many days went by before I had a drink of water that would've made any difference from keeping my body from going into total dehydration. And I didn't know how much time I had left because I was very hungry, and my body was starting to give up. The one thing I could remember is how tired I was becoming. I kept dozing off, and my eyes would pop back open, hoping Julie would come walking through the door. With the last of the H2O that was dwelling within my vessel, beads of sweat started rolling down my face. In my dehydrated, coma-like state, I could not understand how my eyes were producing so many tears.

At that very moment, Rapper's last words invaded my soul! I lay on the floor in a fetal position, and then I locked my hands together as hard as I could, and I started praying. "God, please forgive me for all the wrong that I have done. I am so sorry. Please give me the strength to pull myself back together. God, you know I never meant to hurt anyone, and I try my best not to, but I'm hurting myself right now, God. In Jesus's name, I pray to you. Jesus, please deliver this message to your father. I am so sorry for the things I've done. I will never travel this road again. Please bring Julie back to me. I'm going to do the right things. Amen." Through my lonely tears and sorrowful cries, I went to sleep.

I was lying there on the floor when I started to feel a shake, shake, shake. I don't know how long I'd been sleeping there. Shake, shake, shake. When I opened my eyes, it was Julie! She picked me up off the floor and gave me a very tight hug. She sat me down on the sofa and started gathering some of my clothes and things that she thought I would need including my cat Mr. Mikie. After dressing me, she held me by my face. She told me she was in love with me and that she was taking me away from Hollywood. As we stepped outside, there was a cab driver standing by his vehicle holding the door open. We travel up the famous Hollywood Boulevard and made a right on Ventura, and we just kept going straight forward with no turning. We passed Universal Studios and the Boardwalk and went straight through the city of Encino. Then, we made a right into a city called Tarzana. The only thing I was thinking during this entire time was, *Wow, she does love me. Thank you, Lord.* :)

When we arrived at our destination, I was happy to see where we would be staying. We were in the suburbs of California. She knew how much I loved the outdoors, so she made sure we weren't too far from a place called Balboa Park. She also knew how much I loved swimming, so she made sure that she got a place with a very large Olympic-sized swimming pool. She gave me my own key, and when I opened up the door, Shadow ran up to me, shook his tail wildly, then started running around the apartment like he was crazy.

Instantly, I felt like I could finally call somewhere home. :)

CHAPTER 33

LIFE AND DEATH

The year was 1998, I had been on the run from Ohio for just about three years now, and my life was changing for the better. I was no longer visiting Hollywood, and Julie was no longer taking care of her street business. I met some Jewish people in Tarzana. For some reason, they took a true liking to me, and they gave me a brand-new 1998 Jeep Grand Cherokee for no apparent reason. I met some Bloods who were also living out there, but they weren't gangbanging in that neck of the woods. They had left their neighborhood in South Central and were out here getting their lives together and doing very well for themselves. Julie got a job at a very popular seafood restaurant and made manager within a couple of months.

By this time, I had fallen in love with Julie, and we were actually spending real time together. One day, we decided to go to Universal Studios on the Boardwalk. While we waited in line to purchase our movie tickets, a female walked past us sort of rapidly with her ball cap on and her head bowed down low.

Julie said, "That was Queen Latifah."

Now after all the crying I had done inside the Chinese theater for the role she played in *Set It Off* and her character breaking my heart at the same time, I just had to say hi! So I took off running behind her after I broke through the line of people and yelled her name really loud. Queen Latifah was honestly caught off guard. She turned and looked me dead in my face. I went over to her, and she was so very cool. I told her that I was from Cleveland. She gave me a hug and some encouraging words, and I told her that she would hear about me again. She gave me another hug and said, "Okay." I got back in line with Julie with a big smile on my face. Julie was smiling for me because she knew I loved Queen Latifah! As I stood back in line watching the Queen walk away, the song "We Are the Pros" just started playing in my head!

The next day, while Julie and I were going for a walk, I ran into Henry Winkler and his classic Mercedes at a gas station on Ventura. He was a very cool guy. Seeing him in person gave me a newfound respect for the character he played as The Fonz on the sitcom *Happy Days*. After a brief conversation with Mr. Winkler, I left that gas station with some encouraging words from him and me telling him that he would hear from me again. A couple of weeks after that, I was on Melrose at the beauty salon, getting my hair braided, and Marlon Wayans was there. He was truly a cool individual as well, and now, I was smiling because I was really living a different life!

One day, inside the movie theater, I turned around to apologize to a customer for taking so long to order my snacks because Julie and I were so high off the ganja! The guy turned out to be the yellow counterpart from the group Kid 'n' Play, and he was a true gentleman about the situation. I guess it is true: when you stop running the streets, you get to see the good parts of life, and time was going by with smiles. Me being on the run was slowly starting to fade away as the months changed.

August was just getting started, and I was standing inside the Beverly Hills Hospital with a big smile on my face and a pair of scissors in my right hand staring at the doctor. He asked me if I was ready. I said yes. Then I looked at Julie and asked her if she was ready.

She said yes. Then, I applied the scissors to where the doctor was pointing and cut the cord. As the doctors and the nurses were telling me and Julie congratulations, I was smiling down at my firstborn child! A beautiful baby girl! The first three or four days at home with my beautiful baby were truly amazing, even though something not seen continued tapping me on both of my shoulders, but my happiness shrugged off them eerie feelings. My mind was in the clouds. I couldn't believe that after the short crazy life I've live thus far, I was given the opportunity to be someone's daddy. But here I am, sitting here with a new baby in my life, a very kind-hearted woman who loved me just for the person I was, and in return, I wanted Julie for my wife. Even as all seemed as if it were gold, my gut feeling was hard at work, and I knew it was time to move!

I remember the very first day of being home with my daughter. Whenever I stepped outside, my body would always give me a very uneasy vibe, and that feeling never left as the next few days went by. On the eighth day, I called some of the homeboys over and told them that I would be moving and needed their help. That same day, I started packing things up because I knew something was wrong. I just didn't know what it was. As the hours ticked away, I got more and more nervous, so I decided to go for a bike ride. Less than three blocks away from my house, the police pulled me over for no apparent reason and asked for my ID. Before I gave it to them, I asked the officer why he pulled me over. He claimed it was because I was riding my bike on the sidewalk.

On day number 9, I stepped outside, and the whole street was just too quiet. As I surveyed the area, I noticed that the city water department decided to come and start working on a small piece of sidewalk, which was now blocking the main entrance to my front door. I walked back inside my home, called the Jewish man I was cool with, and told him I wouldn't be coming to work any longer. He told me he would miss eating bagels and Lox with me in the early mornings. I placed the phone down, kissed my little daughter on her forehead, and gave her a promise. "Precious little one, I love you. You're my only child, my firstborn, and I'm asking God to keep an eye on you and keep you safe. I'm going to take care of you. I'm going to be sure that I can find a way to be in your life."

On September 10, 1998, I had just finished strapping on Shadow's harness and hooking up his leash so we could go for a walk. As we were walking, there was a black sports car on my street with the windows tinted so dark you couldn't see anything inside of the vehicle. A little later that afternoon, Julie was playing with the baby and me, and the fellas had just finished eating lunch. We were ready to start moving my things. I picked up two dining table chairs and headed out the door. When I walked into the middle of the street, I just stopped moving because the hair on my left arm was beginning to stand straight up; and a split second after that, I had goose bumps running all over my body. I quickly looked to the left, and there were no cars on my street except for the black car that was there yesterday. I heard noises, so I tilted my head toward the sky and realized there were two helicopters circling.

For a second, I thought it was another amazing bank robbery attempt going on, like the one that occurred in North Hollywood on February 28, 1997, with the two guys covered with armor from head to toe. Then, I noticed a large helicopter was in the distance and a smaller bubble-like one just flew overhead. Common sense made my body turn and look to the right, and that's when I started hearing the throttles of the horses. Three unmarked police cruisers were speeding in my direction. As I dropped the chairs and raised my hands in the air, the officers were already getting out of their vehicles. After a couple of blinks from my trusted eyeballs, I was then staring down the barrel of twelve-gauge shotguns and 9mm service pistols trained on my face.

One of the officers started to shout at me, "You better not run. I will shoot you! Get down on your knees, and place your hands in the air!"

Little did this officer know that if I ever planned on running, I would've been gone, and this little capture-the-bad-guy scenario wouldn't have had the chance to see the day of light with me being the main actor playing in it. Truth be told, I was truly tired of running and was thinking about my new daughter. Shoot! I had already been on the run for three years, and there was no statute of limitation because I had already been charged in Ohio. Besides, I had done some calculating. After doing a little math, I figured, "I'm twenty-five now. If I can get out of this with ten years, I'll be thirty-five when I come home. And I'm pretty sure if I continue working on getting my life together, God will give me a fair path to travel, and I could probably one day be in my daughter's life again."

After lying down on my stomach as I was told, the officer had me place my hands behind my back, and then the handcuffs were applied. As I lay on the hot concrete, peering down the street, I watched as the door to the black sports car opened up. The guy got out with tennis shoes on, a pair of blue jeans, a white polo shirt, and a white baseball cap with matching sunglasses. He started walking toward me with a vanilla folder in his hand, "What's your name?" he asked politely.

By this time, the guys who were helping me move had gone and told Julie what was going on. She was standing there when I answered the officer's question. "I'm Devon Richfields," I revealed to him through a very rapid beating heart and nervous breathing.

He proceeded to place a large photo down by my face. Then he said, "Yup, you look like Brian M. Dixon to me."

That's when Julie started shouting, "His name is not Brian! It's Devon. Everyone calls him D. Y'all have the wrong person! Can y'all please let him go now?"

The marshal looked at Julie, then told the officers to stand me on my feet. Julie was told to come over and talk to me. I explained to Julie that my real name was Brian, and I was on my way back to Ohio. The marshal told Julie to go get the baby, so I could see her for a second. After shedding tears and giving kisses to the two worlds I loved so dearly, I was escorted to the officer's vehicle. I asked him how they found me, and he said they'd known where I was for the last few months, but I wasn't a main target on their radar. They had murderers to track down. "Besides," he said, "we knew you had a baby on the way, so we allowed you to walk through that first, Mr. Dixon. We're not monsters, you know! We just chase them and catch them!" He finished that statement with a chuckle. "Now it's time for you to go back to Ohio because Cleveland wants to talk to you, my little monster." He finished that last sentence with an even bigger chuckle. And to be honest, I found myself appreciating his corny jokes because now it was time to start the beginning stages of facing some very serious charges that were nothing to chuckle about!

Before they could put me on a plane, train, or bus, I had to go through their system first. My first stop was something called the Glasshouse, where we ate burritos for lunch, breakfast, and dinner. At this time, I was bitten by some type of insect, which left a large scar on my left calf muscle. For the next three days, I had puss running out of that scar, but that was of no concern to the officers who were housing us. They just told me to wait till I got to the county jail in order to receive proper treatment. For some reason or another, they continued to call me by my alias name and not my government name. We were now well into the month of September in 1998, when I was placed down on a bench waiting for them to call my name at the Los Angeles County Jail. I was given a sandwich and an apple, then asked if I was a Blood or a Crip because they had special housing modules for gangbangers. I didn't have the chemistry for either one of those housing units.

When we started getting booked in, there were over one hundred of us in there. Sooner or later, I knew my name would be called, and there it was. "Brian Dixon, come to the desk."

But I ignored them because at the Glasshouse, they were calling me by my alias! That's the only name I understand, so that's who I was going to be. The officers went around, asking people their names and personally checking them off a list. When they got to me, I told them that my name was Devon. They continued to look up and down the list. Finally, they were mad because they couldn't figure out who I was, so they took me to a single man's jail cell and handcuffed me to a bench. They only left me about four inches of chains to move around and told me that's where I will sit until I could remember who I was.

With the day's events, I was stressed out. As I continued to only think about Julie and our new daughter. I had no problem falling asleep in such a very uncomfortable position. It seemed as if hours had passed when I was awakened by the cell door opening. About five officers stepped into the cell and asked for my name in a rueful manner. Once again, I told them my name was Devon, and that's when one of the officers grabbed me by my throat, and I flipped out like a madman. I was kicking and screaming, as if all of my stupid heroic Red Ranger tactics were going to break my chains and set me free. All five officers ran out of the room, and less than two minutes later, all I saw were shields and mace after they subdued me. I saw a white alcohol pad, a white nurse, with a white coat on, and I was stabbed with a needle full of liquid! The beginning process of the sedation closed my eyes pretty rapidly. I don't know how long I was out, but when I awoke, I was naked in a dark cell with only a very thick foamy-type blue blanket.

When the officer made his rounds, he noticed that I was awake. He came to my cell and shackled my ankles to my wrists. He walked me over to a table where the psychiatrist was waiting for me.

After a series of questions, he prescribed me Haldol, (mechanism not fully understood; antipsychotics block postsynapitc dopamine receptors in the brain,depress the RAS, including those parts of the brain involved with wakefulness and emesis; chemically resembles the phenothiazines: psychotic disorders.) along with a pill called Cogentin,(imbalance of cholineric and dopaminergic neurotrans-mission in the basal ganglia of the brain of a parkinsonism patient). With no options but to pop the pills, I was spaced out and pretty much unresponsive to anything that made sense around me. But I was pretty much safe because they left me alone inside a twenty-three-hour-a-day one-man cell on the psychiatric unit. Once the psy-chiatrist felt I was well enough to be placed inside a regular mental population cell block, I was given a county orange jumpsuit and was allowed to come out of my cell. But for some reason, I wouldn't come out. I would just pace back and forth while my cell door was open. Since they finally figured out who I was, I was allowed to use the telephone.

As I picked up the phone and made a collect call to my mother, it turned out to be a call that I would carry with me for the rest of my life. My mother accepted the charges, but I could tell that something was terribly wrong, and after listening to my mother's voice, there was nothing I could do except break down into tears. :(My little sister, my beautiful little sister, my only sister at the tender age of nineteen, had just passed away from a blood disorder called Lupus. I didn't know how to react to such a sad discovery, and with all the complications from the medications that was flowing through my body, my system had no choice but to allow me to have a chron-ic-heartbroken-very-sad-watery eyed- episode in front of everybody on that cell block! All I could do is reminisce on the broken home from which I came from, I never had a chance to get to know my sis-ter because I was a soldier to the streets. Never had a chance to see her first boyfriend, never was there for any of her graduations. And now because of all of my stupid acts, I will not be there for her funeral, (Its really hurting me to write this part of the book) so due to my actions in life I will be saying my deepest and my loneliest goodbyes to my little sister from a jail cell on the other side of the United States. :((TCB) "I miss U. Please forgive me for the big brother I was not." Julie actually had a chance to see my little sister before she passed away, because as soon as they locked me up, I had her moved straight to Ohio with my parents.

My nervous breakdown resulted in me being the target of a maced shower, strapped down with five-point restraints, and yet another liquid needle. I don't know how long I was out of reality, but when I awoke, I was back inside of a jail cell, naked, with a blue foamy blanket. I was in and out of that room so many times you could've mistaken me for a Black Linus, from the Charlie Brown series because that thick foamy blanket actually became my friend.

Finally, the time came for me to go back to Ohio. After the marshals read the report of my jail status, they weren't taking any chances with me. We started the trip off on negative vibes, with them not trusting me at all. Once the chains were around my waistline and my feet and wrist shackles were connected to make one body chain, a black box was placed over my handcuffs. This didn't allow me to do too much movement at all, unless I wanted bloody wrists. As we entered the airport and I boarded the airplane, I was surprised! You would've thought this was a commercial airline. There were over one hundred prisoners on here waiting to be transported to wherever, and this would be my very first airplane ride. My first stop was Oklahoma. From there, I would be transferred to a bus. As I walked into the federal facility in Oklahoma, I was extremely shocked. This super maximum-security facility played house to some of the most notorious individuals in the United States. I was locked up with people from all sorts of different countries! I got cool with a guy from Tonga! I wasn't in this federal facility for a good twenty-four hours before they had us all strip naked and went over our bodies with the blue light. They were trying to get some type of detection of blood. After, I was given a thumbs-up, as I walked past the cell where the incident occurred. The six-by-four room looked more like a mini-slaughterhouse than a prison cell. And this devastating scenario transpired more than once during my stay in the Oklahoma Federal Facility. One thing I started to learn early was that when you're in the federal custody system, your life don't mean jack shit to the next man.

As I boarded the bus, I was happy to see that we had TVs to keep our eyes busy. It would be four to five days before we reached Ohio. That meant four to five days of eating peanut butter and cheese crackers, an apple, and two eight-ounce water with two crunchy granola bars. With these delicious kick ass meals, the guards controlled the prisoners' restroom usage during transportation. And trust me, everyone was constipated! Finally, I walked inside the Cleveland County Jail. As I was being ushered into the processing room, someone yelled one of the nicknames that I conjured up out of thin air. "Joker, Joker!"

I turned to see that it was Beans! After three years of not seeing anyone that I knew personally, here was Beans, in the cell next door to me. Even though it was a brief reunion, I was very happy to see my friend, and he couldn't believe I was there. My transition into the Cleveland County Jail was not a pleasant one due to the fact that I wanted to go to a regular county jail population unit because I wanted to be able to talk with Beans, but they felt as if I wasn't ready for general population. That's when the officers and I had a verbal disagreement, to which I ended up with the short end of the stick. For all my hard work in the conversation and my slight physical attributes (which I somehow unknowingly added to the situation), I was awarded a needle with liquid in it inserted into my bloodstream, accommodated by a cold jail cell on the psychiatric floor and another foamy blanket. And the cherry on top? All my clothing was taken away once again.

This went on for a couple of months. One day, they decided to switch up my medication. They put me on something called Trilafon (management of manifestations of psychotic disorders significant for antipsychotic activity). That was just one of the worst things they could've done. When the Haldol and the Trilafon met each other inside my bloodstream, I guess we can say they didn't like each other, and both sides of the medication started gangbanging inside my blood system. This sent my mind into an uncontrollable whirlwind! One second, I was unhappy. The next second, I was happy. Then I was horny, and for a split second after that, I was angry. This was an ongoing thing, so the psychiatrist of the county jail figured it was best for me to remain inside this cold cell with no clothes, forever!

During one of the episodes, two federal agents came to visit me. I believe they were talking about some bank robberies, but I truly couldn't concentrate on exactly what they were saying because one second, I thought they were my friends. The next second, I thought they were my family. The next second, I thought they were trying to hurt me. A split second after that, the first agent sounded like he was a singing feline sitting on someone's fence while purposefully allowing his irritating meows to prevent people from sleeping. When the other agent started talking while his partner was making terrible music, he sounded as if he was a whimpering canine stuck inside the house when he really wanted to be outside raising his leg up on a tree. And boy oh boy did their music suck when they combined there conversation in my direction! I just sat there, watching them do their ugly duet number. The medication really had me stuck on stupid, but my ears were working perfectly. Early the next morning, it was time for me to go to court and answer to the sawed-off shotgun charges. And due to my physical and mental state, it was best that they continue to keep me in a jail cell that was located behind the courtroom by myself until it was time for me to make an appearance in front of the judge.

As I was nervously waiting for my turn to explain my actions, I started hearing voices coming from every direction. I couldn't make out what they were saying, so I started asking them, "Are you talking to me? Well, what do you want?"

That's when I heard a very loud and clear "To put you on fire!" And I truly didn't want to be on fire! Very quickly, my mind went to work to ensure that I would be protected from the fire that was targeting me! I had a lot of hair on my head, at least fifteen inches long, so I put my hair and my head inside the toilet and started flushing it rapidly! I figured once whoever came to put me on fire, when I stood up and shook my head real hard from left to right, all the water from my hair would coat my body like a fire-resistant protection suit. I heard a lot of noise that sounded like chains, so I braced myself for the fire! When the cell door opened, they tried to snatch me up very fast and with a lot of force, but I had my head so deep inside of that toilet that my head got caught on the rim, and they continued to pull even harder, trying to break me free. They had to snatch me up a few times before they finally got me out, and when I opened my eyes, I didn't see any fire at all. It was the sheriff. And he started shouting to the other bailiffs and sheriffs, "He's trying to drown himself!" Instantly, I was slammed into the jail cell wall and was pinned against it until reinforcements came.

I never made into the courtroom that day, but a needle did make its way into my bloodstream. Just as quickly as they pulled the needle out of me, I was back in Lala Land. A couple weeks after that, I had another episode. They introduced me to the five-point strap mobile chair and a bigger needle. When I awoke the next morning, I had on street clothes and was in a regular room with two beds in it, and the door was unlocked and wide open. As I got up to look out the door, I realized I was inside a hospital. It was too lifelike to be a dream, so I knew this was the real deal. But one thing I noticed: there were no exit doors. I walked over to the desk where a nurse was sitting and politely asked her where I was. She told me I was at the Metro North Coast Hospital. I didn't muster under my voice, but what I was thinking just came flying straight out my mouth in a real loud shout, "So you telling me I'm in the loony bin!"

To my disadvantage, a few of the other patients didn't like what I said. They started approaching me, and I became scared because I truly didn't know the power of this medicated gang. I decided to protect myself and ran toward them growling like a bear, but my Yogi the Bear impersonation only lasted a split second as I was forced down into a chair and strapped in, while watching the "alcohol-free" liquid cocktail from that big ass needle slowly disappear into my arm once again!

Whatever was inside that last needle really had an effect on me! For the next fifteen to eighteen hours, I was physically restricted from doing anything. A simple task such as scratching my nose was impossible due to this extreme feeling of unbalance motion running its course over my entire body. As the days started going by, the psychiatrist tried different medications on me. I do believe that they deemed me one of their best lab rats while trying to make me mentally prepared for court. From time to time, my big brother would come see me. Julie would come visit me with our daughter, and I was proud of her because now she had her own place here in Ohio. To my surprise, Mom made her visits to see me because she always said she would never come see me while I was locked up. But here she was with my aunt and my grandmother, and we were giving my daughter a birthday party inside one of the visiting rooms. Later on in life, she explained her reasons about her personal visitations. She said, "By you being in a psych ward wasn't considered the same as me being in jail behind thick glass to be viewed as an animal. This is a hospital, which makes a world of a difference to me."

The eagle even made his visits! As mean as he was to me when I was growing up, he actually stuck with me through my whole prison sentence. He used to always tell me to use my time wisely while I was incarcerated. He made sure that I didn't want for anything. Once a month, he sent me enough money to make it through to the next. I remember the time we had our last visit, looking at each other through the thick glass. He tried to give me hints, but in my medicated state, I didn't catch on to things so quickly or not at all. He kept telling me that he wasn't going to be around for long. He talked to me about getting my life together. He made me make him a promise that I would never be like him. I gave him his promise. At the same time, I needed to know something, so I stood up and motioned for him to bring his face closer to the glass.

I asked him, "Why did you beat me so bad and then turn around and lie to my grandmother that you didn't do it and not one time have you offered an apology?"

Instantly, he started shedding tears. He didn't look at me at first but lowered his head and started repeating over and over, "I'm sorry, Brian." But he never gave me an answer. He just sat there, crying. But the answer was revealed later in life as I was looking at him in the hospital on his deathbed. And there's no doubt in my mind that if I had the hand he had given himself in life, I would be somewhere crying as well.

CHAPTER 34

ATTORNEY SWISS ROLL AND THE AIR MARSHAL

Finally, with all the pills sliding down my esophagus, with all the liquid needle cocktails that has tattooed my arm, and with a lot of nights and days of being stripped and strapped down like a naked drug induce grown baby, the psychiatric hospital had finally accomplished their goal, and I was found competent for court. That meant it was time for me to leave the hospital and be placed back in the Cleveland County Jail. And that made a sad day for me because that meant that I will no longer be able to watch my favorite show. Because due to the medication having me so laid-back, I used to stand in one spot for hours, watching the Metro helicopters take off into the air and land. I promised myself that one day in life, I would take a helicopter ride. Back in the county and pretrial after pretrial, it was finally my day in court. I wasn't feeling all that great about my court-appointed public defender, Attorney Swiss Roll! When I first met this jive turkey, it was a total joke. During our first initial interview, he would doze off and go to sleep! I mean like a real freaking little nap! Attorney Swiss Roll would be sleep for about five minutes, right in front of me! On the day of my trial, Swiss Roll was like, "Okay, me, the judge, and the district attorney have decided that you don't deserve eight to twenty-five years in prison. The district attorney said that she is willing to give you three to fifteen years, and if you take that deal, the judge said that she will bring you back in six months and set you free. Do you want to take it?"

"Of course I do!" I replied to him.

"Okay, I'm going to notify them that you accept the plea deal. Now you are not allowed to speak on this inside the courtroom because we already discussed it. So when the judge asks you if anybody offered you anything, just say no."

"Okay," I politely replied back to this evil nigga.

Finally, I was brought in front of the honorable Judge Greenhouse, and from what I heard, she was a fair judge but strict as well, so I was fortunate to have such a judge presiding over my case that would give a fair shake if the case truly called for it. The judge spoke to me, "Mr. Dixon, how do you plead?"

"I plead guilty, Your Honor."

"Make a note that Mr. Dixon pleaded guilty. Mr. Dixon, you will be sentenced to three to fifteen years. Mr. Dixon, did anyone offer or promise you anything to take this plea?"

The whole time I was standing there thinking, "I'm happy that I do spend my time wisely while incarcerated, and the law library is one of my favorite places." There was no way in the world that judge was agreeing to the deal that Swiss Roll said they were offering me. I turned my body toward my wicked ass attorney, then stretched my arm out and pointed straight at him like the crime he was committing! I answered the judge's question in a slightly loud tone. "He said,"—then I turned my body around and pointed at the judge, so she will know that I'm not as crazy as the try to make me out to be—"that you said, if I plead to three to fifteen years, you would bring me home in six months and set me free!"

Judge Greenhouse looked over at Attorney Swiss Roll and said, "I didn't say that!"

Turning and pointing again, I shouted, "He said you did! And I know what I'm talking about! Because the court system sent me to the hospital for them to make me competent for court proceedings! So I know exactly what I'm speaking on, Your Honor."

The Sleeping Swiss Roll just sat there with his head down and didn't say a word. Then, the judge said, "Okay, Mr. Dixon, I'm going to bring you back in six months."

Seventy-two hours after that, I was back on a prison bus, making my way eagerly into the future. My first stop was back at the Grafton prison system where I was fortunate enough to have a conversation with the female guard that said I looked no older than her son back in 1992. This time she removed me from my unit right then and there and gave me another kitchen job. And this was pretty easy for her to do because now she was a sergeant. A couple of weeks later I was sitting inside of The Richland Penitentiary, and with not too much to do in this joint I just counted the months that were going by too slow for my taste, but I do give credit for every day that sailed by pretty smoothly. I only had one incident that wasn't in my favor too much, but I still came out of it with no harm. The dorms at Richland Prison were split into two different units. You had your A side, and you had your B side. You had little groups that used to wrestle each other whenever someone got caught on the wrong side of the dorm. The bathroom was agreed upon by both sides to be neutral, but some of these guys didn't follow the rules. Whenever I went to the restroom, I would put a lock inside of a sock, just in case.

One day, three guys came in to jump on me, and I explained to them that they already knew the rest room was on neutral grounds. But they weren't trying to hear that because earlier that day, I caught one of them on my side of the dorm, and I put him in a choke hold and lay him down on the floor. So while I was standing in the rest room, waiting to see which frog was going to jump first, I pulled my lock and sock out, and they made an angry retreat. A few minutes after that, their gang leader stepped in front of my face with a lot of attitude. I've never been one to argue. I watched my mother and father do it way too much, so with a fast strike, I connected my fist to his nose, and his attitude flew straight out the ballpark, pretty much like the way the vice cop smacked my little friend at the school playground years ago. He didn't put up too much of a fight. I guess he totally understood and respected the PSI in my punch at that particular time.

At about two or three in the morning the following day, the inmate next to me woke me up. While he was strapping on his shoes to help protect me, he said, "They coming around the back way." I hurried and strapped up my tennis shoes, then grabbed my lock and put some blue soap inside of a sock and went to meet them. I didn't know what I was walking into. There were about seven of them bastards! They had no notification that I was very known and respected in the streets, and most of all, people just flat out liked me for who I am. By the time they got close enough, four of the imprisoned big heads were standing next to me and you do not argue with an OG in prison! This guy thought he was cool with these OGs, but the OGs were from my neighborhood, except for one. He was from Columbus, but he liked me. He was the one that woke me up. They explained to the guy and his crew that there would be no stabbings because these coward ass niggas came after me with homemade prison knives. The OG from Columbus said it would only be fair to me if the guy fought me on his own since he pulled the card. The guy didn't want to do that, so we called in a truce, and that was that. It was never spoke on again.

I had six months in, and I still hadn't received any paperwork from Attorney Swiss Roll showing that he had done his job to get me back in the courtroom, nor was I surprised. With two months left on the actual eight months I was given, I knew it was time for me to do some homework! I started going to the law library and got busy. I already knew that I wasn't available for shock parole or super shock parole due to the seriousness of my crime. However, I was given a promise in that courtroom, and I was determined to see some type of results from that attorney's bullshit that he thought he was going to get off.

As the days went by slowly as ever, I was into the eighth month when my name was called over the loudspeaker. It was my time to see the parole board because of all the county jail time that I had in already! I was well over the three-year period that was required on a three- to fifteen-year prison sentence that was needed in order to see the parole board. After sitting in the little room with four people that had the right to do whatever they wanted to do with my time, they decided that I needed to walk off three more years in the prison system before I see them again to discuss me being set free. As I walk through the prison yard, making my way back to my unit, other inmates were asking me, "What they give you? Three more years?"

I just said with no emotions tide to it, "Yup!" That's when my childhood friend DeMarco started explaining to me that I shouldn't even worry about it, unless Cuyahoga County never comes to retrieve me. That night, the correction officer told me that I will be leaving in a few hours. So I quickly packed my things and headed back downtown for court without ever receiving a letter from my lawyer. After about a week on the mental health unit, I was the next name on the docket to be called for court, and there it was! Dixon! And the same sheriff as before when my name was called came to retrieve me, and when he opened up the door to the waiting cell, I could see the relief on his face because I didn't have my head stuffed down into the toilet! We looked at each other for a split second and shared a quick smiling smirk, his smirk saying, "Thank you," and mine replying, "You're welcome, you fuck."

As I entered the courtroom, my attorney was sitting over there, dozing off as usual with his silly "stuffed" in his suite self. The district attorney was on the other side, preparing her case while totally against me being released! And by the seriousness of her facial expression, I could tell she was prepared to do whatever it took for me not to see the day of light unless it was to be behind prison walls! As Judge Greenhouse came out of her chambers and sat down in her chair, the proceedings started. The judge stated that we were there for my potential release. Attorney Swiss Roll didn't say anything, but the prosecutor had plenty to say. She explained to the judge her justifications for me to continue on with my current prisoner status. She suggested I wasn't mentally ready to go home. She ended on this particular note, "Besides, Your Honor, Mr. Dixon's attorney did not file the proper motions in order for him to be released."

Once again, Attorney Swiss Roll didn't offer anything but a sleepy and tired aura circulating around his large self. For a brief second, when I turned my attention back to the judge, I believe I could read the judge's lips. It was as if she was muttering under her breath, "Mr. Dixon, Dixon, Dixon!" When the judge said my last name for the third time, it was drawn out! I continued to watch as she started tapping her hands against the papers before her. With a slight raise of her eyebrows, I could tell by her expression when the imaginary light bulb above her head popped on! She asked the courtroom to give her a second, and she headed off to her chambers. She returned after a brief few minutes with an envelope in her hand. As I glanced at the envelope, I knew it was the one I mailed to the clerk of courts. After opening it and reading the contents, the judge looked at the prosecutor, then turned a sharp eye toward my attorney. Then, she addressed the courtroom. "It seems here that Mr. Dixon took it upon himself to file his own motions, and from what I can see, everything is filled out properly. Mr. Dixon is free to leave on super shock probation."

That night while I was sitting on the unit waiting for my name to be called, I watched through my cell door as other inmates' names were called and they were leaving the unit to go home. I can't remember when I finally fell asleep waiting desperately to hear my name being called, but unfortunately I was awakened very early in the morning by a sheriff. He told me that my attorney wanted to talk to me. I was thinking, *Wow, Mr. Swiss Roll actually has something to say to me.*

But when I entered the conference room, it wasn't Mr. Swiss Roll at all. This guy was a federal attorney! He extended his hand and introduced himself as federal attorney Mr. Good Fella. I can actually say that his name fit his personality. He was on the straight and narrow. Instantly, my gut told me that he wasn't out to get me, but at the same time, it didn't tell me that he was on my team 100 percent either, but I had a gut feeling that he wasn't out to railroad me as much as attorney Mr. Public Pretender.

As I sat in the chair in front of him, we met eyeball to eyeball for the first time. He asked me what I knew about a bank robbery while he glanced through a folder with my picture on it. I didn't answer him. I just stared at him, not hearing nor caring about a word that was coming out of his mouth! My whole train of thought was on what had just transpired the day before around the same time. Judge Greenhouse had just told me I was free to go home! Now I was sitting in front of another attorney guy! MF! Instantly, he stopped what he was saying and stared back at me. He closed his folder, stood up, and placed his hand on my right shoulder just before he exited the little conference room we shared.

As he squeezed my shoulder, he softly said, "Everything's going to be all right." And I flipped out. As the weeks passed, on December 1, 2000, I walked into the federal courtroom accompanied by two federal marshals and plenty of handcuffs and chains. When Federal Judge Kind Heart entered her courtroom, I asked her if I could look out of her window because we were high up in the air. And for the past few weeks, I've been inside of a jail cell, butt-hole bare, with no window, for twenty-three hours a day, and I really wanted to see what type of view she had. She said yes, to my surprise, and asked the marshals to walk me over to her window. Her window was behind her podium, but she still allowed them to let me invade her space. I can truly say that she was a beautiful-hearted judge. As I looked down, all the cars and people just looked like dots moving about their daily business.

On December 4, 2000, I was ordered to remain in custody with no bond and was immediately transported to a federal medical facility to begin psychiatric treatment. January 23, 2001, I was delivered to a Metro federal correctional center in Chicago, where they ran a series of tests on me. On March 7, 2001, I was found to be competent to proceed to criminal adjudication. On March 16, 2001, my case was turned over to the permanent judge who would oversee everything. His name was Simon Twiss Junior. He reminded me of Judge Mathis from the TV courtroom show. He seemed to be a fair judge, as long as you were a respectful criminal. From April 19, 2001 until my sentencing date of May 8, 2003, I was in and out of psychiatric hospitals all over the country! The US marshals were at the point now from seeing me so much that they actually started calling me Brian since we were seeing one another so freaking often.

I had taken over ten airplane trips and who knows how many bus rides! One minute, we somewhere where it was snowing. After a couple of hours passed, we were somewhere where it's bright and sunny. A couple of hours after that, we were somewhere where it was nighttime, then daylight. My biological clock was totally off the Richter scale. During one of my air trips, the government dressed up one of their wolves in sheep's clothing. Sitting right next to me on the airplane was the young guy that participated in the bank robbery with me. It was a very good thing that I know people who know people who know some more people because I was told through the grapevine that this young guy had gotten busted for something else, and to save his soul, he explained to the police that he knew who the bank robber was from years ago.

Mr. Wolf needed to establish a conversation between me and himself. As we rode through the bumpy turbulence, he continued over and over, trying to get me to remember who he was. I just sat there and let the medication inside my body take the steering wheel while conversing with this programmed clown. I could tell he was upset because this fish wasn't biting. Finally, they placed all of us inside the same cell at a federal holding facility located in Youngstown, Ohio. I had grown tired of the charades, so I needed to find a way to get this guy to stop talking to me! As we lined up to receive our lunch from the officers, I grabbed mine with a smile and proceeded straight to the toilet. I placed my hamburger and my french fries on top of the toilet seat where everyone had previously urinated. After taking a couple of bites, I stripped down to my birthday suit and walked to the middle of the cell. After folding my clothes into a makeshift pillow, I went to sleep in the middle of the cell floor with not even an underwear on, just butt-hole new baby bare! So the marshals placed me in a cell by myself. On May 8, 2003, I walked into the courtroom with all my government-provided platinum jewelry shackled on me, followed by two marshals. Judge Simon Twiss Junior asked me how I plead to the charges found against me, and I said, "Guilty, Your Honor."

Before he sentenced me, he asked me, "Mr. Dixon, did you rob the bank?"

I was answering his question within my thoughts, *Technically, no, I didn't, Your Honor. See what happened was, I went to the bank earlier that week and applied for a small loan, and they rejected my offer. They talked about me bad, Your Honor! They even called me a name! They said I may become an undesirable liability! And that hurt my feelings, Your Honor! So I went back within the next couple of days and made an unlawful withdrawal. The only harm that I brought forth towards anyone would be the IRS because my withdrawal had no taxes to be paid added to it. Because once I made the withdrawal, Your Honor, the insurance company had to pay the bank back. And once the long arm of the law finally caught up to me, to which I knew they surely would do sooner or later, once I'm in prison for the charge, whatever job detail they give me to work while incarcerated, the money was going to go to the insurance company that paid the bank. I believe I'm only guilty of not paying the interest on the money I borrowed.*

But just as fast as that thought entered, the thought was gone, and I answered, "Yes, I did do it, Your Honor."

So I was committed to the custody of the BOP for a term of sixty months, and it was recommended that I get housed at the Springfield, Missouri, facility and continue to receive mental health treatment. I was given credit for time served, so out of the five years that I was sentenced to serve, I was left with only seventeen months of actual prison time to complete. They did give me a cherry on top, and that cherry was three years supervised release to follow, along with over $12,000 to be paid to the courts and over $50,000 in restitution.

After it was all said and done, I asked the judge if I could pass everyone their gifts I made for them for being so kind to me throughout this case. He said yes, and I began passing out all the cartoons of Bugs Bunny, Daffy Duck, Wiley Coyote, and a few others that I colored the night before. I gave cartoons to just about everyone in the courtroom. My mom and dad received one apiece as well. My attorney received one, the judge and the district attorney received one, and I apologized to the court's reporters that I didn't color one for them. A few hours after that, I was in an extra extended van that was occupied from the Rooter-to the-Tooter with both male and female prisoners. For one reason or another, I was fortunate enough to be placed in front of a very beautiful woman who had just received a three-year prison sentence for narcotics. We were allowed to talk on the van because everyone had been sentenced and we were on our way to Youngstown, Ohio to be separated and placed on an airplane to Missouri. During this road trip, me and this lovely young lady was in a very deep conversation about our "Sexual Love Partners" that we were leaving behind, when out of the thin air, Tyrese voice started smoothly sailing out of the van speakers into everyone's ears singing his song 'Why You Gonna Act Like That'. With both of us imprisoned with our chains around our ankles and handcuffs around our wrists, that wasn't enough to prevent us from putting our lips and our tongues together. We French kissed and sucked and nibbled on each other's bottom lip until Tyree's magical notes started to fade away back into the van speakers. Once Tyree's voice went totally silent we slowly opened our eyes back up just to notice everyone looking at us with their mouths "WIDE OPEN" doing the flycatcher dance with Envious-Thought-Patterns protruded from their eyeballs. (Now whenever I hear that song, an automatic smile takes shelter on my lips)

On July 22, 2003, I was delivered to the USMCFP in Springfield, Missouri, the same prison that housed the notorious mafia boss John Gotti. My stay in Missouri was only for a few months. They just wanted to make sure they had me on the right medications. Once it was determined that everything was running smoothly within my blood system, I was placed on a small two propeller airplane with two pilots and three air marshals. With all of us so tightly crammed into this little ice cream scoop of a real airplane, we were on our way. We landed in Pennsylvania. About an hour or so after that, I was at my parent institution, the notorious Lewisburg high-security federal penitentiary, a.k.a. "The Big House!" Lewisburg Federal Penitentiary is one of the many federal penitentiaries that's above ground that was built for the most disruptive and difficult to control federal prisoners from around the country, and they had little old me in here with these monsters! >:)

I was trying to figure out why the officer in California considered me a monster. I wasn't on the level of these guys in here! At least I didn't think I was. As I got undressed and prepared for my blue federal wardrobe, one of the officers was staring at my legs because one of my legs was bigger than the other. So I asked him if he wanted a story. He said yes, so I told him.

Somewhere between all of the airplane rides and all the different modes of transportation, from airplanes to cars to buses, one day I woke up inside my jail cell, and I couldn't stand up. I complained for the next few days to the officers who were running the units, but due to me being a psychiatric patient, my words didn't mean nothing to them. I was no more than sounds of mere nothingness. One day, the officer that worked my unit knew my older brother, so he went and got a nurse. I knew exactly who the nurse was because when Julie used to bring my daughter down to see me, the nurse would come inside of the visiting room just to see my daughter. I can still remember the first time that she saw us three together. She told me that I could never deny my daughter because we looked like twins. After I explained to the nurse what was going on, she ordered an emergency outgoing hospital visit for me. I was taken to St. Vicks (the same place not too far into the future, where the eagle took his last breath), where it was determined that I had a blood clot in my leg which was moving upward toward my heart. The doctor looked at me and said, "Consider yourself very fortunate that the nurse took time to listen to you because within a few days or less, my friend, you might not have made it. And I'm sorry to tell you, but due to the duration that you suffered with the clot in your leg, one of your legs is going to always be bigger than the other."

After I finished the story, I had a cool relationship with the officer for the remainder of my time there.

Before he escorted me to my designated unit, he asked me if I believed in God. I responded yes. Then he asked me if I believed God and Jesus were one, and I answered yes. Then he told me when I got a chance to read 1 Corinthians 13, and I gave him a promise that I would do so. When I finally entered the cell where I would be living for the next few months, I started thinking to myself, "First I was in Missouri, in the same prison where John Gotti died, and now I'm at my second prison, where he used to live as well!" Not only was I sitting where John Gotti used to sit, I was also sitting in the same space where Scarface Al Capone used to sit! Not only was this the home of some of the most top-notch mobsters, it housed other famous men as well, like Bayard Rustin, the civil rights leader, and accused Soviet spy Alger Hiss! And I was not trying to follow in the supposedly mega crime figures' footsteps! I quickly opened up my Bible and started reading 1 Corinthians 13. During my reading, I came across 2 Corinthians 5:17. By the time the morning showed itself, I had a brand-new perspective on life.

My transition into the high-security facility was an easy one. They had my medication regulated correctly, so I was very aware of what was going on, and I started spending my time wisely. The first thing I did was put in requests to see the counselors because I wanted to sign up for parenting classes. Throughout my years in prison, somewhere down the line, Julie had given up trying to be a mom and abandon our daughter, so her brother and his wife took charge, so Julie didn't have custody of our child any longer. She tried to get her daughter back and sent me all the paperwork from California of all the court proceedings of her custody case. But in the end, she lost total custody. Later on in life, she started getting herself together. She even got married and had two more little girls, but she never got over the regret of losing her first child.

After I signed up to participate in the three stages of parenting, I decided to sign up for Spanish as well. Due to the fact that I had a prison job now, I never did take Spanish seriously. I did, however, take my prison job very seriously! Because I was preparing myself to come home. I wanted to already be in the mode of having a strong work ethic. As the months went by, I was cool with just about everyone in the prison, inmates and guards alike. I also stayed in church. I was truly starting to get to know our Father. As the months passed, my every thought was about how my daughter was doing. I knew nothing about her. Julie and I had long since lost contact.

Holidays were hard for me because I made stuffed bears and cards in prison that I couldn't send to my daughter because since Julie's brother and his wife had custody of her, they started refusing my mail. Everything I sent out to her came right back to me. But I did not let that stop me from taking photos with my daughter's picture. Easter of 2004, I painted eggs, made cards, and sat my daughter's picture up with them and took photos. One day, I believed God would bring us back together, and I would show her that the promise I made to her years before inside the Beverly Hills Hospital had never left my soul! I am very determined for my daughter to know who her birth father is! And if it is possible, with me trying to walk with God because I'm not an angel! But Mr. Brian Dixon is going to bring this to light! Amen.

As the days were sliding down for me to be released, everyone in the prison became very comical. I didn't mind. The officers told me that they hated to see me go because I was such a hard worker. Then we both would laugh. The officers I worked with cleaning up trash in the kitchen of the prison warehouse were really cool with me. They were very surprised that I would even come to work on my days off. They didn't mind me taking a little food here and there to supply the prison with because as long as there was food being circulated around, it became one of the substitutes to keeping the riots from jumping off. And believe me, food controlled a lot of different types of attitudes. I saw a guy get sliced up and life flew out of the prison on a helicopter over a case of fish. That's when I understood the powerful pressures of eatery and heartless individuals!

I used to love the days when we had cereal with the nuts in it. Once the servers was finished serving breakfast, all the buckets of unused cereal would have to come down through me. I would hide pounds and pounds of cereal, and then I would come in on my day off and help out. All the while, I had a hidden spot in the trash room where I separated the different types of nuts and put them in their own bag and took them back to the unit to sell for stamps. Any unused portions of meat I made into sandwiches. I guess that's why I made it through Lewisburg so easily, everyone knew me as the walking restaurant. The word of my tasty sandwiches got around the whole prison to the point where I started taking orders.

I became friends with a few members from the Blood organization Sex Money Murdered. They were out of New York, and one of their OGs had taken a liking to me. I had gotten to know a few of the Folks as well. One of their OGs was from Akron, and I knew one of what the OG's from Cleveland to which he associated with and that turned out to be my childhood friend. I spent so many stamps with the Jamaicans, who were making the teddy bears that their whole crew had taken a liking to me after getting to know me a little. I even became real cool with a few Aryan brothers because we would always see each other in church. Right before I was getting ready to leave, one of them made me an all-black leather Bible case, which I still carry to this day.

Working in the trash area of the kitchen turned out to be one of the best things that ever happened to me in prison. As I entered my last week of incarceration at Lewisburg Federal, seven or eight officers handed me recommendation letters. Then, I was called down to the counselor's office, and they too handed me recommendation letters. When I made it back to my unit, other inmates were surprised, and a few others weren't. They said, "Brian, you a good dude. You should have never been in here in the first place. You're not cut like us. You're a good guy, and we know you won't be back! Now get out of here and find your daughter, man! And remember, if you come back, you're going to have to deal with us!"

I was punched in my chest, then stomach, and hit in my head a few times. Then everyone started giving me handshakes and nigga hugs.

PART IV

CHAPTER 35

GOING HOME

I was moved to the going home unit. Being relocated was sort of cool because you didn't have to work, you didn't have to attend any programs, and you didn't have to do anything but eat, sleep, and sit on a toilet that you wished was porcelain instead of cold, hard steel. I spent a lot of time in that unit corresponding with a female I had met from the Philippines due to a pen pal mailing service company. No thanks to the help of the concrete walls that I slept in every night, aiding me to actually thinking she was my girlfriend. (When I get released, sooner or later, I was going to make sure she became my wife. She was a good catch! She had no children, had finished college, had a teaching degree, and wrote English better than I did. She sent me proof of everything. In my possession, I had all her photos and copies of her college degrees and blah blah blah. I couldn't wait to meet her!) In my mind, she was my wife! One thing I learned for sure while being incarcerated, them concrete walls will take your thoughts and let them fuckers run wild! With no real reality of control!

Finally, the day had come, and it just so happened to be my little brother's birthday. After seven years straight, two hernia operations, a sinus operation, one laser growth removal, and a lethal blood clot that left my legs looking the opposite of a set of identical twins, and only that freaking "Count Dracula off of Sesame Street " probably knew the answer to how many psychiatric pills I had taken over this course of time. But yes, I was on my way back into society. And one thing that I've noticed about the federal system is that they consider you a man, and they leave you with the consequences of doing what is right and what is wrong as a responsible human being. So they didn't hold my hand and supervise me on my way to the halfway house. They gave me a bus ticket, $75, a map to the halfway house, and a lift to the Greyhound station. The rest was up to me. The only thing they did, as far as supervision was concerned, was giving me a time to arrive at the designated halfway house.

With being absent from society for so long, the world had definitely changed on me. It did an honest to God switcheroo that I must adapt to! And I already knew there was going to be a lot of new things to become familiar with. I started figuring this out when I was at the Greyhound station. As I was waiting to board the bus to make my way back to Cleveland, Ohio, my body told me that it was time to release some water, so I entered the rest room, just as anyone else would. I released my water just as anyone else would.

As I reached to press the handle to flush my water, there wasn't one where it should be. *Okay,* I thought. *It must be in the back of the toilet or on the floor.* So I started looking around the stall area, but I didn't see anything, so I gave up. After making sure I had everything zipped up, I exited the stall. That's when I heard the toilet flushing itself. I quickly went back to the toilet and tried to figure out what was going on, but I couldn't put it together. Every finger I pointed came up with an empty answer. I walked back and forth in and out of that stall about three times before I gave up, and not one time did it flush again. I went over to the wash sinks shaking my head, filled my palm with the liquid soap, and started rubbing my hands together, making sure the soap was nice and leathery while doing its cleaning job. As I reached to turn on some water, there were no handles or buttons for me to press. So I started walking back and forth in front of the water faucet, thinking it was going to turn itself on, but it didn't. So I started waving my hands in front of it, no results.

Okay, I thought to myself. *I've been gone seven years. I know technology is on a different level, so this must be one of those voice-activated water systems.* So I used my voice. Here I was standing in the middle of the rest room, giving orders to a freaking sink. "On!" I said. Okay, it's not working. "Water on!" Nothing! Just as I was about to mimic the actors in the "clap on, clap off" commercial, a man rushed in with his little son. I guess the little boy had gotten something on his hands. I watched as the man picked his son up and held his hands underneath the faucet for couple of seconds. Then water came pouring out. All I was thinking was, *That still doesn't account for that fucking toilet!*

As I boarded the Greyhound, I made sure to get a window seat because I wanted to see everything on my way to the city. As I eased into my seat, the shade was pulled down over the window, and I didn't see any strings to pull it up. I started waving my hands at it and pausing in different spots, thinking it worked off the same jackass system that the sinks worked on. Then the lady behind me reached over, pressed this little black strip, then the shade automatically started raising up. I looked at the woman with one of my silly faces, and we both just started laughing. Finally, I was pulling into downtown Cleveland. As I got inside Linda's truck, my brother and the eagle were there as well. I told him, "Happy birthday." I told Eagle, "What's up? Thank you for sticking with me." I gave my mom a big hug and a kiss on her forehead.

I didn't mind being in the halfway house down on E. Fifty-Fifth. When I awoke the next morning, I realized how really clean of a facility I was being housed in, and the staff weren't rude like most halfway spots. They were about their business, they weren't trying to overplay their authority hand, and I truly respected that. After getting initiated over the next few days into the about-to-go-home crew, my federal parole officer showed up. As he opened up my folder and started reading, I could tell by his body language that he had no notification about my past before he had just sat in front of me. He didn't get started with any questions or any offerings of information from me, but I sort of figured this anyway because I was watching him steadily and his body language had given me nothing to smile about. So I already knew what he was about to say, and my self-confirmation was right on target.

As soon as he opened up his mouth, he said, "Mr. Dixon, after going over the information in your folder, I'm not going to be able to be your parole officer. The courts are going to have to sign a special parole officer for your case." After a couple of weeks, I was introduced to my new "special" parole officer. He was a pretty cool guy.

Later on that day, I had a surprise visit; it was Beans! I hadn't seen or heard anything from this guy since I first got to Ohio in 1998, and that was seven years ago. I didn't even ask him how he knew I was down there because the streets are always going to talk. We gave each other a nigga hug, and he presented me with a brand-new winter coat.

The next day, my mom came to visit me. As soon as she walked through the door, she already had tears in her eyes, but they didn't show any signs of her being happy to see me. I started wondering, what did the eagle do now? As I sat down with my mom, I started to understand that the tears were due to her feeling humiliated. My mother grabbed my chin and said, "Brian, I have never felt so dirty in my life. I have never been so humiliated in my life, but you are my child, and I would do whatever it takes to see you get your life back on track because I know it's in you to do right! Brian, you better not let me down! You better come home and do the right thing! Because if you don't, I'm going to turn my back on you!"

With that being said, she released my chin. I grabbed my mom's hand and asked her what was wrong. That's when tears started rolling out of her eyes like a faucet was turned on and left running without anyone caring about the overflow. After our conversation, I felt so bad for my mom. >:(

She explained to me that the special parole officer had visited her and her husband and explained to them that if I didn't have anywhere to go, they would be forced to send me back to prison. As soon as the parole officer walked out their door, the eagle told my mother that I wasn't allowed to come to their place. She explained to me that the eagle didn't want me there because I was grown now and he knew that he couldn't beat her or mistreat her while I was around. My mother said she begged him and begged him as he continued to say no. After she got down on her knees and begged him like she was some type of slave, asking her master not to beat her any more, he still said no, called her all type of degrading names, then retreated to his master quarters. (That evil ass motherfucker.) My mom said that's when it dawned on her that she had gotten on her knees in front of the wrong man, and she started praying to Jesus to give His Father a message! My mom and dad were not sleeping in the same bedroom any longer. She was living inside my late sister's room. The very next day, for some reason or another, the eagle knocked on her door that morning and told my mother that I could stay there but only for a few months. She wasn't happy because he was letting me come there. She was smiling because God answered her prayer in such a timely manner. :)

After our conversation, I didn't respond to anything that my mother told me. I just had a lot of thinking to do. As the weeks started going by, I was allowed to go out and look for job, and I landed one pretty quickly. At the same time, this new job just about landed me a one-way trip back to prison. A guy at the facility put me in contact with a guy that owned a car wash, and he put me in contact with another guy that owned his own construction business. In the very beginning, I knew there was something wrong with this chump, but I had to ride it out because I gave my mom my word about trying to do what's right. My first issue was how "sweet acting" this guy was being towards me, when he asked me how old I was and I gave him my answer. This "meat muncher" was like," I can't believe that you're that old! You really look young for your age, and I'm so used to hiring younger guys (a-he-he, chuckle chuckle chuckle) you're hired" But like he said, I only look younger, but I'm not and I would've respected the guy preference if he would've just been straight up with me because then we could've had a quick conversation and he would've definitely known where I stand and everything could be smooth sailing or not. But he preferred to play closet games.

My second issue was, he was always telling me that after a good season of work, he would take all his employees to Florida, and they all would stay inside one cabin and have fun! (Let us not forget people who are reading this book that all his employees were young men.) The third issue was the last darn straw for me. When he picked me up for work, he stated that we weren't going to be working this day and asked me if I ate corned beef. We went to a little restaurant for lunch. His conversation consisted of telling me that he had clothes at his home that fit me, and that I was more than welcome if I wanted them. The one thing that I noticed, every time I spoke, he never gave me eye-to-eye contact. This goofy fuck would be staring at my lips, like most women do. On our way back to the federal halfway house, I asked him if he was gay. With no change in his demeanor, he answered yes. I pondered for less than a half of a second, and then I asked this man if he liked me. He responded with, "Did I say I like you?"

And I responded with, "No, but you showed me all the body language of a female." After dropping me off, I decided there was no way I could work for this guy. This wasn't due to the fact that he was a homosexual because I couldn't care less about that. It was due to the fact that he was lying when he answered my question about liking me. I knew he would probably try his hand later on down the line, so I just got out of his way.

A few days went by and I started working for a telemarketing company. After a week of tutorials, I was actually put on the working floor and set up with my own cubicle, which made me smile because I was looking at it like, "Yesterday a prison cell! Today my own little office! Tomorrow my own company!"

Our job was trying to get business owners to buy credit card incentive machines to help their business grow and have more returning customers. My first phone call to a business owner was the call that got me fired. I also got a "You cannot leave this facility again, Mr. Dixon, for another job interview." (But they still allowed me to go to church. A van used to come pick me up and take me over to the Lincoln West High School for services. I just loved the service at that The Word Church.) The floor managers got mad at me because once I found out the business owner was an exceptionally small business owner, I told him it would be in his best interest not to buy the machine. He was a fireplace cleaner, he worked alone, and from our conversation, I could tell that his education had caught the very short end of the stick. With all the interest fees and service fees that they were going to be charging for this little contraction, he would've been bankrupt the first month. My manager decided to start hollering at me, not knowing that I wasn't taking my medication properly. I showed a little of myself, and with that being done, they felt a little threatened. So the security showed me a little of themselves and escorted me out of their building.

The next few weeks ran pretty smooth. The whole staff had taken a liking to me. I didn't have any issues at all. I had three days left before being released. I spent day one convincing the staff to let me go store shopping for some knickknacks before my big day. After a few hours, they finally agreed. It was time for lights out on day 1, but I didn't go to sleep. Instead, I had one of the inmates bring me back a book from the BMV, and I read that book twice before the sun came up. Day number 2, I awoke and got my pass to leave the facility, but I didn't go shopping. I went straight to the BMV and took the temp test. I passed the exam and went back to the facility. Day 3, my release date. I explained to the staff that I forgot a few things when I went shopping. Since I was going to be released later on in the afternoon, I asked if it would be okay if I went downtown to go shopping. They agreed, and I went right back to the BMV. I had a childhood friend, whose mom treated me like a son, (I will always be grateful for all the days they hid me from the police until I was able to come up with a plan, and the best part about my stay with them, was that her daughter was at one time my little sister's best friend before my sister passed away) meet me down there because I needed to use her vehicle. And I returned to the facility with my driver's license.

As I was standing in the doorway, waiting for my mom to come get me, I could see a big smile on her face as she was pulling up. When I placed my first foot into her truck, my mind retorted back our conversation that we had. On the many stops before we got home, my mom stopped over at my cousin Cinnamon's aunt's house. I never knew Cinnamon during our childhood years because she was the same age as my little sister, so I had no reason to pay my little cousin any attention. She wasn't home at the time, which hurt me a little because I was very curious to what my little cousin looked like now. The last time I saw her, she couldn't have been more than six or seven, and now she was in her late twenties or early thirties. Just so happened that a few weeks after that, I was on my way into the Speedway gas station for a candy bar when I saw a woman staring at me from behind her steering wheel. Then, the woman called my name. It turned out to be my little cousin Cinnamon! :)

Back at my parents' house, the first few days went by with the eagle being quiet. Then one day, I was in the kitchen about to fix me something to eat, and he angrily entered the kitchen and started pointing at his dishes that he had off to the side of the sink. He started cussing at me and threatening me not to use them. As the next couple of weeks went by, he started his process of kicking me out. His conversations would go like this, "Why you living here? You know how to go out and make money! You know how to sell drugs! So why you living here?"

I didn't pay him any attention. I was doing my best ignoring this dirty bastard. I was already used to his evil ways, so there was nothing he could've presented to me to which I hadn't already adapted to. As the morning came into play, he needed my help. I was asked to drive him to his cellular phone carrier, so he could pay his bill. The eagle was walking with a cane by this time because he had had a hip replacement, but what occurred this day had nothing to do with a hip replacement. It had more to do with him telling me not to touch his dishes. As I got out of the driver's seat and walked around to the front of the vehicle, the eagle was lifting himself up from the passenger seating. As soon as he closed the car door and took a step forward, my stepfather went falling straight back and landed on his butt for no apparent reason at all. At least that's what I thought, but he and my mom knew more than what I knew about why he was always fumbling and bumbling. When we returned home, I explained to my mother what happened. As she gave me an explanation that wasn't in cahoots with her body language, I didn't say anything. I just continued to let them think that they were hiding something from me, but I knew something more was wrong.

Finally, the day came when I couldn't take it anymore. I had to find somewhere else to live because this jackass was really putting my patience to the test. It was becoming very annoying having my stepfather tell me day after day, "You know how to sell drugs, so why are you living here? You need to get the fuck out of here."

One Cleveland Browns football weekend, Eagle and I had just finished watching a game on the television set when he got up and went to the store. As soon as he came back through the door, he was at it again, but this time, he went too far. He told me to get out, and I couldn't live there anymore. I told him I wasn't going anywhere because I didn't have anywhere to go at the time. He told me that I was getting out of there, and that he didn't care where I went. I just looked at him like he was crazy. He started storming toward his bedroom shouting at me, telling me he was going to go get his gun. I got up and went to the door and started putting on my shoes because Ike, Linda, my brothers, my grandmother, my cousins, my grandfather, my uncles, and aunts all had guns! And nine out of ten, I knew this guy was serious. There had been so many murders due to stepfathers and sons! I started thinking about Marvin Gaye and my childhood friend Skeleton and countless others, so I decided that I didn't want to be added to the statistic list, so I left and was hoping that I would find a reason not to ever go back.

For the first couple weeks, I was in New York and Florida. I did this against my better judgment, but the young lady that my little brother introduced me to paid me to be a bodyguard. The super woman and her little five-year-old son were on their way to Florida, and she didn't want to travel alone. Given my current living situation, I wasn't thinking about my probation officer or going back to prison, so I decided I needed this little vacation. And I did enjoy myself! She introduced me to a group of motorcycle riders who took a liking to me and had no issues giving me my own bike while we visited them. I flew past palm trees at 120 miles per an hour, feeling so free! I was so happy to be out of Ohio that I started taking pictures of the hotel I was staying in and the Florida's Dade County police cars. But as good things come, good things go, and it was time to go back to Ohio to face reality. At the end of our trip, my brother's friend gave me a very big hug because she was so thankful for me saving her son. On our return trip home, her son's shoestrings got caught inside of the escalator at Cleveland Hopkins Airport. I was walking a little ahead of them, but I sprinted so fast to their location when I heard her screaming my name and broke the shoestring with one quick pull. She said she would always be grateful, and so would he. Later in the future, he would always ask his mom for me to be the one to show up at his school for Dads and Doughnuts. :)

Once back in Ohio, I didn't have anywhere to go due to my pride. It just so happened that I ran into Chopper's father as I was walking down the street. Chopper's father knew how I used to help his mother out, and Chopper and I had known each other forever, so he looked out for me. He gave me a job at his dealership, a house to live in, and a van to drive. As the next couple of months went by, my gut feeling was not letting me feel comfortable about the situation. I felt as if I wasn't going anywhere, so one morning, I gave him back the van and the keys to the house and told him thank you for everything, but I had to go. He wished me well, and I was back walking with nowhere to go, so I went back to the neighborhood with a pocket full of motivation and self-discipline.

I started off living in crack houses, but I wouldn't sell or use any dope. After a few of the major dope boys found out I was home, they tried to put whatever they could in my hand, but I wouldn't accept their poison. Why couldn't they offer to take me somewhere to buy me some clothes so I could start going on job interviews? But they were very quick to offer me four hard adults and a baby or a couple pounds of that grass. Finally, I found a Minuteman service that accepted me and my reckless history. I was only making $33 every other day, but I was doing the right thing. After a few weeks, I saved up enough to buy a Mongoose mountain bike. Now, I had transportation!

A lot of people were laughing at me because they were used to me doing much bigger things in the neighborhood, but I did not let that get in my way because my mind always returned back to my conversation with my mother. I was on my way back to the crack house after I scored some potato chips at the store, but running into Chopper changed my course. I didn't even know he was home from prison. To my surprise, the very first thing he asked me was where I was staying. After sharing my living conditions, I moved in with him and his family, with the agreement of $300 per month. Everything was pretty smooth at Chopper's house. His two daughters and his son treated me as a big uncle, and his wife played the part of a cool sister. I loved every moment being over there, and they did too, except for the fact that I used to steal their cars to go to church. Chopper used to cuss me out about doing so, but he knew I wasn't going to pay him any attention. Every time Chopper and his wife would hide their car keys. Come Sunday morning, they would understand that their hiding places were a no go, and I'll be sitting in church.

Now that I was living with Chopper and his family, I was relocated to a different side of town. I had to find a different temp service company to work for, and boy oh boy did I find one. I was doing everything to make sure I stayed out of trouble, and the new temporary service really put me to the test. I used to ride my mountain bike thirteen miles to work and thirteen miles back to Chopper's house. To put the icing on the cake, with a cherry on top, after pedaling the thirteen miles to work, I had to ride on the back of a garbage truck for the next ten to twelve hours, tossing trash for only six dollars and some change an hour. But I refused to let my mother down. During the course of this, temptation smacked me right in my face, but I continued to keep my cheek turned in the opposite direction so my mother's left hook wouldn't have to do it for me.

CHAPTER 36

OLD FRIENDS

One day, while I was pedaling home, I ran into Quito. He asked me what I was doing for a living, and I told him I was tossing trash and cleaning toilets. He looked at me, smiled, and started laughing. Then he gave me the keys to his brand-new Mercedes AMG. He told me to take it for a spin around the corner. I sat down in the driver's seat with his little son sitting on the passenger's side. I mentally felt my mother's hand smacking me in the back of my head. I got back out the car and wiped my fingerprints off the steering wheel. He started laughing at me again. Within the next couple of days, he came and picked me up, and we went downtown to one of the hottest night clubs. It was no mystery that everyone knew Quito. The line was a quarter-mile long from the entrance door of this club. There was talks that Lebron James had something to do with the ownership, as we walked straight in pass everyone. Once inside, even though it was very crowded, the owner of the club walked us straight over to the VIP section. As we sat there, he started showing me pictures from his cell phone of him and some famous rappers. One was believed to have been Gucci Man.

As we pulled up to Chopper's house to end the night, he asked me what I needed, and he wasn't referring to any clothes, so I could go on job interviews! I told Quito I didn't need anything. Once again, he started laughing and said, "Okay, but, B, whenever you ready to stop cleaning toilets, let me know." As he started pulling away with his brand-new Mercedes, I just started smiling because the temptation that flowed from his lips couldn't pierce this armor suit I was wearing. I didn't know that would be the last time I saw Quito. Not too far into the future from that point, he was picked up by the DEA, and now he's sitting in the federal penitentiary with twenty-five years on his back. Yes, sir, I will continue cleaning toilets! Thank you for this suit of armor, Lord! :)

I had other small incidents where the suit wasn't required, but I was still being saved in some type of manner because Chopper was my suit. With the snow now covering the ground, Chopper figured that I had been home long enough, and it was time for me to have a drink, and that nigga love his liquor. So Chopper, one of his good friends named Jolly, and myself went down to our neighborhood bar for some drinks. Everyone from the neighborhood was at this bar. It was as if I was attending a coming home reunion!

Chopper slid me a long island iced tea. Without sipping, I downed it. Jolly slid me a long island iced tea. Without sipping, I downed it. I was feeling super duper nice. When I looked in the corner, I saw my high school girlfriend. Without sipping, I downed the long island iced tea she slid to me as well. Then, she said, "Let's get out of here, and go to the movies." When I told Chopper I was pulling out, he handed me one of his extra cell phones and told me to call him if I needed him. Within the next couple of hours, I needed him because those three long island iced teas really started doing a number on me that I could not handle. As my ex-girlfriend and I entered the movie theater, everything was blurry to me. Everyone seemed to be talking like they had cotton balls in their mouths. I don't know what I did or didn't do, but my ex-girlfriend left me at the movie theater. When I finally got my mind together enough to call Chopper to come pick me up, I started feeling really hot. When Chopper got to the movie theater parking lot, the phone he had given me starting ringing.

I answered it. Chopper said, "Where you at? Me and Jolly sitting right in front of the entryway."

I said, "Look to your left, nigga. I'm hot."

He and Jolly started laughing because I was sitting on a snow bank with my coat and shirt off. As we made it back to our neighborhood, we went to a different bar to eat. Jolly placed a plate of food in front of me and told me to eat up. Jolly was a cool guy, a Pisces like me. A lot of people don't understand, but a Pisces is a double sign, and some personalities seem to share the same fish. So we connected. After a couple of bites and letting the liquor exit through my mouth a few times, I started sobering up. When I looked around, I didn't see Chopper or Jolly. I went outside, and there was some commotion in the parking lot.

Jolly and one of the bar owners from our neighborhood were having a disagreement. Everyone was drunk, but at the same time, everyone was friends. The bar owner from the neighborhood had taken Jolly's Range Rover without his permission and was gone for hours. With both of them being in the alcohol swimming pool within their own right, this brought forth a boxing match. Jolly was only about five feet and a few inches tall, and the neighborhood bar owner stood at a solid six feet and six inches tall. It will always be in my heart, that if two of my friends are fighting, I will always make sure it is a fair fight because after the fight, we're all going to be friends again. Now, Jolly was really out of shape. He was just round, and every time he threw a punch, his whole body would spin like a box top, and he would fall on the ground. He did this about three times and every time he did this, I had to run over and stop the bar owner from stumping him in his head. The bar owner got mad at me, but I explained to him that we were all drunk, and Jolly wasn't his enemy. As I was talking to him, I saw him glance over my right shoulder. I followed his eyes and saw Smiley and his older brother walking up. His older brother looked and saw that it was me, then looked at the bar owner, and said, "You called me and told me that you were getting jumped? Brian, don't jump people!"

That's when I looked at the bar owner and said, "You called them and told them that you were being jumped?"

He looked at me and said, "Y'all did jump me!"

I told him, "Don't call me a liar," and as soon as he formed his lips to say that we jumped him again, I punched him in his eye. And what in the world did I do that for? That jolly green giant bar owner snatched me up off my feet and slammed me down twice on my back. I was pretty sure that any dollar bill that I had in my pocket had surely turned into quarters! When it was all over, all of us got inside the same vehicle and went back to the owner's bar. The owner and I got out of the vehicle, and Jolly and Chopper pulled off because they had a quick run to make.

I was standing outside of the bar when about five guys I knew from my childhood came out wearing some serious disgusted attitudes upon their faces. One of them was the guy that pulled the gun on me when we were children. I could tell he was the leader of this goofy bunch. "So you jumped, my boy?"

I really don't like conversation, especially when I'm being greeted in a threatening manner. I just put my fist up, stood in a boxing stance, and told them, "I'm going to fight every last one of y'all, but it's got to be one-on-one, you jackasses!"

They weren't trying to hear that! As they started moving closer to me, I stood my ground; and out of nowhere, a dark shadow came from around the bar, sliding out of some evergreen bushes, holding a black revolver in its left hand. Then the shadow spoke. He said, "Y'all all can fight him, but it's going to be one-on-one like the fuck he said. And if one of y'all decide to get froggy and leap, I'm going to put a hot one in you!"

Instantly, I knew that voice, and they did too, and we all knew he wasn't playing and meant every word that came out of his mouth. I hadn't seen him since I'd been home, but this was a nice way for us to have a reunion. I said, "Wassup, Smoke!"

"What's good, B!"

"What you doing out here in the bushes, Smoke?"

"Waiting to bust a lick, on one of these lames." (Quick street education for you, the reader: *Lame* is referring to a corny or goofy individual who pretends to be hard core. "Bust a lick" is referring to committing a robbery on the lame.)

We stop paying those goofy guys any attention and stood on the sidewalk catching up on lost time.

When the next day arrived, I was thankful that Chopper and Jolly told me they'd be back to pick me up because both of them ended up going to jail that night. One went away for a drug possession case, the other one for murder. I packed up my things at Chopper's house and left because I was not about to stay in a house with the wife of a man who was in prison. So now I was back to living wherever a safe place was for me to lay my head. The good thing was, I had a job located about three blocks from where my mom stayed. Even though I was working for a temporary service, making under the minimum wage, I went to work at that job as if I was getting paid $40 an hour. I even got my brother and some childhood friends a job there. For the first two weeks, everyone called me Robo Nigga. The other workers used to hate when they saw me coming through the door because they knew it was time for them to really work. We were working on an assembly line, and I was at the head of the table. I used to open up boxes and push the merchandise so fast down the assembly line that the other workers couldn't keep up.

One day, I upped my own status and gave myself a promotion. I was in control of the power hand jack, when one of the permanent workers came over and took it from me without giving me any type of notification. At the same time, he left his tow motor behind, so I jumped up on it, read the directions, played with the handles to learn what did what movement, then took his tow motor without giving him any notification. All the other temporary workers got mad when they saw me driving the tow motor because they had been there for months, still working the assembly line, and here I was just a few weeks in and already riding around on a horseless chariot. When the foreman came over and asked me what I was doing on the tow motor, I explained to him how I came to have it in my possession. To my surprise, he wasn't upset with me. Instead of telling me not to operate it any longer, he left me in charge of it.

A few weeks after that, my manager got a call from corporate. Some of the other temporary workers had called and complained about me driving the tow motor when they had been working there much longer than I had. The manager came over to me and told me that I couldn't drive it any longer. I didn't like that at all, so I went inside of the manager's office, grabbed his car keys, and went for a drive to cool off. I received a phone call from the manager, and he asked me if I took his car. I said yes.

He said, "I'm going to give you a call back and never touch my car again!" About thirty minutes later, he told me to bring his car back and that he worked out a deal with corporate, so I could still drive the tow motors. One of the ladies that I used to go to lunch with offered me a room at her home, so now my life was starting to point in the right direction. One thing I've learned in life is, you have your good times and you have your bad times, and most of the time, it's a combination of the both.

A few months into the job, the eagle passed away. I was there in his room, watching him on his deathbed. As the machine was helping him continue to cling on to life, I knew he was in his last hours. As my stepfather and I locked eyes, we both knew that would be the last time we saw one another. Within an hour or less, my family received the call that he had passed. My feelings was very mixed. My right eye had a tear fall from it, and my left eye had no tears at all and was smiling! I wasn't the only one who lost a father that year. Chopper lost his father as well, and it was tragic. I received phone calls from a few of Chopper's family members. They asked me if I had seen his dad. I told them, "No, I haven't seen him in a while." He never showed up for his own party. When he was finally found, it was in the back of his own car trunk, with a lifeless female body in the same predicament as his. I couldn't believe what was going on. This guy was very cool and very laid-back. I just couldn't understand it. As soon as I heard the news, I started thinking about Chopper because he was in prison at the time, and I wished I could have been by my friend's side.

I guess with those two negative vibes invading my atmosphere, some of it rubbed off on the lady that I used to have lunch with. When she moved me into her home, everything was fine for the first couple of months because this allowed me time to save money. She had two daughters and a son. This allowed me to have an artificial family atmosphere that I enjoyed, but I did not let myself get too connected. When she moved me in my train of thought was, *Wow, she's pretty cool!* But her train of thought was different because she was hungry like the hairdresser and her weirdo baby daddy, and I wasn't going to feed her hunger pains between her legs! One night, she displayed how hungry and angry she was that I was living in her home, but I was not stroking her kitty cat.

The time was 2:00 or 3:00 a.m., and I decided to turn on my bedroom light so I could read my Bible and try to cope with the freshly new situations. As I was reading, my bedroom light cut off on me, and she walked away and went back into her bedroom. Instantly,

I was thinking, *Fuck! Here we go!* So I got up and turned the light back on and returned to reading 2 Corinthians 5:17. But I couldn't get into my Bible (Basic Instructions before Leaving Earth) because the lights shut off again. I got up, turned the light back on, and waited in the middle of the room for her. When she stuck her hand through the door to cut the light off again, I asked her what was wrong. In return, she asked me why I wouldn't have sex with her. I didn't answer her question. I just stood there staring at her because I had an all-powerful problem with speaking the truth about how I viewed her outer appearance, and I didn't want to hurt her feelings. Besides, it was too early in the morning to be flat-out lying. Since I wouldn't answer her question, she started reaching for the light switch again. I cannot recall what type of vocal cords I utilized when I told her, "You better not touch that light switch again." And she didn't, and I smiled to myself because the nervous look on her face was priceless. I politely requested the horny, lonely lady to just give me fifteen minutes.

But within ten minutes, everything I owned at that particular time was in garbage bags, and I was sitting on the stairs of her porch with nowhere to go. I called my mom and asked her if she could hold on to my things for a while. As I was making my way to my mom's with all my garbage bags, a female that was driving by said she met me at a club before, and she kindly gave me a lift to Linda's place.

I saved a couple of dollars so when the sun came up, I went over to the west side and purchased a car. My car became my house. When we got off work, I would drive away like everyone else as if I was going home, but I was already at home. I would go get something to eat, hit a couple of corners, then pull back into the job's parking lot. They always wondered why I was always the first one there. With the staff managers always seeing me first thing in the morning, and with my performance, I instantly became a hit.

One day, one of the managers called me into his office and told me he did a background check on me. I told him not to say anything else, and I notified him that that would be my last day. That's when he told me that no one knew about it but him. I asked him what made him look into my background, and he told me because I took his car. All I could say was touché. Then this white man, who was my manager, looked me straight in my eyes and bluntly said, "Can you score me some powder?"

Instantly, I thought about my four-wheeled house, and I thought about how cold it was outside. I mean it was really starting to get chilly outside, and I was using a lot of gas trying to stay warm by turning the car motor off and on throughout the night. And my 2 Corinthians 5:17 started fading as I was now starting to go astray. I told him, "Maybe."

At that very moment, my manager and I started a very nicely built negative relationship with one another. I didn't want anyone knowing I was back in business, so I found a guy in my neighborhood that was a few years younger than me, and I turned him into my supplier. I didn't know the guy personally, but my little brother knew him well and spoke well of him. More than a few times a week, my manager would have me running back and forth from my neighborhood. Then, one Saturday morning, he surprised me and asked me if I wanted to make a few thousand dollars. I told him it depends, and he told me to meet him at the job site. When I got to the location, which I was already there anyway because I slept in the darn parking lot, I saw the manager going past me in a very huge box truck. (To you, the reader. If you are wondering why I just didn't go over to my mother's house to sleep, it's because of my self-motivation and my self-discipline all mixed together in a big bowl of strange will power of patience. As long as I continued sleeping in that parking lot inside that car, it took away all my comfortable zones and made me work harder at achieving my goal. So in other words, it's safe to say, I'm showing you a glimpse of being institutionalized.)

I met him at the exact location I was told to be at. As he went into the building, he told me to just a hold on for a second. A couple minutes after that, he was pulling up to the box truck with a tow motor loaded with supplies. He told me to break the boxes and supplies down into separate units and load them into the box truck. Before I could even get started, he was pulling up again with another tow motor, loaded with even more supplies. I guess in a way he called himself looking out for me because there was no way I could get charged with breaking and entering because I was never past the building threshold. After the box truck was loaded to the max with supplies, he had me follow him to the drop-off spot. Once at the drop-off spot, I didn't have to do anything but sit in my car. He went into an odd-shaped building, and as he walked out the door and headed in my direction, I could see a white envelope in his hand. After he handed me the envelope, I opened it straight up, and it was just like he said, a few thousand dollars.

As the next couple of weeks passed, we became pretty cool, and I opened up to him a little bit. After hearing my story, the next day, we were at the same apartment complex where my mother lived, standing inside the renter's office. As the leasing officer pulled up my background, we both saw her eyebrows start to go up in the air. But before she could mutter a word, my manager stood up and told me to wait outside the office, and he closed the door in my face. I do not know what transpired behind that door, but when it opened, the leasing officer handed me the keys to my own apartment, something I never had before. A place of my own. I gave my white manager a nigga hug and a grown man handshake, accommodated by a big "thank you, my brother" smile.

As the next few weeks went by, I continued to supply him powder, and he continued to give me a lot of hours at work. Finally, I was able to purchase a TV, a very nice queen-size air mattress, and a black Italian glove leather sofa. I was happy, but at the same time, my conscience continued to nitpick at me because I knew I was doing wrong. I told God while in prison that I would never sell drugs again. And the 2 Corinthians 5:17 that had started removing itself fully from my gone astray sleep-like state within my soul, started making itself visible again. I called my manager and told him I needed to talk to him. He gave me his address and told me to come over to his house. As we started talking, he started telling me a heartfelt story about his life. He revealed that one time in his life and not too long ago that he was doing very well in life as far as family and work values were concerned, but due to being a participant at "Heroine" parties, he lost everything, including his family. Just as he ended on the word *family*, his wife and two teenage daughters walked through the front door. I was sitting there watching them interact with one another, and I couldn't wait to tell him what I came over for in the first place because this display of family affection just made it that much easier for me to talk to him about cutting away from the drugs. He and I went down into the basement to talk, and I explained to him that I was done. There would be no more powder coming from me. I told him I didn't want to slip back into my past, and I didn't want to dishonor my word to God, no more than I already had. I grabbed his hand and explained to him the gift he was given: to have a second chance at being a father and a husband. We departed from our illegal relationship on good terms. During the course of that same week, I was notified through the word of the streets that the young guy I was getting the powder from was murdered on his birthday at a club on Harvard Avenue. (Rest in peace, my friend, I will always respect the way that you carried yourself in my presence.) (S) :(

As I was going into 120 days on the job, it was time for them to make a decision: allow me to become permanent or let me go due to the choices I made in my past life. I believe there was nothing on the menu of my past that the executives felt they could digest and have trust in me, in order for me to become permanent, so I was released from the job. During this time of financial abstinence, another blessing came my way. I received a phone call from Chopper's little brother. He was starting up his own company doing deliveries for a major supplier. It turned out to be inventory from Best Buy, so I was back in action and working and paying my rent!

CHAPTER 37

LEADING LADY

Being on the legal side of life was a beautiful thing! At the same time, I had a void in my life! By me not truly having a relationship with a beautiful-hearted woman, I didn't have a leading lady in my life to make me feel whole! So I started dating. I was missing in action for seven years, so I really didn't have any dating skills. The best thing I had to offer a woman was simply me, and that was not a big hit with the type of women I was meeting.

The first female I met had me ice-skating! Let me explain. After a few dates and a few hot nights, she wanted me to meet her mother and father. I was in cahoots with her, even after only knowing her for a couple weeks. Her mom and dad stayed in a very nice suburban neighborhood. When they met me, they had a weird expression on their faces, and I couldn't put a finger on it. I didn't get any negative vibe from them; they actually treated me very nice. When it was time for us to leave, her mother came and whispered in my ear, "You are very different than what we are used to her bringing home. And if you last, we would love to have you over again."

As I climbed into my date's truck wearing a puzzled expression on my face, I pondered to myself, "Just what in heaven was her mother trying to hint at?" As we were driving and getting closer to

Cleveland, my date asked me where the marijuana was. I politely told her, "I don't know." She instantly went into a rage and started speeding! We were doing fifty-five miles per hour in a thirty-five miles per hour zone! She told me I was a liar and said I knew where everything was. I blamed myself for this situation because I always tell a woman about my past history as soon as we meet, see if they want to deal with me or not. Every time we came to a stop light, she would slow down a little bit as if she was going to stop, then go straight through the red light. While this was going on, I was timing myself waiting for her to hit twenty miles per hour. When she did, I jumped straight out of her door, and when my gators hit the ground, I started sliding as if I was on ice going for the Olympic gold. And I was doing well for a quick couple seconds until I flipped in the air and landed in some slushy mud. I didn't let that stop me. I was on to the next.

I have a rule in life now, I will not let a woman pick me up for a date until we've been dating for at least three months. Not too long after that incident, I was at a bar with a couple of friends. Well, they weren't friends I considered my A1s, but I did know these guys. When the bar was closing, they were on their way to an after-hours spot. I didn't want to participate, so they found a lady that they all knew to give me a ride home because I do not believe in driving drunk. When I met her, she seemed cool. After making sure my car doors was locked, I was getting into her vehicle when I saw people I knew and some I didn't know, but they all were looking in my direction laughing and pointing. Since it was 2:00 a.m., I didn't put too much effort into trying to analyze what was going on. She asked me if I minded stopping at her house for a second. She wanted to grab some more money because after dropping me off, she was going to treat herself to some breakfast. When we entered her home and she turned on the lights, I noticed she was about twenty-five to thirty years older than me, with a very huge gut that could easily house quadruplets. But this didn't bother me at all because she was nice enough to give me a ride home. She handed me the TV remote and asked me have I ever seen the movie *Baby Boy.* (That was my first time seeing what the R&B singer Tyrese actually look like.) I responded with a no and watched her as she inserted the DVD. She told me she was going upstairs to change. While she was telling me this, she placed a glass filled to the top with wine down in front of me, and then she proceeded upstairs with her own glass of wine. As the few minutes went by, I was really into the movie and never noticed that a half an hour had passed by so easily until she started calling for me to come upstairs.

"I don't think it will be appropriate for me to come up there!"

"Please!"

Then, I thought, *Fuck! Here we go!*

She called me a few more times, and I steadily ignored her. I didn't feel safe answering shit! So she decided to come downstairs. That view will be forever tattooed on my freaking brain! Whenever somebody says *Baby Boy*, whether it's pertaining to a movie, someone giving reference to their son, or a female who had just given birth, the image of that woman standing on her stairs with that gut hanging from skin-tight biker shorts, and I guess her Sunday's best bra, instantly becomes an terrifying horrific rebirth image in my thinking process! And I cannot help but laugh! I didn't want to hurt her feelings, so I told her thank you for the offer, but I was in a committed relationship. She counterattacked that with an "I don't mind! I won't tell if you don't tell."

Since I didn't give in to her charming offers, she told me she was sleepy and couldn't take me home until the morning showed its face. She continued calling my name to come upstairs. This went on for the rest of the freaking night. This sex deprived biker shorts older woman had me afraid to go to sleep. I watched *Baby Boy* five or six times before I was getting out of her vehicle and a block away from where I lived. I refused to have her showing up at my door unannounced.

I didn't let that stop me either. I just decided to try a different method of dating. That's when I turned to online computer dating, and there was no thumbs-up there either. The first female from the online gig, I decided to meet at McDonald's. She was a little older than me, but she was nice looking. She was also a big turnoff instantly. As we sat at the table across from one another, she started telling me I looked like the last guy she just dated, and he took her for everything! Then she asked me if I thought I could live life getting by with my looks. That's when I asked her if she wanted a coffee. She didn't want one, and neither did I, but I told her, "I will be right back. I'm about to go get me a cup of that Jo."

As I was standing in line waiting to meet the cashier, I started telling myself, "Wait for it, wait for it, go!" As most older females do, and she was no exception, the moment she saw I was the second person in line, she whipped out her mirror and lipstick. With her being distracted by herself, I went straight out the side door ran like Fo Joe and cleared a Dukes of Hazzard right through my passenger window and was on my way to the next.

In a way, I was starting to enjoy this because it started to become amusing. I wasn't trying to be rude to these women, but I just wasn't good with explaining my reason for rejection. If you give me a reason, I will take off without giving a reason why. The next female was a bank teller, and I could tell that she knew nothing about hard times. I dated her a couple of times because she truly amazed me. I found it very shocking how she viewed and belittled people with less money. She had a habit of calling people silly monkeys. One evening, we agreed to meet at TGIF. In life, I always let the lady order first because she's usually the one paying for our meal. On this particular day, when it was my turn, I asked for one banana. The waiter looked at me as if I had made a mistake. I reassured the waiter that I would only be requiring only one banana. As we sat waiting for our orders to present themselves on our table, I started to nitpick her brain, questioning her about her views on the way she treated people. Just as her face started turning red, the banana was the first meal placed on our table. I jumped straight up and shouted, "Everyone, everyone, in life, if you act like a good little monkey, you deserve a banana!" Then I exited the building, after placing a dollar on the table.

It was back to the old drawing board when I met the next female at the library. She turned out looking nothing like any of her photos on my computer screen! That sneaky trickster! Another rule I have in life: if you bring deception to the table, you must open your arms, and embrace the monster you've created. As I waited at the library to finally meet this woman, she rudely called my phone cussing at me because she couldn't find the library, and it was my fault she was lost. I didn't say anything due to the fact that my patience and under-standing usually took over before I come to my last conclusion and bring myself down to someone's level.

When she got out of her vehicle, all I could do was stare. I couldn't believe this was the person whose photos I was entertain-ing. As we entered the library, most of the staff started waving at me because they knew me. Before I could finish waving back, the female made a rude comment, asking me if I dated everyone that was wav-ing at me (but there was also a couple of guys waving at me). Yeah, I have really picked a cherry off the Internet this time. I grabbed the basket and went over to the movie section to make a few selections. In a rude manner, very much to my distaste, she asked where the restroom was. I quickly pointed her in the right direction. I forgot to tell her she needed to notify a librarian in order to gain access to the rest room. When she turned the handle and it didn't open, she started shouting and asking how was people suppose to get in there. Once the button was pressed and I saw the restroom door close, I slung the basket off my arm and walked very briskly through the parking lot to my vehicle. I did a very good job of not burning rubber as fast as I was pulling away!

Working and dating were starting to take a toll on me, but I decided to give it one more shot. This time, my little brother decided to go with me on one of these fantastic dates that I be telling him about. We met up with a female that seemed pretty cool. For one reason or another, I was very interested in her, but her lips had a little purple dance going on sorta like Barack Obama lips, and they really needed a hint of lip gloss. I asked her the magic question that I ask every single female whose face I get in front of, and I only ask this magic question if I am very interested in you. I only ask this magic question once, "Do you smoke cigarettes?"

She responded no, and we started enjoying our time at the bar. Afterwards, we returned to my apartment. As she positioned herself on my Italian soft glove leather black sofa, I went into the restroom to brush my teeth. When I came out feeling like a million bucks, there was smoke all in the air, and this ashtray-mouth individual was sitting on my sofa smoking a cigarette. I gave no notification about how I felt about her actions. I just told her that we had to end the night because I had to work in the morning. (To you, the reader. Do you or do you not believe in karma? I believe in God for just about everything. I believe either things are meant to happen in your life, or things are not meant to happen in your life. I truly believe both negative and good things happen in one's life so we can participate in a learning experience, and take that experience towards the future to utilize in life if certain predicaments or obstacles open the door for us, pertaining similarities. So just flat-out lying is a no-no for now on.)

I pretty much had given up on dating and started concentrating on the job with Chopper's brother. One day while I was coming inside the apartment building, I noticed a female I used to work with. She told me her name was Eva. We exchanged numbers as friends. After a few conversations, she knew a little bit more about me, and I knew a little bit more about her. She actually stayed inside the same building I did, but I didn't find this out until the day we exchanged numbers. A couple of weeks went by before we saw one another again, and that came about with a knock on my door. When I opened my door, I could tell she was a little upset. She explained to me that her brother and sisters be stealing her money. She wondered if I would be willing to keep it in a safe place for her. I agreed, and she handed me a roll of money. A few weeks went by before I heard from her again, and that came about with a phone call. It had to be around two or three in the morning. I could tell by the conversation on the other end of the receiver that Eva was very intoxicated. She asked me if I could come pick her up, and I agreed. When we got back to the apartment complex, she told me over and over that she didn't want to go upstairs to her mother's apartment in that condition, so I told her she could stay over. Due to all the alcohol she drank that night, she started displaying the bulimia trick without putting her fingers down her throat. She spent the night inside my restroom with Mr. Porcelain. As the next few weeks went by, we found ourselves spending a lot of time together. She didn't like being at home with her brothers and sisters, so she pretty much always asked if she could come down to my place. I didn't mind because I didn't have anything going on myself.

As the next few weeks went by, we started becoming cooler friends, and one night in particular brought us very close together. A cousin I hadn't seen for over twenty years had come to visit my mom. Eva and I were on our way to go play some pool, so we invited my cousin. While inside the pool hall, I noticed my cousin drinking the alcohol out of cups that were left behind by other customers. When I saw her picking up a beer bottle, I knocked it out of her hand and told her it was time for us to go. On the way back to the apartment complex, I called my mother to notify her of what had happened. That's when I found out that my cousin was a very super seasoned uncontrollable alcoholic. After exiting my vehicle, I thought my cousin was going to stay over my mom's house or even my place to get some rest, but she headed straight for her car. Before she could get her key into her driver's door, I ran over to her and prevented her from entering the vehicle. She started screaming and hollering, as if she was being attacked by a stranger, so I snatched the keys and walked away from her. She called the police on me, but after the police interviewed Eva, along with an innocent bystander in the parking lot that stood up for me, the police didn't bring anything my way. (The very next night, my cousin was in a car accident. While driving very intoxicated, she destroyed her vehicle, another lady's vehicle, and managed to get both of them a free ride to the hospital and a few weeks' stay.) That night was one of many that would bring me closer to the Bedford Heights patrolling officers. After all was said and done, Eva and I were left looking at each other inside of my apartment. We both decided that it would be a good thing if she stayed the night.

CHAPTER 38

EVA

A few weeks after that, she moved into my place. We still didn't know each other well enough to be doing so, but we did. It had most to do with two people helping each other out with bills and freedom. I needed help paying rent, and she wanted to get out of her mother's apartment, so the situation was good for both of us. After a couple of months, the sweetness of our relationship started turning sour very rapidly. Before she met me, she was messing around with a married guy, and this was still going on as we lived together. By the time I found this out, she was already six months pregnant. During the last three months of her pregnancy, we separated. She moved back in with her mother, and Chopper's little brother and I got an apartment together. We all were still living in the same building.

As the next couple of months went by, it was getting closer for her to have the baby. During this time, I learned that the married guy she was seeing was white, and he had no plans of going to the hospital with her. With 2 Corinthians 5:17 weighing heavy on my heart, I decided to go to the hospital and be by her side. Truth be told, there was a fifty-fifty chance that I could be the father of this child. As Eva pushed and pushed, she delivered a baby girl. As I was cutting the cord, I shielded my true feelings because I was going through an unemotional event within myself. This little baby right before my eyes was as white as white could get. But I was very confused because the baby didn't have a big head, like most white babies do, and she didn't have big lips like most of us black people do. So at the same time, I was just dumbfoundead! My feelings were at a standstill on who was this little girl's father.

I left the hospital for a couple hours just to get my mind right. Later on that night, I had a conversation with Eva. I explained to her, "Whether the baby is mine or not, I'm going to go purchase an apartment because I know you don't want to go back to your mother's house, and I know a hard worker when I see one. So you can live with me for one year if you wish, just be sure to save your money because as soon as that year is up, we go our separate ways." Three days after the baby was born, we were downtown getting all three of our mouths swabbed so we could determine exactly what was going on with this situation. As the weeks went by, we were living together like a little family. When the day came and the results were delivered, it was finally revealed that I was 99.9 percent the biological father.

Before I had the chance to even soak in that I was a new daddy, I received a phone call from my parole officer. She told me to make sure that I could make myself available to be at her office the following day because she was locking me up. I did not know what was going on, but I did as I was told. When I arrived at my parole officer's office, there were two marshals waiting for me. Without any explanation, once again, my hands and my ankles were united with the platinum prison chains. Within a couple blinks of an eye, I was walking off the prison bus and being ushered into a federal holding facility in Youngstown, Ohio. After a couple weeks of sitting inside a cold cell not knowing what was going on, a piece of paper was slid underneath my door. I couldn't believe my eyes! It was an arrest warrant request dated for August 23, 2007. It read as follows: "This report serves to inform the court that Mr. Dixon has been essentially living a parallel alternate life while on supervision. He has repeatedly misrepresented his lifestyle and circumstances to this officer over an extended period of time. When confronted, the officer categorized the misrepresentation as confusion, misunderstandings of probation conditions or indicative of mental disorders. A number of the misrepresentations related to the areas of his life which would not have represented violation behavior, as such misrepresentation may be a cover for illicit activity. The probation officer became suspicious of the offender after receiving a phone call from a distraught person following a domestic dispute in which the Bedford Heights Police Department was called to the scene but no charges were filed. The caller indicated that the mental disability presented by the offender was feigned to the probation officer, for illegal activities. That the offender giggles loudly, paces and tremors, stumbles and bumbles, and unable to remain focused on one topic for any length of time, in order to sell drugs. According to the person, however, the offender intentionally wears two left shoes when reporting to the probation office in order to destabilize his gait, and present in a completely different manner in the community. The person portrayed the offender as crafty, and resourceful."

After reading everything, what was going on was very clear now. Eva was trying to get my probation officer to send me back to prison. She did this over a year ago, but due to the fact that the federal government likes to do their own investigations first, they waited a whole year before telling me to turn myself in. As I continued to read further, there were a lot of bogus charges and that was enough to get me back into a full swing with this platinum prison jewelry and this luxury concrete six-by-four one-man cell condo, with uniformed butlers that brings me food. (Yeah, you must know how to utilize your imagination in order to do prison time.) My first charge was Failure to Report Address Change due to the fact that I moved into three different apartments. Even though they were all on the same floor of the same building, they charged me with escape. My second charge was Failure to Report Employment. My probation officer was mad that I was working with my cousin on his truck, and I didn't report it to her. She even drove out to the Best Buy warehouse and tried to coerce the management into obtaining information about me, but they had nothing they could offer. Truth be told, technically, I didn't have a job. I was only a helper on an as-needed basis, but the paperwork the probation officer had portrayed me as a truck driver with Class A license. My third charge was False Statements to USPO. They stated that I misrepresented situations to this officer on a number of occasions, sometimes for no apparent reason. I had no idea what in the world she was talking about.

All this came about when I only had about four months of probation left, before I was totally released of all paperwork and set free to start getting my life together! I couldn't believe that after two and a half years into this dance, they were trying to make the music to stop! I believe a month and some change had went by before I was finally brought back to the Federal Courts in Cleveland and right back in front of the federal judge that I colored the nice picture of Bugs Bunny for. As I was standing there watching the judge shake his head back and forth, he was reading the arrest warrant reports. I took it upon myself to survey the courtroom. I glanced over to my left to take a peek at the US District Attorney, and he didn't have a concerned expression written anywhere on his face. He looked more like he wanted to hurry up and get this over with because he had other important business to tend to, and this was a waste of his time. I glanced over to my right. My attorney was sitting there with a smirk on his face. He was watching the judge as well and was just playing it cool while making another simple free paycheck. As I looked past him, I was locked into eye-to-eye contact with my probation officer. Her eyeball stare made me feel like a bull's-eye for actual daggers! I couldn't help but smile to myself because the harder she stared at me, the more I knew she was in the wrong business. She would've made a great character in the Roger Rabbit movie because she was truly animated. As the thought passed through my mind, a little laugh slipped out, and everyone in the courtroom looked at me. Due to past court appearances, I guess the judge figured, "Let's get this show on the road before Mr. Dixon flips out."

As the federal judge started presiding over the courtroom, he directed his attention straight to my probation officer. He stated to her, "It says here that Mr. Dixon is in sales of narcotics. Do you have any evidence to support that Mr. Dixon was in sales of narcotics?"

My probation officer replied no.

The judge stated, "You had two FBI agents follow Mr. Dixon for over a year, and within that time, they reported that Mr. Dixon gave no signs of illegal activity. So how did you obtain information that he was in sales of narcotics?"

The response was, "Eva."

The judge looked at me and asked if I sold drugs.

"Not since Hollywood, California, Your Honor. I think I might've had a couple of bumps in the road but I'm not exactly for sure."

"It says here that you charge Mr. Dixon with an escape charge. Where did he escape to?"

My probation officer replied that I changed apartments without giving her the correct number to the apartment into which I lived. The judge looked at me and asked me if I ever left the premises. I told him, "No, I never even left the same floor, Your Honor."

The judge said, pretty much talking to himself, "So how did he escape? Mr. Dixon, your probation officer charged you with giving fake statements, as far as your work ethic is concerned. Explain this to me."

I explained to the judge that sometimes my cousin asked me to be a helper, nothing more. They give me a few dollars under the table.

I could tell by the judge's expression that it was time for this circus to come to an end. He laid down his last decision. "I find no justification to send Mr. Dixon back to prison. Furthermore, I find no reason to extend Mr. Dixon's probation sentence." Now, the judge turned his attention directly toward me. "Mr. Dixon, you only have a couple of months of probation left. Do the rest of your paper the right way, please! And word of advice, you see the young lady sitting back there? The only reason you came before me is because of her. I strongly advise you to get away from her." As I turned my head to look in the direction to which he referred, Eva was sitting inside of the courtroom.

I completely understood what the judge was saying, but it was too late. We were living together now, and when she moved in, I had no idea that she was bringing hell along with her. After being released, our relationship started snowballing in the wrong direction at the speed of light! Things were so bad with Eva that I did not know what to do, especially when she hooked up with one of her friends from Akron, Ohio. Some nights she wouldn't even come home or even call giving me a reason why she wasn't coming home. I didn't want to start any arguments with her because I never knew where an argument might lead, and I was already afraid of this woman because she had already sent me back to jail on some false bullshit.

Two days had gone by, and I hadn't heard a word from Eva. I picked my daughter up, and we headed to the store to get her some corn twisters. While standing inside the store, I met a lady that owned a few daycare's with her mother. She told me her name was Malina. She was holding a little girl in her arms that was about the same age as my daughter. We exchanged phone numbers and instantly became telephone buddies. As my daughter and I walked back into the apartment, Eva was home and very intoxicated. I asked her if she was okay. Then I asked her can she notify me ahead of time the next time she planned on being away for so many days. She said yes and passed out on the sofa. As the days went by, Eva was never home, but she would call me and tell me that she couldn't tell me where she was. One day when I returned home, I ran into a guy that I knew from the apartment complex. He told me Eva was a stripper. Then he went forth to explain the whole story to me. Eva had a best friend in Akron that was a stripper, and they had teamed up and started doing private parties together. I couldn't believe what I was hearing, but at the same time, I didn't doubt it because I really didn't know her.

About six days had gone by and I hadn't heard anything from Eva. That's when she came stumbling through the door. She was very intoxicated and wanted to pick up the baby, but I wouldn't allow it. I asked her to go take a shower first so she can pull herself together. Instantly, she started getting mad and threw things at me. She threw one of my tennis shoes at me, and I caught in midair. I've always been known to have fast reflexes, so just as fast as I caught it, I threw it right back at her. Yes, I meant to hit her with the Nike Air Max, but I didn't expect for it to hit her point-blank in her nose. Blood started gushing out of her nose like a faucet. I found this to be kind of odd because just too much was coming out. (A few months into the near future, it was discovered that the tennis shoe wasn't the main factor for her nose becoming a faucet. Eva's nostrils were very good friends with Mr. Powder Cocaine). Eva started crying and went over to the Bedford Heights Police Station and pressed charges on me.

So here I was once again, in a six-by-four concrete condo, with my personal butlers bringing me some of the world's finest foods. As I was standing in front of the judge explaining the situation, Eva walked into the courtroom and tried to offer the prosecutor a letter that was created to get the charges dropped against me, so the prosecutor just had her read it out loud in the open courtroom, "To whom it may concern: My name is Eva, and I am writing this letter in regards to a restraining order I had placed on my "Baby Daddy". I truly regret making that decision" etc.

I was just standing there with my mouth wide open when Eva finally reached the conclusion of reading that fake ass letter inside of the open courtroom, I was not the only one looking at her like she was on something that had the exact-equivalent-effect of a "Freaking Sugar Field" that was rushed into someone's vein with some type of new technology of a syringe. And she gave the courtroom spectators, "including my unbelievable eyes" the perfect reason to be wearing a very super shock expression on our faces. First off, her court appearance had me standing there with a dunce hat on my head, and I'm pretty sure if anything would've caught a reflection of me, it would have purely brought to focus an image of a Super Jackass! For allowing my goofy self to become a victim of this type of super-induced-energize-powdered nose of a woman. I was just standing with my eyeballs shooting upwards and reciting to myself more than a few times, 2 Corinthians 5:17. *"You are a new creation!"* I know now that this is going to be some hard work! (This road that I'm about to travel will not be a walk in the park) But I must turn the other cheek! The old me is gone! Just suck it up!

Eva was standing in that courtroom with a weave on her head that wasn't properly cared for. I'm sure if the Dark Mistress Elvira would've had a chance to view this statue of a synthetic mess, she would have stopped whatever horror movie she was showing to her dedicated fans of an audience and stepped into some real-life boxing gloves and ask Eva if it was okay for them to step into a boxing ring and have a private one-on-one woman talk about her wig. The stilettos that she produced on her feet to hold her high in the air would've made any short person in that courtroom with a small man complex, super jealous of her and running for the border to purchase some boots from Mr. Dove's Cry! I'm more than certain that Prince would've been jealous as well. Now the slope that made up her cleavage was open wide enough to support any type of skiing expedition. Her miniskirt was so short that it gave any dirty old man a reason to be proud. Even with this distracting image standing in front of the judge, the judge did her best at remaining professional as others in the courtroom was whispering and explained to her, "The letter may or may not be taken into consideration. The fact is, you have already pressed charges on him, and we just can't take them back." I was given a bond and walked back to my concrete condo.

During the next couple of days, a neighbor from the apartment complex came to visit me. I really didn't know this neighbor too well, but they stayed down the hall from me. They alerted me that there were all types of people coming in and out of my apartment at all hours of the night. I started thinking to myself, when I saw Eva in the courtroom, I didn't even know who she was. So I did not doubt anything this neighbor was relaying to me. I really needed to be set free, but with all of this technology leading our lives in this world of computers in the palm of our hands that when I got up that morning to contact the people that I needed in order to get released, my dumb ass couldn't remember any phone numbers that would accept collect calls!

During the course of Eva's absence, Malina and I were truly on the verge of becoming friends. I gave her a call, and since my bond was low, she had no issues whatsoever giving me a get out of jail-free card. When Malina displayed that act of kindness upon me, I had a newfound respect for her. There was nothing she could do to make me look at her in any type of negative light, because for guys like me, that was accustomed to the revolving door of freedom and no freedom. For someone to go out of their way and bond us out, they instantly get a special place in our hearts. (But only if I could see into the future, I would've returned her get-out-of-jail free card, and stayed my ass in jail). So this was the new way I view my beautiful Malina.

("I'm a very hungry cat! I'm truly at the point of starvation. I'm searching for food as I go from alley to alley, but with total control of my patience in search for the right puzzle piece to forever carve my hunger. With my self-motivation and 100 percent determination, I finally came upon what I was looking for! A nice juicy mouse! This one course meal of mine was trapped in the corner of my alley of a dining room. The only way out for this four-footed meal of mine is to be crafty enough to get past me, and my hunger would never allow for that juicy "RAT" to initiate one of the type of programs. As the glands were hard at work, my mouth continue to water like nothing I've ever experienced before. I slowly started approaching my meal with strategy and my focus on full force, and just as I was about to strike pay dirt! My paw landed on a piece of broken glass! As the pain rippled through my entire body, my meal could have easily slipped away from me, but my meal didn't do that at all. To my surprise, the mouse walked over to me with no fear and removed the glass from my paw. That's when my respect for this mouse became solid. And the only thing that could ever take away this view, would be "Supreme Mistreatment" by the mouse.)

After being released from the city jail, I was not allowed to go to my apartment. I had places that I could've gone, but I decided to sleep inside my car because my issues with Eva were unresolved. I wanted to make sure my daughter was safe and that none of my furniture left that apartment complex. The money that I had given Eva for the rent did not go to the proper bill collectors, so my apartment complex issued me an eviction notice. And the courts ordered me to go to anger management classes for the tennis shoe incident. By this time, Eva was so deep into the street and stripper life. I was never allowed to see my daughter. I never knew where my daughter was or who was keeping her. Every time I went to her mother's house, she would say she wasn't there. I didn't know what was going on, and Bedford Heights Police were getting tired of me complaining to them about me not seeing my child.

After weeks of sleeping inside my vehicle, it was time for me to appear in court for the eviction notice. A few hours before court, I received some help from some of the apartment complex managers. I didn't have keys to go inside the apartment where I used to live, so the apartment manager gave me a ladder and explained to me how to pry the sliding glass door open with a Car Jack. Once I was in, the apartment manager and I removed my black Italian soft glove leather sofa and my big ass TV. Due to the fact that I didn't have a pot to piss in, we put my things inside empty apartments around the complex. He would warn me every time when one of the painters or maintenance men was going to go into one of the places where my things were being stored. We would move them to another empty apartment. This went on for a few months. I left everything else inside the apartment because I knew she needed those things for my daughter. I knew I was going to miss my extra king-size bed, but I truly wasn't concerned at the same time, because only Eva and the walls of that apartment knew exactly what went on inside of that bed since my absence.

Finally, I was making my way into the Bedford Municipal Courtroom, (the entire way there, I was mentally kicking myself in my backside for adding Eva to my leasing agreement) and even though both of our names were on the eviction notice, I was already pretty certain that Eva was going to be a no-show. As the charges were read down to me, I just turned into a human calculator and started adding up everything. It started off with $1,462 for the missed rent payments, then there was a charge for carpet stains, an additional charge for drywall repair, more charges for cleaning the kitchen, two more extra charges for cleaning the bathroom and removal of a miscellaneous thing, then came the cherry on top, which was the court fees.

At the end of this bout that I was losing, I was over $3,000 in the red.

CHAPTER 39

MALINA

As I left the courtroom, pondering how was I going to pay back over $3,000 for something I didn't do, it was the butt end of October 2008, and the weather had become very chilly. I pulled into the complex where I used to live and parked my car right up underneath my mother's balcony. I turned the heat on in the vehicle and grabbed my little portable DVD player. With so much sadness going on in my heart, Steve Harvey and I spent many nights together inside that vehicle. Watching him on *Def Comedy Jam* always brought a smile to my face. My favorite routine of Steve was the talking eyeball. When the morning came, I would grab a cup of coffee from Speedway and watch Steve Harvey again because watching him was the only thing that seemed to get my day off to a good start.

Even though I was sleeping in my car, I would still go to my mom's house to wash up, make myself something to eat, then head straight over to the gym. The whole time, I pondered where my daughter was and what I was going to do for money with a past criminal record like mine. Because the moving job I was holding down was long gone, and I knew no one was going to hire me because of my past record. So due to the time I spent in jail, I lost my little part-time job with my cousin. The company no longer allowed anyone with a felony to participate with distribution. Once again, I believed God was feeling my pain. Most individuals with my type of constructed genetic makeup always walk a very thin line when it comes to survival. We have no problem slipping back into old habits, if we feel that it is a matter of life or death. Sleeping outside in a freezing car with Steve Harvey, due to my stubbornness, certainly put me on the rim of life or death and my dark side was trying to breathe life again.

As I entered the gym, for some reason, I didn't walk my regular five miles first, that five-mile walk was something that I participated in, just about every morning, and I really enjoyed it, because there was a group of senior citizens always walking with me. As bad as I needed it, I never had the time to show up at one of their prayer groups that they continued to invite me to, but I kept a promise that one day I would make it. As the future came near, that promise was brought to reality. So I bypassed the inside walking track and went straight into the weightlifting room. As I was pushing steel up and down, I overheard a guy talking about he needed help with his cleaning company. I went over and introduced myself, and later that night, I was at work with him! So my dark side didn't get the chance to full bloom again.

During this time, I was still searching for my daughter, so I turned to one of the best sources in the whole world, Facebook! As November of 2008 hit, sleeping inside my vehicle was really becoming a nuisance, and running around, trying to locate my daughter, was becoming a very big headache. Just as I was on the verge of exhaustion and in need of some honest rest, a woman I met on the dating website was truly feeling my pain. The only problem was that she stayed in Bermuda. But she did not let that faraway distance between the two of us stop her from coming to the USA to meet me. She boarded an airplane with her sister and her little dog, Pebbles, and came to my rescue. The woman had money, but the money she controlled did not control her heart. She explained to me that I needed me sometime alone so I could get my thinking straight, and that she was willing to help me as far as I would let her go because she truly believed in me. She moved me into a fully furnished home that she owned and gave me keys to a new Ford Explorer.

She was a seven-day churchgoer, so I attended church with her one Saturday morning. Sunday night, Bermuda and her sister gave me hugs and kisses, and she told me her house and vehicle were at my disposal. I dropped the three off at the airport and drove back to the gift she had given me and got some rest. As the next couple of days went by, I just lay in bed and watched TV, and with the refrigerator belly full of food, I did a lot of good eating and swallowed my vitamins because I knew I had a tough road ahead of me to travel, and my health needed to be ready. This was nice and dandy, and I was very thankful, but I'm still the man that I am, and the place Bermuda offered me was on the side of town opposite from where I needed to be. As soon as Bermuda notified me of her safe return to her country, I mailed her the house keys and the truck keys and told her thank you for everything. (We remained friends over the years to come. Summer of 2012, she paid me a surprise visit.) I got in my own car, fresh and rejuvenated, and drove back to my apartment complex and parked underneath my mother's window. I turned my heat on, and then I woke up Steve Harvey and let the Def Jam play.

I don't know when I dozed off to sleep, but when morning showed its face, I was back searching for my daughter. During this time span, Malina and I stayed in contact. She decided it would be a pretty good idea if I moved in with her, her little daughter, and her cat. Malina told me to get my silly ass out of the cold. (To you, the reader. Is this statement true or false: You really don't know a person at all until you've lived with them?) I found this new situation to be pretty cool under the circumstances. Her little daughter had begun to look at me as a father figure, and I was very cool with that especially due to the fact that she was just a couple of months younger than my own daughter. Being around her took some of the monkey off my back from missing my own child. At the same time, I learned more about Malina, and she learned more about me. After learning more about her, I began to have a soft spot for her because she was diagnosed with the same blood disorder that my sister passed away from. As she revealed more of herself to me, I understood that she was a little nutty in her thought patterns. She started to show me all the warning signs of a woman that have been done very wrong in a past relationship, and by the things that was flowing from her lips was as personal and direct as flying daggers through the air. I truly believe that she had forgotten who I really was and she was viewing someone else that she had been with before meeting me while steadily using her words as if she was pouring hot grits all over my body. But due to the similarities of my sister which gave me a sense of false hope, all I could do is stand there and absorb the heat as I wonder why haven't anyone smacked her teeth out? So the best thing for me to do was to turn my cheek to a lot of the things that she poured on top of me. As the days went by, the negativity in the atmosphere just grew stronger and stronger with the King standing over me because she had done a total face transformation while scalding me and the views I was seeing was very manly. Her opinions about me begin to follow behind one another like ants marching to store food for the winter. And I actually believe on her good days, that she truly believed that I were a crawling insect and she was verbally stomping on me. She said a few things that just about any man that honestly didn't have any type or respect for a woman, would've knocked her face-off. And then patted himself on the back for a job well done. The one thing I truly have learned in life is that words only hurt your feelings mentally if you allowed it to occur. I've never seen words do any physical damage to the outer parts of a body. One day after one of Malina's "Verbal Beat Downs" was over, I noticed that my arms and my legs were still in working condition, so I left her house and decided to have a conversation with my mom about what was going on and she told me not to pay it any mind because everything that she was saying to me was because of the illness that she was suffering through. My mom said that my sister suffered hard from the same symptoms as Malina.

Linda said, "Don't let the evil things that she says travel to your heart. And never give into retaliation on her level, because you are a much better person than that and you know that's not your character." I gave my mom an okay and went about my business.

With so much going on in my life, I decided to go for a long drive and with the way my brain was processing all of the events, I didn't pay too much attention to the fact that it was now dark outside, so my goofy self was driving around with my headlights off. I figure this out when I saw the red and blue lights flashing in my rearview mirror and the police cruiser loudspeaker was telling me to pull over. I pulled over to the curb and cut the power on my engine. As the officer made his way to my driver's window, we already knew one another from me running back and forth over to the police station complaining about my daughter's mom. He told me to follow him, and we pulled up into the Speedway gas station. We both went in and got coffee, and then we stood in front of his police cruiser to talk. After a brief and very educational conversation, on November 20, 2008, I had tracked down Eva and I went to the Cuyahoga County Juvenile Court system and filed for my parenting visitation rights. They were granted to me! I was back in my daughter's life! (I will always have respect for you, Officer V, and your Asian partner, Officer C. Thank you guys for my first step toward gaining custody.)

Things weren't too great over at Malina's house, but who could hold her thoughts against her? She had an ex-felon living in her house with her and her adopted daughter and the cat. She was not charging me rent money, and she started letting me know she wasn't charging me any rent money with this statement. "It's getting close to two months for you being here, next month, you have to go. It's nice that you keep the cat litter box and the house clean. I really appreciate you keeping the driveway shoveled for me. And thank you, for driving to my job and getting all the snow off my vehicle and letting me sit inside your car with you while mine's warm up. But that's not enough. I don't know how you're going to get an apartment because your credit can't be too good. It's nice that you have a little job, but all you do is mop floors and clean toilets. The only way I can see you taking better care of your daughter is with my help. Look at your vehicle. It's on its way out the door, and don't think you're going to be using my vehicle to go clean the accounts. It's embarrassing enough that my neighbors have seen you use my car a few times already. I feel sorry for you. To be honest, sometimes, I feel like I'm feeding a grown kid. I mean let's really be honest, look at you! You will never have another woman like me in your life. You don't have nothing! Only worthless dreams about writing a book. I don't think you're going to ever be successful at anything!" (And there it was! "The old kick a Nigga while he's down maneuver"). But I just took it on the chin, because she wasn't the first person to step on me, and I was pretty sure she wouldn't be the last. Because I know God is going to pick me up when the time is right! So I'm going to really be honest with myself! Because I'm truly not the one to let human words transform into a "Stopping Obstacle" in my life. So I just keep on pushing forward.

When Malina finished revealing her true feelings about me, all I could say was "Okay." I left her standing in her kitchen and went down into the basement. I sat down on the futon that I utilized as a bed, and let my faucets do their job because I was so hurt from her words! Not because she said them to me, but because they were true, except for the part about my credit and the worthless dreams about me writing my autobiography. So I just sat there as the tears started pouring from my eyelids, her cat must have sensed something was very wrong with my heart. The cat walked over to me, looked at me for only a few seconds, then jumped up on the futon next to me and laid down. I found this to be very surprising because every time I gave this cat a bath, it would hiss at me as if I was trying to drown him. Maybe this cat sensed that I was leaving and the litter box wouldn't be changed as often. He would be back to her regular cleaning routine. Yuck. I guess this was the cat's way of showing me that he appreciated me, so I smiled.

As I sat there, I had to reevaluate what my mother said because after everything Malina had just laid down on me! It didn't sound like it was coming from some type of blood disorder. That bullshit was from her black ass heart. At the same time, it was all true because I was truly downing in the bottom of the bucket. And the real man in me couldn't get mad at her. She was just letting me know that she was not going to be the one throwing a lifeline down for me to climb up. (But fortunately a smile was sent on my way for brief second, because out of nowhere, Eva dropped my daughter off at my mother's house unannounced doing the holiday season. That was nice and dandy, but Eva wasn't following the court order properly that she was ordered to do.)

When Christmas came around, she had gotten my daughter a few things, and I resented it. But at the same time, I did not let my pride get in the way of my daughter's happiness. I was poor, and I accepted that fact. I knew how to go out to make money, but at the same time, I gave God my word that I would no longer live my life to that degree. So as my daughter opened up her gifts from Malina, I just put my head down, tucked my tail between my legs, and started praying for my life to get more financially in order.

CHAPTER 40

SCALES OF LIFE

Finally, 2008 had ended, and I was standing with my eyes closed in the middle of Malina's driveway with my arms stretched high and wide toward the clouds. I was doing two very important things at one time. The first thing I was doing was giving God a hug. The second thing was welcoming home 2009 with open arms. (As I'm sitting here writing this book, I'm thinking maybe I shouldn't have had my arms so far apart when I gave 2009 a hug!) This new year set off a chain of events that left me pretty much on the sour side of life! The balance scale of my personal journey was pulling strongly in both directions, as far as my negative and positive energies were concerned.

I made sure I was making the right steps into this new year. I sat in the manager's office inside my mother's apartment building while I filled out a renter's application. The manager asked me if I had a cosigner. I said no.

She said, "You know you have to earn triple the rent in order to live here."

"Yes, I know."

"Not only that, your credit would have to meet minimum requirements."

"Yes, I know."

The manager went to her office desk and ran a credit check on me. I had known this woman for a couple years now, and her facial expressions never changed, which made it very hard for me to read her body language. After running my credit, she sat back down at the table with me. I was waiting for her rejection, but instead, she told me that my credit wasn't as bad as I thought it was. She said it was good that I paid back all the money that was owed to the apartment Eva messed up. Not only that, but Linda had just moved out of the apartment she was renting and moved into a bigger one down the hall, so I moved straight into the one she just left.

My mom was very pleased with my stubborn self because she no longer had to walk out to her balcony and look down to make sure I was all right. Later that day, as Malina walked through her door, I gave her the good news, and we separated as friends. She even opened up a phone line for me so we could continue to stay in contact. After all the paperwork was cleared and a sizable amount of security deposit was pulled from my bank account, I had the keys to my door in my hands. Like a bolt of lightning, the maintenance men and I moved my things into my new place. Now I was ready for business! I went straight downtown to the juvenile courts and gave them my new address. During this time, Eva was not following accordingly to the visitation rules the courts ordered, and I knew in my gut this was going to become a terrible ordeal later on down the line.

One night, I put one of my favorite Hungry Man dinners in the oven. After removing it from the oven and preparing to take the first bite out of my breaded fish patty, my phone started ringing. It was sort of late in the evening, so I automatically knew it could only be one of two people: either Malina, which would be out of the question at this point this time of night because at this point we were only speaking every blue moon, or my mom, which would be unusual for Linda to be calling so late.

As I glanced down at the phone, I didn't recognize the number, but I answered, and my cousin Cinnamon said, "Hello." This truly caught me off-guard because we really didn't keep in contact at all, and we didn't have any reason to because we were more strangers than we were blood. But that one phone call was the one that took us from being unfamiliar first cousins to viewing one another as brother and sister. Instantly, I knew something was a mist by the tone of her voice, so I said, "What's up?" She notified me she got my number from Linda. As she prepared herself to tell me the reason for this phone call, the whole vibe made me feel a little uneasy. She started explaining her situation, and before she could get partially into the reason for her conversation, I jumped inside my Nike Air Max, grabbed my favorite aluminum baseball bat, and did a Flash Gordon to my car! As I pulled out of the apartment complex's parking lot speeding like a bat from hell, getting pulled over by a cruiser was of no concern. I just hated the fact that after I utilized my favorite aluminum baseball bat on someone's head, I would have to relinquish it inside one of my secret fireplaces.

Then another thought crossed my mind. I wondered if Cinnamon would become compelled to spill the beans to the authorities about any of my premeditated actions. I was on Cinnamon's street in less than two and a half minutes. I parked my car eight houses down and ran to her doorstep. She opened the door and let me in, but the Situation at hand was absent from the scene. We sat down and started to politic. She revealed to me, in detail, about her past marriage. I totally understood why she didn't allow anyone to ride in her back seat now. Then, she explained the reason for calling me over to handle the Situation instead of calling the police? Then she explained to me that she didn't want the police to be involved in this goofy ordeal due to personal reasons, she just wanted the Situation to be gone without any hurtful doings to anyone's career, and her older sister told her I was the best option for the job.

The next day, I was at Cinnamon's house early in the morning. She relieved herself of her house keys, and to be certain, I asked her one more time, "Are you positive that this is what you want?" She said yes. I told her it would be done before she gets home from work, and if I ever come over and the Situation was present again because all was forgiven, I would never look at her as a cousin again because I was putting my life in jeopardy. She told me she knew this already because her sister had notified her of how guys from the streets have a code. As the Situation appeared at the door, I introduced myself in a very polite manner, but he knew exactly who I was! Because the first time I went to my cousin's house, a few months prior, he stayed down in the basement area and never came up to introduce himself. I went and found him, and before I extended my hand to give him a handshake, I asked him, "What type of man lets another man come into his home, and he don't come and introduce himself?"

Before the Situation could even give me some type of superficial explanation, I grabbed his hand and shook it while applying a little pressure to my grip. Now that morning, before he could step inside the house he occupied with my cousin, I stepped out for a serious one-on-one. I explained to him that Cinnamon didn't want him there any longer, and his first expression and body language were of refusal. I counterattacked that with my mom's deer-stopping stare, and that grabbed his attention because he started explaining how he had been living there for the last two years and had stained the wood and done a lot of work on the house. I reassured him that I understood all that, and then I had to let him know where he went wrong.

I said, "I feel for you, my brother! I have nothing against what you just said. You just fucked up by making the mistake of moving in with a woman you are not married to, and your name is not on the mortgage even though you helped pay it. And she's asking you nicely to leave so you both can move on with your lives without any incidents. I'm here to help accommodate you with the procedure of removing all of your belongings." He understood and was a gentleman about the transition. The Situation even gave me a gift because after sizing me up; he knew I participated at a gym. So he left me a pair of twenty-five-pound dumbbells.

As the weeks followed, my cousin and I were becoming friends. One thing that I've learned through experience in life, just because we're blood bound does not mean that we are friends. I woke up the next morning and started stepping to my regular routine. I headed over to the local gas station to grab a cup of coffee and some breakfast cakes. After doing my dance decorating my cup of Joe, with the free sugar and creamers that they offered, it was time for me to start my five-mile walk. As I moved my legs faster, I was brought to an abrupt stop by someone calling my name. Her face looked familiar, but I couldn't put a finger on it. She didn't disclose who she was, or even offer a simple good morning. She just said, "You have a son!"

I smiled, but I surely wasn't laughing because every inch of this woman's body language gave me no reason to doubt what she just revealed.

"I have a son by whom?"

She got closer to me, then offered her lips to my earlobe. "Please don't tell her that I was the one who told you, but the little boy looks just like you, and I don't think it's right what she's doing. Do you promise not to tell her that it was me who told you?"

I nodded my head yes.

Then she whispered, "The Lawyer."

Before she could even pull her lips away from my ear, my body was already ravaged with goose bumps. As I was standing in the middle of the gas station parking lot, my thought pattern went into cardiac arrest.

The admission door had just opened up wide for another possible child custody case, and I was just standing there prohibiting traffic from moving about in a natural way for a gas station parking lot, when my mind automatically started reminiscing. (As we both were busy folding and exchanging our clothes from the washing machine to the dryer inside of the "Wash-In-Spin" that was located across the street from my apartment complex, I ran into a guy's wife that is a member of the same church that I would frequently attend from time to time. As we both stood there trying to figure out which one of the other customers will be finishing first with their clothing detail she decided to ask me if I was still single. I said yes, and she asked me why is that?

I started explaining, "It's so hard to find someone who will not judge me for my past mistakes and who will want me just for me, and not look at me because my pockets are flat, but look at my heart and the goodness that I have to offer to a healthy relationship, and not because of my past living. I'm at the point now that I'm hoping to find someone who understands, that it's not behind every good man, but beside every good man, you will find a better woman. And to be honest with you, I had a letdown in my life before. I had met someone that made me fall head over heels. I loved the way she looked, and I loved the way she smelled every single time she exited the shower. I liked the way she laughed, and I enjoyed making love to her. But the feelings were not balanced. And I made a fool of myself. I never looked at this woman for how much money she made. I always looked at the way she made me feel in the beginning. I used to tell her all the time that her job, her car, or her house don't mean anything to me. All I care about is how she treats me.

"And with so much false pretense circling our relationship, I was into this thing with a blindfold on. Anyway, I decided to ask her to marry me. So I took what little money I had and purchased a very small diamond ring. It was all I could afford at the time, but to me, it was big because I'd never weighed love by material things. I went to my favorite flower store and got a dozen long stem roses. With her bachelor's and her master's degrees, I drove to the hospital where she was the head nurse. I got down on one knee in front of her and all her coworkers, and I asked her to marry me. She said yes, and she looked as happy as she could be. Then all of that changed very rapidly. As one of the other nurses came over and asked her to see the ring, the other nurse looked at the ring and turned her nose up, and the entire body language of the woman whom I just asked to marry changed. In the days that followed after that, she made it her job to belittle me every single day. But I didn't let it bother me. I remained holding my head high until I had enough money to move away."

As the man's wife was finishing up saying "amen to that," I noticed one of the other laundry-goers approaching my direction. With a beautiful smile, she said hello, and I noticed she had a tear in her eye. (As I'm sitting here writing this book, I'm thinking, when I saw that smile and that tear on that woman's face, I should've thought she was nutty and ran for the border.)

The woman with the beautiful smile said, "I'm sorry to intrude. Please forgive me, and I do apologize if you feel I'm crossing over the lines by being nosy, but me and a few of the ladies over there washing overheard your whole story [I was thinking me and my big ass mouth!], and we all agree that you are a very handsome-looking man with noticeable standards, and I have the perfect person for you to meet. She's perfect for you. You guys will make a perfect couple! She's a thirty-eight-year-old lawyer. She has no children. She's one of the heads on the Catholic Council, and I was wondering if you would like to meet her. I could give her your number, that's if you say yes."

At this time in my life after dealing with Eva and Malina, I was really just about open to all positive notions, so I decided to be in cahoots with the beautiful smiling lady with the one tear hanging from her eye.(At that time, I didn't catch this because that smile and that tear threw me off! But why is a woman who is thirty-eight, a lawyer, with no kids, single, idiot? And this smiling teary-eyed lady really liked saying the word *perfect* just a little too darn much. I now know that my reading body language and my sensitive spidey senses had a major flaw going on!) Not a good twenty-four hours went by before I received a phone call from the Lawyer. Surprisingly, we had a very decent conversation. I was really digging her intellect. One thing for certain, if the chemistry is right, a very knowledgeable street person and a very knowledgeable college graduate could create one hell of a team together. So we decided to meet at a bar.

After a few drinks and some laughs, with the mixture of both of us having lonely voids in our life and both suffering from other people's hands not touching our bodies, I agreed to accompany her to her house. Once we pulled into her double-car garage, the garage door began to let itself down. It became the perfect place for two wild animals' energy to ignite. With both vehicles' freshly turned off engines, each hot car hood instantly transformed into comfortable beds! And that was just round one. We picked our clothes up, and neither of us bothered to put any of the clothing back on our bodies as I took a peek out of the garage and into the moonlit midnight, and we started laughing as we skipped across her driveway and made it to the side door of the house nude, truly not caring if we were spotted by a neighbor or not. As I entered her home, I smiled as I looked around because she was a neat freak like me.

As we tried to make our way up to her sleeping area, we got stuck on the very soft-covered carpet stairs. This thirty-eight-year-old (Head of the Catholic Council) was honestly showing me moves and making noises I wasn't used to from someone her age, and I enjoyed every second of it! As our sweat and other bodily fluids was starting to moisten the carpet on her stairs, all I could think was, *Wow! Now I see why she's one of the Heads of the Catholic Council! Because she really knew how to take charge and control a situation! Because the way her watery mouth baptize my purple headed warrior, she just about had me begging for mercy!* Even as round 2 was exercised in such a compact area, we surely managed to make it a total success by both of us reaching our peaks and releasing at the same time while staring into each other's eyes. Before we could initiate round 3, we stopped at one of the first rooms located upstairs. When she flipped the light switch, I couldn't believe my eyes. It was a bedroom filled with furnishings for a little boy.

Before she could say anything, I blurted out, "You said you didn't have any children!"

She responded, "I don't. This is for when I have one, silly!" Then she snatched my hand and dragged me into her bedroom, and that night, I saw more sparks than I had ever seen at any Fourth of July show! When the morning came, she was already dressed and standing over me with her briefcase in her hand, just smiling at me. I said good morning to her, but she didn't say good morning back. Instead she replied with, "I wish I could put you inside of a jar, and just keep you on my nightstand!" After she said that, my eyes went straight for her eyeballs, and I didn't see any tell-a-tale signs of her joking around with the statement she just said. As she double checked to make sure she had everything in order for her courtroom meeting, she looked at me and said, "Well Monday morning, just another day in the Cleveland courtroom of chaos. The refrigerator is full and enjoy the cable because I have every single channel open that's available." Then with a twist of her heels, she was on her way to work like the "wicked witch" that I did not know that she was. (But surely I will be finding out).

I lay there for about an hour, and then my stomach decided we were hungry. I'm one of those guys that just has to have potato chips with everything I eat. So I put my clothes on and laced up my Nike Air Max. I went to the side door and opened it, but I couldn't leave because the security door was locked. I went to the front door of the house, and the results were the same. I located every single window inside of this woman's house, and every single window had bars on them. I was trapped! When she finally made it home, I questioned her about her actions, and she went haywire! She started punching me and spitting on me and kicking me simultaneously! And while she was doing all these things, she kept saying over and over until it started to sound like a schizophrenic chanting, "What are you going to do, with your record! What are you going to do, with your record! What are you going to do, with your fucking prison record!" And there it was! The truth was now out! That this woman is "Super Nutty". And I knew it was time for me to play chess with this self-proclaimed "Boxing Kangaroo!" Yes, chess will be the game that I play, because there was no way in the world I was about to walk away from that good sex. Flat out!

"So please, please don't tell her that I told you!" With the sound of her voice, I snapped out of my delusional state and told the woman okay. I told her she had my word at the time! (Wow, I have a son?) At that moment, I decided against my five-mile walk. Instead, I walked away from the gas station with mixed and confused feelings and headed home so I could figure out my next move.

Later that afternoon, my cousin came to pick me up so I could tell her what transpired that morning. After the story ended, she asked me what I was going to do. I replied with just a shrug of the shoulders and a fictitious laugh. Then I started to ponder. I really needed another job, and with the way my daughter's mother is going about being a parent, I needed something where I could control the hours. I tilted my head to my right so I could just stare at the sky out of her car window. That's when I noticed we were passing a beauty school, and I told Cinnamon to park. As soon as we walked through the door, I started surveying the whole school. As I was processing my surroundings, a shapely grown woman with a very pretty face and a first-rate I-mean-business demeanor about herself sat down with me and my cousin. Her name was Instructor Robinson and showed us what the school had to offer. I went into my pants pocket and handed this soft-spoken woman the few hundred that was required for me to start school for nail technician license. Cinnamon and I walked right back out of that school door with a receipt! And my little cousin was smiling, and telling me that she was proud of me for choosing school over the streets. Because she knows the thin-line that ex-felons walk, but she knows that is also very walkable, if a person truly give up their old negative ways.

The next day, I woke up thinking, *Is it true that God wouldn't put anything on us that He feels we can't handle?* I was about to find out the answer to my own question because my life plate had just gotten full with a four-course meal and dessert. Time was of the essence, so I immediately start eating! My first course was going to be finding out who my biological father was because I was curious why he didn't want me. Since I had a son, I was going to be sure not to follow in my father's footsteps. I called my mother and told her I needed to talk. I already knew as soon as I started asking questions about my biological father, Linda was going to get real stubborn and tight-lipped. I entered her apartment and didn't beat around any bushes! "Linda! Who's my father?"

She turned and looked me straight in my eyes, and to my surprise, she wasn't doing her deer dance. She just started shaking her head. Then she said in an angry tone, "I can't stand your father. He pointed a gun at me." I asked my mother what happened, and she started explaining. "Me and your father were living together. It was raining outside. He came into the house and took a brand-new coat that he had just bought me. He didn't say anything to me. He just walked right back out the door. I went over to the window and looked out, and he had placed my coat over another woman's shoulders. I raised the window up and shouted at him. I told him don't ever come back. That's when he pulled his gun out and pointed it at me and told me that if I didn't get my head back inside the window, he was going to blow it off. So I pulled my head back in the window because your daddy was crazy enough to pull the trigger." My mom finished telling the story.

I didn't say anything for a few minutes because I wanted to watch her and get a feel for what exactly was going through her mind at that very moment. My mom's body language showed me no signs of her being sad about the situation, but she was definitely angry. I waited for the coast to clear, and then I asked Linda to give me his name, and my mom said through gritted teeth, "John Doe."

"Okay," I said softly, then asked her where did John Doe lived. She said, "Cedar with his momma."

I went down the hall to my own apartment and jumped straight on my computer. I eliminated all the different addresses down to one, jumped in my car, and started making my way toward Cedar. When I turned on the street where the GPS was leading me, there were a lot a guys in front of the designated location. I braced myself because I had to be careful in this neck of the woods because I didn't know anyone from this area. There was no doubt that I was in the hood, and I had no issues with any hoods that I knew of. But at the same time, I was showing up unannounced, and I had stopped carrying guns, so I felt naked. Here goes nothing! I stopped in front of the house and let my passenger-side window down and shouted, "Do any of you guys know if John Doe lives here?"

"No John Doe lives here. You have the wrong address, partner!" Their body language had all the signs of stranger danger.

Right then and there, I knew I was at the right place because my mother had already told me the whole family was crazy. I shouted again, "Check this out, homeboy. John Doe might be my father. I never met him before, you dig?"

One of the light-skinned guys with Chinese-shaped eyes started walking toward my vehicle. As he got closer, I started laughing to myself, but my facial expression didn't show my laughter. But the guy that was coming up to my window favored me so much, he could've been my brother or nephew. As soon as he looked into my vehicle, he was like, "Wow! Hey, y'all come here. This dude looks just like John Doe!"

I parked the car and got out and started meeting everybody. It turned out that I was related to everyone standing in front of the house. One of them said he had just called John Doe and that he was on his way over.

When he pulled up and got out of the car, I was looking at a six-foot-three, older version of myself. We gave one another nigga hugs for a quick second, then started talking. He told me that the last time he saw me was when he was in prison. "They were showing your face on every news channel, for like a month straight. The first time I saw it and they displayed your name, I was like, 'Wow! That's my son!'"

The night ended with pictures being taken, me meeting my grandmother, aunts, uncles, a few more cousins, my brothers, and sister. I invited my father to lunch the next day because just for once in my life, for some reason or another, I just wanted to see my biological father and my mother in the same room together.

As the next day came to life, I gave Malina a call. We had become good friends again (Don't judge me people! I know I'm not the only one reading this book that have played the back-and-forth game because my heart was confuse), during our separation from one another so I asked her to accompany me if I can get my parents to meet. Also, her adopted daughter and my daughter were growing up like best friends. I had to beg Linda to get on board with us, and she eventually gave in. As we were waiting in the restaurant for John Doe, he suddenly appeared at the table with his sister and her husband. After a few dances, drinks, and a couple more pictures taken, everyone went their separate ways. A few weeks after that, I went back down to Cedar to visit John Doe. He was drunk when I arrived, and he asked me to call him Daddy. I asked him never to ask me to do that again. He told me I could get out of his house. I gave my grandmother a hug, not knowing if she even remembered who I was because she slipped in and out of "reality consciousness." After over thirty years, of not knowing who my biological father was, I was just given a reason not to ever go back over to where he live. But I did accomplish what I went after, because I actually had the opportunity to be in the same room with my biological dad and my mom.

Now let me move on to the second course of my plate, "The Lawyer". After finding out I had a son, I went to her house to inquire as to whether or not the information was correct, and it was. When I saw the little boy, I had the biggest smile in my heart as well as on my face. Even though I knew his mother was mentally off the Richter chart, this was my son, my only son, so I had to see if we could be a family. After all, the smile my son gave me whenever he saw my face was priceless. The Lawyer asked me to move in with her. I realized that she had just made a major chess move. So I retaliated with the same game play but only left her only to take a pawn, allowing me to execute my knight. I agreed to move in, and I pretended that I shut my apartment down, so I moved my Italian soft glove black leather sofa into her house, along with my computer desk. With these two objects moved into her house, I had her really thinking I let my apartment go. The first week was pretty cool, but the second week had me on edge. By the third week, it went down!

It started off with me in the basement getting her work clothes together. She came down the stairs mad! And I didn't know why! She knew I was scared of her, but on the flip side of that coin, she didn't know that I don't mind a good challenge. I was studying and taking a mental note of her as she started to mumble to herself as if I wasn't present. Then she says something rude under her breath. Like the sometimes smart and cautious man that I am, I refrain from saying anything back; I just continue to observe. Another day into the third week, I managed to have my daughter with me and while my daughter and my son were playing in the living room together, I notice that the Lawyer had her eyes trained on my little girl without ever taking a break to blank. That's when the magical light above turned its self on above my head, so I decided to go into her bathroom and did a very thorough search and found an outdated bottle of antidepressant medication. The last day of the third week was crazy. I woke up early and gave my son a kiss and notified the lawyer that I had to go pick my daughter up that morning, and I left for my mission.

Upon returning, after parking my car in the garage, I walked over to the security door, turned the knob, and found that it was locked. I was standing there with my daughter. I was back wearing the sucker hat on my head again. I called her cellular phone over and over, but she wouldn't answer. So I called her office, but I didn't give her secretary my real name. When the Lawyer's voice came on the line I casually asked her what was the reason for locking the security doors? She told me her neighbor said there was a man lurking around. In other words, that was just her way of telling me that I was that man. Now, I could've easily broken into her house to remove my things, but she had an alarm on the house, and I didn't know too much about being a burglar. I drove my daughter to my mom's and I called Chopper's brother with the big Best Buy truck. It was just in my favor that he was off work that day. After kissing my mom's forehead, I jumped in my vehicle and drove down to the lawyer's office building and the secretary notified her of my presence. She came walking out of her office with a very angry facial expression, and she was mumbling rapidly. The only thing I was thinking was, *Here we go!*

She started shouting at me and told me how wrong I was for coming down to her job. She still didn't know that I knew about the antidepressant pills, so I just started playing my cards. As she was shouting at me, I looked in her eyes with a half a deer stare and told her I wanted to get married. I then explained to her how I just wanted me and her, and my son to be a family. I told her I was signing over my rights to my daughter. She gave me a really big smile and said, "Really?"

I said, "Yes. Let me go home and put something together real nice for both of us to enjoy. Call your mother and ask her to watch our son for tonight." I gave her a kiss on her lips and started walking away. Just like clockwork, she called me back and gave me the security code numbers and the key to the security door. As soon as I made it back to her place, Chopper's brother was waiting for me. We loaded my things into his truck and were ready for blast off. But before we left, I went over to her neighbor's house, the one she said saw a man lurking around. I had her neighbor call her office from his phone. As soon as I heard her voice, I simply explained to her that I was leaving and that she can get her house keys from her neighbor. Last thing I heard the Lawyer said was, "You have nowhere to go! And don't ever asked me to see your son!" as I was hanging up.

After a couple weeks went by, we continued to remain in light contact through short phone conversation. And throughout them short conversations, we managed to agree to meet at a bar. After a few drinks and some laughs, Cinnamon announced that it was time for her to start making her way back home so we all decided to separate with that same plan in mind. I lived right across the street from the bar, so I didn't drive over there, which opened up the "Fantastic Idea" for the Lawyer to offer me a ride home. As we pulled into the parking lot, she asked me if she could come up for a second and talk. Against my better judgment, I agreed. The conversation quickly boiled into an argument. I jumped up out of my seat and notified her that I was turning on my video camera and gave her my reasons for doing such a thing. I told her about the schizophrenic chanting she was doing. As the camera was running, she couldn't handle the very arrogant remarks I gave to every question she shot at me. More than once, she walked up to the camera and talked to it personally. I guess that was due to the mixture of alcohol and a lack of taking her own prescribed medication. She took a look at my camera and said, "Turn it off."

I said, "No. Because with my record, I need proof of everything." She truly couldn't take my arrogant remarks any longer, and after about three or four times of me asking her to leave my place, the lawyer shouted, "I don't care no more!" Then, she looked at the camera and shouted, "Put it on tape! Let's go!" She punched me in my face as I was sitting down in my desk chair and threw her keys at me. She had me cornered in my chair, and she was standing over me, so I kicked her a couple of times trying to get her away from me! Because I knew if this wild woman gets close enough to my face, she's definitely going to swing! She gave me a couple more punches and eventually grew tired and sat back down on the sofa.

I asked the Lawyer to leave my apartment a couple more times, but she wouldn't go. That's when I figured that maybe she needs directions. "There's the door. Just turn the handle and leave!"

She told me, "No! I'm not touching your stuff." When I heard her say that, I had to pause for a second! She caught me off guard with that shit! I didn't even understand what the fuck that was supposed to mean. She sat there being motionless like a snake, daring anything to come close to it until her second wind kicked in. Then she was back up fighting. All the while, I was getting everything on camera. Finally, after I put my head down and let her hit me, she realized her punches had no effect. All of a sudden, I felt a sharp pain in my head. Sometimes, I have very fast reflexes, so before she could strike me again, I introduced my right hand knuckle sandwich to her nose. That's when she decided to lay down on my carpeted floor. As I lifted my head up, I could feel wetness sliding down my neck and my back. I knew I was bleeding sorta bad, so I didn't bother to touch the injured hole in my head. Instead, my eyes shot straight over to her hands to see what it was that she used. Of all things, it was her high heel shoe. As she lay on my floor, she told me she needed medical attention. As I watched her make her next move, I knew I was definitely not dealing with any ordinary woman. Because this woman pulled such a powerful move on the chess board of life that it made me step my game up!

The knuckle sandwich she received seemed to have ruptured her nose, and she was sucking as much blood into her mouth that she could get. Then, she spat it into my carpet and started rubbing her face in it. She stood up and stared at me for only a second. She spat a load of blood into her hand and started walking around my apartment, streaking my walls and my door frames with it. Then, without out a word spoken, she left my apartment. As soon as the door closed, I locked it and ran to my camera to make sure it was still recording. And sure enough, mission accomplished! I gave her a few minutes to make it to the police station, then jumped in my Air Max and ran straight over to the Bedford Heights Station. When I made it into the parking lot, I noticed her car wasn't there. You would've thought the way she was chanting that song, "What you going to do, with your record," this would've been her first stop. After showing the officers the video and explaining my past history to them, they told me to press charges.

Now, it was time for me to move on to the third course of the meal. As I walked through the door for the first time at the beautician school as a student, all eyes were on me. The women there couldn't believe I was a student at their school. Everyone acted very decent toward me, even the staff. All this was due to my daughter. She made me a very big hit there. It had even gotten to the point that they told me I wasn't welcome unless I had my daughter with me. My daughter really liked the instructors because while I was doing nails, they were keeping her full of M&M candies. I loved going to school. Not only was it keeping me out of trouble, but being there was helping me pay my tuition as well. I would take my rent money and ride with Beans to New York City and bring back some merchandise to sell to the ladies, like designer scarves, logo design socks, sunglasses, etc. I would make my rent money back first, then make sure my daughter was okay, and the rest I put on my school tuition. So yes, I was making life work, but at the same time, I was really going through some things.

Eva was truly a piece of work! Even though I had visitation rights, she couldn't care less about court orders. I wasn't seeing my daughter as scheduled:

> April 22, 2009, 1600 hours, Patrolman. C_interference with custody_ complaint filed on child's mother. Mother is not following the custody paperwork from the domestic relations court. Mr. Dixon is advised to contact magistrate.
>
> April 23, 2009 16:46 hours, Patrolman. M_interference with custody_ mother, the child was just seen entering apartment building, Mr. Dixon has proper paperwork for visitation rights, Mr. Dixon on the phone with police when he asked for the child. Female would not answer door. Mr. Dixon was advised of his options.
>
> June 24, 2009 16:00 hours, Patrolman J, R, C,_interference with custody and domestic dispute_Brian Dixon is trying to exercise his visitation rights to pick up his child. Mother of the child refusing to let him have the child. Male that was with female was from Michigan, he gave false statements to police, and was arrested.

This went on many times with Eva, but I would never forget June 24. As I walked into the building where her mother lived, Eva and some man were getting off the elevator, and he was holding my daughter. Eva was trying to leave the building before I got there, so I couldn't get my daughter. I walked over to the man holding my child, slid my hand inside his arm, and lifted my daughter away from him. I told him I meant him no disrespect, but I needed to know his name because he was holding my daughter. Eva started hitting me while this guy walked away stating he didn't want anything to do with it. I handed my daughter over to Eva and followed the guy outside. As he ran to his vehicle, I jumped inside my 2004 v8 Grand Cherokee and hit the gas and blocked him in so he couldn't go anywhere. Then, I called the Bedford Heights police. I don't know what was going on with this guy, but they took him to jail and gave me my daughter.

After that day, Eva took my daughter away from me and moved to Portage County illegally. I had to track her down! While all this was going on, I had a couple other issues as well. I couldn't afford the payments on my truck no more so the repo man came and borrowed it forever one night. But one of the students, nice-looking woman named Tracy, had a big heart for what I was going through with my daughter and let me use her vehicle to go clean accounts during the daytime. I knew she was married, but she told me that she and the husband were separated, so I didn't think anything of it. I had too many of my own problems going on. I did, however, catch the part where she told me she slept in the upstairs bedroom with her children and her husband slept in the basement.

As our conversations carried on for the weeks that followed, I came to understand many things about Tracy. For one, her body was very deprived of other people's hands touching it, so we both may sure that her body would not be suffering no more after meeting my purple headed warrior. It got to the point that her and her "Beautiful Body" were spending so much time over at my place in the early mornings that we both knew we were wrong for being there when we were supposed to be in school! Tracy spent so much physical time with me that she never acquired the mandatory hours in order to go to state board for testing. But the more I got to know her, the more I truly saw the coolness in her. She was a one-of-a-kind (Sexual Machine) in my bedroom as well. She was also a team player. She would come pick me up to make sure I got my accounts cleaned, and she had no problem going out of her way to help me while I worked. It had gotten to the point that the game we were playing of "no strings attached" had truly became our favorite game and she was a serious team player. And she had no problem showing me that she had my back. Now somewhere throughout this course of time within our secretive relationship that was hidden from everyone at the school, we started to fall for one another but we understood that that was the wrong thing for us to be doing as we argue with our inner feelings about the intimate relationship we were illegally having.

One early Tuesday morning in school, Tracy stories to me about her husband finally decided to surface. That morning she was explaining to me that her husband was mad because she was now walking around the house smiling. When he questioned her about her newfound happiness, she told me she showed him the court date for their divorce hearing. I gave a small laugh while shaking my head, got her car keys, and went to clean an account. On the way back to the school, I called her and asked her if she wanted me to bring her lunch. She said yes and told me to come pick up the money because she was treating me to lunch as well. I walked into the school, received her money, and got back inside her vehicle. By me living in South Central, California, for second, I have an automatic habit of always looking in my rearview mirrors while driving. As I made a left on the green light, I noticed a Scooby Doo–looking van closing in on me very rapidly.

At that time of day in that particular suburban area, whether you lived out there or not, if you knew about that area, you knew not to speed in this neighborhood because you would definitely get pulled over. My gut told me this speeder was for me, so I had to create a quick test. I sped up and entered the right side of the roadway, and Scooby Doo performed the same maneuver.

Okay, I thought, *this guy's definitely hunting for me.* Now let me create an escape route form this goofy guy. I slid back over to the left lane, and just as I had hoped, he copied my movements with a reckless performance. I said, "Wait for it, wait for it, go!" I made a hard turn back into the right lane and easily slid between two cars within inches of touching them. He didn't have the skill to perform the same maneuver this time around, so he was stuck in the left lane and fell about five cars behind. As I was starting to make my right turn onto the freeway, I looked into the rearview mirrors. That's when I knew this Scooby Doo driver was very determined and nutty. When he saw that I was about to escape on the freeway, he turned out of the left lane and drove on the wrong side of the road, heading toward the oncoming traffic. I found this to be amusing, so I slowed down to see if he was going to make it, and he did! All I was thinking was thank God for that because no one needed to become a casualty of his curious anger. I lightly applied pressure to the gas pedal so the transmission would change courses properly, and I could start climbing to the top speed of this vehicle. At 105 miles per hour, I became a fan of Mazda vehicles for the next few exits. Due to experiences in life, I understood that just because the sun was shining, that didn't mean you wouldn't see rain fall, so I've learned to always keep an umbrella. I called Tracy while I exited the freeway. Scooby Doo was nowhere in sight. I politely asked her what her husband drove. Before she could answer the question, he was calling her on the other end of her phone. I called one of my umbrellas, which was actually one of the students at the school. I had her bring Tracy to me. We all met up at the school and had a quick conversation, and then everyone went their separate ways. I truly didn't know what her and her husband had going on within the household, but the very next day, she handed me the keys to the vehicle again while she was telling me that he put her and the children out of his house.

As time went on I was halfway finished with school when I received a letter in my mailbox indicating that I had a court appearance to make in Bedford Ohio. The letter explained that the Lawyer has been arrested at her job, so a hearing has been set forth for both of us. After Tracy gave me a yes, that she will be going with me, when the day came we both walked into the courthouse together. As we were sitting there, something made me look down the hall because it started looking a little dark as if the lights were automatically lowering their wattage, but my view became very clear! First in line was the Lawyer, followed by four other black trench coats, and all of them trench coats that were floating towards my direction were being held up by long snooty white faces and they all were carrying big black briefcases. As she passed me, she gave me a smirk of intimidation. I politely pulled my triple black trench coat to the side and offered her a view of my camera as if I had a gun in my waistband. Then I counterattacked her smiling smirk with a 100 percent full blown deer stare, accommodated with a pure mixture of intimidation.

Finally, the prosecutor called us into the conference room. All four of her henchmen got up following one another like children in a lunch line, but the prosecutor assured them that was not necessary and only allowed one of her goons to attend our little session. After the prosecutor viewed my video footage, she passed it over to the chosen henchmen. After he finished viewing it, he said, "That's not going to hold up in court. For all we know, the footage could've been manipulated." The prosecutor just said okay. The next week, while I was sitting in the courthouse, the Lawyer came walking down the hall by herself. There was no loss of light and not one of her henchmen was by her side. They had left her hanging! Finally in front of the judge, she decided to plead no contest.

Now it was time for me to initiate plan number two, which was getting visitation rights so I could start being a part of my son's life. Since my son's mother was part of the court system, she got wind of the visitation rights that I filed, and she counterattacked me! I was coming from the store and headed back into my apartment when my cousin Sweet Pea drove past me. She handed me a letter that had been sent to her apartment. It stated that a criminal complaint had been filed on me by the Lawyer. I didn't know what was going on, but I was about to find out because I was due in court the following week. When I entered into the court room, my son's mother was already there, and to my surprise, she was alone. No henchmen needed, I figured. As the judge started presiding over the courtroom, he asked me to explain my actions. I explained to the judge I didn't know what was going on and asked to what actions he was referring to. He responded, "The actions that you signed your signature on, when the sheriff presented the protection order to you, Mr. Dixon."

"Your Honor, I never signed any protection orders or been in the presence of any sheriffs lately."

"Mr. Dixon, you're denying signing your signature on the protection order?"

"Exactly, Your Honor," was my only reply.

Right at that second, we all knew what was going on in that courtroom! The Lawyer had falsified some paperwork! The judge then asked me to explain my relationship with my son's mother.

"Your Honor, me and my son's mother don't have a relationship. Our relationship was based only on sex. After I stopped giving her sexual favors inside her garage on top of her hot car hood and letting her bathe me with her big mouth, she turned very evil, Your Honor. Even beat me up! She's on probation for it as we speak."

I have some respect for the Lawyer sitting there and not denying anything, and the judge knew I wasn't fabricating any stories. At the end of the day, he placed a restraining order on both of us, until the year 2015.

Now it was time for me to continue eating the meal I had created on this life plate of mine, which was making sure that I got my nail license. When I started the nail gig, I didn't know it was going to be so deep into the medical field! It was so many words and meanings that I've never heard of in my life! And by the time I learned everything while getting the hours I needed for state board, I could've been a light level LPN or a midlevel nursing assistant or somewhere along those freaking lines. But I actually did it! Here I was on the heels of being a forty-year-old man that grew up in the streets and never had a real solid day in school, along with ten years of prison under his belt, had come home and finally done something for himself to be proud of.

CHAPTER 41

SINCERE

With nail school being complete, it was time for me to go to state board for my exams. I called Malina, and we started our three-hour trip. As I looked in the backseat, her daughter was passed out before we even pulled out of her driveway. One thing I could say about Malina, even though she didn't want me in her life as nothing more than a friend, when it came down to it, she would always have me and my daughter's back. This made me really respect our friendship! Even as I yearned for it to be more, I understood the fact that she had some past hurts from other guys, and she always reminded me that she made way more money than me.

The clock finally struck the hour for me to go take my exam. Malina told me she was going shopping and said, "Don't worry about the exam because you know that you already passed." As I entered the exam room, I was the only African American hood nigga in the session. The other men present were Asian, and boy oh boy, did they overpopulate this little room. As the instructors entered and started explaining the procedures about the first exam, I realized I either had a real friendly face or a very pleasant demeanor because they started picking with me in a joking but professional manner as soon as they introduce themselves to me. After we took the physical exam, we moved along to the computers for the written exam. This time, I hit all three instructors with a couple of my own professional jokes. After all was said and done, we all sat inside the waiting room, waiting for our names to be called for our exam results. I sat there and watched very nervous facial expressions transform instantly after opening up their envelopes and reading their final score. The new transformed expression by most of them was that of sadness. A lot of the females had tears in their eyes, and some were actually crying out loud. I continued to sit there about to blow with anticipation that had built up inside me. Finally, I was one of the last names called. As I opened my envelope, about twelve of the other exam goers surrounded me as if we were in a football huddle, and they were waiting for me to give them the next play. I started reading my numbers, and one of the Asian guys said, "It's okay, Brian, we all have our hours in. You can come right back and take the exam over." I didn't say anything. I just handed him my results and walked to the desk to pay for my license. At this time, I was feeling very Italian, with extra-large Cojones.

The following week, Malina and I were back on our road trip. This time, we left her daughter with her mom because Malina told me after I took my manager's exam, she had something she wanted to share with me over lunch. As I exited the state board building with my manager's license in my hands, Malina yelled, "Boy, you knew you were going to pass!" We both started laughing and were on our way to lunch. As we sat there across the table from one another, I noticed when I ordered my long island iced tea she ordered a virgin strawberry daiquiri. I was very surprised and stunned by her choice of beverage because this woman and her family likes to drink. She waited until my long island iced tea was nothing more but a memory, and then she blurted out while looking down at her virgin daiquiri, "I'm pregnant."

The ride back to northern Ohio was kind of silent. I really didn't have too much to say because the woman who didn't want me in her life as a partner just told me she was Prego! And I knew that there might be a 50-50 chance that I was or was not the father because we both were very sneaky snakes when it came to us seeing other people for sexual desires. Now that I am thinking about it! This woman is very argumentative! There's no way we can be around each other! Now with me being a professional nail tech and having my manager's license, it was time for me to get busy and put what she said on the back burner!

I was sitting in my apartment looking through the local salon magazines, so I could find somewhere to work, but first, I needed to come up with a name for myself. I started calling myself Nails by Sincere. I posted an advertisement in the same magazine I was looking through. Later that day, I received a phone call from one of the instructors at my nail school. She told me there was a beauty salon that didn't have a nail tech and hadn't had one in years. She said many nail techs had tried to get into the place because it was a prestigious salon. All the Cleveland Browns players' wives and Cleveland Indians players' wives get their services there, along with newscasters and blah blah blah. She told me she thought I had the right looks to get in there. And she was right. I was hired after my first interview. At this time, I didn't have a car of my own, and I had to travel a long way to get there. One thing I've learned and embraced due to the course of my experiences is I am not afraid of change.

After a couple of months of work, I had to let the prestigious salon go. The next salon I went to was from a reference from my cousin Nina who used to work there. After a few months, I had to leave there as well, due to the fact that I was not an ordinary nail tech that follows the ordinary rules. The next salon I was in wasn't bringing in the money fast enough do to the winter season. So I went to Best Buy and bought a mini refrigerator and stacked it with Angus cheese hamburgers, Red Baron pepperoni pizza, chicken and rice and cheese burritos, along with an assortment of popsicles, ice cream sandwiches, potato chips, crackers, and water and whatever else you may find at your local corner store. It had gotten to the point where people weren't even coming to get their nails done; they were coming in just to buy food. Needless to say, they kicked me and my little restaurant out of the salon. But it happened at a good time.

The same day they released me from my duties, Julie decided to leave California and pay me a surprise visit. While we were loading all my things into Julie's vehicle, I received a phone call from the student whose husband chased me. She told me to come work inside her aunt's shop. After a couple months, I had to leave there as well because one day, the ex-husband came in to pick up his children and saw me sitting there making money and told me he didn't feel comfortable with me working there. He didn't want to see my face every time he came in for his children, so it was best for me to pack up. I just had to respect his request because it wouldn't be cool for me to be seeing a man's face working with my ex-wife, knowing he might have been sexing her while we were still under the same roof.

The next salon was my final straw, and that was when I knew I had to get myself together and open up my own place. The mother of Quito's children had a cousin that owned a shop. They told me I could come work there. Then one day, the woman that I shared the Mickey and Minnie Mouse bond with was under the hair dryer staring right at me as I walked to my desk, and this sent pain to my heart. After about two weeks of working there, things were going very well. I finally had a real clientele. But one morning, when I went to open up the shop, all the locks had been changed. Come to find out, the cousin didn't own the shop at all. Her child's father was the owner. He decided to kick her out due to infidelity within their lives and everyone who worked at the shop was affected by it. Once again, I was sent packing, so I turned my apartment into a miniature nail salon, accommodated with a full spa chair.

CHAPTER 42

SUPERSTITION COMES TO LIFE

As 2009 was coming to an end, I was sitting down the hall from my place in my mom's apartment having a discussion about my daughter because we haven't seen her in a while. We lightly brushed the conversation to the side because we both knew my heart was in pain, and my mom told me not to forget to be at her door at twelve o'clock midnight, and I promised I would. Now let me explain the reason behind this. Linda is very superstitious, which in turn makes me very superstitious because that's my mom, and over the years of knowing this woman, I'm finally coming to realize how brainwashed I am! Linda will not let any woman into her home after twelve o'clock midnight on New Year's Day unless she lived there.

But a woman would be allowed to come in after a man who does not live there comes in and walks through every room of the house first. To prove this point, the year before, all my female cousins were at my mother's home on New Year's Eve. They decided to go out and get some drinks to bring back before the New Year presented itself. As the ball was dropping in New York, my cousins were knocking at my mother's door, and she would not let them in. Finally, with all the noise they were creating, a Bedford Heights male officer showed up and walked through my mom's place to ensure that the superstition will stay at bay for that year. Now sliding back to the past for a hot second, my mother was very upset when one of the New Year's was coming in in the late 80s. She directly told me and my brother Earl not to let any of our little girl friends into the house until the New Year Day was gone bye-bye. But Earl did the exact opposite, and not only did he let a female into the house on that very forbidden day! He also washed some clothes on that holiday which was also a forbidden rule. So every year Linda talks about these actions by Earl were part of the reason her and the Eagle lost the house we grew up in.

The year 2010 was only seconds away, and I was standing at Mom's door waiting to do the walk through. After completing the mission, I gave Linda a kiss on her cheek, and I headed back toward my own place. Less than ten minutes later, I got a knock at my door. When I opened it, Eva was standing there with our daughter, crying. I asked her what was wrong, but she wouldn't tell me. My daughter had already walked into the apartment and took her coat off because she knew she lived there. Eva started asking me repeatedly if she could come in. I did not want to let her in because she did not live with me, and this was the first time I've seen my daughter in months! She started to get hysterical, so I put it in my head that since we used to live together, maybe the curse wouldn't bother me, so I let her in. Boy oh boy, was I wrong, big time wrong! The next morning, I made breakfast for them. As soon as I started a conversation about her not respecting the court order, she grabbed our daughter and left. I called the police, and they told me there was nothing they could do, and I would have to go back to court.

For the next few months, I resumed trying to find out where Eva lived so I could give the courts an address. Try after try, I finally located her Facebook page. I did a search of her friends, I did a search on her family, and I studied everyone's photos until I finally pieced a location together. I jumped in my car and headed towards Portage County to make a police report. On my way there, a lot of road construction was going on, so I was detoured to another road. That road swung me around to the location where she lived, so I decided to go pay her a visit and see if my daughter was there. I already knew things were bad because I received a phone call from Eva's father telling me I needed to get a hold of my daughter because Eva was leaving our child with just about anyone who would keep her, so she could run the streets. The conversation with him truly set me in motion. One thing he said that tattooed itself on my brain was that he blamed himself for all this because he left the home when she was a little girl, and I was not about to play copycat to his footsteps!

Finally, I reached the parking lot where Eva lived. After arriving at the basement part of the building, I started knocking on the door pretty hard. Eva came to the door and asked who it was from behind it. That's when I shouted, "Where's my daughter at?"

She didn't say anything. As I put my ear up to the door to listen for sounds coming from my child, a very heavy, freshly smoked marijuana smell crept up into my nostrils from under the door. Then I heard Eva and a male's voice talking back and forth to each other. Due to the previous encounters I had with her and other men, I stepped a few feet away from the door and produced my Samsung Galaxy from my pocket and set my camera on burst mode. As the door opened, a pretty big guy came out and started walking straight toward me. I didn't move a step. Instead, I started snapping pictures at one hundred miles an hour! All those flashes in this guy's face really got him angry, and I could tell he was sizing me up because the first thing he said was, "What you want to do nail tech?"

I politely explained to the angry guy I didn't want to do anything. I just want to know where my daughter was. I guess he took that as a soft gesture because he started talking to me very rudely. I guess any rude guy would do the same thing with what they saw presented in front of them. He knew I worked a job geared toward females, and I was wearing glasses, and I wasn't letting off any negative energy. I am sure he viewed me as a sugar cookie. But when he started making threats about what he was about to do to me, I threw my glasses down the hall and pulled my shirt off. I know I couldn't see it, but I know I had a killer deer stare going on when I said, "Waz up then, bitch nigga!"

He paused for a split second, taking in all of my, "I tried to be a gentleman chump, but now, I am about to release ten years of prison stress on you." I was truly off my square. He knew it too because his whole demeanor changed. He then said, "You know what, that's between y'all!" He went out the door and started heading toward his car. While all this was going on, Eva had slipped out of another door somewhere in the building. When I followed the guy outside, Eva was already standing next to his car, and they both jumped in and started to pull off.

I was hitting on the glass, shouting, "Where's my daughter at?" I had already alerted Kent police before I knocked on the apartment door, so I knew they would be on their way. As I stood in the parking lot of the apartment complex waiting on a cruiser to show up, I noticed a window open, and it was definitely her apartment. I ran over to the window and opened it wide enough to fit through. It turned out to be my daughter's bedroom. Once inside, I couldn't believe my eyes. The only thing this place was missing was dead bodies and maggots with animal feces smeared around the walls. I could not believe how nasty the place was, so I rushed to make sure I got a photo of every room. I could hear police sirens in the distance, so I made my way to her front door and let myself out. I was standing outside when the first cruiser pulled up. I gave him the description of the vehicle they left in, and then I started showing the officer photos of Eva's apartment.

The first thing the officer asked was, "How did you get the photos?"

I politely explained to him, "In their haste to get away, before you guys showed up, the front door was never locked. I didn't touch anything. I took a couple of photos and came back outside and waited for you guys." A call came back to the officers that they couldn't locate the car Eva and the guy fled in. The officer had me file a report with the apartment complex office, and upon filling out the report, the manager revealed to me they had numerous complaints from that address. After I finished in the office, the officer had me follow him back to the police headquarters. As we were pulling up, Eva was walking down the street. The officer questioned her about the condition of her apartment, and she told him I broke into her apartment and did all the damage. The officer didn't hesitate. He called Eva a liar straight to her face.

Then, he said, "There is no way in the world, from the time frame that Mr. Dixon called us, to the point we showed up at the location, that he could have done that, even if there were three of him!" The officer gave me his card and told me to go to Cuyahoga County Juvenile Court system and file for a new court hearing.

I said, "Okay, but I still need to know where my daughter is at." Eva said she was with her grandmother, so that meant that my daughter was right across the street from where I lived! Her mother and I stayed in the same apartment complex, just different buildings!

I jumped in the car I was using and peeled rubber right in front of the police station and made my way to the freeway. I called Bedford Heights Police and verbally delivered to them what was going on and that I was on my way there. Two police cruisers met me in front of her mother's building. After going over my paperwork, making sure I had a right to have my daughter, we went upstairs and knocked on the grandmother's door. I could hear my daughter's voice inside, so I shouted her name!

My daughter ran to the apartment door, and with about an inch of a locked door between us, my daughter started screaming,

"Daddy! Daddy!" As she was screaming my name, the officers and I could hear my child's screaming was starting to fade away. That's when the police started knocking on the door very hard. As the grandmother started to open the door, they asked me to step to the side, and they entered the apartment. After about ten minutes, the one officer who looked like a black Incredible Hulk pulled me to the side. He grabbed me by my shoulders like a father would do his son and said, "Brian, there is nothing we can do. Even though you have visitation rights, we cannot take the child if they don't hand her over. You have to go back to court, and I advise you to do it right now! Go and file for you a new court date, Brian! And a word of advice, do not come back over to their house. Don't even go back over to the mother's house in Kent, Ohio! As soon as I release your shoulders, you go downtown and file some paperwork! Do you understand me?"

All I could say was yes, with tears running from my eyes because my daughter was right behind that door. Even though I had the proper paperwork, I was not allowed to see her!

As I walked out the door and mentally prepared myself to head downtown, it dawned on me: this was a weekend day, and the courthouse was closed. That night, I called one of Eva's family members (this is from the actual police report):

On or about the date of July 18, 2010, I was at home missing my daughter KM Dixon. I, Mr. Brian M. Dixon, have not seen my daughter since Father's Day of June 2010. The child's mother and I had yet another situation where I had to call the Kent police due to her keeping KM Dixon away from me on June 24, 2010. The child's mother and I can never have a conversation because her attitude is so rude. So I didn't call the child's mother to see how KM Dixon was doing. The attitude of the child's grandmother on the mother's side is very rude as well. So I called a cousin of the family because he is around the child's mother and my daughter. He answered his phone.

I said to the cousin, "Hey, how you doing, man?"

"Shit, nothing. I've been wanting to get in contact with you, but I didn't have your number."

"You should have gotten it from Eva."

"I don't really be around her anymore. She's something different. I'm not cool with the way she's living."

"I feel you, so what's up with your little girl?"

"Baby mama drama, same as usual."

"The reason that I'm calling you is because I haven't seen KM Dixon since Father's Day."

The cousin interrupted me before I could finish what I was saying. "Yeah, I know, and that's some bullshit!" I guess the cousin realized at that point, I didn't know what was going on. "Hey, you don't even know what's going on do you?"

"What are you talking about?"

"Man! Eva mother called the social work people and told them that you be touching your daughter."

"What the fuck you mean?"

"Man! I think that the Children's Services have been over to their house and everything."

"What?"

"Man! We fell out! I haven't even been over there. I told my aunt that I'm not on that. If the nigga didn't carry himself like the way he always do, then I would have an issue. My auntie told everybody not to say anything to you about it. Man, she told them people that you be having sex with her and that you be putting your fingers inside of your daughter's anus, and that you be going down on her."

"What the fuck!"

"Man, that's some bullshit. Man, if this shit go to court, I'm on your side. Even though we really don't know one another, I've seen you with your daughter. When I last spoke to Eva, I kept telling her that she needs to speak up. That's that man's life! Man, I love my aunt and all, but she is the most money hungry person I know. I told her she was wrong for doing this."

As the cousin continued talking, I began walking down the hall to tell my mother what he just revealed. The cousin was on the phone while I stood there, explaining to my mother what he said. I watched as my mother frantically started shaking her head and stated more to herself than telling it to me, "I told you to never let a woman be the first person through your door on New Year's Day."

As I started making my walk back down the hall toward my apartment, the thoughts of this retired street gangster being accused of being a pedophile had my facial expressions bleeding premeditated murder in the first degree! Each step I was taking started transforming my heart into something dark and evil! Joker has been lying dormant for years, but this new situation gave Joker a reason to breathe again! Hibernation season was definitely over with! Within my reasoning mental capacity, there was nothing there to think about except the walls that was going to become my painting canvas with the spray of blood coming from their bodies with whatever caliber I thought fit for the occasion. As I continued to walk, my right shoulder transformed into Mr. Denzel Washington in the movie *Man on Fire* because he told the little white girl he would never leave her!

As I made my next step, my thinking pattern was now with the darkness, as I felt my left shoulder transform into Samuel L. Jackson in the movie *A Time to Kill* because he was determined to see revengeful thought patterns being played out in real life. The next few steps, the good in me started taking over, and my right leg turned into Taraji P. Henson in the movie *Taken from Me* because she was not going to let distance get in the way of her being a parent, so I needed to be smarter than the average bear. That thought was quickly pushed to the side as my darker side began wanting more control in this very ugly situation. My next step transformed my left leg into Doldh Lundgren from *The Punisher* because he was ready for war and retaliation for his family. It was inevitable! But for some reason or another, when I got to my apartment door and turned the knob to let myself in, my torso transformed into Kevin Costner when he played in the movie *Waterworld*. With everything connected, my head transformed into Bruce Willis from the movie *Armageddon*. With the mixture of Kevin Costner making sure that little girl saw adulthood and Bruce Willis giving up his own life to make sure that his daughter had a life, when I stepped back inside my apartment, I took all six characters and combined them into one, creating a brand-new Mr. Brian M. Dixon. With her cousin still on the phone with me, I asked him, "Why hasn't Eva called me and told me about this crap?"

"I don't know."

So the cousin and I called Eva using three-way calling. When she answered her phone, I asked why she hadn't called me to tell me what was going on. Eva said she didn't know what was going on and that some detectives called her from Portage County and said they wanted to meet with her the following day. Little did they know, I would be showing up at that meeting as well. I got the detective's phone numbers from Eva.

Before the night ended, I got a knock at my door. It was Eva, and she had my daughter with her. She pushed my daughter in my arms and told me that she had some business to take care of. She turned her back and started walking down the hall to exit the building. By the time the morning came, I hadn't heard a word from Eva, so I called the detectives to find out where and when this meeting was supposed to take place. After the detective gave me the information, I gave my daughter a bath and made us some breakfast. I borrowed a car and made my way to Portage County. As I entered into the room, there were two detectives sitting there. They both stood to shake my hand. After a brief conversation with me, one detective slid back from the table and said, "Wow," and the whole time he was looking at the other detective. That's when the other detective followed suit and slid back from the table and clasped both of his hands behind his head as if he were about to lay down and take a lap. While they were staring at each other, I intervened and asked them what was going on. They both looked at me, simultaneously.

Then, I guess the detective in charge said, "You don't fit the profile of this report we have in front of us. We did a background check on you before you came in. Your past history just doesn't fit this profile." Just as the last word rolled off his tongue, Eva came walking through the door and had a seat right next to me and our daughter.

August 2010, Eva, our three-year-old daughter, and I were sitting across the table staring at two detectives in Portage County. In return, two detectives were staring right back at the three of us. I guess the main detective who was presiding over the case decided to get to the matter at hand.

With a deep breath, he said, "Okay, here we go. On July 15, 2010, Portage County Department of Job and Family Services received information stating (KMD) was sexually abused by her father, Brian M. Dixon. Information disclosed includes, father putting his nose, mouth, and face on her 'birdie,' along with her anus. Report also states he licked her all over and inserted himself." (God, please forgive me for the hateful thoughts that travel through my mind every time I have to read this book over.)

Instantly, Eva went into a rage and started shouting, "I never made no allegations like that. Me and this nigga have our issues, but I would never say nothing like that just to get back at him!"

That's when the detectives told Eva it was the grandmother that made the call. Eva just started shaking her head and repeated, "No, no, no, he's not like that. Him and my mother do not get along. I don't know what in the world she is talking about or why she even made that call. She never said anything to me."

At that moment, I pulled out all of my documents and started showing the two detectives everything I had been going through with Eva and her mother. With a nod, the lead detective said, "I understand, but at this time, you have to turn your daughter over to the mother." I tried to explain to the detective that that was not a good idea, but he reassured me due to the circumstances, I had no other choice but to do so. I handed my daughter over to her mother, and as she was accepting her, she just shook her head saying "I don't believe this."

The detectives advised Eva not to let me see my daughter because now it was an ongoing investigation. With that, I just watched as Eva started to walk away with my daughter calling my name over and over, "Daddy! Daddy! Daddy!"

As I drove back to my apartment, I couldn't believe what just happened. I could tell by both of the officers' demeanor they didn't want to give Eva the child, but in any situation, they must uphold the law. I could respect it even though I didn't agree with it in this particular situation. I can still remember the look in Eva's eyes as I handed over our daughter to her. Her whole expression read, "I can't take her right now!"

As I entered my apartment, even with so much going on in my head, I continued to do my regular routine. I took my shoes off and placed them by the door, sat down on my sofa, and turned the TV on. I got up and walked to the kitchen to grab a bottled water because I knew I just might get dehydrated this night. As I felt the tears building up inside my soul, I knew it was going to be a rough night.

I woke the next day still in disbelief of the prior day's event. I was not in the mood for anything. I just sat staring into empty, unanswered, cloudy thoughts. That's when my phone rang. It was Eva! She said she was in my building and was bringing me our daughter. When I opened up my door, my daughter smiled and said, "Daddy." Then she put both of her arms up in the air for me to pick her up. I asked Eva why she was bringing our daughter over to me after the officers in Portage County told her not to do that. She stated she didn't know what was going on with her mother, and she didn't have any ideas about what was going on. With that being said, I told Eva, "Let's just let our daughter get comfortable for second." As she got into her routine of playing with her toys and dolls, I asked her to come over to me and her mother. Then I asked her, "Baby, who told you to say that daddy touched you?"

Instantly without hesitation, she replied, "Grandmother and Aunt T." Then, she went back to playing with her toys.

Eva looked at me and said, "I don't know what my mother is up to. All I know is that my cousin told me that no one was supposed to say anything to you about it."

After more brief conversation, Eva prepared herself to leave. When she was at the door I asked her, "When will you be coming back to pick her up?"

"As soon as I get the chance. But I'm not leaving her with my mother because I don't know what she's up to."

At that time I didn't know, nor did I care, if Eva could read facial expressions or not. If she could, I'm pretty sure she understood that my face had transformed into a picture book, and the pictures was describing, "You can call me silly, you can call me serious, but you cannot call me naïve, stupid, goofy, or dumb." As Eva turned her back and began walking down my hallway, I softly closed my door and walked over to my daughter. I sat down on my sofa and braced myself as if I were on a roller coaster because I knew my brain was about to take off! Here I was, a man with ten years in prison, being called a pedophile! As soon as I started thinking about the word *pedophile*, that's when my brain started revving its engines! As I felt my brain starting to go down the first big hill of this roller coaster ride, my body followed suit!

August 2010, I called over to the Bedford Heights Police Station and explained the situation to the dispatch. After a couple more questions, we hung up. As my brain resided in neutral while contemplating its next move, I received a phone call from a Detective Sinbad. He asked me if the child was still with me. I answered yes. He told me to give him a few seconds and he would be right over. The detective was true to his word because within a few minutes, there was a knock at my door, and boy oh boy, did his name fits his physical aura. This detective had to be about six feet and four inches in height! He truly resemble, at more than a glance, the actor-comedian Sinbad. And for split second I was wondering was this the same "Vice Officer" that yanked me out of my car when I was younger in Cleveland? But with the seriousness of what was going on at hand, I pushed that thought to the back burner.

As Detective Sinbad entered my apartment, he was followed by a detective just the opposite of him. He was a little shorter in height and more on the darker skin level than Detective Sinbad. He was much younger and a rookie into the detective playing field. He introduced himself as Detective Chestnut. As they made their way over to my black sofa, walking on my carpet with their shoes on, all three of us sat on the sofa. I felt comfortable sitting next to Detective Sinbad because even though I didn't know him personally, we would always see each other around the city at the bar where he orchestrated law and order or just seeing him riding around the city freely on his Harley Davidson. As we sat there, neither detective asked me any questions as I explained the events that started the night I received that terrible and horrible news from my daughter's mother's cousin, all the way up until the two detectives knocked at my door.

Now it was time to question my daughter. I conducted my own interrogation right in front of the two detectives. I asked my daughter, "Baby, who touched you?"

She pointed at me and said, "He did," then pointed at detective Sinbad and said, "He did." Then she went right back to playing with her toys.

Both detectives looked at me but didn't say a word. I looked right back at them and didn't say a word, either. Finally, Detective Sinbad spoke, "So the child isn't supposed to be in your care right now?"

"No, she's not, and I don't know what to do. I've never been in a situation like this before. That's why I called you guys."

Both detectives stood up simultaneously. As I was shaking their hands before they exited my door, I could see the concern written all over their faces. It made me feel good because I knew some type of action was going to take place. As the next few hours passed, I never heard anything from Eva. She didn't even make one phone call to say hi to our daughter.

August 2010, Thursday, at four o'clock, twelve minutes, forty-three seconds, I received another knock at my door. As I opened it, Detective Sindbad and Chestnut were standing there. Standing right next to them were a white man and a white woman. They explained to me that they were from Portage County Children's Services. After a brief second, everyone entered my apartment with their shoes on. Detective Chestnut asked me to step inside my bedroom. He began asking me all types of questions that were not in any type of order. Purely an amateur's tactic, but that was his job, so I had to respect it. That's when I knew he was only a mere distraction as the other guys were preparing to take my daughter away. After everyone was finished taking part in whatever position they had to play, they allowed me to hug my daughter before her removal from my custody. As the white man and white lady tried to hold my daughter's hand, they started walking down the hallway. My daughter snatched away her hand from them, looked back at me, and said, "Come on, Daddy." With tears running from my eyes, I explained to my daughter that I couldn't go with her, and they allowed me to hand her Doggie.

December 30, 2013, at 7:33 a.m. (It's very hard for me to write this part of the story. It's taking everything in me not to let one tear fall from my eyes. Even though it is three years later, but the pain of watching my child being taken away from me is still fresh in my heart, as if it is happening today as I'm writing this.) On that day, I asked the Portage County Children's Social Workers to hold on for a second. I ran back inside my apartment and got Doggie. Doggie is a stuffed animal I got for my daughter when she was two years old, and she loves Doggie. Doggie is an all-white stuffed animal that would remind you of an overly large and very stuffed pound puppy, with very bright eyes, and pink eyelids accommodated with pink ears and a pink nose. To add to the appearance of Doggie, she was given a little pink tail with all four paws colored in pink. Whenever it was time for her to go to sleep, she would always ask, "Where's Doggie?" She would not allow herself to go to sleep unless Doggie was with her.

As I got down on my knees and gave my daughter another hug, I placed Doggie in her arms and had a conversation with both of them. "Baby, you and Doggie have to go with these guys, but Doggie is going to go with you everywhere you go to make sure that you are okay." Then I looked at Doggie, and I said very seriously with tears falling from my eyes (and yes, ladies and gentlemen, I was down on my knees speaking to a stuffed animal!), "You protect my daughter, Doggie, and you make sure you bring her back to me!"

Once again, I gave my daughter and Doggie a hug, and this time, she allowed her hand to be held as I watched the four of them walk away from me.

The two detectives stayed behind and asked me a few more questions. I knew this was just part of the distraction as the social workers made a getaway with my daughter. I had to respect their job. After a few more questions, which may or may not have been of any significance, the two detectives made their way down the hall. For some reason, I just stood there, watching them walk away. Then on cue, Detective Chestnut turned around and started briskly walking back toward me pulling out his pen and his little notepad. I don't believe he even knew I was still standing there. He seemed to really be in his own world thinking to himself. For all he knew, I could've went back inside my apartment. But I was still standing there watching him as he was making his way back down the hall like he had something very important on his mind. Finally when he noticed me he said, "Mr. Dixon, I'm trying to understand a couple of things. You mind if I ask you a couple more questions?"

"Of course you may. I don't mind at all."

"When did all this take place?"

I asked him if he could he be more specific.

"Where did all of this supposedly take place?"

"I don't have the slightest idea. I didn't know anything about the situation until I talked to her cousin, and he notified me as to what was going on."

"I'm just trying to understand a little something," Detective Chestnut said, "because if it happened here in Bedford Heights, why did the grandmother call Portage County instead of calling us?" At this time, I could tell the detective was within his own thoughts. Even though we were standing there together, this rookie was actually thinking out loud. He started to walk away from me without really saying another word.

I broke his concentration by saying, "When you get a chance, look at all the police reports that I have submitted dealing with that family! Then do a check on my background. I have nothing on my police record except for bank robberies, drug sales, and guns! I don't fuck kids, Detective!" As soon as I closed my door, the tears running from my eyes seemed as if they were trying to give Niagara Falls some serious competition.

As the minutes quickly went by, the tears were pouring more than ever! I started pacing back and forth inside my apartment. Something purely evil was now build up and living inside me. The darkness was removing all the goodness in me. My arms and legs started feeling very light as if I had no control to whatever they might do next. My brain seemed as if it were being drained of all morals. The only thing left was the dark side of me. I never noticed that my tears had stopped falling, and my nose had flared up. That look I was now wearing would give any raging bull a run for his money! As my pace began to slow, after imprinting a beeline inside of my carpet floor, Spice One, 187 started playing in my head and the frown I wore had formed itself into a wicked smile. Sawed-off shotguns started jumping around inside my head as if I were counting sheep. This wasn't about my daughter any longer, now it was about me! It was about my character! It was about the type of gangster that dwelled within my soul! It was about them calling me a child rapist! And now I must hold court in the street for their fucking lies! A vampire would've looked like a mosquito standing next to me! I was out for blood!

As I stood in the middle of my living room floor, the smiling scowl on my face was so hard that the left side of my eye and nose was jumping rapidly! Avenue after avenue opened up of all of the street people I know, from New York all the way to California, where I had access to some of the world deadliest guns! I'm a man, and I've never lied about something I have done! I told the truth in court! When they asked me if I was the one wearing the dress when I robbed the places of my choice, I told the truth! When they asked me if I robbed them banks, I told the truth! And when I get questioned about this family, I'm about to hold court too! I will tell the truth again!

As I reached 99.5 percent of evil rage, calculating the seconds of the spin of a .40 caliber short nose Bulldog with hollow point tips, I fell to my knees and started praying to God. God knew I was on my way to go pay that family a visit! As I was on my knees, I got a knock at the door. I answered to the knock on the other side, and who knows what type of tone was released from my vocal cords.

"Bedford Heights Police Mr. Dixon," the voice answered from the other side.

As I opened up the door, there were three blue uniform police officers. As they made their way into my apartment, I closed the door behind them. Before they could even state the business they were there for, I beat them to the punch and asked the leading officer, "Are y'all here to arrest me for that bullshit?"

As the leading offer answered my question, it was apparent that every last one of these officers knew about my past history. He stated, "No, Mr. Dixon, we are not here to arrest you, but we are here to tell you to let us do our job! We don't want you going nowhere near that family! Let us conduct our investigation, and we will see where we'll go from there. Give me your word that you understand where I'm coming from."

Before I could answer this gentlemen, tears begin to pour down from my eyeballs again and it wasn't from me being sad about what was going on. It was because in my heart, I knew God felt my pain and He was saving me! (James 1:19–20: "Know this, my beloved brothers: let every person be quick to hear, slow to speak, slow to anger. For the anger of man does not produce the righteousness of God.")

As my body began to slow down and be at ease, I couldn't speak to the officer because my vocal chords was either not focusing enough, or I pretty much just didn't have anything to say. But just as a handshake is an agreement to a deal, I just nodded my head in response as if I was at an auction. Either this officer was good at reading body language, or maybe now because he was very familiar with my past history. Whatever the case was, he didn't pressure me anymore after I nodded my head. It was as if we both had a powerful understanding, and he knew I wasn't going to disrespect what he asked of me.

(In 2014, I locked my keys in my car and had to call the Bedford Heights Police to help. When the officer got out of his cruiser, it was the same officer that made me promise that I wouldn't go after that family. We haven't seen one another since that day, which put our distance at four years. When he approached me for my identification, he was wearing a puzzle expression on his face. So I intervened with a "Do you remember me? Do you remember telling me not to go nowhere near that family and let you guys do your job? "

He started smiling, then said, "Mr. Dixon! Wow! Look at you! You smiling! You were such an angry guy back then!" We both started laughing! And as the saying go! "When two or more come together, I will be in the mist." So when he started talking about God and how He can change the worst of the worst! (I butted in for split second during his speech and said, "I know that's right") All you have to do is open up that door and let Him in. After a good handshake, Officer JM and I departed with him handing me his card and me promising to give him a copy of my book when it's released.)

After closing my apartment door once again, I slowly made my way back to my sofa and just sat there. My mind was trying to get its engine going again because it knew we had a task at hand. My mind continued to send messages to my body saying, "Hey, body, we have to get going! We have a very large obstacle that we must jump!" But my body was not going to let my mind tactics go into action right then. We needed actual rest involved before any moves would be taken.

For two weeks straight, I did not leave my apartment for anything! I just continued to breathe deep breaths. I continued to pace back and forth just shaking my head and ponder. I continued to unconsciously dehydrate myself because there were times I just could not stop the tears. After my two weeks of mourning, I decided it was time for me to get my mind and body right because I truly didn't know what road I would have to travel in this very unhealthy mental situation. For some reason, I am a person that always picks Monday to be the day I'm going to change something in my life. The day I'm going to get things going. The day my faith, self-esteem, and self-motivation all come to a focus point. So on Monday morning, I grabbed my gym bag and headed over to the Bedford Heights Recreation Center. Now I was no stranger there. I had been attending that recreation center often since 2005 when I came home from prison, so people were very familiar with me. We didn't know each other personally, but we did know one another's face if we were passing in traffic. I tried my best to stick to my regular routine. First, I went to the indoor track and started stretching. Then I set my cell phone to play music from Tupac, then proceeded to walk a mile. After my walk, I headed toward the weight room, lay down on the bench, and did a couple sets of bench pressing. I swooped up the arm curling metal bar and started putting my work in. Then, I proceeded to do a couple of squats to get my legs and my gluteus maximus back on the grind. By the time I was done with that, it was on to the elliptical machine. This was early morning, so the gym was mostly filled with senior citizens. Every time they saw me, we loved saying hi to one another and having a quick chat. For some reason, it just made the morning seem bright and right.

Everyone knew I had a dark cloud hovering over my head. No one turned their back on me. One of the prayer members walked over to me and asked what was wrong. I explained to him the issue. He told me to go home and get everything I had to show him. It was very fortunate that I stayed right across the street from the recreation center, so I hurried home and grabbed every piece of paper pertaining to my custody case that I could find and ran straight back out my door. Within thirty minutes, I met him inside the prayer room. He was not alone. He was accompanied by four or five other people, all members of the prayer group. As each of the prayer members sat in individual chairs, it formed a half-circle around me. Everyone was looking at me. I don't know who it was, but one of them said, "What's going on?"

I started explaining everything to them, and within minutes, Niagara Falls appeared on my face again. There was no way I could hold my tears back from the semistrangers. As I verbally started to come to the conclusion of explaining my situation, I opened up the folder and displayed the proof of everything on top of the tennis table. Each member got up and started going through everything I had to offer. After a few minutes of close surveillance of my material, they all started to place paper on top of paper until it all came together, and everything was back in the folder. Then we all grabbed hands and formed a circle and started praying to God. As we finished up, a white guy named Mr. T, who I would always see while walking on the inside track of the recreation center, told me to meet him in the prayer room the following day because he had some Scriptures for me. As it was time for us to finally leave and carry on with our individual day, each one of them came over and gave me a hug. To my surprise, each one of them said the exact same thing as they were hugging me, "Place everything in God's hand, and let it go!" As I hugged the last member, who was actually the first guy I talked to, he told me to go home and put all the paperwork I had in some type of order.

Finally, I was back in my apartment, and I actually felt better. As I walked over to my black sofa and sat down, there was a knock at my door. As soon as I opened it, I started smiling. It was my next-door neighbor, her sister, and the reverend that lived right above my apartment. They came to tell me they heard what was going on because all three of them were very familiar with me and my daughter. We all grabbed hands, and once again, we asked Jesus to send His Father a message. The next morning when I awoke, I couldn't believe the way I was feeling! I truly had no worries, and my heart had honestly placed everything in the Lords hands. I had my mojo back 100 percent! I was off and running. That next morning, I was back at the gym and got my workout on and told everyone who came over to me, "Everything's going to be all right. Thank you." After the gym, I found a hair salon located in Bedford Heights, so I was back doing nails right across the street from where I lived. Once the nail technician job was secured, I got in contact with a guy I knew who had a cleaning company. So now I had two jobs locked down, and both of them allowed me the flexibility to work the hours in any which way I chose to maneuver them, which was priceless.

After about a month, I received my first court date to appear in Portage County. Even though I was never charged with that horrific crime, I was still treated as a criminal. After being given no choice but to accept a court-appointed lawyer, I was ready to begin the fight for my child. My lawyer and I entered the courtroom, and they ushered us over to a little corner where they placed two little wooden chairs. As Eva entered the courtroom with her lawyer, they were placed at the courtroom table where they sat with the social workers and the attorney for the child. My attorney and I looked like outcasts due to everything that was going on in the room. I was truly considered the bad guy. As the proceeding's ended, my mother, Cinnamon, along with my uncle and my aunt, and I met with a second attorney, that said the Portage courts appointed him to my custody case to aid me. So we all were inside of this little room that was connected to the courtroom. Just before my attorney was about to speak, the social workers who had my daughter in foster care entered into the room.

When the door shut, the second attorney decided that he will be the one to start this party off. I pretty much let everyone in that little room know where I stood as soon as he spoke his first few words. "Mr. Dixon, I do hope you understand that if you are charged with this crime, you are looking at life in prison." Before he could even mutter another word, I broke the silence of the room. With pure control over the rage and anger I had brewing inside of me, I'd bluntly stated, "I'm Not Trying To Hear What The Fuck You Talking About. I'm Not About To Listen To That Dumb Ass Shit. Those

Mother Fuckers Are Lying On Me! What I need to know from you and obviously those two social workers standing right there is what I need to do to get my daughter back."

As my family and I sat there listening to the attorney and the social workers, my mother and my uncles asked them some key questions. Cinnamon just stood in the middle of this little room with her back to the wall, soaking in every word spoken from everyone and continued to write a lot of things down on her notepad. Finally, the social workers asked if anyone had any other questions before we ended the meeting. That's when I came to understand that I really didn't know my little cousin at all. The one thing I found out that day was that she had a very big education, and she carried herself with very well-pronounced professionalism. By the time she finished questioning the attorney and the social workers, they were actually sitting there with their mouths open and a blank questioning stare. Finally, the male social worker spoke up and asked my cousin Cinnamon, "Who are you? I've noticed you haven't said anything since we've been in this room until now. Are you one of Mr. Dixon's attorney or something of that fashion?"

Cinnamon just smile, and answered back, "I'm Cinnamon Dixon. And no, I am not Brian's attorney. I'm his very concerned cousin." Due to the way my cousin Cinnamon spoke and the way she was dressed, the attorney and the social workers were still in disbelief to what her true position and interests were to the case. They still believed that she was lawyer.

As the next couple of weeks went by, I continued to stay focused at the gym and be productive inside of the hair salon. Due to Cinnamon being the greatest cousin in the world, I was able to pick up a couple of cleaning accounts of my own because she would have me drop her off at work and allow me to utilize her vehicle anyway I seen fit. Even her sister stepped into the caring cousin role, she tried to come to my aid as well! Cinnamon's sister call me from out of town and told me that she was on her way to Ohio to offer her home to the courts for temporary placement for my daughter. I tried not to let my daughter's situation drive me insane or toward a depressed state because I did not know where my daughter was. I knew nothing about her health or how she was doing. The one thing that continued to keep me in a positive stride was my prayers and the fact that I knew she was in temporary foster care. I knew she was under a microscope by the social workers. Finally, I got a call from Portage county. This call was to arrange a meeting for my daughter to be placed with one of the family members, whether it be someone inside of my family or someone from the mother's side of the family. One thing I was not going to let happen: I was not going to allow them to place my daughter anywhere near the mother's side of the family.

As I arrived at the Portage County Social Service Center, Malina and her daughter were chaperoning me because Malina wanted the courts to know that I'd been around her daughter for the last four years and that she leaves me alone with her when she have things to do. As the meeting got going, Eva's father and his wife were willing to take temporary custody of my daughter. My mother and my uncle and his wife were also willing to take custody. As the meeting ended, I was given a list of homework chores that I was due in order to prove that I qualify to be a father. (That Was If I Was Not Charge With Being A Fucking Pedophile!) They sent everyone else over to the Sheriff's office to be fingerprinted so they could conduct a background check on everyone.

As the next few weeks went by, I started checking off the list and jumping through the Hula-Hoops that were given to me. The first thing I started with was something I had three of even before I had my daughter, and that was parenting class. Even though I already had three certificates for parenting classes, Portage County figured they wanted me to have a certificate from their system as well. Get on your mark, get set, go!

Within two days, I was sitting in parenting class. As the next few weeks passed, I had completed everything that was required of me. Everything except the At Risk Evaluation! During this time, I started doing my homework on Eva's father and his wife. From my own investigation, and due to the fact that a couple of people within Eva's family knew I wasn't a monster and aided me in my investigation, it came to light that Eva's father didn't even live in the house with his wife, and they were knee-deep with their own family issues. I was definitely going to bring all that to the table. Even though I was about to throw a monkey wrench at Eva's father's plans for him and his wife to gain temporary custody of my daughter, I still had respect for the man because at one of the meetings, he stood his ground, and he let everyone in that room know where he stood.

While a little commotion was going back and forth between all parties, this man stood up and said, "Listen to me," with his voice loud enough for everyone to stop what they were saying and pay him some close attention. "I really do not know what's going on, but all of our main concern should be to get my grandchild out of foster care! I do not understand why these things are being said about Brian because every time I've seen this young man, he has always carried himself as a man. He was always a gentleman in my presence. So can we please get back to the matter at hand?"

Even though Eva's father was on the other side of the playing field, I respected that he took the time to evaluate situations in everyday life. At the same time, he was still on the other side of the fence so I had to stay focused on my main goals.

As soon as the meeting was over, I asked my attorney and the social workers to come have a talk with me, and I did not want anyone else involved in this conversation. As we entered into the exact small conference room where my cousin got into their ass about this "Horrible Insane" situation, I started to explain everything about Eva's father and his estranged wife. I ended my conversation with

"Until we have a full understanding of these allegations against me, I do not want my daughter going to their family or my family. I'm asking you guys to keep her in your custody until we can resolve this matter." For one reason or another, I was granted my wish.

A few more weeks passed before I received a phone call from Detective Chestnut. He asked me to come over to the police station because he wanted to have a meeting with me. As I entered the detective's conference room, I was followed by my mother, Malina, and my cousin Cinnamon. I really appreciated how these women were in my corner, and they had every reason to be because they actually knew me. The next couple months were filled with more orchestrated social work meetings and more Hula-Hoops for me to jump through. Then, finally, I got an actual court date. When that date came, my mother and I teamed up with my uncle and his wife, and we were on our way. It had been well over ninety days since I had last seen my child, and I had no idea that I was going to see her that day. As we finally made it to the courthouse, I was very surprised at what I saw.

Being from the streets, my street thoughts were the first thing to kick in, and I started wondering, *What is really going on here?* The reason I was thinking this way was because I had been to this court house more than a few times, and for one reason or another, the waiting room chairs were rearranged. After a brief conversation with the guard that protected the metal alarm, my family and I were standing in the middle of the waiting room. To the right side of the room was Eva and her family. On the left side of the waiting room, the chairs had been rearranged to form a horseshoe and the opening of the horseshoe was pointed directly at Eva's family. To my surprise, every chair within the horseshoe was already occupied with authority figures in the case. There were three or four social workers, along with the Portage County sheriffs, that I talked to in the very beginning. Bedford Heights detectives Sindbad and Chestnut were sitting there as well, along with the guardian of light, who was actually the attorney for my daughter.

With very few seats in the waiting room, my family and I were sort of forced to sit in the corner away from everybody. If you came inside the courthouse, you wouldn't have even seen us because we were blocked by a wall. As we were all waiting for the bailiff to call us inside the courtroom, each group of people was busy in conversation within their own entourage. For one reason or another, my aunt was just sitting there watching everybody who entered into the courthouse, as well as everyone who was leaving. My aunt called my name as she hit my knee with her knee. She spoke in a soft tone, "Brian, isn't that your daughter walking in with that white woman?" At first, I couldn't see what was going on because the wall was blocking my view. So I stood up and walked closer to the wall so I could look around it. Sure enough, it was my daughter that my aunt had seen. I stood there stuck for only a couple of seconds watching because I was so happy to see my daughter. As three or four seconds passed, I watched the white woman hand my daughter over to Eva's mother. Just as a director would call action to a movie, I was the director of my life. And until my daughter is old enough to stand on her own two feet, I am destined to be the director to which what positive direction her life should be flowing too! So I'm the HNIC! Until my daughter is educated enough to take that title away from me and control her own life! And I will always be her protector just as she became mine on that very day.

So I yelled "Action!" to myself. I walked from behind that wall and stood in the middle of the waiting area floor. I was standing between all the authorities and all of Eva's family. Eva's mother was holding my daughter between her legs. I did not care who thought what because everyone was invisible to me except for my child. I did not care who had anything to say about the action I was about to make. All I knew was that I cut the cord on that child! As I stood there looking at my daughter, I transformed my anger into a lion's roar! I yelled my daughter's name. Instantly, she stopped what she was doing and started looking around the courtroom waiting area. But a little boy with the size of a teenager head, who was her cousin, was standing in front of her, and she couldn't see me. Without hesitation, I let out another roar! As my daughter started leaning inside her grandmother's legs so she could have a view around the little boy, she spotted her daddy!

At this time, my daughter was only four years old, and even at such a young age, she released a roar just as loud is mine! She screamed, "Daaaddy!" I could feel the presence of everybody looking at my daughter because for her size, she made a lot of noise. As my daughter started wiggling, trying to get out of her grandmother's holdings, I could see her grandmother tighten her grip. That's when my little girl let everybody know that she was a force to be reckoned with! My daughter and I looked at each other eye-to-eye, and I could see the grandmother tighten her grip some more, and that's when my four-year-old broke concentration with me and turned her attention to her grandmother. She roared at her just as loud as she could and screamed, "Daddy!"

My child had started struggling with her grandmother which automatically made the grandmother loosen up her hold, but she still had her hands wrapped around my child. With the grip being loosened, my daughter turned around and was facing her grandmother eye-to-eye. Then she roared again, "That's my daddy!" She started pushing her grandmother, trying to break free. This little four-year-old was really putting her work in! That little girl was going beyond the call of duty to gain a release from her captor! She started to struggle so hard to escape her grandmother's little holding cell, that it looked as if she were fighting her grandmother and the grandmother knew this was not a good look for her, especially due to the fact that she was the one who started all of this chaos! She had no choice but to release my daughter. Even though my daughter and I were more than thirty feet apart from one another, as soon as she realized she wasn't being held down, she took off running! She ran those thirty feet as fast as her little legs would carry her! I quickly got down on my knees and just opened up my arms and my daughter jumped straight into them! As I raised up, I put my gator shoes and my black hit man trench coat into action! My daughter and I started spinning in a circle! I raised her high above my head and continued to spin while we were smiling at each other.

I said, "I've missed you, baby!"

And she responded with, "I missed you too, Daddy!"

As we came out of the spin, I gave her one of my biggest kisses and hugs.

After a couple minutes, the social worker walked over to me and said, "Okay, we have to go now." But I was very satisfied because right then and there my daughter and I! We let everyone know where we stood! We were one another's protectors! One thing I happened to notice, when the social worker was walking away with my daughter she didn't return my child back to the grandmother or her mother. Instead, I watched my daughter leave with the white woman she came with. I don't know how much time I spent with my daughter after she jumped into my arms, but one thing was for certain: I was not concentrating on the scene around me. When I turned my head away from the door because my daughter was no longer visible, I noticed the waiting room was empty of all authority figures. Only my family and I and Eva's family were left in the waiting room. Finally, I saw my attorney walking toward me. His conversation was very, very brief, but he was smiling. All he said was, "You and your family can go home, Brian. Court has been rescheduled for another day." He patted me on my back, gave me a handshake, and walked away from me. My family and I didn't know what was going on.

Then my mother spoke up, "Brian, as soon as your daughter ran across that floor and jumped into your arms and you guys started spinning around with your coat looking like something out of a Batman movie, the Bedford Heights detectives were the first ones to get up and leave. Then everyone else went in their own directions."

A couple weeks later, I received another court date. I don't know why, but I didn't tell anyone that I was going. I went on my own. I was starting to feel bad for my family because they had been with me since the beginning. They were riding up and down the highway with me for every single court date, every single meeting, and some of the meetings didn't even make any sense or have any concrete motive. It was as if they just wanted to see if I would show up. Then it got to the point where it was just my mom and I because I told the rest of my family members, "I got this, but if I need you, I will let you know." On this one particular day, I was not going to drag my mother out of the house. She really had my back, and I truly appreciated how she stuck with me. But something inside me told me it was time for her to rest her mind, body, and soul, and I could now go on alone.

As I entered the courtroom, I walked over to my usual seat in the courtroom that was the designated "The Bad Guy Corner" and waited for the judge to preside over the case. After everyone had given their speeches, except for me and my lawyer, we noticed that Eva and her attorney were having a disagreement. He continued to tell her, "No, no, no, it's not a good idea!"

But in response, Eva continued to say, "But I want to. I really, really want to!"

So against her attorney's advice, Eva took the stand, and her attorney started to ask her questions that really didn't have any relevance. Against his better judgment (I could see it in his face), he popped the magic question. He took a deep breath, then asked Eva, "Ms. Eva, do you believe that Mr. Dixon did anything wrong?"

Her response was, "Yes, I believe he did something! No, I take that back. I know he did something."

Everyone in the courtroom saw her attorney's eyeballs go straight up into the air. I sat there with my anger boiling. My attorney could feel the heat coming off me because he grabbed my knee and applied pressure so I could stop moving. He started patting my knee as if he were telling me to "chill out, nigga" or "be easy, dude."

Eva's attorney took another deep breath, and then he asked his next question. "Ms. Eva, what makes you believe that Brian did something wrong?"

Her response was, "Because my mother said so!"

At this time, my attorney had no restraint over my next move. I stood up in the courtroom and looked at every body aside from Eva and shouted, "She Needs To Get The Fuck Out Of Here With That Bullshit! Because Them Two Motherfuckers Are Lying On Me!"

As I was standing there looking at everybody looking at me with their opened mouths, I heard the judge call my name. He said, "Mr. Dixon, would you like for me to put you out of my courtroom?"

I replied, "No, Your Honor. I apologize. But she's lying."

One thing I noticed from the judge while he was asking me if I wanted to be put out of his courtroom was that he didn't say it in a rude way. It was as if he could feel my pain. As the courtroom proceedings were coming to an end, I heard Eva's attorney telling her she shouldn't have gotten up on the stand. Even though all the mouths were open when I was making my speech in the courtroom, no one looked at me angrily when it was time for me to exit at the end of the proceedings. It was as if everyone were in their own thoughts of the event and was putting two and two together that maybe that guy is not a monster.

A few days after that, I received another call from Detective Chestnut. He wanted to have a quick meeting with me. As I entered the conference room, I noticed he was alone. Detective Sinbad was not there. I questioned the young detective about the whereabouts of his partner. He didn't give me much information and went straight into the interview. He asked me questions like, "Where did the alleged activity take place, Mr. Dixon?"

In response, all I could give him was "I don't have the slightest idea. I did not know anything until I called one of their own family members and he told me what was going on." (To you, the reader. Has anyone in your life ever passed away and you never had the opportunity to tell them how much you appreciated something that they have done for you? Today's date is January 5, 2014. I just received a phone call revealing to me that the guy who alerted me as to what was going on about his family trying to frame me had just passed away in a car accident. I am very, very, very saddened by this. Other than thanking him over the phone, I never had a chance to show him my true appreciation. I was trying to wait until I finished this book so I could find him and hand him his own personal copy. As the days go on, I will always be grateful to this guy. Where ever you are, KI, I just want to tell you thank you again, my brother! It's because of you that I was able to fight for my child! You will always have a spot in my heart, and I will never forget you! I will be dedicating this biography to you. Much love to you, my brother. Rest in peace!)

The detective took a short break while he was thinking to himself. Then, he asked me another question. "Mr. Dixon, I have a little daughter as well, and sometimes, I pick her up and just nibble her little legs. You know, I just I love my child! Have you ever did anything like that?"

"No, Detective" was my response. After a few more questions I just can't remember at this time, the detective looked me straight in my eye and told me he was going to be making his way out to Portage County to go interview my daughter. If she told him that I did something wrong, he wanted me to come over to the police station and turn myself in. If she told him I didn't do anything wrong, he would be calling me to tell me to go and fight for my child. As I got ready to leave the interview room, it was my turn to look the detective straight in his eyes.

I explained to him, "Between me and you, I am one of those guys that would be in your cell with a knife, if you came in to the prison with one of these crimes." As I was walking away from the station, because I stayed right across to street, I was thinking to myself, *Where was Detective Sinbad? Why am I explaining everything to this rookie who just may use my situation to gain a name for himself and leaving me with the short end of the stick? One thing I know about Detective Chestnut is that he doesn't remember having a conversation with me when he used to be a math teacher in one of our neighboring cities. So I know darn well if his mental calculator is very efficient to add that truth, he will eventually put the right answer to this equation of a fake ass case!*

During the next couple of hours, I had a brief conversation with a couple of police officers with whom I was familiar with. They explained to me that Detective Sinbad had a heart attack and he may not be returning to the force. I couldn't believe my ears. It never crossed my mind that young Detective Chestnut didn't have the proper ability or the right credentials to oversee my case. It was just the fact that he was new to the detective field and I didn't know the guy, so I was hoping that this younger Detective was the type of officer that always put good police work in front of everything else that could easily be slipped into place. I was hoping not to become his personal "Stool Pigeon". But my thumping heart told me that he wasn't for me or against me, something just kept telling me he was a good officer that pays attention to the evidence from all parties. 'I guess it was by the way he actually stood up out of his chair and acted out the type of father he was to his own daughter while playing with her. But only time would tell. So I had my personal reasons not to be afraid of him. So I decided to push the negative to the back burner and only have positive thoughts! So I started gaining confidence in the young brother because every time he talked to me, he would looked me straight in my eyes and he never looked down at the ground or up in the air when I had the feeling that he was on some "Trick a Nigga" bullshit. So that actually prove to me that he was really paying attention to every little aspect from everyone he interviewed.

As the next few weeks passed, I was sitting inside the salon doing nails when I received a phone call from Detective Chestnut. "Mr. Dixon, I've already called Portage County, and I explained to them that you would be coming up there to fight for your daughter. Mr. Dixon, when you get your daughter, I want you to put all this behind you, and I want you to be the best father that you can be." I don't know if Detective Chestnut could sense it or not, and I didn't care who was looking, but I had tears rolling down my face. I responded with a thank you. Then, I explained to my client that I had to go and told her to grab any nail polish she wanted, and she could have it for free. I ran across the street to tell my mother the good news, and then I called Portage County and asked them when I could see my daughter. The officer told me as soon as possible. I was out there the very next day!

As I was waiting in the waiting room, I thought to myself, *My little daughter has no idea what is going on. This time, when she comes walking through the door, I'm going to be standing right there waiting on her.*

As I peered out the window, I saw the same white lady I saw before walking up the sidewalk with my little girl. As soon as they came through the door, my daughter didn't miss a beat! She jumped up in my arms and said, "Daddy." As the foster mom and I introduced ourselves to each other, it was as if she'd already had a talk with the social workers. I could not detect any negative energy being released from her, which made us an instant hit. As we started our conversation, she went on and on about how my daughter always talked about me. She explained to me the one thing she knows for sure: she'd never had a foster child that cared so much about her father. As we were talking, my daughter came over to the foster parent to ask her a question, and I noticed that my little girl was calling her mom. This didn't bother me at all because after meeting this little smiley-faced white woman, I know God made sure that my daughter was in good hands. After the foster mom and I were done with our introductions, my daughter and I followed the social worker to the visiting area. This was our first time spending time together after about four or five months. I guess the social worker understood that I wasn't a monster because me and my daughter played with each other and talked as if we never missed a beat.

As the next few weeks passed, the social workers started letting their walls down. I could tell because every time I would come to visit my daughter, it was unsupervised. The first few times I came down, the social worker sat in the room with us. Now that I was becoming a regular at the foster care center, I went back to being the person I always was whenever I went to visit my daughter! I was now bringing a thirty-two-inch flat screen TV, a PlayStation with video games, and movies. The day before my visit, I would always stop at the library to get some books to read to her. I also would always bring us lunch, and some days since they had a microwave inside of the visiting room, I would just bring some food and make our lunch there. During this time, Malina and her daughter went with me a couple of times, as would my cousin Cinnamon and her son. Malina even gave my daughter a party there for no reason at all. A just-because party.

After about a month and some change flew by, I had another court date. As I entered the courtroom, I started making my way over toward my this-is-the-bad-guy corner, but to my surprise, the corner was empty. The chairs had been removed. That's when I heard someone calling my name. It was the social workers and the lawyer for my daughter. They were sitting right next to each other with only a chair separating them. One of the social workers started pointing at that chair and said, "Brian, this is your seat. Come sit down before the judge comes out."

Wow! She actually just called me Brian! Okay, I see the tables is starting to turn! We are now on a first name basis! Woohoo! I did what I was asked to do, and I was feeling pretty damn good about myself. I settled down right between the two with a big smile on my face, even though you couldn't see the smile on my face because I was smiling from within. As far as my appearance was concerned, I continued to wear my serious court face on my outer shell. To my surprise, I was greeted again with something I had never seen before. When the judge came out of his chambers and we all stood up, he looked directly in my direction with a smirk on his face. In the words of Jim Carrey, I said to myself, "All righty then!"

As this court day came to a closing, the doors had been opened and exposed Eva's drug usage. She failed two drug tests issued by the social workers and other key administrators. All I was thinking, in the words of Rick James and Katt Williams, "Cocaine is an addictive drug!" and "This must be that Frankenstein weed!"

During this time, I was having car troubles and Portage County was not around the corner from where I lived. It was an hour or more away! I was using my brother's car, and he had just came home from prison the same day I had court and took his car away from me. With so much going on, I didn't even notice I had not paid rent for the past two months. The only reason it slipped my mind was because the management never sent me a bill. Now with the way I think, I looked at this as an act from God. So with two months of rent not being paid, I was working with $1,600, and I needed a ride because I did not want to go and start asking people to use their car. I jumped on Craigslist and found a van for $1,400. The van looked nice, but it definitely had its issues! And bless Malina's heart, she came and picked me up so I could go get it. After I got my plates that same day, I drove straight to the manager's office and explained to them that they hadn't sent me a rent notice in two months. They checked their computer and found the mistake and told me, "It's okay, just pay everything back next month" and "Congratulations on how things are developing with your daughter." I really appreciated the management team where I lived because they were involved with my case since day one. They even went out of their way to write a few letters to the courts on my behalf.

After running around all day, I finally made it back to my apartment. I was back to regularity, so I closed my door and took off my shoes, then walked across my clean carpet and sat on my black sofa. Within three minutes, I was starting to get comfortable with my legs kicked up on my ottoman, and that's when I received the phone call from the social workers in Portage County. They asked me how I would feel about bringing my daughter home every weekend. I just started smiling! As soon as we hung up the phone, I started calling junkyards because my van had no seating in it, except for the driver's chair and the passenger chair. On a Thursday morning, I was out of the house, and I hunted down four backseats to put inside my van. Friday morning, I was at Walmart buying a car seat, a couple of toys, and some food and snacks for my daughter. Friday evening at 6:00 p.m., the foster mom was handing my daughter over to me. As raggedy as that van was, my daughter said, "Daddy, I like our car." I just started smiling. That old raggedy van ran me up and down the highway. It made sure that I was always able to pick my daughter up and drop her back off. I can't even count the times it just sounded like it was going to die on me, but it never did during them times.

Everyone was happy to see my daughter again. I'm sort of known around the barber and beautician world in Cleveland, so my daughter and I made many stops to barbershops and beauty salons to say hi. One day, after leaving one of the salons, I received a notice in the mail for a court hearing, which came around the corner for me just a little too fast, because it was set for January 25, 2011, and that was just a couple of days away! I was ready for it until my phone rang. It was the social workers from Portage County. They told me I must have an at risk assessment interview done before we went to court. After hanging up the phone, I needed some rest because I knew the next day was going to be hectic! I woke up the next morning and started making phone calls. As I was talking to the secretary of the At Risk Program, she explained to me they had no available openings for the next three weeks. That's when I explained to her I must have this done because I had to go to court in two days.

Then, she said in a very polite voice, "I am sorry, Mr. Dixon. There is nothing I can do. I can schedule you for later on in the month if there's an opening." That's when God stepped in! As I was telling her I understood and was getting ready to hang the phone up, she said in a louder voice, "Hold on, Mr. Dixon! We just had a cancellation, like right now while we're talking! Can you be here at three p.m.?"

"Yes, I can!" was my reply! I grabbed all my paperwork, and I made my way to Portage County. After mutual greetings, the psychiatrist conducted the interview. After the interview with the psychiatrist, I was still laughing at the way I explained everything. He shook my hand and gave me his seal of approval, then told me to go fight for my child. Later on that night, Cinnamon came to visit me to see how I was doing. I broke down with tears running from my eyes and told my little cousin I was getting tired, and she went off in a different direction. She started crying and shouted at me not to give up! She said she could never imagine her father giving up on her and told me never to give up on my child! I just said, "Wow, okay" :)

On Monday evening, January 24, 2011, I received a phone call from the foster mom, asking if I could meet her that night because she had something for me. Of course I will! I met the foster mom at the foster care facility. She and her husband were waiting in their van for me. As soon as we stepped out of our vehicles, she gave me a big hug! She smiled at me and said, "Everything is going to be all right. I don't know if you know it or not, but her mother was never allowed to remove her from the foster care. Neither was her grandmother. You were the only one allowed home visits, and here, I want you to have all of your daughter's things! We've all been watching this situation very closely, and there was no way I was going to give these things to the mother!"

She handed me two large garbage bags full of stuff. This time, I gave her a hug, and right before we departed, I promised her that I would always stay in contact with her because she really did care for my daughter as if she was her own. (God bless you, Mrs. P! I am very thankful that you were the one chosen to be the foster parent! You will always have a place in our hearts.)

When I got back to my place, I sat down on my black sofa with the two garbage bags in front of me and started to pull the materials out so I could place everything inside of my daughter's bedroom. The garbage bags were jet-black and large, so you couldn't see inside them. I had to stick my arm down into them to remove the things. I came across all types of toys and clothes. The next time I stuck my arm down a little further and came across something that was soft. By the texture of this object, I knew exactly what it was! I started smiling!

As I started pulling, this object passed everything inside this big old garbage bag. As soon as it came to focus, I said, "Hello Doggie! I see you found your way back home!"

So I grabbed Doggie and placed it on her bed.

CHAPTER 43

HEART AND SOUL

January 25, 2011, I was the only one on my side of the field sitting in the courtroom. Eva and her entire family were there, but Eva and I were the only ones allowed into the courtroom. As the proceedings began, we finally got down to the determination of where the child should go. The judge asked all the authorities in the courtroom, "By a show of hands, who all agrees for the child to be placed with the father?"

My lawyer stood to his feet with his hand raised. The guardian of light stood to her feet with her hand raised, the prosecutor stood to his feet with his hand raised, and the social workers were standing to their feet with their hands raised. I even sat in my chair with my hand raised! The only two people who didn't have their hands raised were Eva and her attorney. Eva's attorney got up and handed the bailiff a piece of paper, and the bailiff turned the paper over to the judge. That's when the judge called for a short recess.

After a few minutes, the judge came back out of his chambers and looked directly in my direction and started to speak, "Mr. Dixon, it has been brought to my attention that you already have a case opened in Cuyahoga County, and by law, I cannot overrule any of their decisions. I do apologize, but you have to take this case back to your county. I must now turn the child back over to her mother."

As the judge exited the courtroom to return back to his chambers, everyone who had stood up to raise his or her hand on my behalf was now shaking their head. You could hear each one muttering to themselves, "I did not see this coming." As Eva was leaving the courtroom, she looked in my direction and said, "Ha-ha, bitch, the mother always gets the child."

The social worker walked over to me and gave me assurance that if I ever needed anything from them in the future, they would be there for me. My lawyer asked me if I was I okay. I looked him straight in his eyes and asked him if he remembered what I said to him the first time he told me I was looking at life in prison for this crime. He nodded yes. Then, I told him, "I'm fine, I'm just waiting for them to clear out the parking lot." As soon as I saw the last car of Eva's entourage leaving the courthouse, I jumped in my raggedy van and made my way to downtown Cleveland and picked up some paperwork to modify visitation rights and file for emergency custody.

January 26, 2011, I had all my paperwork notarized. I had my money order in my left pocket, and I was standing in line at the Juvenile Clerk of Courts to submit everything I had so I could receive a new court date. Since I was feeling froggy and like a super dad, I jumped and also filed for visitation rights so I could start seeing my son on that same day. After all the paperwork was done, I drove my raggedy van home. I figured my van felt it had done its job because after that night, it never started up again. My little cousin Cinnamon came to my rescue! She started given me her car and having me drop her off at work and told me to go take care of my business!

As February flew by, on March 1, 2011, I was back in the courtroom with Eva. She was ordered by the judge to start keeping the visitation order as ordered until our next court date. I picked my daughter up later that day. March 3, 2011, on my birthday, I was right back in the same building right back in another courtroom receiving visitation time with my son. Over the next couple months, I had my daughter and my son at the same time exercising my visitation rights. Everyone kept asking me if they were twins because they were only six months apart.

As summer passed and we were entering into the fall season of 2011, I noticed that my son and daughter would fuss over toys. My son's mother had a vengeful hate toward me for getting her locked up. What did this woman expect? She literally sucked the blood into her mouth and spat it into my carpet and rubbed her face in it, then left streaks all over my wall as if she was really in a terrible struggle! Of course I got her locked up, and of course I figured she had the right to have a hateful vendetta toward me.

So that fall season while in the courtroom with my son's mother, right before the judge was about to order for me to gain regular visitation with my son, I stood up in the courtroom and started waving a homemade flag I made that morning that said, "I give up!"

Then I gave the judge my explanation for the homemade flag. "Your Honor, my son and my daughter are only six months apart. Due to the fact that they truly don't know one another, it's like they're playing with strangers. Both of them argue over toys, and I already know what his mother is capable of. She lied on me more than once with no avail. I also know if I ever bring my son back to her with the smallest scratch on him, I will be right back in your courtroom charging me with abuse, neglect, or some form of child endangerment. My son's mother has already taken me through enough. I honestly believe that it would be in my best interest to drop my visitation pursuit right now. I wish to not go any farther with this case, Your Honor."

The judge looked at me really hard, and I know she could see the seriousness in my face and the concern. Then she glanced at my son's mother and spoke, "Make a note that Mr. Dixon has dropped his visitation rights pursuit of his son. We are allowing Mr. Dixon's case to be dismissed without prejudice. Mr. Dixon can reopen this case back up whenever he chooses." Then she just looked at my son's mother and said, "This man didn't make you have the baby. That was your choice. By him being the father, he has rights as well. It was your choice to sleep with this man."

As soon as the judge was finished with her speech, I raised my hand as if I was in grade school and asked if I could be excused because I had to get to Portage County and pick my daughter up.

Finally, after everything I had been through, I was standing inside the courtroom on September 28, 2011, when the judge granted me joint custody of my little girl! When summer vacation of 2012 came, my daughter didn't understand what was going on when I wasn't taking her back to her mom that Sunday night. She looked at me with a very big smile on her face and said, "I don't have to go back right now, Daddy?"

I just started laughing and gave her a hug and responded with a "No, you don't have to go back right now. You're stuck with me for the next thirty days, kiddo. Now you and Doggie get in there and clean your room while I make us something to eat."

My family was so happy to have my daughter back around us. She did not know how many cousins, aunts, and uncles she had on my side of the family as I began letting her meet them one by one. And in other parts of Ohio like clockwork, Eva was back to her shenanigans! My daughter's school was in talks about charging Eva with truancy. Not only was court orders not being following, our daughter was not doing well in school. And once again, I was missing a ton of days out of my daughter's life do to the Eva. I knew everything was about patience and physical proof.

Once I had enough school reports and police reports, I submitted paperwork to the courts to modify the joint custody. I asked the courts to make me the dominant parent for school purposes. So now

I was off to another waiting game. During this time, Malina and I were getting very distant from one another. She had really started being mean to me due to my financial status. She didn't believe in anything I believed in. As the new year of 2013 came to life, I was on my way to see Malina. I looked her straight in her eyes and said, "You already know I will be turning forty this coming March. We have a child together, and I am in love with you. I know I don't make money like you, but I can be a good man. Do you want us to try to have a serious relationship? Because when I turn forty. I am making sure that my life takes a dramatic turn towards a positive walk and lifestyle. You will no longer be able to look at me like my name is 'Little Jimmy'." (To you reading the book, Little Jimmy is a character that I created within myself, in order to stop myself from giving Malina a piece of my mind and allowing me to respect my mother's wishes. So every time she belittled me and made me feel like she was talking to a child, I wouldn't retaliate back. I would just say, "okay okay Little Jimmy hear you" because if it wasn't for Little Jimmy, one of the other seven personalities that dwell within me would've definitely had a conversation with Malina about her nasty habits and her disrespectful ways. "Box Car: in order to survive in the game, you must become different characters")

Malina looked me right back in my face and said, "I'm scared! I make over $100,000 a year, and you have nothing. I'm afraid if we have a relationship you're going to get lazy." I didn't say anything to her response. I just understood that I did not meet her criteria for what she wanted in a man, and I could respect that. While I was studying my train of thought, it was broken because she still was talking. So I started to continue listening.

"And furthermore," she said, "with your money problems, and this dream about this book you're writing, you should move into a one-bedroom apartment because you know it's hard on you trying to afford that two bedroom you have. Now that you have joint custody of your daughter, you should really consider downsizing." As she was sitting there giving her expert advice about what I should do with my life, my mind started retorting back to the story of "The Cat and the Mouse." (After the mouse stood there holding the piece of glass that was pulled from the cat's paw, they instantly became friends. And now since the cat was very grateful, the mouse took it upon itself to take advantage of this cat's life that it just have saved and started disrespecting the cat. The cat was very grateful for what the mouse had done! So the cat let the mouse get away with a lot of disrespectful things. Because the cat knew he could have never pulled a piece of glass out of his own paw by himself. But one day, the mouse went too far and started pulling the cat's whiskers out in front of all his friends! That's when the spell was finally broken that the mouse had over the cat's head. The cat took a very deep breath and didn't even bother to let out a roar as he was preparing to eat the wicked little mouse. But the mouse said, "Hold on for one second cat. I'm on my way to Canada tomorrow! Just give me a break and eat me when I return?" So the cat understood and agreed to what the wicked mouse asked of him. As the cat turned to walk away from the "CONNIVING" little mouse, he heard a sweet voice that stated in broken English, "Wow, now that's something that you don't see every day!" The cat quickly turn his body towards the direction where the voice came from and he couldn't believe his eyes! Then he said, "Wow, now that's something that you don't see every day! What kind of cat are you sister? Because I know you're not from around these parts of the woods." The voice replied, "I'm from the Asian parts of the world, I am what you call a Siamese cat". After the two cats sniff each other for good measure, they wrap their tails around one another and started walking towards the future. Months later when the mouse return from Canada, he kept his end of the bargain and was searching for the cat so it could be eaten. But when he found the cat, he observed that that cat was now married to a very delicious looking desert of a feline. So it was no need for that "Rat" to give that cool cat a bad taste in his mouth.)

That day, I turned my back on Malina and started walking away. I could still hear her talking. She was explaining to me while I was getting my stroll on that most of her friends were not married, and all have big jobs, and they prefer to be single parents. "I should have done what your son mother did to you, and never told you that I was pregnant. Matter of a fact, I don't want you in her life! I don't even want her knowing who you are! Your daughter would not be playing with them, and if you come by my house I'm calling the police." Right then and there, I understood that she was not going to let me be a father to our child, and I could deal with that because I did not ever want to go through what I went through to get custody of my daughter with Eva! Because the Cuyahoga County juvenile court system was making me run around in a very big maze thus far. And then I had a thought, *Is it really true that this is how Lupus have people acting? Am going to find some time to do some research on that Lupus. Because I don't think that's the case here.*

When I got home that night, I was saddened because my apartment was flooded. The will power inside me was not going to make me downsize to a one-bedroom because of a major water spill! Instead, I moved into a luxury two bedroom. It cost more than my flooded apartment, but it was priceless because now my mother was my next-door neighbor. It was in the weeks of March 2013, and my birthday was in the next couple of days! For one reason or another, God allowed me to see my fortieth birthday! Woohoo! So when my birthday came around, I didn't have anyone to spend it with. All of my friends were from the hood, and they didn't like driving out to where I lived because of the police. Most of my family members didn't know too much about me because I pretty much shut down from everyone so I could complete this book I was writing. So I spent my birthday on Facebook, and I was very satisfied and happy to be receiving happy birthday messages from my childhood friends and some of my family members. It was very special to be receiving happy birthday messages from people whom live all around the world that didn't even know me. They were just showing a sign of kindness. As I was sitting on my sofa corresponding with Facebook, Cinnamon called and told me to put some clothes on and get out of the house, and she was sitting in front of my building waiting for me. We went around to a few bars. We even visited some friends that had invited me to come see them from off the social media site because they were having a birthday party on that very day. Finally, my night was coming to an end, and I was back home sitting on my black sofa, and it was getting very close to midnight. Without a cake for me to blow the candles out, I didn't have a reason to make a birthday wish, but I did do some praying to God.

I got down on my knees, and I said, "Jesus, can you please deliver this message to your Father? Over the years, God, I've been so lonely. Relationship after relationship not going anywhere. I do feel I have a clear plate. God I am asking you. Can you please bring someone into my life that will treat me as I treat them? That's the only thing that I am asking for God. I just want someone who will treat me exactly as I treat them! Amen."

The next day, I set up a profile on a black people dating site. After a few glances, I saw the profile of this Asian woman, so I contacted her along with a whole bunch of other women. Before the day was over, she was the only one who responded. After about a week of phone conversation, we met in person, and she was as cool as she could be. I could tell that she'd been around black people a lot. After we had a brief discussion of both of our living situations, I asked her if she wanted to be my roommate. She said of course, and she moved in. When she and my daughter met for the first time, it blew me away because my little girl had accepted her just like an ATM accepts your debit card! After about a month of us living together, I awoke to see my daughter laying on her lap, and she was hugging my daughter. They both were on my black sofa watching cartoons. As I stood there watching them, I knew I wanted that woman to be in my life and if only for a season.

As the days started flying by everything was going so well. We had even cruised into a regular smooth sailing routine. I would get up and make us breakfast and then take her to work in the morning, then make it back home to start back on my book. One day, I got two phone calls from both of the movie casting companies I stood in line for! In one of the movies I got to be in, I had a chance to meet Kevin Costner, and he is a very nice guy. While we were shooting some of the movie footage, as soon as the producer yelled "Cut!" Kevin Costner walked straight over to me and introduced himself with a handshake. I couldn't believe it! I'd been wanting to meet this guy ever since I seen *Waterworld*, and here I was standing there shaking his hand and having a brief conversation with him.

Later that day, while we both were in the lunch area, I had to shake his hand and hold one of his shoulder like he was my brother and give him his respect for the speech he gave about Whitney Houston's at the funeral. As my days were coming to an end on the set of that movie, I found myself just a couple of days later running around in downtown Cleveland while the shots were being fired on the next up-and-coming superhero movie! I even had the chance to meet Samuel L. Jackson's stunt double who did all the driving shots in the movie. Of course I collected as many used bullet shells as I could find! So being an extra in a couple of movies did have its advantages.

A few weeks down the road, I asked my roommate to marry me! A few months after, we were married. While we were on our way out the door, sticking to our regular routine, Immigration pulled up and took my wife away! I jumped straight into action.

Tuesday, 9:30 a.m. November 19, 2013. As my wife and I woke up, instantly we fell into our regular routine. She was the first one out of the bed; that's only because she made sure that she beats me to the bathroom. Just as I'm sure that most caring wives would do, she always stopped on my side of the bed first. She would lean over and give me a hug and a kiss on my cheek while whispering good morning in my ear. The whole time while she's doing this, she's holding both of my wrists because she knew if I'm given the opportunity, I would grab her and throw her back on her side of the bed and run into the bathroom and lock the door. As soon as I heard her close the bathroom door, I jumped into my second routine.

That's grabbing my Galaxy Note 3 so I could try to get a couple of games of racing in before she comes out. Now we're both off into our third rotation of the morning. I'd go into the bathroom, and she'd jump back into the bed and grabs her Galaxy S4 and continues playing this pet puzzle game, which she's been trying to beat for the last couple of weeks. She had made it all away to board 56, and that is where she was stuck. It really frustrates her, and I just add on to her agony by giving her a little pet name. Whenever making a reference to her, I called her Number 56.

She could easily pay for extra hammers or little bombs that explode to help her out, but she's just as bad as me. I don't believe in paying for extra things to help me win a game. I relied solely on my skills, my patience, and my determination. As we moved into the fourth cycle, we'd meet inside our kitchen. As she was preparing the coffee, I was toasting the wheat bread and frying up some turkey sausage. As we ate and sipped our coffees, we just sat there, staring at each other while we have conversation and play toe games with each other's feet under the table. Today's conversation consisted of "This is going to be our first Thanksgiving together."

After we finished our brief breakfast, we separated and accordingly went into our fifth rotation. She occupied the bedroom and the bathroom simultaneously, while preparing herself for work. I went to my office desk and went over the last installments to the biography *When a Soul Stops Running*. As we both put a closing on our fifth cycle, we easily glided into our number six installment, and this was putting on shoes and locking the door while we make our way to the car so I can drop her off at work and get back to my book. I told my beautiful wife that I would be done before the year ends.

As I escorted her to the passenger side of our vehicle, I opened the door as usual, and she slid in and said, "Thank you." I walked around the car toward the driver side, and I saw a newer model Explorer pull out of the parking spot in our complex. It made this maneuver kind of rapidly, and within just a couple of seconds, I understood why!

As their vehicle blocked my vehicle off, and due to past experiences of life, I knew it was the police, and by the type of vehicle that was being utilized I knew it wasn't city or state! My spidey sense was yelling, "This is Federal! Run, nigga, run!" But I didn't run because I knew my plate was clean, and that's when I turned my head toward my right shoulder and looked at my wife. Quickly, I turned my head back toward my left shoulder, and two white guys were already out of the vehicle! Before any physical action was made, the driver was holding his hand out at me as if telling me to stop. Then he spoke, "Take it easy, Mr. Dixon. [As soon as he said that, I knew that he had reviewed my past history.] We are here for your wife. We are with the Immigration Service. We have a warrant for her arrest."

Once they had total confidence that they had control over the situation, the passenger of the Ford Explorer walked over to the passenger side of my vehicle and removed my wife and asked me, "How did you guys meet?" The driver presented a large vanilla colored folder. As he opened up the folder, I noticed there was a very large photo of my wife. He pointed out that she had missed a court date, so they had court without her being there and the judge ordered her to be deported out of the country. After giving me their business cards and telling me to call after 12:00 p.m., I kissed my wife on the lips and gave her a hug. Then, I just stood in the parking lot of our apartment complex as they drove away with my wife in the backseat of their vehicle.

When their vehicle was no longer visible, I went straight upstairs to my mom's apartment and explained to her what just happened right in front of her bedroom window. After explaining everything, I went next door to my own apartment and did the only thing that I could do. I paced back and forth for the next few hours, waiting to call the number on the card. Within those hours, somehow my wife was able to call me from her cell phone, and she told me that they would be taking her over to Bedford Heights Police Station, which turned out to be beautiful in a cruel way because we stay right across the Street from the station. As the hours went by, I finally got in contact with the arresting officer.

He really didn't give me too much information; he just provided me with the case number for her, and that was the end of our conversation. At this point in time, nothing in life mattered to me more than to get my wife back home! (To you, the reader. So far, since you've been reading this biography, you pretty much have a clarification of my persona, my will to make it, my determination not to be defeated if I can help it, and my patience on waiting for results to reveal themselves. So now it's time for my brain to start thinking.)

After getting the information from the immigration agent, I started making phone calls, and every lawyer I called told me that they wanted $10,000 up front. One of them even sent me a text message that read, "I'm in court right now. I received your message about your situation. Bring me $8,000 cash. That should hold me for a bit." This went on for the next three hours.

By this time, I believe my brain felt as if it had exhausted every possible avenue that could have been looked upon for this day. We were heading into 7:00 p.m., and most lawyers would not be taking any calls at that time, unless you were already a client. As my brain started slowing down and getting back into its regular rhythm, it knew it was time for my heart to take over. The clock was steady ticking the seconds of the day away. My heart sent a simple message to my brain saying, "Hey, brain, let's send a message to Jesus, so he can relay it to his Father." After their brief prayer conversation with Jesus, I took my pointing finger and scrolled down the last names of the lawyers in the Yellow Pages. I stopped on a female attorney's name. I called her phone and left a message. When she got back with me, it was close to 7:30 p.m., and she explained to me that she didn't handle the type of case I was referring to and redirected me to a male immigration attorney.

We were already into the evening, but to my surprise, the attorney answered his phone when I called. I explained the situation and gave him my wife's case number. He told me he would call me back. As thirty minutes went by, he did what he promised, and my phone rang. The attorney explained to me he needed $2,500 in the morning in his hands, and that would put a stop on her deportation and open her case back up because she was ordered out of the country within seventy-two hours. With an okay, I clicked the little red button on my Galaxy Note 3 and just shook my head because I did not know what money tree was going to sprout up in my life. Now it's time to put your belief up front and leave everything in His hands.

As I was pacing back and forth, Cinnamon came walking through my door, and I explained the whole situation to her. "$2,500," she said. Then, she asked me what I was going to do. That's when my heart closed the door on my brain because with that one little question from my cousin, my brain started revving its engine. As the RPMs got higher, Cinnamon said, "Here's $500 to get you started. You have six months to pay me back. I know you, and I know you're going to take care of your business. You are not about to try to find an easy way out because you've been through too much in life to slide back into bad habits."

And with that being said, all I could do was respect it. Cinnamon usually came over to my house to work on some editing for me. I truly believe everything happens for a reason, just as He moves in mysterious ways. So I was very thankful for her little talk because each day of my life is walked on a very thin line.

Cinnamon left my place with my life story downloaded on a little flash drive so she could work on it at her home. After locking the door behind her, I sat down on the sofa. My cell phone started ringing. To my surprise, it was one of my wife's coworker's husband. After a quick conversation, he told me to drive over to his house and pick up $1,500. After shaking the attorney's hand, I followed him to his office. After giving him all the information about who I was and who my wife was, he told me to tell him my story, and he truly didn't realize the can of worms he just allowed to be let loose. I sprang into action! I started with letting him know that I did not have $2,500 right now, then I showed him the newspaper clippings of the not-so-nice guy I used to be, then I showed him how I changed my life around, then I showed him what I went through fighting for my daughter, all the way up to my biography. I pulled it out and put it on his table and let him know I did not have a real job, but I would be sure that he got his money I just needed him to believe in me. Then, I asked him if he would accept $1,500 for now so he could put the motion into the system in order to stop her deportation.

He said, "God must have really sent you to me. Have the rest of the payment by December 20, and I have some homework for you." As I took a look at the homework lists, I found it to be pretty simple. He wanted me to bring him proof that I was living in the apartment around March 2013, and he wanted proof that my wife was living there as well. He needed my birth certificate and some of her paycheck stubs. With a handshake, I was leaving out of his office and transforming into Super Husband.

As I entered my apartment, I went straight to work. I found an electricity bill from March, as well as my leasing agreement. I found her paychecks, but they had no address on them at all. I wondered if this was going to create a problem. I found some cable bills that were in my wife's name with our address on it, but the cable bills were dated early April, and the attorney said he wanted something from March. I wondered if this was going to create a problem as well. As I was sitting there, pondering, my cell phone rang. It was the manager from my wife's job. He told me to come down there and pickup $1,500.

Thursday morning, November 21, 2013, I found myself waking up to me and my wife's teddy bears. We had two teddy bears, and they complimented each other in their dress. Just as the saying goes when two people get married, "Something old, something new, something borrowed, and something blue." My wife's bear had on a pretty blue dress and a blue bow on the left side of her ear with the whole outfit traced in silver, sparkly-looking diamonds. My bear was dressed with a blue vest on and shiny silver pants, with a hat on his head that complimented his wife's bow. Both bears had 2013 written in sparkly diamond writing on each of their left paw. I just lay there, staring at the bears as they were staring at me. I guess we were all wondering if my wife would ever be coming back home. After a few more minutes, I collected myself and prepared everything that was needed. I had to meet the lawyer over at the city jail where my wife was being housed. I sat at our kitchen table wishing she was across from me, making her little jokes and playing with my feet. After taking a deep breath, I was out the door.

First stop was to change $1,000 of this $1,500 into a money order. I had to pocket $500, so I can take care of other business. As I was sitting in the police parking lot, the attorney parked right next to my vehicle. I jumped in his car with him and presented to him everything he had asked for, but in my hazy state of mind, due to the absence of my wife, I forgot a few things. He went into the station to visit my wife, and I went back to my apartment to grab what was missing. As I waited in the parking lot, the attorney returned from the visit, and he was paler than Casper the Friendly Ghost! He said it was freezing inside of there. He said it was so cold that my wife couldn't concentrate because she was shaking so badly, which was totally understandable because it's like 100 degrees all year long in her country. In order to get the interview going, he offered her his trench coat to keep her warm, and he took on the role of shaking just as badly as she was. After he visited with my wife, we sat in his vehicle together, I watched him as he went over everything. He said everything seemed to be in order and gave me a receipt for the thousand dollars I handed him.

After that, I was off to Walmart to go by my wife some warm underwear that she was allowed while in custody. I was very thankful for the female salesperson who helped me out because after I explained the situation to her, she went straight to work and got me everything I needed. Friday morning, November 22, 2013, I got a call from the attorney. He explained that everything looked fine, then told me it would really be helpful if I had something that proved that she was with me in March. That's when my head did a transformation into a cartoon light bulb! It dawned on me, as I explained to the lawyer in the beginning, that my wife had been living with me since before March 15, and that's when I popped myself upside my head! Around the early part of March, my wife was pulled over by Bedford Heights Police, and since the police knew me, they called me to come pick up her and the car. They issued her a ticket with our address on it! The lawyer called over to the police station, but they told him the system was down. I told the lawyer to give me two hours because I was about to rip my apartment apart and find that ticket. Less than eight minutes into my search, I found it! I jumped in my vehicle and headed straight down to the lawyer's office! As I presented the ticket to him, he looked over it and stated, "Perfect!" As the weekend started floating in, I was always cleaning up our apartment, rearranging furniture, and continuing my conversation with God. This went on for a while; my OCD was at its best!

Wednesday morning, November 28, 2013, I awoke feeling better than my last seventy-two hours. I was a little excited because it had been eight days since I'd seen my wife, other than looking at the photos that made their home on our apartment walls. As I sat there, waiting for her to enter the visiting room, I prepared myself to try, to keep on smiling for her. When she finally sat down, she did not look the same. In such a short amount of time, she actually looked five pounds lighter; she was already thin. Her eyes looked like darkened sockets. I couldn't hold back and tears just started rolling down my face. After the visit, I got in my car and drove home feeling lonelier than the first time they took her away. Before I could even turn the handle to my apartment door, my brain started running again, and I was on the phone with the state board ordering my contractor license so I could start back doing nails. Then I was back in a car in search of a salon, so I could start working.

As I was driving, I gave a beautician I knew a phone call. It was a little after three o'clock in the afternoon when she gave me the location of her salon and told me it was all right for me to come. When I stepped into the salon, my first thought was, *I could really work here.* But you know when you get that feeling that someone's looking at you, and instantly, your head turns toward the direction where the energy is coming from? As I was talking to the beautician, my head slowly started turning toward my right shoulder, and there was a big light-skinned guy sitting down staring right at me. I decided to do my Jesus meek thing, and I turned away from him, but the energy was still there. When I turned my head in the same direction again, this guy was still staring at me very hard. I walked over to him and extended my hand. As we shook, we both applied pressure to our grip, and I could tell that he was just as strong as I was, maybe even stronger. I spoke to him and explained that the reason I came over to him was because he kept staring at me and I was wondering if we knew one another. He explained that he was from down the way and that all his friends were either dead or locked up. With an okay, I walked back towards the beautician's chair. As the beautician and I were talking, this big guy got up and walked over toward us. I politely, without making a scene, turned my feet and planted them for scoop a nigga-up position. But as he got closer to us, he turned his attention toward the beautician and told her that her food was getting cold in the back. I could tell by the way she rolled her eyes that this must be her dude. I just took the card she offered me and told her yes when she asked me if I'd be coming in that Friday. As I started up the vehicle, I knew that would be the last time I visited that place.

There is a very well-known fitness center where I live. Not only does it have a workout gym, an inside track, steam rooms, swimming pools, and whatever else you can think of to get the body right, but it also has a salon inside, and they were in need of a nail tech. I drove there to go introduce myself. After being told that I must submit an application online, I headed back toward my car. That's when I got a message from my lawyer telling me that my wife may have to stay in jail past Christmas. That was sad to hear because Christmas was also the day she celebrated her birthday.

Thanksgiving Day, Thursday, November 28, 2013. I was sitting in my apartment alone. I wished my daughter was there, but she would not be coming over until the next day because I had her the previous year for Thanksgiving. It was her mother's time. I knew there was nothing I could do, or anything anyone else could do for that matter because we all had to wait to see what the judge was going to say. This was the holiday season. For all we knew, he might not be back in the courtroom until after March 2014 came into play. At that moment, my spirit was not into the holiday season but my spirit was into what it did best, and that was to proceed forward. Don't let life live me; I live life! So for this Thanksgiving Day of 2013, my writer's block is over because with so much going on I stop sitting in front of my computer! My typing Mojo was back! So I started preparing to make *When a Soul Stops Running* a finished product.

As the months floated by without making too much noise, I finally had an actual chance to watch the seasons of my life and others close around me change. My wife was back at home with me. In 2014, the courts gave me my daughter for the entire beginning of summer with no visitation from her mother. So I took it upon myself to go back to the salons for extra hours. Then, I went to Columbus and received my instructor's license, and it was so ironic that all my students were Asian! After receiving my license, I got certified for CPR and AED because my daughter loves the water, and I wanted to make sure I was capable of protecting her 360 degrees. I took a deep breath and exhaled very slowly because just like my mom came from around the corner of her car to catch me with the five-finger discounted gum, I knew the true party was definitely about to start. As I exhaled, I also braced myself for the next plate of life experiences that I must eat. Because one thing I'm truly learning about life is that true stories never end. They just continue to grow with no exit in front of them. Even in death, someone is bound to speak your name, which will add something to your life even if the story is a recycled one. And in my heart, I do believe as sheep of the Creator, our lives are truly already written. And I believe God is the only author! Sometimes, He calls us home early, which is not a bad calling at all. For the rest of us, I believe all our lives can possibly have an ending with a smile to them. It just determines on the steps we take to bring forth the outcome of our journey. So what's on this plate of mine that I have to eat? It's the beginning of *When a Soul Stops Running Part II 'Shady Paths of Lights'*..

I have a multicourse meal, and the dessert will determine how well I clean my plate. I have a portion of my last pretrial date for my daughter by Eva. It's in October of 2014. Then we moved to trial. So as of now, I'm making visits at the Cuyahoga County Diagnostic Clinic. They want to be sure if I'm playing with a full deck of cards or not. :) My next portion consists of my wife. She came to the United States on a K-1 fiancée visa, so it's not looking good because her first marriage didn't pan out. August of 2014, I received a phone call from my wife's immigration attorney stating she needs to show more evidence that she actually lived in Florida with her first husband. But she has no more evidence to give. She has already drained herself to give her all. My wife's final court date is set for December 2014. That's the day she finds out if she will stay in America or board a plane to Thailand, where she hasn't seen her family in over six years. And because of the K-1 visa, the attorney has already notified the both of us that our marriage is not recognized in the court of law. My three side dishes consist of the following: In 2015, the ban will be lifted off me and my son's mother The Lawyer, so I will be putting in the paperwork for my visitation rights. Then, it's back to California to schedule a DNA test to see if I actually am the father of Julie's beautiful daughter, and I am wishing for the best! Julie have stopped visiting me since I got married, but I do stay in contact with our daughter through the media site.

As all this is taking place, my youngest child will be a little older, so I'm looking forward to seeing The Nurse in court in 2015 as well. So for dessert, I'm hoping to be on my knees in the future saying thank you to God, with a copy of *When a Soul Stops Running, Part II, Shady Paths of Lights* and all my children and wife beside me.

This book will definitely touch the lives of many, and I would recommend it to anyone no matter what circle of life they live."

P.S. To you, the reader. I do hope this book gave you a glimpse of a man that comes from a broken home, but that does not mean that he has to stay broken. Now I suggest that you read this book again, but this time, read between the lines. Because every author puts a secret message inside their book. All it takes is good old common sense. Peace. (BMD)

ABOUT THE AUTHOR

Brian M. Dixon is a native author from Cleveland, Ohio. By him having to become a man at the tender age of 12, he managed to experience the most negative aspects of the street life on a different channel than most. After running from state to state and soaking in so much, his natural creativity was born. This allowed him to produce his first work of readable true art. He now is devoted to true story telling for others enjoyment. *When A Soul Stops Running* is his first introduction into the world of writing.

CPSIA information can be obtained at www.ICGtesting.com
Printed in the USA
BVOW08s1107071015

420841BV00003B/4/P